Marble Road

Life was never meant to be easy. It is a phrase sixteen-year-old Alexa Samson not only knows, but lives. The orphaned child of a heroin-addicted mother, she has spent her life being shunted around, never wanted by anyone except the sister she has been forcibly separated from.

It is an injustice she is determined will not continue beyond her eighteenth birthday. Her only goal in that time is to somehow keep her sister from following their mother to the grave at the hand of the very poison that brought her into the world.

Naomi Metzl was born in Sydney in 1981. A former research scientist, Marble Road is her first novel. It is the first of four books in the Marble Road series, following the life and struggles of Alexa Samson.

Marble Road

Naomi Metzl

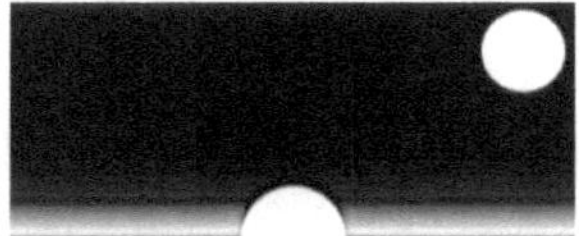

Midnight Sunrise Publishing

This book is dedicated to my grandfather Joe
You supported every one of my dreams. You believed me capable of
everything I wanted to do.
In life and death, your love has guided and inspired me. I will never
forget you.

Stone walls do not a prison make,
Nor iron bars a cage;
Minds innocent and quiet take
That for a hermitage;

If I have freedom in my love
And in my soul am free,
Angels alone, that soar above,
Enjoy such liberty.

To Athea, From Prison
Richard Lovelace

Chapter One

BLINDING SUNLIGHT STREAKED through the half-open curtains, stabbing painfully at Alexa's eyes. She screwed them up against the intrusion, but knew resistance was futile. Her arm was still wrapped around the waist of her sleeping sister, whose knotted brown hair lay tussled across her face. Slipping carefully out of the bed so as not to wake Bethany, Alexa trudged to the window to look hatefully – jealously – out on to the manicured lawns that surrounded them. The suburban world mocked her. It pranced in front of her as if it were real – as if it was a world she could one day belong to.

Turning from the window to keep the bitterness at bay, Alexa suddenly caught her reflection in the mirror. Walking casually over to investigate, she realised that it had been a long time since she had bothered to really look in a mirror and decided not to start now. She had enough problems without worrying about her appearance. It was not as though she considered herself ugly, but she also had enough self-awareness to realise she was not what the world called pretty either. Her legs were short and stubby, accentuated by her slim waist and small chest. Yet, as unremarkable as she had always found her body, it had never been short of attention – wanted or otherwise – so she knew it had all the basic requirements.

However, when Alexa did bother to find something to admire about herself, she always came back to her long blonde hair and sparkling blue eyes. The shimmer of her golden hair in the sunlight and the colour of her sea-blue eyes were entrancing. When she saw colours like that, she could not help but believe – her heart occasionally aching at the possibility – that the world had really been created as something wonderful, something to be enjoyed.

Looking away from the mirror, Alexa noticed that Bethany's tall and lanky body lay immune to the glaring sunlight that was now filling the room. The sight brought little comfort. Bethany had slept well, but Alexa could only question how long it would last. This time Bethany had relapsed within five months, and the length of time she stayed clean between periods of using was quickly shrinking.

It was almost impossible to believe Bethany was just fourteen years old. Bethany had been fighting her heroin addiction since birth. Alexa tried not to let herself believe that Bethany was beginning to lose her battle, because if Bethany succumb to this Alexa knew she would lose her one lingering connection to the world – her only reason for existence.

Long suppressed images began to swirl in Alexa's mind. The battles – won and lost – the near misses and the hatred all pulsed through her brain. She could still clearly picture the face of her mother, the woman who brought this plague into their lives, and remember the horror of watching her give Bethany heroin. Their mother had put small amounts on Bethany's tongue or up her nose, just to stop Bethany screaming, and then later to reward good behaviour.

Alexa had always tried to stop it, but with constant exposure over her lifetime, Bethany's craving for heroin at times was stronger than her desire for oxygen. The only grace was that Bethany did not want to be an addict, and never truly resisted Alexa's attempts to get her clean. Bethany's struggle was staying clean. It was worse now that Bethany was older. At home with their mother, Bethany had only ever snorted it. After their mother had died, the only place for Bethany to source the drug was from the streets, introducing her to the world of needles.

Bethany had been a fortnight on the streets this time before Alexa had been able to bring her back to Bethany's foster parents' place to withdraw. It had taken Alexa many days to find Bethany, and several more to rid Bethany's body of the toxic poison. They were the worst days, the hardest to convince Bethany that she could beat her addiction and that she wanted to. Now Alexa had achieved that feat, she was being forced to leave Bethany, knowing there was nothing she could do to prevent Bethany from relapsing in her absence.

The bitterness of their situation struck like a knife, but Alexa knew she had to suppress it. Bitterness, anger, jealousy, they did nothing to help their situation.

"Bethany, wake up. You have to get up. We need to get to school," said Alexa, sitting gently on the bed and caressing her sister's arm.

"Don't worry about school. It'll still be there tomorrow,"

Bethany yawned, pulling the covers up over her head.

"But I won't be. And I'm not leaving until I get you there."

"Good, then I will never go to school again."

Alexa bowed her head and pulled the covers off Bethany's face before wrapping her arms around her.

"I will stay if you need me to," Alexa said, hugging Bethany tight. She would do just about anything for Bethany. She only wished she knew what she could do to save them from this horror.

"Will they let you?" asked Bethany with a hint of hopefulness.

"No, but I'll work something out. I'll get a job, try and find a place to live."

"What job can you get at sixteen?"

"Don't let that worry you. Just say the word and I'll start looking," replied Alexa sincerely. The means did not matter if they could be together.

"I'm getting up," sighed Bethany grumpily.

It took Bethany over an hour to shower and dress. She was in no rush and Alexa could not hurry her. Alexa had not eaten in two days and though her stomach rumbled, she paid no attention to it. Her only thoughts were for Bethany and making sure she made it to her first day of school. Besides, Alexa knew that Bethany would be running too late for a sit-down breakfast and the Christies would not look fondly on her helping herself to the food in the cupboards. They had never looked fondly upon her.

On the way out the front door, Mrs Christie handed Bethany a bag of food along with some money.

"I will see you tonight," Mrs Christie smiled at Bethany, only to throw Alexa a dark glare before shutting the door.

Alexa scoffed internally. Mr and Mrs Christie had not spoken to her once while she had been there. If Bethany had not wanted to eat or drink, they had not offered her anything. It was like she was invisible, except for the scowl that came across their faces whenever she came into their view. Despite having asked her to find Bethany and bring her home, they had never once expressed their thanks for her doing so, and it was not the first time either.

If the Christies' hatred of her were not the reason she had been separated from Bethany for the last four years, Alexa may have found the whole situation amusing. As it was, she tried not to let the disdain she felt towards them boil within her. While they housed and supported Bethany, she would show them some level of respect.

"Why don't they like you?" asked Bethany as they trundled down the street.

"I don't know," answered Alexa honestly. "I was the evil sister, I guess. They loved you from the start." Everyone had always liked Bethany. "I was more trouble. They still treat you well, don't they?"

"Yeah, I guess," muttered Bethany.

"What do you mean 'I guess'? Yes or no. They don't hit you or anything, do they?" asked Alexa anxiously.

"Why would they hit me? No, they treat me fine," waved Bethany dismissively. Alexa sighed quietly. There was so much Bethany had never noticed, never seen. "I just wish you could still live there," sighed Bethany. So did Alexa. She would have lived with the devil if it meant she could live with Bethany. "How's your latest family?"

"The Whites? Yeah, they were all right. They got me a job over the summer – although I ran out on it to find you." Alexa smirked as she turned to Bethany, so that Bethany knew that it was nothing she should feel guilty about. "Don't reckon they'll take me back, but least I've got a bit of money saved. If I scrape some more work in the other holidays, I'll have enough money for you to come and live with me when I turn eighteen."

"That's two whole years away," groaned Bethany.

"I know," sighed Alexa, but after four years apart she was starting to realise they would have no choice but to wait their time out.

Running away so they could be together had never convinced their social worker to place in the same home. As the years had gone on it had only made their social worker threaten Alexa that her actions would risk her even being allowed to see Bethany. That was one thing Alexa would not accept.

"We'll get there. I don't care what I have to do, I'll find a way. I promise," said Alexa sincerely.

"Do you want this?" asked Bethany, holding out her lunch as they reached her school gates just fifteen minutes after the bell.

"No, I'll grab something at school. You take it," smiled Alexa. She would never take anything from Bethany.

"Then do you want the money?" asked Bethany kindly. She was such a sweet and generous person when she was clean.

"No, you keep it," smiled Alexa, brushing Bethany's cheek tenderly. "Just as long as you promise me you won't buy any drugs with it."

It was a worthless request, and Alexa knew she could never hold Bethany to any promise she made like that. Once Bethany was on drugs she was a different person and promises meant nothing.

"I promise," nodded Bethany solemnly, allowing Alexa to take heart from the fact that Bethany still wanted to stay clean.

"Good. I want to see you healthy. I don't want to lose you," Alexa said, trying not to let her voice break. Bethany nodded, but she was looking past her to a man standing across the street. Alexa followed her gaze. "Who's that?"

"I don't know," replied Bethany, shaking her head, her eyes wide and wary.

Alexa was not sure she believed Bethany by the fear in her eyes and voice, and turned to survey the man intently. He looked like he was in his early twenties, but his eyes were mean. He made Alexa uneasy by the way he continued to stare at them.

"I should go before I'm late," said Bethany, her eyes still wide and scared. "Thanks for coming and getting me."

Bethany turned and rushed towards the school gate.

"Hey, Bethy," called Alexa, dropping her bags and rushing to hug Bethany. "I love you."

"I love you too, Lex," gasped Bethany, hugging Alexa tight before quickly pushing her away and running into the school.

The world suddenly seemed so empty. Turning back to her bags, Alexa noticed that the man across the street had disappeared. There was no one else around and she found it hard to force her feet to move on from the place where Bethany was. When she did start walking, it was a slow shuffle, her body straining to lift her leaden legs.

"Oi! Where are you going with all those bags? Shouldn't you be in school?"

Alexa skidded across the footpath and away from the man yelling at her from the passenger side of a car. She had been so consumed by her sorrow as she trudged slowly down the street that she had not noticed the police car pull up beside her. In no mood for trouble, Alexa moved closer and answered the officers' questions quickly and politely. It did no good to deny who she was or where she was supposed to be. They always found out anyway.

"Do you realise that you were reported missing a week ago?" asked one of the officers, pointing at the small screen in the front of the car.

Alexa shrugged. Apparently the Whites had cared enough to notice her sudden disappearance. She would have to write and apologise – and thank them. It would probably be the last contact she had with them, and they really had been very nice as far as foster families went. Most had never cared if she left and never came back. As long as she had turned up to school for the start of the next term, there had rarely been any fuss.

The officers grabbed her bags and tossed them into the car. Alexa shrugged as she slipped into the back seat. At least they were promising to take her straight to school and not to the police station. They also did not see the value in meaningless conversation and let her be as they trawled through the heavy remnants of the peak hour traffic. Alexa could not help but smile when the officers put on their lights and siren, instantly speeding up their progress. Apparently they were as sick of her as she was of them.

It did not take long for the familiar, yet daunting, turrets of Redgrove College to come into view. Alexa sighed heavily at the sight. She was back.

If it had been set in the open, rolling hills of the country, Redgrove College might have been enticing. Situated within the sprawl of the city and surrounded by eight-foot fences and large steel gates, the fortress-like stone campus looked more like a prison than a fairy tale castle. That was the very reason most of the boarders were sent to Redgrove College. The school was run like a prison. Students were not allowed out of the school grounds at any time – except at the holidays – and only then if they went home.

Now entering her fifth year at Redgrove College, Alexa knew every inch of that school – every entrance and every hidden exit. She knew that her tardiness meant that she had missed the start of year assembly, but that did not worry her. It was always the same old crap. If there was anything interesting about the start of the new school year, it was the mystery of who would be their next year advisor.

With a quick glance at the clock as they pulled into the school grounds, Alexa knew that her Principal, Mrs Taylor, would be angrily watching over her grade as they gathered in the dining hall. She could even hear their raucous laughter as she strolled towards the dining hall door, the two officers shadowing her progress. They had not taken up her offer to simply drop her at the gate.

“Good morning, Year Eleven,” Alexa heard Mrs Taylor cry,

calling the grade to attention.

"Good morning, Mrs Taylor," the students chorused flatly in reply.

Alexa could not help but smile. Everything was exactly as she had imagined.

"Welcome back. I hope you all had a wonderful summer and have come back with the intention of achieving great things in your last two years ... for a change," Mrs Taylor muttered loud enough for everyone to hear. "I'm hoping the importance of your final two years here will distract you from your usual antics." A quiet chuckle rippled through the grade. "As you may have noticed Mr Knight has consented to be your year advisor."

"Didn't anyone else want us?" asked Sam Michaels.

"As a matter of fact, no – and I really don't think that it is anything to be laughed at," cried Mrs Taylor, as the grade smirked. "Well, on that note I think I will let you all get acq–"

Alexa strolled casually into the back of the dining hall, as if unaware of her escort. She did not acknowledge their existence as Mrs Taylor looked up and glared at her.

"Ah, if it isn't our missing person!"

Alexa watched the grade turn as one to face her. There were several broad grins among the faces and she could not help but return their smiles. Sam was shaking his head, but Alexa only shrugged in reply. Her turning up with police in tow should not have been completely unexpected.

"We found her across town," said one of the officers to Mrs Taylor. "We thought she was playing truant, but when we realised she was listed as missing we brought her here."

"Thank you, officers," sighed Mrs Taylor, not sounding very thankful at all, making Alexa smile more broadly. "I will deal with this. I will let you deal with your students," Mrs Taylor added to Mr Knight as she left the hall with raised eyebrows.

All eyes suddenly switched to Mr Knight. Alexa even heard a few of the girls sigh as they took in the sight. He was handsome and just twenty-six. His wavy dark brown hair fell casually across his forehead directing all attention to his deep chocolate eyes. His face retained a boyishness about it that had made him popular among the female students, but Alexa did not care for his looks. She just wanted to know what she was up against.

"Good morning," smiled Mr Knight, taking a step forward. "I hope you were all inspired by your Principal's words." Alexa exchanged a glance with Sam Michaels, her frequent partner in crime – or punishment, at least. It had been so long since they had really committed any real misdemeanours, but this school has a long memory. "Now, we have two big years in front of us and –"

"Two years? Ah, I think you mean one," called Nick Poulos. "Haven't you noticed no one's lasted in your job for more than a year?"

"Some say the job is cursed," added Alan Chan to the grade's amusement.

"This is not Harry Potter, Mr Chan, and I don't believe this job is cursed. I think you've simply been waiting for the right teacher."

There was open laughter from the grade while Mr Knight simply smiled assuredly back at them.

"Optimism. That's a great thing to have in your position," chimed Sam.

"C'mon, Sir. What are you doing taking this job? We like you. We don't want to have to hurt you, but you're gunna have to face facts. You won't last more than a year. It's just the way things go," said Chad Olsen sincerely.

It had begun. The G7 – Alexa, Sam, Chad, Nick, Alan, Stacey Verloc and Chris Appen – had begun their initiation. They were the reason – in the school's eyes at least – that no year advisor had lasted more than a year. It was always them who tested out the new year advisor. They were the ones who always bore the brunt of their disciplinary proceedings anyway. However, Mr Knight seemed determined not to be intimidated and was much less flustered than his predecessors had been at this point.

"Now, I'm always here if you need help," said Mr Knight in a tone that conveyed his desire to wrap the meeting up, after he managed to get in a quick run-down of all the essentials. "I'm sure you all know where my office is. Any questions?"

"Yeah," shouted Alan, smiling brightly. "How do you think you're going to bow out? Big scandal? Nervous breakdown? Sacked? What's your preference?"

"I will be here when you finish your final exams next year with a smile on my face, congratulating each and every one of you," replied Mr Knight confidently, gaining him a mixture of laughter and sighs in response.

"You have to admit that the man has optimism on his side," said Nick cheerfully as the meeting finished.

Alexa smiled. She knew Mr Knight would not last out the year either. No matter how enthusiastically they started, there had only ever been one, inevitable conclusion.

"Oh, one other thing," called Mr Knight over the departing students. "I need to see the following students in my office."

The majority of the students continued to exit the dining hall. Only seven bothered to wait in a state of annoyed compliance.

"Sam Michaels, Alexa Samson –"

"Anyone other than the seven of us you want to see?" asked Sam politely, his eyebrows raised as he gestured to the lingering students.

Mr Knight quickly checked his sheet of paper against the seven students who had not departed.

"Err, no."

"Right, we'll see you there then," called Sam, and he left the dining hall.

"Miss Samson, you can go and put your bags in your room first," said Mr Knight.

Alexa turned and left without acknowledging Mr Knight. It was always the same old crap.

Chapter Two

MARCUS KNIGHT LOOKED at the clock on his office wall. He was not sure why he had agreed to go along with this. It was half-past eleven and he still had one student left to see. He was supposed to see all the members of the G7 individually – to 'break the group' – but he would have been here all day. Instead, he had gone in pairs: Chris and Stacey, Sam and Chad, and Nick and Alan. To Marcus, those seemed like the natural groupings.

It was strange. Marcus had never even seen the G7 as a group of seven – unless they were getting in trouble. Never before, occasionally after, and he wondered if the group actually existed. He had even ventured to ask that question in the first two meetings. Stacey had vehemently denied its existence, while Chris had just sat in silence trying to comfort Stacey. When pushed, all Marcus could get out of him was, "Whatever you believe, man. You won't believe us anyway."

Sam and Chad were different. They had smiled broadly at the question – as they had to nearly every question – before Chad responded with, "If it gives you a purpose, sure, we exist, Sir."

Marcus had been tempted not to bother asking again, but curiosity eventually got the better of him. Alan and Nick were two of the top students in the year. They had brilliant minds and it had always astounded him that they would be continually grouped in with the trouble-makers. So when he asked them about the G7, he was surprised by Nick's response.

"Of course we exist, Sir. If we didn't, then we wouldn't be having this meeting."

"But we just don't think that our 'existence' means the same thing to you as it does to us," added Alan.

Marcus thought he sensed bitterness in their voices as they had spoken. Despite this, in general, he thought the meetings had gone well. Perhaps not a complete waste of time, though certainly not what he had been expecting. All of the students chatted freely and confidently. Marcus had never seen students respond to a teacher's questioning with such nonchalance, arrogance, even. But he had to guess that this was a process they were used to and suspected that they used these meetings much the way he did – to size up the opposition.

Marcus looked at the clock again. Alexa had been sitting outside before he had called Nick and Alan into his office, so he wondered why she had not entered when they had left. With a frustrated sigh, he pushed away from his desk and stalked across the room. At the door, he expected to hear chatting and laughing, something to explain Alexa's delay, but it was quiet and he sighed again at the thought of having to pull her out of class. These meetings were next to useless, but he could not have a student defying him so early in the year.

However, Marcus only made it one step out the office door before he stopped dead. Alexa was there, curled up asleep on the old couch that had always lived outside this office. She looked so small and fragile. She looked exhausted. Placing a hand on her shoulder to gently wake her, Marcus could not help but jump as Alexa startled herself awake, her bag thudding to the ground.

For a moment, Marcus noticed that Alexa's eyes were wide with fear as she looked up at him and quickly moved herself into a corner of the lounge. However, seconds later she was recomposed, picking up her bag and striding silently into the office.

Watching her walk, Marcus realised that Alexa really was small – just a little over five feet. She quickly tied back her long blonde hair, leaving just a few wisps floating across her face. That was when Marcus noticed her eyes. They were an amazing deep-sea blue, but they were also somehow cold and sad, and as emotionless as her youthful face. Marcus found himself intrigued by Alexa instantly as she, too, sat confidently before him.

"I haven't seen much of you since my year seven geography class," Marcus said as he sat down at his desk.

He was not sure Alexa had changed much, though he was struggling to recall any defined memories of her. For the most part she had been quiet and unassuming, as though trying to be as small and indistinct as possible.

"Most people round here would say that's pretty lucky," Alexa replied casually to his statement.

Her tone was almost bored, but Marcus could feel her eyes boring into his, gauging his response, and he realised that she, like the six students before her, was using this time to size him up. He could not help but wonder what she saw.

"Would you like to tell me where you've been these last few days? You've had a lot of people very worried," Marcus continued, wanting to find some way to connect with Alexa.

It was clear Alexa did not find any enjoyment from these proceedings the way Sam, Chad, Nick and Alan had. However, of all the students in the G7, Alexa was the one most staff put forward as their ring leader. Looking at her, Marcus struggled to believe that, but she was such a closed book that he knew he could be easily mistaken on that count.

"I really doubt that," answered Alexa sceptically. Her lips moved as if she had more to say on that point, but she stayed silent.

"Really? Why's that?" asked Marcus. It was true, there had been little real concern among the staff, but he wondered why Alexa would think such a thing. Everyone had made the right noises in front of her.

"I was looking for my sister," Alexa said dismissively, answering his earlier question.

That did not bode well and it must have shown on his face. Alexa crossed her arms and scowled heavily.

"From what I've seen of your file, when you mention your sister, you are usually getting yourself into trouble," Marcus said gravely. He had been forewarned that Alexa's sister was a trouble magnet. There were rumours that plans had been in place for her to attend Redgrove as well, but after the trouble Alexa caused in her first two years they refused to take her.

"Nice to know," replied Alexa. Her voice was no longer bored, or calm, but her face remained unchanged as she slid further into her chair.

"So this took you six days?" asked Marcus, seeing that this was really a major source of trouble in her life.

He had not read Alexa's full file, but would have to now. He was determined that, as her year advisor, there was much that he could do to assist her. The few teachers who were sympathetic to Alexa and her situation always lamented how little had been done to help her over the years. Now he was in a position to rectify that situation.

"No, it took me two and a half," Alexa replied scathingly, as though he were a fool to believe it would take any longer. "I spent the rest of the time helping her through withdrawal and this morning I went with her to school in an attempt to guarantee she attended at least one day."

Marcus gasped internally, though he managed to control his external reaction. Alexa's manner was cold and detached, but it was clear from the pain that had just streaked through her eyes that she was anything but. He could not comprehend how she could speak of things so casually, as if it were almost normal to have to help your little sister through withdrawal. He had a little sister and shuddered at such a thought.

"Why did you need to go and find her?" asked Marcus. It was obvious, but he wanted to keep Alexa talking.

"Because her foster parents told me she was missing. They thought I'd be able to talk her into returning to their home," Alexa continued in her bored tone, though her eyes were roving around the room, refusing to meet his.

"The two of you are not living together?" That surprised Marcus and he knew it was evident in his voice. "Why not?"

"Does it really matter?" Alexa asked agitatedly. "Who's the girl?" she asked quickly, before he could answer. She was looking over his shoulder to a photo on the bookcase and he was surprised by the sudden lightness in her voice and a slightly playful smile on her face.

"My girlfriend," Marcus replied curtly, returning his gaze to Alexa, unsure of where this was going.

"What's her name?" Alexa asked, her voice still light and friendly.

"Jackie," Marcus answered, slowly frowning. He had always been strict about keeping his personal life very separate from his school life and, in particular, his students.

"Nice. What's she do?"

"Does all this really interest you?" asked Marcus finally, his voice stern as he tried to make it obvious that the topic was not up for discussion.

"No, not really," answered Alexa, and Marcus could tell from her voice that she really did not care. "I just thought we were getting to know each other. Thought it'd appear rude of me if I didn't give the impression I cared."

Marcus did not allow the smile he felt reach his face. It was dangerous to reward his students' petulance and he knew he had to set a hard line with this group right from the start.

"Can we expect more disappearing acts from you this year? I really hope not," Marcus continued, wanting to quickly move on from his personal life. This was not the first time Alexa had disappeared. Last year she had run away from school no less than five times, the longest for almost a week. "Your marks are still relatively acceptable. You may want to work on them, even though you're not on an academic scholarship."

"No, I'm here on the 'Ease Our Moral Conscience' scholarship," Alexa sneered, rolling her eyes as she looked away.

"I don't think anyone sees the situation like that," Marcus lied. That was exactly how Redgrove saw it, but he was a little surprised the students had picked up on it. Redgrove's reputation was spotless. "From what I've heard, this scholarship is helping you be a damn side better than your sister."

Alexa's eyes flashed hatefully and Marcus knew he had crossed the line.

"Yeah, well, I guess I had the advantage of not being born a heroin addict," Alexa replied harshly, her eyes delivering him a threatening look of the likes he had never experienced as she rose and left the room without being excused, the door slamming behind her.

Marcus sighed long and low, covering his face with his hands. He had always prided himself on his ability to maintain a strong wall between himself and his students – approachable, but never too friendly. It was essential, given the small age gap between himself and the older students, and in all his years as a teacher it had never been tested, even in his first year at a mere twenty-two years of age. However, as he stared at the door Alexa had just stormed through, he suddenly felt the smallest of holes form in his protective wall.

***

Alexa climbed the steps towards her next class, her meeting with Mr Knight fading with every step. She did not think Mr Knight would give her too much trouble. He seemed like he wanted to help too much to be purposely problematic. If she kept a low profile then she was sure he would have no reason to bother her.

However, as Alexa reached the landing, it was not Mr Knight that was troubling her. It was the relentless aching in her stomach. As her stomach growled more forcefully, she could do nothing more than place her arms around her middle and trudge towards class. She would make up for the forced starvation at lunch.

"Miss Samson, my office, please," called a deep voice from behind.

Alexa smiled. Turning, she watched the history teacher, Mr Marsh, stride back towards his office. She followed his tall, well-built frame. He was thirty-eight, but his hair was already greying. Alexa had always wondered how it had not made him look old. He called it the Richard Gere effect, but Alexa had never really understood. She had no idea who Richard Gere was.

Year advisor to the current tenth grade, Mr Marsh had his own private office. Alexa could count on one hand the number of times she had been in there. Mr Marsh waited at the door for her to enter and shut it quickly behind her. Before Alexa could even turn back to face him, he had pulled her towards him and was kissing her feverishly. She kissed him back, curling into the warmth of his body that wrapped so easily around her own. As his kissing increased in intensity, her head started to spin and she was forced to push him away.

"Sorry, Clinton, but do you have any food? I feel like I'm about to pass out," said Alexa, stumbling out of his arms and into the nearby chair, slightly breathless.

"When was the last time you ate?" asked Clinton, his curiosity no greater than if he had been asking her the time. She liked that.

"Saturday morning maybe," Alexa replied gingerly. That world seemed so far away now and her stomach ached again, but for a completely different reason.

"Here," said Clinton, passing her a chocolate bar as he knelt in front of her.

Clinton watched her, stroking her hair as she shoved the chocolate into her mouth. The sugar rushed instantly through her veins, making her realise just how dazed she had been. It was as though her brain was suddenly working at full speed again, able to take in more than just what was right in front of her. Even her limbs felt suddenly more connected to her body.

"I'd better go before I'm late for class," Alexa said, realising just how much of the day had passed already. It seemed like a lifetime ago that she was with Bethany. "I can't get myself into trouble – well, more trouble – on the first day."

"What class have you got?" asked Clinton, his hands moving from her head over her shoulders and down to her waist.

"Double maths," Alexa sighed. It was not the way to start the new school year.

"Surely you don't prefer to be there. Surely you'd rather be here with me."

Alexa knew it was not a question. The grip of Clinton's hands on her waist was leaving little room for refusal. When Clinton leaned forward to kiss her, she did not push him away. She pulled him closer and allowed his body to press against hers.

***

"Your meeting with Mr Knight didn't really go this long, did it?" asked Alexa's best friend, Ezra Singh, when Alexa arrived halfway through her maths class.

Mrs Jackson had not even questioned her. The members of the G7 were always late on the first day of school. It was a ritual so entrenched in the start of each year that they had often made the most of it and skipped their first class if they could not be bothered going.

Alexa shook her head as she slipped into her seat. Ezra looked confused before sighing heavily and shaking her head.

"I shouldn't ask then, should I?" huffed Ezra.

"Not unless you've changed your opinion over the summer," replied Alexa with a hint of a smile, trying to keep the conversation from becoming too serious.

Ezra knew about her and Clinton Marsh, and did not approve. Alexa knew there was very little to approve of, but things were never that black-and-white in her world. Mr Marsh was a respected teacher, but he was not universally liked by the student population. He could be hard and soft in equal, but unpredictable measures. Alexa had seen the softer side of Clinton and it had made her more accepting of his harder manners, perhaps because he had never been particularly hard on her. Still, even she had to admit, theirs was not a love story that would go down in history. It was hardly even a love story.

If Ezra ever heard the full story, Alexa was sure she would approve of their relationship even less. It was complex and Ezra had never wanted details, much to Alexa's relief. Ezra was not a boarder, and Alexa was not sure they had enough free hours in the year to fully explain this story, whose seeds went all the way back to their very first year at Redgrove.

Redgrove College prided itself on being an exclusive, well-respected educational institution. Parents paid good money to have their children educated at the school, whose reputation was regarded throughout the state, if not the country. It was no surprise then that Alexa had felt out of place when she had arrived. Alexa was still unsure how she had managed to receive the hardship scholarship that supported her tuition and boarding at Redgrove, but at Redgrove she was, and there were more than a few who resented her presence.

The very worst of them was the matron of the girls' dormitories. Ms Carter believed people like Alexa polluted the sacred halls of Redgrove College by their very existence. From the beginning, Ms Carter caused trouble for Alexa. There was nothing Alexa could do right and there were punishments abound for all she did wrong. In her first year, Alexa was sure she scrubbed all the girls' toilets over a hundred times. After a while, Alexa even found some pride in their sparkling appearance. There was just no point being angry. The other scholarship students had it just as hard and this was not her first taste of life's injustices.

By the time Alexa reached year ten, she had become all but immune to the punishing routine that marked her life at Redgrove. However, that year things took a dramatic and horrifying turn. She had been dating Sam Michaels for almost two years. Sam was the best thing that had ever happened to her. They were practically inseparable, but being together meant taking risks and breaking rules. Alexa had never cared. She was punished no matter what she did, and would have broken every rule for Sam. She just never guessed the consequences would be so dire.

When Ms Carter caught her trying to sneak into Sam's room after curfew, the fury in Ms Carter's eyes was unparalleled. They seemed to glow red. Alexa knew the normal punishments would not suffice for this misdemeanour, but how much more she could never have guessed.

After being dragged into Ms Carter's office by her upper arm, Alexa had stood in the middle of the room waiting patiently for the tirade to end. It was the same as it always had been, so when it stopped Alexa knew to take her opportunity to leave.

"Now you will listen here, you filthy, little drug addict!"

Alexa could still remember the angry hiss that was Ms Carter's voice that night and the fear that had pulsed through her when she felt a hard stick being pressed into her windpipe, pulling her back towards the centre of the room.

"I will not stand for you spreading your filth around this school. Do you understand?"

Alexa could not reply. The pressure of the cane was threatening to cut off her air supply. She tried to nod, but Ms Carter had hold of her hair. The pressure released suddenly, but the next Alexa knew, she was face down on Ms Carter's bed in the room adjoining her office.

"I have tried my very best to discipline you over the years in an attempt to make you a better person – to make you deserve your place here – but it seems nothing I have done has had an impact on you. Perhaps it's time you truly understood the consequences of you actions."

The consequences came down on Alexa's back again and again. Alexa bit the quilt to stop herself from crying out in pain, though the tears could not be prevented from streaming down her face.

"You will learn to accept punishments for your wrongdoings. The world has been too easy on you and I won't have it. I won't tolerate you, you filthy, little drug addict!" cried Ms Carter as her cane continued to strike Alexa's back.

When the savagery was finally over, Alexa rose gingerly to her feet and headed across to the other side of the school. It was a painful trek, but she was glad that she had been wearing a cardigan that day and that Ms Carter had not pulled her clothes up to expose her skin. Wiping her eyes, Alexa steeled herself for revenge. As wrong as her actions might have been, she knew Ms Carter's were worse.

However, although Mrs Taylor's face paled at the sight of her back, she refused to believe Alexa's accusations. Mrs Taylor accused her of having the other members of the G7, probably Sam, inflict the injuries on her in a bid to get Ms Carter into trouble. Mrs Taylor wanted proof, proof Alexa knew she could not provide. Mrs Taylor's ultimatum was for Alexa to prove her accusations were true or risk the security of the scholarships for the G7 members – her and Sam.

Alexa never told Sam what happened that night. Mrs Taylor could have been bluffing, but Alexa could not be sure and she did not want Sam in trouble because of her. Mrs Taylor might not act against staff without proof, but she would act against the G7. There was no way Alexa was going to let Sam's place in the school be put in jeopardy because of her.

Keeping that horrid secret took its toll. Sam refused to let the issue drop, and their relationship ended just weeks after the incident. However, as time went on, peace returned. Alexa and

Sam could not keep themselves apart no matter how scared or angry they were, but that proved to be only the beginning of the brutal punishments. Alexa never scrubbed another toilet again.

When it dawned on Alexa that these assaults would never end, she began running away from school. It was at the peak of these assaults that she first started to notice Clinton Marsh. It was like he appeared out of nowhere. She had never once paid him any mind, but soon he was everywhere, smiling warmly at her, asking her how she was. When Clinton eventually asked her into his office for a chat, she was so desperate and alone that she confessed everything.

The moment the words were out of her mouth Alexa was trying to take them back. She could not trust the teachers here, but to her never ending surprise, Clinton had believed her and even taken her side. However, Clinton knew the workings of Redgrove better than she did, and knew there was nothing official that could be done. He reassured her that he would handle it personally.

The relief that had flooded Alexa in that moment had been so profound that she had rushed up and hugged Clinton. No one at Redgrove had ever been so kind or understanding. She could still remember the fluttering of her stomach as Clinton's arms had embraced her and his lips planted a kiss on the top of her head. But more than anything, Alexa remembered the feeling of security when Clinton said, "Don't worry, Alexa. I will take care of you."

Alexa had looked up then, and Clinton's eyes met hers. When he leaned down, she moved in to meet him. It was wrong. She knew that. But he cared. She did not love Clinton the way she had loved – still loved – Sam, but she had been so alone since her and Sam's breakup and needed someone to be close to.

Deep down Alexa knew that as long as she stayed with Sam, Ms Carter would use that as an excuse to keep up her violence. One day Alexa would explain to Sam why she had hurt him so badly. It did no one any good to get themselves wrapped up in her life.

Chapter Three

ALEXA WAS THE first of her roommates to reach their bedroom at the end of a long first day. With her late arrival that morning, she still had no idea who she was sharing a room with for the next two years. She grabbed her bags that she had dumped on the floor next to the door that morning and made her way to the bed closest to the window. It had clearly been slept in the night before and there were a few personal items on the bed and bedside table. Looking around, she found the unclaimed bed in the middle of the room.

Without a second though, Alexa picked up the bedside table in front of her and quickly swapped it with the empty one in the middle of the room. She then removed the personal items from the bed next to the window and placed them on the middle bed. She was in the process of making the window bed when Martha Henderson and Natalie Wang arrived.

"This isn't one of you, is it?" asked Alexa in a friendly voice, pointing at the bed by the window.

"Nope," replied Martha with a smile. "We knew who we were sharing with. We're this end."

Martha pointed to the two beds furthest from the window, chuckling slightly as she dumped her bag on her desk. Alexa thought Martha seemed quite pleased that she was stealing someone else's bed.

"It's the new girl, Bianca Ross," explained Natalie. "We did tell her that was your bed, but she insisted on first come, first serve. She won't be happy," she added with a grin.

Lizzie Chatri arrived in that minute and surveyed the scene. Alexa had never shared with Lizzie before, but Lizzie had the reputation of being one of the nicest people in the school. It was immediately clear that Lizzie was not happy with the bed-swapping, but her comments made it apparent that was because she did not want her roommates fighting. She had known the window bed was Alexa's from the start. Everyone had always known that.

"I hope you're planning on moving that bed closer to the

window," said Martha when Alexa had finished making the bed.

Alexa examined the area and realised the bed had not been moved yet. Pushing against the bed with her thigh, she found it unwilling to budge.

"Need help?" laughed Martha.

Alexa smiled and nodded. Martha, Natalie and Lizzie all came over and started pushing the heavy, four-post bed. They laughed as they pushed, joking at how remarkably weak they felt up against the bed.

"You'd think we'd be better at this by now, huh," huffed Martha, smirking to Alexa.

"Um, that's my bed," said a trill voice from behind them.

All four girls finished moving the bed before turning to face the newcomer. She was tall with long brown hair and furious brown eyes. Alexa recognised her immediately as the angry girl from her maths class who had taken offence to her rumbling stomach and her and Ezra's giggles.

"We told you Alexa always has the window bed. You'll thank us later," said Martha pointedly, making no apologies for their actions.

Bianca stood at the door, her gaze moving from Martha to Natalie and then on to Lizzie. Martha and Natalie both sneered at Bianca slightly before sitting down at their desks and pulling out their books. Lizzie said nothing, just ducked her head and rushed to join the others at her desk. Bianca stormed to the bed in the middle of the room without a word. Alexa felt bad, but there really was a very good reason she had always been assigned the bed next to the window – and it had nothing to do with her tendency to climb out windows.

"Hi, Bianca," said Alexa cautiously. "Look, I'm really sorry about the confusion with the beds. Anyway, I'm Alexa Samson."

"Yeah, I worked that much out for myself with your dramatic entrances this morning," snapped Bianca. "You don't have much respect for other people, do you?"

"Um, well, I guess that all depends on the person," was all Alexa could stammer in reply before heading to her bed, stung by Bianca's manner. "I'm going to bed. Don't worry about waking me for dinner."

Alexa had eaten about three meals at lunch, making up for the last week, where food had been such an infrequent luxury, and all she wanted to do now was sleep. This day had been long enough already. Laying down and closing her eyes, Alexa was asleep within minutes and did not stir once as her roommates went about their normal business.

So deep was her slumber that Alexa did not wake until early the next morning. She had not had a full night's sleep since leaving her foster home. Her stomach once again rumbled with hunger as she showered and dressed so she did not bother to wait for her roommates before leaving for breakfast. There were only a few other early risers in the dining hall when she arrived and made her way to the food, grabbing a stack of toast and a large bowl of cereal. She was still making her way through the toast when her roommates joined her at the table.

"Hungry?" asked Martha smilingly.

"Starving," replied Alexa between mouthfuls. Bianca rolled her eyes and trudged over to the queue for breakfast. "Not really a happy one, is she?"

"It's her first time at boarding school and she's missing her family," said Lizzie with genuine kindness.

Alexa stared at Lizzie in awe. Martha and Natalie just shook their heads, smiling as though they pitied Lizzie.

"I guess that explains some of it," said Alexa, trying hard to be as forgiving, but found herself drawn towards Martha and Natalie's reactions. It was obvious that yesterday was not the first run-in Martha and Natalie had had with Bianca. "But she'll be missing more than that soon enough. Freedom, for one."

"Good food for another," added Natalie, looking down mournfully at Alexa's breakfast.

The others went to get their breakfast, and Alexa was surprised when Bianca returned with them. Bianca did not speak or even engage in their conversation, and as soon as she had finished eating, she left with the same determined silence.

It did not stop there. Alexa noticed Bianca working hard to ignore her whenever they were close, even in English when they all had to form groups of three or four. Ezra had tried hard to catch Bianca's eye to make their third, but Bianca teamed up with Stacey and Carly, who were seated next to her. Instead, Alexa and Ezra teamed up with Sam and Chad for the assignment, much to Sam's delight and Alexa's relief. She was not sure she could really handle much more of Bianca's disapproval.

However, as the day progressed, Alexa's mind began to drift away from Bianca's stubbornness and towards the afternoon.

Senior students had Tuesday afternoon classes free and this year it was the time Clinton had arranged for them to meet in private. He did not like them being seen together too frequently at school, and Alexa was still surprised he had risked the rumours yesterday, but the truth was she was called into teachers' offices so often that no one would have bat an eyelid.

When the lunch bell rang, the senior students scattered. The boarders were not allowed to leave the school grounds, so most headed back to the dormitories or the library after grabbing their lunch in the dining hall. Alexa slipped away from her classmates and headed out into the grounds. She walked to a far corner, in the opposite direction to the departing day students, and slipped unseen through a small gap in the eight-foot-high hedge fence. She walked quickly down a small street and then into an alley. It was only a few minutes before Clinton's car pulled up in front of her. With a relieved smile, Alexa hopped in and sat low in the seat as they sped away.

Alexa noticed Clinton's apartment was messier than usual, perhaps a product of the long school holidays and more hours spent at home. Lunch was a quiet affair, with few discussions about their time apart. Their relationship really was not like that and Alexa was glad. She did not want to discuss her life with Clinton. This was something she would walk away from as soon as she left Redgrove and believed Clinton felt the same way.

"I have to clean up," Alexa sighed, feeling the grip of Clinton's hands on her arms as she washed the dishes.

Clinton always had food available in the apartment, but it was Alexa who made their lunches and cleaned up afterwards. It was something she had always done willingly. In return for escaping Redgrove for even just a couple of hours, she would have done much more.

"Forget the washing up," said Clinton, kissing her neck as his arms continued to gently restrain her. From the burning heat of his body against her back, Alexa could tell he was completely naked. "I'm quite capable. I will do it myself tonight. Now come with me."

Alexa complied willingly, though not as quickly as Clinton wanted as she tried to dry her hands. He was insistent, wrapping his arm around her waist and pulling her forcefully to his bedroom. With burning intensity, Clinton stripped her naked, running his fingers over her body before leading her out on to the balcony. It was a hot day, but the shutters that enclosed the balcony allowed the breeze to blow in while keeping the direct sun off them. It also afforded them a great deal of privacy, though Alexa knew Clinton liked the mixture of voyeurism and privacy. When she had once voiced her fear of being seen, he had stood her against the shutters, her naked body free for anyone to see, and laughed at her as the world took no notice of what he did with her.

Today Clinton laid her down on the large daybed that occupied much of the balcony. Alexa smiled at the look in his eyes as he knelt down and again stroked her body. It was nice to feel wanted. Clinton leaned forward and kissed her fervently. When her arm wrapped around his neck, he climbed on top of her, pressing his body to hers.

***

It did not take long before talk of the summer among the students began to fade. It was too depressing to reminisce about moments of freedom when they were all being held in captivity. Instead, they talked about homework and assignments as though they truly cared, mixing up the conversations with gossip about the latest romances. This year the pickings were relatively slim, meaning there was just one romance that had all the year elevens enthralled.

"You have to realise how much he still likes you," Ezra said to Alexa in an incredulous voice as they sat in chemistry.

Alexa did know and it made her stomach churn. They had been spending so much time with Sam and Chad working together on their English assignment that it was impossible not to notice Sam's intentions. It took every ounce of willpower Alexa had to try and be oblivious, but she was beginning to realise that she was going to hurt Sam again no matter what reaction she had.

"Sam? No, we're just friends," Alexa replied with a dismissive wave of her hand, trying to convince Ezra of her impartiality. "We haven't been together for almost a year now."

"Yeah, and no one knows why you guys broke up. You seemed like such a sweet couple."

"We *were* a sweet couple," said Alexa, trying to contain the bitterness she felt over how their relationship ended. "But we did break up and you can't turn back the clock and change things. It just doesn't work that way."

"He has to better than Mr Marsh."

Alexa knew Ezra had never understood her infatuation with

Sam, but it was obvious that paled in significance to her incomprehension about her relationship with Clinton.

"Does Sam know about you and Mr Marsh?" asked Ezra, looking at her thoughtfully.

Alexa shook her head forcefully. She did not want to think about what Sam would do if he ever found out about Clinton. She was sure there was a chance Clinton may not survive the revelation. It was clear Ezra guessed as much and it made Alexa worry what Ezra might say in front of Sam, but nothing slipped from Ezra's lips during their many hours together with Sam and Chad.

At the start of week four, all their time together working in the library culminated in their group gathering at the front of their English class. They had submitted their written assignment that day and the four of them now stood nervously preparing to act out a scene from the play they were studying. Bianca's group had just taken their seats, Bianca in a huff from the lack of effort from the rest of her group. The sight made Alexa smile.

Ezra was fairly unenthusiastic in her reading compared the other three. Alexa could not help falling into the groove with Chad and Sam. These four weeks had really served to remind her how much she had missed hanging out with them. It made her encourage Ezra to be more animated in her acting, but Ezra had stated previously that her main contribution to this part of their assignment would be not giggling hysterically. However, Ezra could not contain herself completely and the rest of the class joined in as Chad and Sam overenthusiastically performed their roles. The loudest cheer of all was reserved for the finale, when Sam unexpectedly kissed Alexa to celebrate their victorious ending.

"I'm not sure that was quite the way the play ended, but good improvisation, I guess," said a grinning Mr Pollock as the group made their way back to their seats. "Let's see if the next group can top that."

Sam smiled nervously as he walked past Alexa to his seat. All she could do was smile and shake her head in reply, but that only widened Sam's grin.

"Now do you believe that he likes you?" asked a still giggling Ezra.

"No, it was just a gimmick to get us marks," Alexa replied dismissively. Ezra frowned at her, and she understood why. "All right, perhaps he does still like me," she conceded reluctantly. "But that doesn't change the fact that I don't like him that way."

"Then why don't you tell him? Put the poor guy out of his misery. Not to mention Chad and me. It's really not that easy watching Sam make a fool out of himself over you and not being able to laugh."

Alexa sighed. She paid no attention to the rest of the class as she mulled over Ezra's words. It was not fair. There was really no reason for Sam to still like her after everything she put him through last year. She loved that he did, but wished he would forget her. He was too good a guy to get wrapped up in her problems.

When the bell rang, Alexa made her way back to Sam's desk, her heart beating erratically. Under different circumstances – under almost any other circumstances – she would not be doing this, but she knew Clinton was a package deal. Without him, she had no protection from Ms Carter – and Sam had no protection from her. There was no other way, and Alexa knew she was going to have to hurt Sam again, just when they had really started regaining their friendship.

"Hey, nice touch there at the end," said Alexa, forcing a smile on to her face. "Might just earn us a few extra marks."

"Yeah, maybe, but that wasn't really the effect I was going for," replied Sam, a glint of hope in his eyes.

Alexa's stomach twisted painfully. She hated herself so much right now.

"I know," she replied sadly, walking out of the classroom before stopping in the passageway and turning to Sam. "Look, I know you want things between us to be different and for things to go back to the way they were, but it's just not going to happen. I'm sorry."

"But why? What happened?" asked Sam desperately, his hands grasping hers. "I realise you got in a lot of trouble that night we got caught together, but it can't be that. I love you, Alexa. Please."

Sam's eyes were now devoid of hope and full of sadness. Alexa felt her stomach tie in knots and her heart begin to split. She wanted to be cruel to get it over with, but knew Sam deserved better.

"I'm sorry, Sam. This is all just more complex than you understand. Things happen, things change and no one can change them back," Alexa said softly, explaining as much as she could. "Your friendship is all I want and my friendship is all I can offer. I can't ..."

Alexa held back the tears that were burning in her eyes as Sam surveyed her closely. She was so close to letting in all out, but she could not do it to him.

"Are you in trouble?" Sam guessed. He knew her so well. "You can tell me. I'll always back you up, you know that, right?"

"I'm okay, Sam," Alexa lied automatically. "I can take care of myself."

"But you're in trouble, aren't you? Who are you trying to protect?"

"Everyone," Alexa gasped, then turned and ran as fast as she could before she could say more.

***

Alexa paced anxiously as she waited for Clinton. With her nerves still on edge from her talk with Sam the day before and trying to avoid him since, she did not even know if Clinton was running late or if time was just dragging itself out to torture her. When Clinton did arrive, it took Alexa most of the short drive to his apartment to realise that he seemed as agitated as she felt. They did not speak and the silence continued all through lunch.

"So I hear I have some competition," said Clinton smartly, as she stood to clear the table.

"What?" asked Alexa, not comprehending. She had been in her own world.

"Surely you know what I'm talking about?"

Alexa shook her head, honestly not seeing where Clinton was going.

"So you haven't been kissing other boys in the middle of your English class, then?" Clinton continued mockingly, but there was a distinct edge to his voice.

Alexa's stomach turned to lead. Mr Pollock must have been discussing her and Sam's kiss in the staffroom. Of course the teachers gossiped!

"Are you talking about Sam?" Alexa asked, trying to sound innocent, but her heart was racing. "That was just a part of the play. He thought the added drama might earn us a few extra marks."

"You were quite the couple once. Are you sure there wasn't more to it?"

"Yes! There's nothing between Sam and me. We're just friends.

I don't have to explain myself to you," Alexa spluttered indignantly. She was not used to explaining herself to anyone. "I had nothing to do with the kiss. It was his idea. And what does it even matter? It was *just* a kiss."

Clinton did not answer straight away, so Alexa began washing the dishes, her arms shaking with anger and indignation.

"I will tell you why it matters," said Clinton suddenly, rage swelling in his voice as he pressed in against Alexa's back. "Because you are mine. And I don't want that boy's slime all over you. So you make sure you wash your mouth out before you come to bed."

With that, Clinton scooped up a hand-full of soapy water and rubbed it across her mouth before pushing her away from him.

The water trembled as Alexa finished washing the dishes in a state of shock. She had never seen Clinton so angry before. She found it strange that he would be jealous when it was his apartment she was in. When she finished the washing up, she walked to the bedroom and saw Clinton lying naked on the day bed. She diligently removed her clothes and went out on to the balcony and sat down next to him.

"I'm sorry you thought there was something going on with me and Sam. There isn't, I promise," Alexa said with soft sincerity.

Clinton placed his hand gently on her face and pulled her down next to him. She was relieved when he kept looking at her with soft eyes as his hands ran over her body.

Then he pounced.

Clinton's lips locked down on her neck as his hand ripped off her underwear. He climbed on top of her without a word and pushed between her legs. He was not gentle.

"Ow. Please, Clinton, stop. You're hurting me," Alexa cried.

Clinton slowed as he looked down at her. He placed a finger on her lips before thrusting hard and continuing unabated. It took all the strength Alexa had not to cry out in pain.

Walking back up to her room after sneaking back into the school grounds, Alexa tried to ignore the burning pain in her pelvis. She hoped the hot water of her shower would help to cleanse her and wash away her fears, but all it did was mix with her salty tears.

As she dried herself, Alexa noticed spots of blood on the towel, but the tears did not fall as she slid down the wall and slumped on the cold tile floor. This was not why she was with Clinton. If he had been this way from the start, she would have taken Ms Carter's beatings. Clinton was supposed to be protecting her, not hurting her.

The problem was Alexa did not know where to go from here. She could not tell anyone else about the abuse she had suffered at the hands of Ms Carter; she could not be indebted to another person. If she dared to tell anyone about Clinton, she knew she would be in as much trouble as him. Her only choice would be to avoid Sam completely in the hope of appeasing Clinton.

If she could stay away from Sam then she could stop the rumours and talk of them getting back together. It would hurt Sam more than she already had, but she did not want to experience another afternoon like that with Clinton. It was more important that she just survive these next two years and make it out to Bethany.

Despite the anguish and confusion she felt over Clinton's misplaced anger, Alexa had to admit that not everything was going so badly. Bianca's cold stare had started to thaw as the weeks had gone on and she came to realise why Alexa had been banished to the farthest end of their bedroom.

Alexa's talking in her sleep was no worse than the occasional snoring of Martha and Lizzie. It was Alexa's nightmares that disturbed her roommates most. They disturbed Alexa. She hated looking down and seeing her five-year-old body, three-year-old Bethany by her side, as fear pulsed through her veins, because she knew what was coming. It was the same every time.

In every dream, Alexa and Bethany ran as fast as they could, desperate to outrun the shadowy figure they feared would be around every corner. When Bethany got tired, Alexa would pick her up and keep running. She always handled Bethany carefully, to ensure she kept the bloody knife in her hand away from her precious cargo.

However, no matter how many times Alexa had the dream, no matter which direction she ran in, they always found themselves in a large field full of oversized pipes. Trying to hide, they searched for one big enough to crawl into and then waited, Alexa's grip on the knife never loosening.

"Alexa," a voice would call from the end of the pipe.

Alexa's heart always started hammering as she edged forward, the knife out in front of her and Bethany safe behind her. The end was coming and there was no avoiding it.

At the end of the pipe, a young round-faced policeman waited for them. He always smiled and told them that they were safe. Then, without warning, a shot would rip through the air. Alexa was never able to look away from the policeman's lifeless body at the end of the pipe or the shadowy figure kneeling by his side, calling her name as it reached for Bethany.

Most of the time, Alexa simply woke from this dream in a frantic sweat, her heart pounding furiously. Occasionally, she would wake in tears. It is when she woke up screaming that her roommates were most disturbed.

A week after Clinton confronted her about Sam, Alexa's nightmares continued on as usual. The policeman was kneeling at the end of the pipe, smiling at them, assuring them that everything was going to be all right now. It was all over. Alexa held Bethany in her arms, but she was so heavy. The policeman held out his arms to take Bethany, but Alexa clung on tight, her heart beating frantically.

"I won't hurt you. I promise," said the policeman gently. Alexa wanted to believe him, but her body still tensed as she slid her way out of the pipe. "It's okay. I'll carry Bethany. I won't hurt her."

Alexa did not want to let Bethany go, but finally gave in to the kindness of the round-faced policeman. However, as soon as she surrendered Bethany, the policeman disappeared.

"You obey me, Alexa. You obey me or I will have to take Bethany instead," said Clinton in a malicious voice, holding three-year-old Bethany in his arms.

"Give me back my sister," yelled Alexa desperately, transformed into her sixteen-year-old self, pointing the knife at Clinton.

"No. Perhaps I like her more. You're too disobedient. I can't trust you," growled Clinton, before he leaned down and placed a kiss on Bethany's tiny lips.

A pained scream woke the entire room and shook Alexa from her sleep.

"No," Alexa gasped, as she sat up in her bed. Her face was wet with a mixture of sweat and tears as she looked frantically around for the images that had distressed her so badly, but all she saw were the curtains around her bed.

Drawing back her curtains, Alexa looked around the darkened room. Lizzie and Bianca's heavy shadows propped up on their arms told Alexa that she had woken them. Natalie and Martha simply rolled over and went back to sleep. This was not a new experience for them.

Alexa closed the door to the bathroom and turned on the light. Her hands were still shaking along with her insides. She slid down the wall and sat on the cold, tiled floor, trying not to let her eyes close to the vision that seemed burned on to the insides of her eyelids. Absentmindedly, Alexa reached into the bathroom cabinet and pulled out a small toiletries bag. She felt around without looking until she pulled out a small silver blade.

Without a second's hesitation, Alexa placed the blade near the top of her upper arm and pushed it into her flesh. Her eyes carefully examined the wound as her hand guided the blade around her upper arm in a precise, deliberate circle. Blood seeped slowly from the cut and, with it, the images from her dream drained away from her eyes and mind, and out of her body.

Alexa circled her arm five times. Pinpricks of pain issued from her arm. She concentrated on each of them, almost wishing they were more painful so that they would distract her mind more completely. Resting her elbow against her knee so that the blood did not soak into her pyjamas, Alexa continued to sit on the cold floor, thinking only of the pain in her arm, until her mind was completely blank.

Chapter Four

"SO, UM … DO you have nightmares very often?" asked Bianca at breakfast the next morning.

Alexa could see the concern etched on Bianca's face, but wondered how much of it was for her and how much for Bianca's own anticipated loss of sleep.

"Yeah, sometimes. Sorry," replied Alexa carefully. There was not much else she could really say. "I didn't mean to wake you. Martha and Nat seem to be used to it, but I guess it must be a bit awkward for you and Lizzie."

"It's a bit freaky, but you can't help having nightmares, can you?" replied Bianca with a slight smile. "What are they about anyway, to make you scream like that? Monsters or something?"

"Yeah, something like that," Alexa replied, not meeting Bianca's eyes. Even she did not know why she had these nightmares or why they continued to scare her after all these years.

When they finished breakfast, Bianca moved off for class, saying goodbye to Alexa for the first time.

The thawing of relations continued in English, when the class was again asked to form groups of three or four for their next assignment. Alexa could not help her eyes from glancing back at Sam's table, but he was not looking in her direction as he and Chad formed a group with Nick and Alan.

"Do you guys have a third person yet?" asked Bianca anxiously, standing in front of Alexa and Ezra, drawing Alexa's gaze away from Sam.

"No," answered Ezra with a welcoming smile.

"I couldn't join you guys, could I?" asked Bianca tentatively.

"Yeah, sure," replied Ezra, and Bianca smiled as she sat down next to them.

"What about Stacey and Carly?" asked Alexa wryly.

"Argh, they did nothing on that last assignment. I had to practically write the whole thing myself," complained Bianca bitterly.

"Yeah, I never thought Stacey did much work on her

assignments," said Alexa casually.

Stacey was a day student and had always enjoyed the social aspects of school over the academic ones. She and Alexa were very different people and had very little in common, except for their inclusion in the G7. However, they did share a strange bond because of that, and Alexa could not help but sigh when Stacey caught her eye, her gaze flicking to Bianca and back before her eyes rolled and her tongue stuck out slightly. This was going to be harder than Alexa expected.

"I actually thought it'd be you guys who'd be really crap," said Bianca judgementally. Alexa turned and glared at her. "Only because … well … you know …"

"Because I'm in the G7?" retorted Alexa, much less casually. "So's Stacey. Or didn't anyone tell you that?"

"Actually more because of the way you acted on the first day of school. The police … and you coming into maths so late – then talking the whole way through."

"Ezra, Sam and me are all scholarship students," said Alexa, ignoring Ezra's exasperated rolling of her eyes. "We kinda have to do the assignments or they tend to kick us out."

"I guess," answered Bianca warily, clearly not sure what to say next. "But it was still a bit hard not to be surprised that a group with three G7 members did so well – I mean, with everything people say about you."

This time it was Alexa who rolled her eyes. There were so many things fighting to be said, but she managed to contain them all. However, she was sure the look on her face conveyed many of her thoughts when Bianca responded quietly, eyes downcast, "I know. I was wrong."

"Great! I'm glad we got that sorted then," said Ezra, frustration evident in her voice despite the smile on her face.

And somehow with that comment Bianca's resentment of Alexa seemed to vanish. Alexa could not be so easy. She had been the subject of Bianca's glares for too many weeks to believe all that anger could simply dissipate in an instant. Turning away, Alexa was not comforted by the sight of Stacey and Carly giggling into their hands. Stacey suddenly flicked up a piece of paper with the word sorry scrawled across it. Alexa responded with, you're not forgiven, which sent Stacey and Carly into a fit of hysterics that did not impress Mr Pollock, but thankfully Bianca seemed oblivious to the fact that the whole exchange was about her.

However, when Tuesday afternoon arrived, Alexa could no longer care about what Bianca thought of her. All her thoughts focused on the afternoon and what mood Clinton would be in. After spending the entire week avoiding Sam as completely as possible, Alexa hoped that things would improve. They didn't.

Clinton refused to forgive her for the kiss she shared with Sam. He was cool and harsh when he spoke and when they moved to the bedroom the sex continued to be rough and unpleasant. Alexa would have preferred that Clinton's anger made him not want to touch her at all, but it seemed as if he wanted her to feel just how angry he was. It hurt, and more than just her body, but she could not understand his continued anger.

When Alexa tried to talk to Clinton about the situation he only became more agitated. The mere mention of Sam's name or the suggestion that he was blowing the situation out of proportion threw Clinton into a terrifying rage. He did not scream or yell or throw anything. His temper was deep and dangerous and all Alexa wanted was to find a way to calm it.

It was all so crazy. It may not have been a love story, but Alexa had liked what she had with Clinton. She had liked it for what it was and had always enjoyed Clinton's company. They used to talk, never about their personal lives, but about everything else. Now there was nothing but angry, painful sex.

The result was that Alexa withdrew completely into herself. She barely spoke to anyone, particularly boys, terrified that Clinton would see or hear and misinterpret the situation. The entire week was spent wondering what the next Tuesday would bring, hoping it would be better, while also trying to come up with different strategies to please Clinton. Alexa knew the only thing she had to offer or entice Clinton with was her body, but hated the idea of him touching her again if he was intent only on causing her pain.

"Hey, guys, what you doing for lunch?" asked Bianca breathlessly, as she danced up to Alexa and Ezra outside their chemistry class at the start of lunch on Tuesday. Alexa guessed Bianca was finally getting used to boarding school. "We can go and work on our English assignment after. What do you reckon?"

Alexa sighed. But not so used to it that she had noticed her absences on Tuesday afternoons.

"Oh, um, sorry. I can't. I have to be somewhere and Ezra goes home early on Tuesdays," Alexa replied uneasily.

"I don't have to go home and we really should get started on the assignment," said Ezra, looking at Alexa with a slight smile. Alexa stared back at her with a warning look. "Why don't we go do it now?"

"Can't we meet tomorrow? I'm free then," replied Alexa desperately. She could feel the seconds ticking away as they spoke and she did not want to be late. Clinton did not need another reason to be angry with her.

"Where do you have to go?" asked Bianca with suspicious curiosity. "It's not like we're allowed out of the school on Tuesday afternoons."

"Oh, Alexa gets special lessons on Tuesday afternoons," said Ezra serenely before Alexa could reply.

Alexa glared at Ezra angrily, biting her lip to keep the hateful words burning on her tongue from being spoken.

"Huh? Special lessons? From who?" queried Bianca confusedly.

"Mr Marsh," Ezra smiled smugly.

Alexa felt a fiery stab of hatred for her best friend.

"Shut up," she hissed, hoping there was still some way she could keep this information from Bianca.

"But, Alexa, you don't take history, do you?" asked Bianca, now thoroughly perplexed.

"Oh, no, Alexa hasn't done history since year eight. Like I said, they're 'special' lessons," answered Ezra provocatively.

"What? No – you mean Alexa and Mr Marsh …"

"I have to go," said Alexa, stalking off without turning to see the confusion on Bianca's face or the triumph on Ezra's.

An empty street was all that greeted Alexa as she approached her and Clinton's usual meeting spot. She sighed in relief, thankful that he was also running late. Within a minute, Clinton's car screeched to a halt beside her and she immediately hopped in.

"How dare you keep me waiting!" Clinton fumed, as he changed gears forcefully. "We're just a just a few blocks from school and you want to keep me waiting in the street."

Alexa did not reply. Her stomach turned to lead. As hard as she tried, she always managed to do the wrong thing.

The short trip was spent in simmering silence, Alexa too scared of Clinton's temper to speak, but as soon as they entered Clinton's apartment his barrage began again.

"Well? Are you at least going to apologise for being late today?" stormed Clinton.

"I'm sorry," Alexa replied unconvincingly as she lingered by the front door. She really did not want to go into his apartment.

"Not good enough," hissed Clinton, as he grabbed her around her upper arm, making her wince as his grip tightened over cuts she had made a few days earlier.

"I'm not at your beck and call," Alexa spat, pulling her arm from Clinton's grip.

"Really," replied Clinton smilingly. The sight did not ease Alexa's racing heart. "Now I know you know that's a lie. You've never dared refuse me before, even if you have wanted to. You're mine for as long as I say so. That is unless you want things to go back to the way they were."

Clinton smiled again. Alexa walked into the kitchen to prepare lunch – anything to get away from him.

"You can forget about that for now," Clinton commanded, still smiling. "We have other business to be attending to."

Alexa walked out of the kitchen and followed Clinton into the bedroom, her stomach in her mouth. Perhaps if she gave him what he wanted he would be kind. Indeed, Clinton was gentle as he took her hand and pulled her down to the bed. As he rolled on top of her, he ran his hand tenderly along her face.

"You just have to understand how things are and start showing me a bit more respect," cooed Clinton, his voice kind and gentle.

"I'm sorry," Alexa replied sincerely.

"Good," Clinton continued more menacingly, wrapping his hand around her throat. "Because if you dare keep me waiting again or continue with this attitude of yours, there'll be hell to pay."

Alexa did not dare reply or even move. It took all her restraint to stop herself from crying as Clinton gave her a hint of what hell would look like. The encounter left her shaking and less than keen to get back into the car with Clinton, but she knew that back at school she would be away from him and his anger for another week.

Trudging slowly up the dormitory stairs, Alexa's day was not made any better by the sight of Bianca waiting on her bed for her. Alexa ignored her, walking straight to the bathroom and locking the door. The last thing she wanted to do was talk. There was no way she could convince anyone she was with Clinton for love after this afternoon.

Waiting until she heard everyone leave for dinner, Alexa finally crept out of the bathroom and dashed towards the door. There was no way Bianca could confront her in the dining hall in front of everyone.

"So was Ezra telling the truth? Are you and Mr Marsh really … dating?" asked Bianca, startling Alexa as she closed the bedroom door to prevent her from leaving.

"Yes, Clinton and me are seeing each other, okay?" replied Alexa mechanically, staring at the firmly closed door.

"Alexa, this – this is not a good thing," said Bianca a little condescendingly.

"It's none of your business. You don't know anything about it."

Alexa tried to open the door, but Bianca continued to block her way with her body pressed against the door.

"You're my friend, of course it's my business."

If Bianca was her friend, this was really the first Alexa had heard about it.

"If you're my friend then support me, don't harass me," Alexa replied aggressively, pushing Bianca's hand off the door and rushing out. It was the kind of friendship she could well do without right now.

Clatter and confusion greeted Alexa in the dining hall the next morning. She had not seen Bianca at dinner and she was nowhere to be seen now. It did not put Alexa at ease. Her friendship with Bianca, if it was possible to really call it that, had always been fragile at best and she had hoped that they could talk this morning. She wanted to try and get Bianca into the accepting state Ezra had once been in, and breakfast was as good a time as any. Everyone was far too busy eating or waking up to listen in to private conversations.

Instead, Alexa spent her morning classes in silence. She was unsure if Bianca had forgiven her for not wanting her help, as Bianca also remained in stubborn silence, and was still far too angry at Ezra to talk to her.

"Miss Samson, can you come up here, please," said Mrs Lux towards the end of biology, handing her a note. "You can go now if you like. We're basically finished for today."

Alexa read the note with a sinking feeling.

Please send Alexa Samson to my office at the end of the lesson.
Mr Knight

Alexa noticed Bianca watching her intently as she made her

way back to their bench. She gave both Bianca and Ezra a scathing look as she packed her bag and stalked out of class. Her mind was racing as she walked unsteadily to Mr Knight's office. She needed to know what Bianca had told Mr Knight. It would help her decide how much she should confess. Perhaps she was better off simply returning to her dormitory, packing her bags and leaving before anyone noticed. She knew she was not a very good liar unless she had time to prepare herself, but about this, she was prepared to lie.

However, even as Alexa thought that, she realised that there was a big part of her that did not want to lie any more. She wanted it all to be over, but knew she could not take that risk. Mr Knight would want his pound of flesh as well.

***

Marcus looked at the clock and found himself strangely anxious. If Alexa came, she would be here in less than ten minutes. It worried him that this fact made his stomach flutter just slightly and he convinced himself that his anxiety stemmed purely from his concern.

"Come in," he said on hearing the knock at the door, his voice slightly strangled by the thump of his heart.

Marcus looked up as Alexa slowly entered. She was very hesitant, but that was not what concerned him. When they had spoken on the first day of school Alexa had looked tired, but lively and almost seemed to enjoy the verbal contest they had had. Now she looked drawn and had dark rings under her deep blue eyes. For a moment, Marcus was sure Alexa was about to cry, but as soon as she took her seat and looked up at him, her eyes were full of anger. It was strange, as her face was completely emotionless.

"Are you aware of why I asked you to come and see me today, Miss Samson?" Marcus asked gently.

Alexa did not answer, but continued to glare at him angrily. Once more, Marcus thought he noticed tears, as her eyes began to lose their anger, but it was so hard to tell when her face was so blank.

"Your friend, Miss Ross, came and saw me this morning. She's worried about you," Marcus continued, watching Alexa's eyes intently, but she turned her face away from him. "She says you've been having nightmares on a fairly regular basis."

"What?" gasped Alexa, turning to back to him with a stunned expression.

"You certainly don't look like you've been sleeping very well," added Marcus tentatively, thrown by Alexa's shocked reaction. She had thought she was in trouble, but for what, he wondered. "Are you okay, Miss Samson?" he asked, hoping she would confess.

"Yeah, I'm fine," replied Alexa in a soft voice that betrayed some emotion.

"It doesn't seem like this was the reason you thought I asked you to come and see me. Is there anything you want to talk to me about?"

Talk to me, Marcus thought wildly.

"No," Alexa replied, shaking her head.

Marcus was unconvinced.

"Let's talk about your nightmares then," he said, desperate to get Alexa talking about anything. Alexa just crossed her arms and raised her eyebrows. "Miss Ross is concerned about you and so am I. I can't help you unless you talk to me."

"I don't recall ever asking for your help," Alexa countered, her voice stronger now.

"Miss Ross, your friend, asked me for my help."

"They're dreams. I doubt there's much you can do to change them, unless of course you think you can give me sweet dreams," Alexa said maliciously.

"I'm not happy with what you're insinuating," replied Marcus, confused and shaken.

"Well, how exactly do you think you're going to help me? I have bad dreams. Have had since I was a kid."

"What are the dreams about?" Marcus asked cautiously, though part of him was screaming to get Alexa out of the office now before her insinuations became allegations.

"Is knowing that really going to help?" asked Alexa in repellent tone.

"Perhaps," Marcus replied, his concern for Alexa winning out over his concern for himself. "It might give us an idea about what is triggering them."

"I doubt it, but, you know what, thanks for the chat. It's been great and I really hope we can do it again sometime," said Alexa, grabbing her bag and heading towards the door.

"I never said that this meeting was over," Marcus said sternly, urging Alexa to resume her seat.

"I think you're forgetting something. I don't care," replied Alexa casually, turning and walking out.

The door slammed shut and Marcus fell back in his chair. Whatever crazy feelings that had been swirling in him fifteen minutes ago were gone. There was something going very wrong in Alexa's life, but he did not care any more. She was a ticking time bomb and would take out anyone who happened to come close. He wanted nothing more to do with her.

***

Simmering anger kept Alexa quiet until she had time to calm down with a free period and her razor. Blood continued to ooze from the cuts that spiralled around her upper arm when she left for class so, despite the warm weather, she pulled on her school cardigan.

"How was the meeting with Mr Knight?" Bianca asked nervously in the last class of the day, obviously having garnered the courage to speak to her despite the scowl on her face.

Ezra looked on, equally anxious. It made Alexa ponder if they were more worried about the outcome of her meeting or her reaction to the question.

"Oh that, it was really good," Alexa replied with biting sarcasm. "We sat down and talked about my nightmares. Mr Knight got out this book on dream analysis and we worked through all my deep-seeded sadness and repressed memories."

"I'm serious," said Bianca in a slightly hurt voice.

"They're nightmares, Bianca, what do you really expect Mr Knight to do about them?" Alexa spat in an annoyed voice.

"So you didn't tell him about Mr Marsh?" asked Bianca tentatively.

"Why the hell would I do that?" asked Alexa, wondering what was wrong with Bianca. "If either of you get kicked out of here, you have a home to go to. I don't. As shitty as this place is, I really don't have anywhere else to go, so I'm not about to say things that are going to get me kicked out."

"What? Why would *you* get kicked out? *He's* the one in the wrong. Don't you understand that?" Bianca asked incredulously.

"You've been here for all of five minutes," groaned Alexa. "You don't understand how this place works. I'm in the 'G7'. We're half the reason we've never kept a year advisor longer than a year and we're blamed for every bad thing that happens here. No one will back me up against a teacher, especially not one like Clinton Marsh."

"She does have a point," conceded Ezra, earning her a disbelieving look from Bianca. "They'll do anything to keep a scandal under wraps here. They'd be much more likely to expel Alexa than sack a teacher."

"Now you get it," muttered Alexa darkly, hating that Ezra could not have remembered that before and kept her mouth shut.

"I still think you need to end this relationship, Alexa," said Bianca, though Alexa did not appreciate her demanding tone. "It's not right. I mean, you don't really love him, do you?"

"I have my reasons, okay," Alexa replied, not wanting to justify her decisions to Bianca. "I can take care of myself. Please, just support me and lay off with the lectures, and that includes the ones from Mr Knight."

Alexa could tell that any reprieve she got from Bianca would only be temporary, but she would take it. She really did not need to be fighting more battles right now. The trouble she continued to have with Clinton was about all she could take.

Even though she made sure she was never late and minded her tone when talking, things with Clinton had changed. It was no longer the carefree and fun relationship it had started out as. The sex was rough and painful, even worse if she let slip a scream or plea to stop. Alexa was filled with fear every minute they were together. The problem was that she did not know how to get away – how to not turn up to meet him. Every week, she was sure it would be the turning point, the moment that things got better, because she was sure they could not get any worse.

She was very wrong.

Three weeks out from the Easter holidays, Alexa noticed that the heavy dread that seemed to now always fill her stomach had a nauseating twist to it. She tried hard to ignore it, positive it was just stress, but there was something else niggling at the back of her mind. When the nausea continued and her period failed to materialise, that niggle exploded into outright panic.

Alexa did not tell anyone about this troubling development, particularly Clinton. His reaction was the one that scared her the most, but day and night, she spent every spare moment trying to find a practical solution to her situation. Even when she slept, her predicament followed her, subtly changing her familiar nightmares.

"You can come out now. It's okay, I promise," said the kind, round-face policeman in a soft voice as he sat at the end of the pipe.

Alexa held Bethany tightly behind her and the large knife out in front of her. "My name's Ben."

"Hi Ben," called Bethany from behind Alexa.

"What's your name?" Ben asked gently.

"Bethany," Alexa answered for her, holding her tighter.

"And she's Alexa," called Bethany happily, cheerfully reciprocating her actions.

"Do you want to come out of there? I can take you both somewhere safe," said Ben kindly, his hand reaching out for them.

"No. He'll find us and hurt her," Alexa answered, shaking her head as Bethany curled into her.

More than anything, Alexa wanted to race into Ben's arms, but she could not trust him. She could not trust anyone any more.

"You take good care of your sister, don't you? Protect her?" asked Ben, and Alexa nodded. "I can help you. I can help you so you can protect her forever. It will help keep your baby safe as well."

Alexa looked down at her five-year-old stomach and felt a small baby under the skin. Her heart pounded painfully in her chest.

"Here, take these. They will help you."

Ben took something from his pocket and rolled it towards Alexa. She picked up what looked like a small marble with the number eighteen in the middle. While she was still inspecting the small marble, Bethany picked the second marble and held it tightly in her hand. Four more marbles rolled towards them, each containing a different number. Alexa scooped them up and inspected each of them.

"Eighteen, six, twenty-eight, forty-two, twenty-three. What are these? How will they help me protect them?" Alexa called, but Ben's lifeless body lay at the entrance of the pipe.

Alexa continued to repeat the numbers, trying to solve the mystery of how they would help her protect Bethany and her unborn baby before the shadowy figure came for them again.

Chapter Five

"I THOUGHT YOU said they were just dreams. Don't read too much into it," said Ezra, as they worked through the maths questions on the board the next morning.

"I know, but there's an answer here. Ben said that they would help me protect Bethany and the ... they have to mean something," Alexa said desperately.

"Maybe they stand for letters or something," suggested Ezra offhandedly.

"No, there's no forty-second or twenty-eighth letter in the alphabet," said Alexa sadly. She had already thought of that. "Maybe I need the sixth marble. Bethy picked up the second marble Ben rolled down. I never even thought about it."

"Ha ha. Maybe they're the winning lottery numbers," Ezra joked casually, not looking up from her books.

"They could be, you know," said Bianca, suddenly excited by the conversation she had previously ignored. "It sure would help you, wouldn't it? If you won the lottery, you could take care of Bethany yourself – get her help and off drugs."

Alexa and Ezra both looked at Bianca sceptically. Alexa was looking for a practical solution to her predicament, not a fairy tale.

"It's just a dream," said Ezra, speaking as the voice of reason.

"Maybe, but what if they are the winning numbers? We could be millionaires," Bianca continued with a wild glint in her eyes. "It's worth a shot, isn't it?"

"Maybe, but I only have five of the numbers, not six. I never saw the number in Bethy's hand," Alexa murmured, not really keen to go down this path.

"We can just enter enough games to cover all the possible combinations," said Bianca, now completely ignoring the work in front of them.

"Are we forgetting that we're just sixteen and can't legally buy lottery tickets?" asked Ezra.

"I'm seventeen," Bianca added indignantly. "And more likely that the two of you to pass for eighteen. Alexa sure won't."

"Yeah, but you're stuck in this school twenty-four-seven. Plus, how are we going to pay for all of it?" asked Ezra, continuing throwing a damp rag over the whole idea.

"I have money," Bianca smiled. "So if *you* can somehow buy the tickets, we're all set."

Alexa and Ezra exchanged unsure looks and shrugged their shoulders.

"I guess it's worth a go," said Alexa eventually, though holding out little hope. It was Bianca's choice to waste money on her dream.

"This is so cool," said Bianca in a high-pitched squeal, attracting a disapproving look from Mrs Jackson. "We're going to be millionaires," she added more softly, but no less excitedly.

Ezra lodged the tickets that weekend for as many games as they could afford, barely raising an eyebrow from the teenage sales assistant. The trio had spent almost an hour making sure they had all possible combinations of numbers to cover the missing sixth number from Alexa's dream.

"Easy as," said Ezra with a smile, as she handed over the wad of tickets to Alexa on the Monday morning. "Now all we have to do is survive our maths exam."

Alexa shoved the tickets in her bag, wondering why she did not just throw them in the bin. It was ridiculous to think they could win. She had never learned how to calculate the exact odds of winning the lottery, but she did not need to know how to do the maths to know that it was all but impossible.

It took some effort for Alexa not to concentrate on the stupidity of their actions as she sat down in maths. She was not in the mood for a test, despite having studied all weekend. It was not that she was a particularly conscientious student; study was just one of the few things that distracted her from her life – and Bethany's absence.

However, just when Alexa felt herself getting into the groove of the exam, her concentration was broken by the announcement that came over the PA system.

"Can the following students please make their way to the Principal's office: Alexa Samson, Sam Michaels, Chad Olsen –" at which point everyone else returned to their exam.

Only Alexa, Stacey and Nick rose from their seats. They exchanged looks that immediately conveyed their lack of knowledge of any incident that could have sparked this disciplinary proceeding. Once upon a time they had enjoyed the notoriety of the G7 and shared mischievous grins after being caught out for their exploits. The novelty had worn off very quickly when the punishments significantly outnumbered the incidents they had actually been involved in.

"Sit down," said Mrs Jackson sternly as they tried to leave. "You're not missing your maths test because you're being blamed for whatever form of chaos has just befallen the school. Sit, sit. You can go when the exam is over."

They sighed as they took their seats, knowing they would be blamed for their lateness too. However, try as she might, Alexa could not regain her concentration. This situation was really more reflective of her life – not five useless numbers from her dream, weighing down her bag.

***

Marcus paced along the far end of Mrs Taylor's office. This was ridiculous. He had been here all period, waiting. Why this meeting could not have been delayed until lunch was beyond him. Dispose of the evidence, he scoffed. Mrs Taylor's notions of these children seemed outrageously biased. He had already given two of them alibis, but she would insist.

There was no knock at the door when Alexa, Nick and Stacey entered. They looked around the room and took their seats in silence. Marcus stayed in the corner behind Mrs Taylor's desk. He did not want to give them the impression that he was a party to this.

"I'm glad the three of you finally decided to join us," said Mrs Taylor smartly.

"We were in the middle of a maths exam," said Stacey, handing Mrs Taylor a note from Mrs Jackson.

"Like we told you they were," Alan added angrily.

"So what are we supposed to have done this time?" asked Nick.

It shocked Marcus that they all appeared prepared to be blamed for this. They just sat there, not arguing, barely even questioning.

"I see. So the seven of you are all going to deny all knowledge of why you've been called here," said Mrs Taylor severely.

"You know I think there are a few crimes the police haven't solved that you haven't blamed us for yet," said Sam angrily. "Is it one of them?"

"I won't have that tone from you, young man. This is no

laughing matter. This incident is very serious."

"We understand it's serious. We're being blamed for things we've never done," said Stacey, her frustration evident.

Mrs Taylor rounded on the group, giving each of them one of her harshest stares, but they simply stared back. If the situation had not been so serious, it almost would have been laughable. Although the students had started to talk back, Marcus could see that was only because Mrs Taylor was trying to get them to confess. If she just told them what they were suspected of doing and the punishment, he was not sure they would have done more than weakly protest their innocence before accepting the situation and moving on.

"Some string was run across the top of a flight of stairs," Marcus said calmly, wanting to move this along. The G7 let out a simultaneous groan of disbelief. "It was found before anyone tripped, but I'm sure you can understand the seriousness of the situation."

Marcus watched all their reactions closely. If they were guilty, they were very good actors.

"And you think we did that?" cried Chad. "Honestly, you think we'd do something that stupid?"

"I wouldn't put anything past the seven of you. You have all shown what depths you can sink to and I know you had a hand in this," scowled Mrs Taylor.

Marcus noticed the students fold their arms as they slumped down in their seats. It was a clear display of defeat not guilt and it made him realise just how normalised this scenario had become for them.

"So when were we supposed to have run this string along the top of some staircase?" asked Sam bitterly.

"This morning," said Marcus, talking before Mrs Taylor could. "Sometime after assembly, we think. The string was found just before the start of recess."

"We were all in class in second period. Mr Knight can vouch for Chad and me," said Sam, looking at Mrs Taylor and smiling hatefully.

"It's true, Mr Olsen and Mr Michaels were in class and neither were late or left class early," replied Marcus for their benefit alone. He had already told Mrs Taylor this. "We need to speak to their teachers. We can't keep blaming them without any proof."

"I don't care whether any of them were there or not," replied

Mrs Taylor, her voice bordering on hysterical as she turned on Marcus. "If they weren't the ones to physically tie the string across those stairs, then they know who did and put them up to it."

Marcus could not believe what he was hearing. It was a level of unreasonableness and irrationality he had never witnessed before. No wonder these students had tried to dispose of every one of their previous year advisors, if they were going to be presumed guilty without any evidence – worse than that, without any desire for evidence.

As Marcus looked at each of them, he noticed that they held out no hope. They were agitated, sure, but resigned. Then his gaze fell upon Alexa. She was staring at her shoes and did not look well at all. She had not spoken a word in her own defence. He knew he could not allow this injustice to happen to her. He could not allow it to happen to any of them.

"I don't think these students had anything to do with this unfortunate incident. We can talk to their teachers and if any of them were absent or late we can bring that person back. I see no point in continuing to hold them when they clearly deny any knowledge of, or responsibility for, the incident," said Marcus, looking intently at Mrs Taylor.

"You don't seem to understand," replied Mrs Taylor incredulously. "These seven are a group. They work as a group. One cannot function without the others' say so."

"I really don't think that's true. I've never seen them in a group, except when we make them one," Marcus continued determinedly. "And even if they are a group, that does not make them responsible for every incident that happens in this school. We cannot hold them responsible for something without any proof."

Marcus tried not to smile as he took in the shock on the seven faces that had suddenly turned to him. Mrs Taylor seemed just as surprised and it left her momentarily speechless.

"I think you seven can head off to lunch, but mark my words," Marcus said sternly, as the seven students rushed towards the door. "If I find that out that any of you were involved with this stunt, you will be expelled. You've been given a chance to own up and I believe you when you say that you weren't involved. Don't betray my trust in you."

Marcus turned his gaze back to Mrs Taylor and from the look on her face, he realised that the next few moments of his life were not going to be pleasant.

***

The G7 stood in a loose circle, still a little shocked at what had just transpired. They did not ask each other if they were responsible for the string. They all knew they were innocent. However, as they knew they would still be blamed in the end – no matter how much Mr Knight stood up for them – they did care about finding out who was responsible.

"Any ideas?" asked Chris.

"Maybe," said Sam, looking at Nick. "Please tell me it wasn't your little brother."

"How would I know? I only just heard about it," replied Nick defensively.

"It does sounds like something he'd do," said Chad with a shrug of his shoulders.

"I promise, I don't know. If he is involved, I'll kill him myself, okay?" said Nick, looking around at the group.

"He is stupid enough," said Alan consolingly.

"Meanwhile, we take the blame for the stupidity of your little brother," said Stacey angrily.

"It's not Nick's fault," said Alexa quietly. "I don't think Con even wants us to take the blame. Con wants the attention Nick gets, but doesn't have the brains. This isn't the first thing Con's done that we've been blamed for, but it is the most dangerous."

"I'll talk to him," said Nick, giving Alexa a faint smile. "If he did have anything to do with it, I'll make sure he's sorry."

In the silence that followed, they heard Mrs Taylor yelling, but could not make out the words. Chad and Sam moved closer to the door, but in that instant Mr Knight came flying out of it and collided heavily with them.

"I thought you would've gone to lunch by now," said Mr Knight, his voice flustered as he righted himself.

"Did you just get in trouble for backing us up?" asked Nick in awe.

"You could say that," replied Mr Knight, grinning slightly.

"Why?" asked Alan finally.

"Why what?" asked Mr Knight, and Alexa could hear the confusion in his voice.

"Why did you stick up for us?" replied Alan, annunciating every word as though Mr Knight was a bit thick.

"You're all innocent, right?" asked Mr Knight in a slightly

concerned voice. They nodded slowly. "Well then, I saw no point in you all sitting there continuing to take the blame for something you didn't do. We should be spending our time looking for the real culprits. Someone could've been seriously hurt."

"Sure, but why'd you stick up for us?" asked Chris, trying to make Alan's point again.

"I really don't understand. I just explained that to you. Why would I not stick up for you?" asked Mr Knight turning his gaze between them with a perplexed look on his face.

"Because no one ever has before. Didn't matter if we were innocent or not," said Sam, as though pointing out the blatantly obvious.

"That's unfortunate," said Mr Knight, truly understating the situation, but it was apparent that he was not about to go against the school and Mrs Taylor any more than he already had. "I can understand some of your frustrations, but I'm asking you to please just stay out of trouble and continue to concentrate on your studies. Don't give Mrs Taylor more reasons to suspect you."

Alexa felt as sceptical as the others looked. Then she noticed Mr Knight looking at her and quickly turned away. She definitely did not want him questioning her now.

"Well, thanks for the support, Sir. We'll see you around," said Stacey as she and Chris walked off.

The rest of the group began to depart, so Alexa lifted herself off the wall she had been leaning against. Darkness suddenly clouded across her eyes and her legs gave way beneath her.

"You okay?" asked Sam, as he tried to hold her up.

"Yeah, I'm fine," Alexa replied gingerly, using Sam's support to find her feet.

"Come and sit down," said Mr Knight, guiding them to the nearby stairs. "Are you sure you're all right, Miss Samson?"

"Yeah, I'm fine," Alexa replied more forcefully as the spinning in her head began to ease. She wished Mr Knight would go away. "I think I just need some food."

Alexa stood and walked off, catching a glimpse of the concerned looks on Sam, Chad and Mr Knight's faces as she turned the corner. If Sam's place in the school was not at risk because of her, she would have curled up in his arms and confessed everything. The problem was that she loved him too much to ever destroy his life by tying it up with hers.

"Alexa! Alexa, wait." Alexa stopped, unable to ever walk away from that voice. "What's wrong? Please talk to me," pleaded Sam, catching up to her halfway to the dining hall.

"I'm okay," Alexa replied softly, trying to convince herself it was true. She had to protect him. "There's nothing you can do. I'm okay."

"Look at me."

Alexa wished she could have resisted that command, because she could not hold back the tears that spilled down her cheeks as their eyes met. She desperately wanted to tell Sam everything – about Ms Carter, about Clinton and about the baby.

The baby.

The thought of it caused more tears to stream down her face. Sam wiped them from her cheeks and wrapped his arms around her in a tight embrace, not letting go until her face was dry.

***

The nausea that continued to punctuate not just Alexa's mornings, but her whole day got the better of her as she and Bianca made their way to class the next morning, necessitating a detour back to the dorms. It had already been a disappointing day. Alexa had convinced herself that she had not believed, but her heart had pounded earlier that morning when she had gathered around a computer in the library with Ezra and Bianca to check the winning lottery numbers from the night before. One number. That was all they had.

"You're pregnant, aren't you?" asked Bianca, pulling Alexa from her memory as she stood hunched over their bathroom sink, washing out her mouth.

Alexa just hung her head and nodded. She felt arms wrap around her, Bianca's head resting in her neck.

"What are you going to do?" asked Bianca softly.

"I don't know," Alexa replied sadly. "What can I do?"

"Have you told Mr Marsh?"

"No. I wanted to be completely sure I was pregnant before I told him. I can't keep it from him for much longer. It's going to be obvious soon enough."

"But what about the baby? What are you going to do? You can't have a baby," said Bianca, turning Alexa around to face her.

"What would you have me do?" replied Alexa heatedly, pushing past Bianca and into the bedroom. "Abortion seems really easy until you're actually pregnant. There's a living thing inside of me and forgive me if I don't find killing it the best option."

Alexa knew her anger at Bianca was unjustified. She believed in a woman's right to choose and had always believed that she would have made that choice too. She even realised it was the most sensible option, but she was not feeling sensible. She felt obliged.

"I'm not saying it's easy, but you're sixteen. You have no home, no money and if you have a baby now, you'll also have no education. It's just not an option to have a baby, Alexa, especially to a teacher."

"Don't you think I know all this?" Alexa cried, hating Bianca's self-righteous tone. "I don't want any of this. I don't want to be pregnant. I don't want a baby and I don't want to kill my baby. It makes no difference anyway. If I survive telling Clinton, the baby sure won't."

"You don't honestly think he'd hurt you, do you?" asked Bianca in a tone that betrayed her disbelief in the dangerousness of Clinton.

"He sure isn't going to hug me and tell me we're going to live happily ever after," Alexa sighed, deciding not to bother setting Bianca straight about how frightening Clinton truly was. "C'mon let's just get to class while I'm not throwing up."

Alexa's relief from the nausea was short-lived. As she and Bianca walked up the stairs past Mr Knight's office, another wave flowed through her body. She stopped and leaned against the wall, waiting for the sickness to pass.

"Maths is almost over," said Bianca. "We should just head over to English, if you're okay."

"Yeah, I'll be fine in a minute. Why people would voluntarily do this to themselves is beyond me."

"Are you ladies all right?" asked Mr Knight, as he walked from his office, startling Alexa and Bianca.

"Alexa was feeling sick. We were just coming back from the dorms and were about to go to English," said Bianca.

"You still not feeling well, Miss Samson?" asked Mr Knight.

"It's just a stomach bug, Sir," answered Alexa, not meeting Mr Knight's eyes. She could not understand why he had to always appear at the worst moments.

"Perhaps it's best you don't spread that bug to the rest of your classmates. Go to back to your room and rest. I'll make sure your teachers are informed of your absence," said Mr Knight firmly.

"I said, I'm fine," Alexa argued, marching past Mr Knight and

Bianca, but she only made it a few metres before another wave of nausea flooded her body. She clapped her hand over her mouth and tried desperately to keep the little contents left in her stomach inside.

"All right, Miss Samson, let's go," said Mr Knight. Alexa felt his arm gently press against her waist, guiding her towards the dormitories as she continued to curl her body against the nausea. "You can go to class, Miss Ross. I will take Miss Samson back to her room and make sure she's all right."

Although Alexa noticed, with no small degree of alarm, the comfort of Mr Knight's slight touch, she threw off his guiding arm as soon as the nausea passed and allowed her to stand up straight.

"I can make my own way back. I don't need an escort," Alexa said bitterly.

"You are clearly ill and I am your year advisor. It's my job to make sure you're all right," Mr Knight replied gently, as they reached her room. "I will make sure some lunch is brought to you and I'll be back to check on you this afternoon."

"Fine," said Alexa, closing the door in Mr Knight's face, unsure if she was happy about this complication or not.

There was no way she would be able to sneak out to see Clinton if Mr Knight was going to check on her. However, she was worried that Clinton would say it was her fault all the same.

Chapter Six

MARCUS COULD NOT stop thinking about Alexa all day. He even mentioned her illness in passing to other teachers, but true concern for Alexa was sparse. She was a troubled and troublesome student. Her full history did not seem to be well known, just that her heroin-addicted mother had overdosed when she was eleven and her sister continued to battle a heroin addiction. During the year, Alexa was passed between foster homes, a place often only being found for her holiday stays in the last few days of term because no one ever wanted her back.

As Marcus walked towards her room, he felt a stab of sympathy for Alexa. He, like the other teachers, could not comprehend what her life must be like. Knocking on her dormitory door, he resolved to have more patience when dealing with Alexa. It did none of them any good to expect her to be like every other student at Redgrove, not when most of them came from some of the state's wealthiest families.

"Good afternoon, Miss Chatri. I'm just here to check on Miss Samson," he said. "She's not been well."

"She's asleep," said Lizzie, smiling up at him.

Marcus moved into the room, watching Lizzie's smile become more embarrassed. Lizzie had been smiling at him like that since year seven and it made him wonder why he had never thought about her. Alexa had never once smiled at him.

"Has she been having nightmares?" Marcus asked, looking over at the far bed, the curtains pulled closed around it.

"No, not today, anyway," said Martha, looking up from her desk. "She tends to scream or cry when she's having nightmares. Right now it's just happy, talkative sleeping,"

Marcus was about to ask Alexa's roommates more questions about her sleeping habits when they heard whimpering and laboured breathing coming from Alexa's bed.

"Yeah, see now that's a nightmare," said Martha sadly, turning back to her desk, her head hung slightly.

Marcus walked over to Alexa's bed and drew back the curtains.

Alexa was still asleep, but he noticed tears seeping down her cheeks. It was horrible to see a young girl look so fragile in her sleep. Kneeling beside Alexa, Marcus placed his hand gently on her shoulder. A second later he was falling backwards, startled by Alexa's frightened reactions to his light touch. From the floor, he watched Alexa scuttle, wide-eyed, away from him.

"I'm sorry. I didn't mean to scare you. You were having a nightmare," Marcus said cautiously, looking into Alexa's scared blue eyes. She did not answer. "Are you all right, Miss Samson?"

Alexa continued to look at him with terrified eyes.

"You didn't ... you didn't give her ... to ... give her to him," said Alexa in a barely audible voice.

"What are you talking about? You were having a nightmare. Are you sure you're all right?"

"Was I talking? In my sleep, was I talking?" Alexa asked anxiously, wiping the tears from her face.

"Not just then, no. Miss Henderson says you were earlier. We heard you crying. That's when I woke you up," Marcus replied, trying desperately to read the thoughts in Alexa's eyes. "Come on, come, I want you to come to my office."

Alexa nodded slowly, wiping her face dry, and followed him out of the room.

"That must have been some nightmare you were having," said Marcus, as they walked towards his office.

"No worse than any other," Alexa replied dismissively. Her voice was stronger now, angrier too.

Marcus stopped and turned to face Alexa, trying to read her eyes, but realised that chance had passed. Her eyes were now as hard as steel.

"You said before you've had these nightmares since you were a child. This same nightmare still scares you after all this time?" he asked with gentle curiosity. "What was the nightmare about?"

"I don't think that's relevant," replied Alexa in a hard voice.

"I think it is," Marcus replied decidedly, especially as she had implied that it involved him.

"Yeah well, you think you can stop my nightmares by knowing what they are," said Alexa calmly. "You think I need to be helped. You think you can actually help me. There's a lot of things you think, few of which are actually right."

Alexa turned and stalked away. Marcus did not try to stop her. She was right. He did think he could stop her nightmares and he did think she needed help, but he was not so sure that he could help. He just hoped desperately, too desperately, that he could help her and that she wanted him to.

Marcus had no idea what had happened to his plan of staying away from Alexa.

***

Alexa rose with Bianca on Friday morning and they headed quickly to breakfast before meeting Ezra outside the library. The trio entered the library and found a computer at the far end, away from all the other students. Ezra immediately navigated to the website with the lottery results.

"Thirteen, eight, thirty-six ..." said Bianca, reading the winning numbers from the draw the night before.

Alexa glanced at the screen and knew instantly that they had not been successful. Despite doing her best not to raise her hopes too high, she had found herself counting on this being the correct interpretation of the mysterious numbers from her dream.

"We still have Saturday night," said Bianca, trying to sound upbeat.

"Let's just face facts, the numbers meant nothing," Alexa said, standing up and collecting her bag. "It was all just a fantasy. You were right, Ezra, it was just a dream."

"Don't give up hope just yet. We still have another chance. You just never know your luck," Ezra smiled at her.

"No, actually, I do," Alexa replied. She knew her luck all too well. "And it's pretty damn crap."

Alexa stormed out of the library unsure of who she was angrier at – Bianca for encouraging her to believe or herself for believing. After many moments alone, Alexa decided on herself. Of course Bianca would believe. In Bianca's world these sorts of things were possible, if not likely. Miracles like that just did not happen in her world. Alexa had always known that, and accepted that long ago, but with one stupid dream she had been convinced to forget everything she had learned through bitter experience.

It was the one thing Alexa truly disliked about Redgrove. None of the other students could comprehend that their world was not her world. She could not just make things better. There was not some simple solution to her problems. She did not have anyone she could turn to. All those things her friends, including Sam, took for granted, they just could not fathom that she too did not have access to. It was what left her feeling like an outsider, an intruder, after all these years. It was ironic, because Redgrove was more of a home to her than any of them.

That thought did not cheer Alexa as she trudged to her next class. This home, like all her others, was likely to abandon her in her moment of greatest need.

"Cheer up. At least you're not throwing up so much any more," smiled Ezra, as they sat down together in chemistry.

"I just wish those numbers had really meant something," Alexa replied, grateful for an outlet for her frustration. "Even if it they weren't the 'winning numbers'. I just wish they meant *something*."

"Even if we do win that money, it won't really help you now. We're sixteen. You have to work out what you're going to do without money."

"Did Bianca talk to you?" Alexa asked, deeply annoyed that Bianca could not keep what she knew to herself.

"I can work things out on my own, you know," said Ezra with slightly raised eyebrows, not completely convincing Alexa that Bianca had said nothing. It seemed too rehearsed. "You never get sick. I knew it wasn't a stomach bug."

"You don't think anyone else knows, do you?" asked Alexa, looking across the bench at Lizzie and Natalie, who were both deeply immersed in their own conversation.

"No," answered Ezra seriously. Perhaps she had told Bianca not to spread the news any further. "Do you know what you're going to do yet?"

"I haven't even told Clinton. I don't know what to do. It's not like any option is all that enticing. I can't exactly have a child, but I really, really don't want to have an abortion. I wouldn't even know how," said Alexa, bowing her head slightly.

That was the real problem. There was no way for her to even contemplate her options when she could not leave the school grounds and there was no one within it who could or would help her. She had no choices.

Bianca refused to believe that, refused to believe there was no one Alexa could call or turn to. That the school would not take her side was also completely beyond Bianca's comprehension. Alexa knew that whatever Clinton's solution was would be her choice. Trying to find options beyond that or people she could confide in was just a waste of energy. That was also something Bianca refused to accept.

Now that Ezra knew about her being pregnant, Bianca maintained a constant conversation about it. Alexa continued to be suspicious that they had been discussing her situation behind her back when Bianca appeared to psychically know when Ezra had discovered the truth, but decided it was not worth the fight. It would look like she was avoiding the real issue, which was probably true too. Alexa would do just about anything to avoid Bianca's patronising advice about what she should do.

"She can't have the baby," said Bianca sanctimoniously as they sat together in English.

"Don't you think it's up to Alexa?" replied Ezra quietly. Alexa knew that Ezra was not pro-abortion, though she rarely imposed her views on others. It made her think that Ezra did not like Bianca dictating what was the right thing to do either. "It's her body, her baby, her life. If she wants to keep the baby then she should be able to."

"She's sixteen. Why should she throw her life away?"

"A child's not a waste of life," Ezra hissed back.

"So you truly think Alexa should have this baby?" asked Bianca incredulously.

"I never said that," replied Ezra with a slight sigh.

"Right, so what's she going to do, have a cot by her bed in the dorms? Bring the baby to class?" argued Bianca, none too kindly. "She doesn't even have a family or a home. She has a kid and she'll just be breeding yet another welfare recipient."

Alexa was stung by the vehemence of Bianca's assessment of the situation. Of course she was concerned that she did not have the means to take care of her child, but really believed that there was more than just her responsible for this child. Ezra clearly agreed, as she pointed out Clinton's role in the whole situation.

"Alexa's the one who got herself into this predicament. She's the one that's pregnant. If she didn't want to be, she should've taken more precautions," countered Bianca simply.

"I think you've covered both sides of the debate pretty well now," said Alexa, trying to sound dispassionate. "You think we can drop it now? Anyone would think I wasn't sitting right next to the two of you."

Bianca and Ezra looked at each other before nodding and turning their gaze back to their work. When they went to lunch Bianca tried to explain that she had not been attacking her, just pointing out the difficulties of anyone being a mother at sixteen.

Alexa simply nodded and agreed. It was easier than arguing. No matter what she said, they were never going to understand.

*****

Sun blazed through the window on Monday morning, waking Alexa from yet another restless sleep. Her heart pounded with sickening anticipation. Saturday night had been their last chance to win the lottery and she would now have to face whatever fate had in store for her.

She and Bianca left the dining hall early to meet Ezra outside the library before assembly. None of them read the numbers aloud. It was immediately clear that they had not won. Alexa walked out of the library without a word, leaving Bianca and Ezra sitting glumly in front of the computer.

Alexa felt strangely unprepared for this result. As much as she had tried not to let herself believe that those numbers were winning lottery numbers, she clearly had. Bianca's enthusiasm had been contagious, along with her optimism. It was only now that Alexa realised that the money had represented her chance to choose, to choose what she did and what would happen to her baby. Now that choice was gone and it lay in the hands of Clinton Marsh.

When the bell rang to signal the start of lunch on Tuesday, Alexa walked out of the chemistry lab with her heart thumping painfully. Ezra wished her luck as she headed towards her secret exit to meet Clinton. This was the last week of school before Easter and Alexa knew she had to tell Clinton about the baby today. Within minutes of arriving at their meeting spot, Clinton pulled up. Alexa jumped in, her nerves gearing into overdrive.

"Hi," Alexa said quietly, trying to gauge what mood Clinton was in. "I'm sorry about last week. I caught a stomach bug and was vomiting. Mr Knight made me go back to my room. He said he'd check on me so I didn't think I'd be able to risk meeting you."

Clinton did not respond, but placed his hand on her leg and ran his fingers along the inside of her thigh. Alexa felt a chill run down her spine and did not attempt to speak again while they drove. When they entered Clinton's apartment she did not go to the kitchen to begin lunch as she usually did. Instead, she sat down at the table and waited for Clinton to close the front door.

"There's something we need to talk about," Alexa said slowly, watching Clinton's reaction closely.

"There sure is," said Clinton, dropping his keys on the kitchen table and moving in front of her. "It seems that you've been quite the busy slut."

"What?"

"I thought I made it quite clear how I felt about you and that boy."

"I don't know what you're talking about," Alexa stammered. She had barely been near Sam over the past week.

"Don't lie to me!" Clinton yelled, slamming his hand down on the table, his face inches away from hers. "I saw the two of you together. In the middle of the school. For everyone to see. His filthy hands all over you."

"What are you talking about? When?"

"Last Monday, that's when. In the corridor leading from Mrs Taylor's office," snarled Clinton.

"Oh shit," Alexa gasped. She had been avoiding Sam since that day, trying desperately to forget how close she had come to telling him the truth. "You don't understand. That was nothing. I was sick," she tried to explain. "I fainted and Sam was just helping me – walking me to the dining hall."

"I told you," barked Clinton, grabbing Alexa by the hair forcing her to look into his wild eyes. "I did not want that boy's filth on you. You are mine!"

"I'm sorry," replied Alexa desperately.

"See now I don't think you are, because the very next day I watched you as you led Marcus Knight into your room." Alexa could not speak as her eyes bulged in disbelief. Clinton's grasp on her hair was so tight she could not even shake her head. "You sure are spreading yourself around, aren't you, you filthy, little slut."

Clinton let go of her hair, pushing her head hard towards the table as he stepped back from her. She could feel herself shaking and tried to control her fear.

"I did not lead Mr Knight anywhere," Alexa said forcefully, determined not to let Clinton speak to her this way. "I told you, I was sick. He took me back to my room. He insisted. I had no choice but to go with him."

"Really? I don't think I believe you. After all, you assured me there would be no further incidents with that boy and yet I find you, myself, in his arms."

"It's not like that. He – is – my – friend. I was sick and upset. He gave me a hug. There's nothing sinister about it and I'm not going to apologise for your paranoia."

Alexa knew she had gone too far. Rage flickered in Clinton's eyes as he grabbed her by the arm and led her forcefully to the bedroom.

"You're mine!" he growled, throwing her on the bed and wrapping his hand around her throat. "You owe me some loyalty, girl, after all I've done for you."

Clinton lifted Alexa's skirt and began to pull at her underwear.

"No," cried Alexa, not wanting Clinton's hands to ever touch her that way again.

"No? Don't you dare say no to me! You wanted this relationship. You wanted what I could provide. Don't you dare tell me you will not keep your end of the bargain," Clinton growled as his hands continued to grope.

"You touch me and this is all over," said Alexa, finally finding the courage to end the relationship. She would rather deal with Ms Carter. At least Ms Carter left marks – evidence – and if Mr Knight was so keen to help her, then maybe he could stop that.

"Don't you dare threaten me, you little slut," Clinton growled, tightening his grip around her throat.

"I'm pregnant," Alexa cried, so desperate for Clinton to stop she could not control her mouth. "You lay a hand on me and the whole school will know you're the father."

Clinton released her at once and she crawled backwards up the bed, rubbing her throat. It was not what she had meant to say. Nor was it the way she had intended informing Clinton of her pregnancy, but it had had the desired effect.

"How dare you … don't lie. You are not pregnant!" Clinton roared.

"I am pregnant with your child," said Alexa calmly, glad she finally had the upper hand.

"You expect me to believe that it's my child? A slut like you, it could be anyone's," snarled Clinton viciously, trying to intimidate her, but she knew the truth.

"A simple DNA test will prove me right," Alexa replied with a slight shrug of her shoulders, trying to prove that she was not frightened by him.

"Are you threatening me?"

"I'm simply making a point," she replied casually.

"Get out."

"What?"

"Get out!"

Alexa took her chance and raced from the room. Grabbing her bag, she dashed out the door, running until Clinton's apartment was out of sight. Once she was sure Clinton was not coming after her, she walked more slowly back towards school, allowing her heart rate to slow with her steps. She was glad that the walk was long enough that everyone was at dinner by the time she arrived back. However, she was not surprised to see Bianca slipping into the room just minutes after she arrived.

"What happened? Did you tell him? How did it go?" asked Bianca anxiously.

Alexa lay on her bed exhausted, looking up at the ceiling. She was not particularly keen to relive the last few hours, especially as she was not sure how much Bianca really cared. At times she felt like entertainment, or a project – something for Bianca to sort out.

"Yeah, I told him," Alexa replied dully when Bianca kept staring at her. She avoided Bianca's eyes, while trying not to remember what had really happened. "But he tried to make out that it was someone else's child. Then he kicked me out," she summarised.

"Really? Whose kid did he think it was?" asked Bianca, sitting down on the bed looking suddenly more intrigued.

"I had a choice. Sam's or Mr Knight's"

"Mr Knight? How does that work?"

"He saw Mr Knight taking me back to my room last Tuesday. Clinton assumed there was something going on."

"There isn't, is there?" asked Bianca in a scandalised, but not wholly disbelieving voice.

"Do you think I just go around sleeping with teachers?" asked Alexa, hurt by Bianca's insinuation.

"No. I'm sorry. So what are you going to do?"

"Clinton got really agitated when I mentioned that a DNA test would prove that he's the father. So if he wants me to keep that little detail a secret, he can pay me the money I need look after the baby."

"Oh no, Alexa. You still want to keep this baby *and* you want to blackmail a teacher. That's never going to work."

"Yes, it is. I'm going to keep my baby," said Alexa forcefully, finally deciding on that point. She would not be forced to give up her child just because it was Clinton's as well. "Clinton won't want anyone finding out that he's the father, and no one has to know. I'll leave here if I have to. It's the best plan I have to look after my baby. It's the only plan I have," she added softly to herself.

Bianca said nothing as she walked away, but as soon as Ezra turned up at school the next morning Bianca was blurting out Alexa's plan. Ezra stared at Alexa as Bianca spoke. Alexa knew why. At Redgrove, you did not just go around telling other people's stories. It was hard enough to have privacy as a boarder without other people gossiping about you, but Alexa said nothing. Bianca would learn the ways of Redgrove soon enough.

Ezra agreed Alexa's plan was not likely to work very well, but did not think it was necessary to try and talk her out of it.

"It's his kid," said Ezra, shrugging her shoulders. "He should pay for it. But you know he's not going to like to being told what to do. I've had him for history. I know what he's like when he goes off. You don't want to get on his bad side. Maybe try asking rather than blackmailing."

Bianca was left gobsmacked by Ezra's response and sat there with her mouth opening and closing as she tried to gather her reply. Ezra smiled slightly and turned back to Alexa.

"So when are you going to talk to him about it?" Ezra asked her. "Before the holidays?"

"Oh shit, the holidays. I haven't gone to Mr Knight to get permission to go back to the Whites yet," Alexa said anxiously.

"Who are the Whites?" asked Bianca.

"They're my foster parents. Most recent ones, anyway," replied Alexa dismissively. "I've been staying with them since the spring holidays, my longest stretch with one foster family for years. They don't put too much pressure on me. I'm considered a guest in their house rather than a member of the family, but it works well enough."

"What about you? You getting out of here, Bianca?" asked Ezra, clearly happy to continue this new topic of conversation.

"No such luck. My parents are bringing me back home for Christmas and I'm hoping to get out of here for at least one of the other breaks, but it's not going to be this one."

The bell rang and Alexa made her way up to Mr Knight's office to have her departure approved. In a way, she was looking forward to returning to the Whites. She had thought that her absence before the start of term may have convinced them not to ask her back. They would certainly not be the first family to do so.

She had been placed in so many foster homes since her

mother's death she had lost count, and had been surprised when the Whites had asked her to return for the long summer holidays. Staying with the Whites was not an unpleasant experience. They were kind and friendly with two children of their own; Brett, fourteen, and Hayley, nine, who were happy and secure and seemed to enjoy her occasional presence.

"Come in," said Mr Knight when she knocked on his door. Alexa entered, but did not look up. "What can I do for you, Miss Samson? You're feeling better, I hope."

"Yeah, I'm fine. I just need your permission to go back to my foster parents for the holidays."

"The same ones? The Whites?" asked Mr Knight. Alexa saw him looking down and realised that he must have her file permanently accessible. "This should have been done last week. Do you a have letter from them? We've received no correspondence."

"Yeah," Alexa nodded softly, her eyes still downcast. She passed Mr Knight the letter from the Whites she had received the week before. It was nice that they wrote to her inviting her back rather than the school. She found it polite. "I just forgot last week, being sick and all."

"Fair enough. This is fine. Have a seat while I fill out your permission slip. You seem to have recovered well from your stomach bug. I assume you still don't want to talk about those nightmares of yours."

"You assume well," Alexa replied firmly, taking the permission form from Mr Knight's desk as soon as he had signed it.

"I'm glad you're feeling better. Have a good holiday and I hope to see you back here without the police escort this time."

Alexa glared at Mr Knight as she left, hating his last comment. It was ridiculous to think that in her moment of terror in Clinton's apartment that she had thought he was somehow better than all the other teachers here.

Walking away from Mr Knight's office, Alexa forced herself to focus on the few good things she had going on in her life. By tomorrow afternoon she would be escaping the school for over a week, and she would have convinced Clinton to pay for the upkeep of their child in return for his reputation remaining intact. All she had to survive in the meantime was Bianca's constant monologue about how stupid she was, how her plan was doomed to fail and how ridiculous it was to even consider having a child at her age.

"Look, can you please just drop it," said Alexa finally. "This is the only plan I have, okay. I realise it might not work. I realise it could backfire badly, but I have no choice. There're no other options for me. I know you think that it's going to end badly, but you also thought we were going to be millionaires, so forgive me if I don't trust your instinct on this one."

Alexa could see Bianca was hurt by her comments, but she could not afford to start doubting herself. She really did have no other options.

When Alexa arrived at Clinton's office at the end of the day the door was locked. It threw her slightly, wondering if he had left early, but she knew he had a class last period and was sure she would have seen him leaving. Heart pounding, she tried to think of a back-up plan. If she did not see Clinton today, she would have to wait until next term to confront him, but feared her foster parents would find out the truth before then. She had no idea how they would react, but doubted it would be kindly.

"I don't remember us having a meeting scheduled," said Clinton from behind, causing Alexa to jump in fright. She had almost convinced herself she had missed him.

"I need to talk to you," Alexa said, her heart pounding.

"I don't know that we have anything to discuss," said Clinton calmly, as they entered his office and he shut the door behind them.

"How can that be? I'm pregnant with your child. Or have you forgotten that?" said Alexa, wondering why Clinton was choosing to play it so cool.

"I can hardly forget an accusation such as that."

"It's not an accusation."

"I've always been careful. If you're pregnant, then it's to one of your other boyfriends," Clinton snarled.

"Like I said before, a simple DNA test will prove me right," replied Alexa smilingly. If he was going to act cool, she was going to appear assured.

Clinton glared at her fiercely before knocking the pencil holder on his desk across the room. Alexa continued to smile, needing to seem confident. Her plan would never work if Clinton knew how terrified of him she was. She held Clinton's angry gaze as he walked towards her. He was trying to intimidate her with his silent fury, so she kept her ground. When he stopped a metre from her, she held her breath to prevent him from hearing the way it was quivering.

Alexa had never appreciated how large Clinton's hands were until he lifted his right hand above her head. She turned her face, but it did little to lessen the impact as the back of his hand struck her cheek. The force of the blow knocked her to the ground, the right side of her face on fire. When she rose to her feet, Clinton was back on the other side of the room looking out the window.

"No one has to know that you're the father," Alexa said slowly, her face still burning. Clinton turned and glared at her. "Just give me enough money to look after the baby and I promise no one will ever find out that you're the father."

"Are you blackmailing me?" Clinton growled, his look becoming more menacing with every passing second.

"I don't want to hurt you," Alexa said earnestly. "It's a win-win situation. You won't have any hassles and I can take proper care of my child. You don't have to have anything to do with the baby. All I want is some money to take care of it."

"You have got to be joking? Do you honestly think I'm going to give you a cent to bring some bastard child into this world?"

"What choice do you have?" Alexa asked, trying to sound defiant, but her voice shook so much that it was barely even a threat. "If you don't do this, I'll tell everyone the child is yours. You'll lose everything."

It took just two steps for Clinton to cross the room. Alexa took a step back, but he was on top of her before she could even reach the door. His hand wrapped around her throat and pulled her closer to him.

"How dare you threaten me," Clinton growled, his face just millimetres from hers. He tightened his grip and she felt her feet lift off the ground. "How about I show you my own win-win situation."

Alexa watched Clinton's face change from one of anger to one of sick delight as pain speared through her pelvis. He punched her twice more in the stomach before releasing his grip on her throat. She fell to the floor in a crumpled heap, her shaking legs unable to carry her weight.

"Now there'll be no baby and I don't have to pay you a cent," Clinton growled, looking down at her.

Alexa looked up at Clinton and saw his leg pull back. Quickly covering her face with her arms, she realised too late that that was not his target. She cried out in pain, her arms wrapping around her stomach. The intensity of the pain threatened to make her sick as she watched Clinton's feet move away to the other side of the room.

"Get out," snarled Clinton when she continued to lie on the floor of his office in a curled up ball.

It was a few minutes before Alexa could even try to comply. Moving was agonising, but she struggled to her feet. Clinton's eyes watched her uncaringly from the other side of the room. She opened the door and staggered out into the deserted corridor; it did not take long for the school to empty on the last day of term.

Alexa made her way to the back of the gym and collapsed, her pelvis in agony. She would lose the baby, of that she was sure, and she cried at the thought of its painful death. Her child was dying and it was her fault.

When the tears finally ran dry, Alexa felt her body fill with empty nothingness. It consumed her, blocking the pain, tearing her away from everything but the knowledge of her failure.

Walking in a blind haze, Alexa made her way to the train station. She supposed she was going to the Whites, but there was no conscious decision to do so. There was just nowhere else to go. Sitting on the platform, she saw a train coming. She knew it was an express and would not stop, but found herself on her feet all the same. Each deliberate step took her closer to the edge. She was just two metres away when the train sped past.

Sitting back down next to her bag, Alexa did not think about anything. The nothingness did not allow for conscious thoughts or feelings, but her subconscious soon had her back on her feet. She knew what she was doing and she was not sorry it had come to this.

One step after the other. The edge of the platform and the front of the train were merging more precisely this time. Two more steps. Two more seconds.

One more step.

Alexa closed her eyes as a horn blared, calling her name, drawing her forward. This would hurt. One moment of excruciating pain and then an eternity of blissful peace.

It hit her chest first. Front then back. Pain ripped through her, but it was not so bad. She had been wrong. Death was not as painful as she imagined.

Chapter Seven

MARCUS WATCHED THE train screech to a halt several hundred metres from the end of the platform. His heart was pounding. He looked down and saw Alexa pressed between his body and the fence at the end of the platform. He had caught her in time.

It took a moment before Marcus could think about anything other than the fact that Alexa was not a broken body under the train that was now slowly moving away. Then he realised just how hard his body was pressed against hers and stepped away. He held an arm out just in case Alexa collapsed, but she did not move. She did not look at him. She did not respond in any way at all.

Alexa slid slowly down the fence, her body curling into a tight ball. Marcus brushed the hair back off his face and looked down at her.

"Don't move," he commanded, pointing his finger at her as he turned to collect his bag that lay abandoned on the platform.

When Marcus returned, Alexa had not moved a muscle. She just sat there, looking blankly down the platform.

"Are you going to explain to me what the hell that was about?" he asked, his voice shaking, but Alexa did not respond.

A minute later, Alexa rose to her feet. Marcus turned to see another train approaching, slower this time, but he could not take any risks. He grabbed her arm and did not let her move. Alexa's eyes flicked to an abandoned bag several metres away. With her arm still firmly in his grasp, Marcus went to collect the bag and dragged her on to the train.

The train journey was spent in silence. Alexa made no attempt to acknowledge his existence. Marcus just sat and watched her. There was not an ounce of emotion on her face and her eyes were dull and glazed. He had always believed that Alexa's emotional weakness was her eyes, but the life and pain they once reflected was gone and he knew something had gone very wrong for this sad, little girl.

"Come with me," said Marcus as kindly as possible, guiding Alexa through the crowded station to a small coffee shop when they alighted the train in the city. "What do you want to drink?" he asked as he sat Alexa down. She did not answer. "You don't move, understand?" he said with unintentional harshness.

Marcus ordered a strong coffee to calm his nerves and brought back a hot chocolate for Alexa. She sipped it immediately, calming him slightly, though all her actions remained strangely automated.

"Do you want to explain what the hell happened back there?" asked Marcus, as soon as he noticed the dull, glazed look fade from Alexa's eyes. "What happened, Alexa? You would've been killed. Do you realise that?"

"I always thought that was the point of suicide," replied Alexa in a flat voice, the usual defiance returning to her gaze.

"Why would you want to die? You have your whole life ahead of you. Alexa, please, what's wrong? Let me help you."

Alexa smiled grimly and shook her head.

"Why don't you think I can help you? Please, let me help you," Marcus pleaded again, desperate never to see someone in that state again.

"What will it cost me?" snarled Alexa, throwing him a dark look. Marcus did not understand, but then Alexa suddenly keeled over. He placed a comforting hand on her shoulder. "I asked you, what will your help cost me?" she said through gritted teeth.

"I don't understand. Why would my help cost you anything?" asked Marcus confusedly. He knew she was talking about money, but did not understand. Teachers were not allowed to charge added fees for their assistance. The students paid enough as it was.

"Everything has a price, right? I want to know what yours is," said Alexa, sitting up again.

"Price? I don't have a price. I want to help you."

"No. Everyone has their price and I think I deserve to know what it is beforehand this time."

Marcus could do nothing but stare. He was starting to doubt that Alexa was talking about money, but that made even less sense.

"I don't want anything for helping you, Alexa," he replied cautiously, concerned where this conversation was going.

"I'm not interested in playing these games," cried Alexa, her arms wrapped around her waist as she glared up at him.

Alexa seemed pained. Marcus looked intently at her face, trying to decipher her cryptic words. Then he noticed a red mark on her check and something sickening stabbed his gut. He must have hurt her when he had pulled her back from the edge of the platform. He had not tried to be gentle. He had only tried to save her life.

"You want to help me. I want to know what it will cost me," continued Alexa in the same vein. "You already know I have no money, so that only really leaves one thing, doesn't it? If you want to help me, name your price first."

"What? No … you have the wrong idea – it's not like … I don't want …"

Marcus was unable to speak, unable to think. He suddenly realised the currency in which Alexa thought she would be made to trade.

"Alexa, I would never … I would never ask for you to repay me for help that I offered you and I would never ever ask for –"

"Really? Well you sure have been keen to thrust you help on me," spat Alexa angrily.

"I do want to help you, but I have never wanted to help you just so that I could sleep with you. My God. This is ridiculous," Marcus gasped.

"I agree," said Alexa, collecting her bags. "Thanks for the drink, but I think I'll stick to helping myself."

Marcus wanted to stop Alexa from leaving or follow her to make sure she made it home all right, but was far too stung by her accusations. If she felt that way about him, he could never touch her again, never go near her, never do anything that could compromise his integrity. He thought over every interaction they had ever had, trying to find actions or words that could have been so badly misconstrued. He thought of Lizzie's smiling face and wondered if he had led her on. Did he give the general impression of wanting to sleep with his students?

Scared that the answer might be yes, Marcus did not do what he knew he should. He knew what the law required of him right then, but he did not want to report Alexa's suicide attempt if it meant that she was going to accuse him of trying to sleep with her. Redgrove College got rid of scandals and it would get rid of him rather than risk a bad reputation. He had spent years building his career and he would not let one troubled child destroy it. Alexa could go throw herself under some other train, Marcus thought harshly, but then the memory of her walking steadily towards the last one came to mind and he pushed his half-finished coffee away. He needed something stronger than that.

Finding the nearest pub, Marcus ordered a double bourbon and downed it in two gulps. Ordering another, followed by several more, he drank until he could not order any more.

***

Alexa woke the next morning to immense cramping pain in her lower back and abdomen. She felt as though three months of periods had come at once and wondered if she would notice when her baby left her body.

When she did not come down for breakfast, Alexa's foster mother, Pam, came up to her room to check on her. Alexa saw the concern in Pam's eyes as she scanned her face. She was afraid Pam might ask difficult questions, but Pam seemed appeased by her story of very bad period pain. It was something Alexa knew Pam suffered from herself and she was glad when Pam returned to her room with pain killers and orders to rest.

The rest lasted less than an hour. Bethany called. She had convinced the Christies to allow her to spend the Easter long weekend with them. Pam looked concerned by the request, but when Karl nodded his consent Alexa rushed upstairs and packed a small bag. She was out the door half an hour later. The pain moving caused did not worry Alexa now. She was going to see Bethany.

Bethany had stayed clean since her return to school. It was a wonderful achievement and Alexa was impatient to get to the Christies'. She could not remember the last significant amount of time she and Bethany had spent together that did not involve wandering city streets together or battling through Bethany's withdrawal. It was not that Alexa cared where or how she saw Bethany, just that the clean Bethany was her real sister.

Alexa arrived at the Christies' just over an hour after leaving the Whites'. Bethany was sitting on the front steps waiting for her and at first sight ran and wrapped her arms around her. Despite the pain of Bethany's crushing embrace, Alexa did not push her away. She reciprocated the gesture, stroking Bethany's long brown hair.

Bethany had grown since the start of the school year and she was now not only taller, but starting to tower over Alexa. Years of drug addiction had left Bethany's body thin and underdeveloped, but it had been making up for lost time during the past few, drug-free months. It was heartening to see. Alexa always feared the health consequences of Bethany's drug use.

Mrs Christie prepared a large lunch for them. It was an unusual development and made Alexa wonder what had been happening over the past few months. Bethany's letters were never very descriptive, and she worried what Bethany had gone through to get these concessions. However, the way the Christies doted on Bethany reassured Alexa that it would have been nothing too severe.

The food was good, and Alexa was starving, so ate everything that was put before her. It did not seem to impress Mrs Christie, but Alexa refused to care. They hated her anyway.

"How's everything going, Alexa?" asked Mrs Christie, though it was clear she did not particularly care about the answer.

"Okay," replied Alexa, between mouthfuls of food, not bothering to elaborate too much. "School's school."

"Are you sure? You don't look so good," said Mr Christie, looking at Alexa's pale face.

Bethany sniggered. Alexa had hurriedly put make-up on to cover the bruising across her face before leaving the house.

"Yeah, I had a stomach bug for a couple of weeks. That's all," replied Alexa, elbowing Bethany in the ribs.

Bethany elbowed her back and they tussled at the table until Mr Christie ordered them angrily to Bethany's room. They complied immediately, Bethany grabbing Alexa's hand and pulling her from the table. They continued to wrestle as they walked, loving that they were actually able to touch each other, but when Bethany's hand came to close to Alexa's beaten midsection Alexa had to pull quickly away.

"So who hit you?" asked Bethany, as she closed her bedroom door behind them. "You always were terrible at make-up. Do you want me to do it for you tomorrow?"

"Yeah, thanks," nodded Alexa.

"You going to tell me who hit you? Or am I going to have to beat it out of you?" asked Bethany with a cheeky smile.

"Clinton," nodded Alexa sombrely, not yet detached enough to joke about it.

Bethany knew all about the affair with Clinton and how it had started, and Alexa was glad. She was not sure she was up to telling the story now.

"What happened?" asked Bethany, her voice more serious as the smile fell from her face.

"I fell pregnant."

"That will do it. You still pregnant?"

"Nope," said Alexa, shaking her head. "He took care of that too."

Bethany took Alexa's hand and led her to the bed. Alexa lay down on her side, trying hard to keep the tears at bay. Bethany curled up behind her, wrapping her arms around her and holding her tight.

"It gets worse," Alexa said tentatively. She did not want to confess this, but she had never kept secrets from Bethany. "Yesterday, after Clinton did this, I … I tried to finish things – you know, for good – but a teacher stopped me."

"I think that's a good thing," replied Bethany instantly, pulling Alexa closer.

"No, it's not," Alexa gasped, knowing the terrible situation she had put herself in. "I owe this guy my life now. I don't know what he's going to want in return."

"Maybe nothing. You help me all the time and you don't ask for anything."

"That's different. You're my sister. He didn't have to help. He's going to want *something*."

"I don't care, I'm glad he stopped you," snapped Bethany, unable to conceal the hurt in her voice.

"Oh, Bethy, I'm sorry," said Alexa, turning to face Bethany. Yesterday, she had not once stopped to think of her. Right now, she could not imagine how that had happened. "I just didn't know what to do."

"I know," said Bethany sincerely. "But next time, you find me first. You're not going anywhere without me. You go, I go."

Alexa stroked Bethany's face and looked into the blue eyes that conveyed the same sadness as her own. She had to try and suppress how much she wanted that outcome – both of them free from this life forever.

"Did you really want to die?" asked Bethany mournfully.

"More than anything," Alexa replied truthfully.

"I want to die, too, most days."

"No, don't say that. I'll take care of you, okay. I promise," cried Alexa, her heart aching with the very thought of Bethany dying. She had feared such a thing her entire life, and knew that if Bethany died she would not survive her for very long.

"Not if you're dead, you can't," said Bethany, her lip quivering.

If Alexa could have truly believed Bethany wanted to die, she would have happily agreed to take her own life right there and
72

then, but Bethany was not suggesting that. Bethany still had some will to live and Alexa knew she had to find some of it too. While Bethany wanted to live, she would find a way to keep herself alive as well.

"I'm not dead and I swear that I'll always be here to look after you," Alexa promised, squeezing Bethany tightly. "I'm going to get us out of here. I'm going to find us somewhere to be together."

Bethany nodded and reciprocated Alexa's embrace. Alexa closed her eyes and concentrated only on Bethany and her continued survival. She could not think about her own life if she had to find a way to survive it.

They stayed like that for hours, wrapped in each other's arms, until they fell asleep, not waking until the early hours of the morning.

The next few days were very soothing for Alexa. Bethany helped put her life back in perspective. It made her remember that her life was not her own, and that she could never again put her own pain ahead of Bethany and her needs. Bethany would have to be her focus for every decision as she tried to get through their final two years apart.

They did not do much over the course of the long weekend. Neither of them cared to. All they wanted was to be together, but it was not always so easy. Despite not having taken heroin for over two months, Bethany's cravings could be powerfully strong and Alexa stayed by her side whenever they came. Bethany tried hard to control her temper when the cravings hit, but Alexa did not care if she was successful. She would take any mood Bethany was in just to be with her, knowing it was her fault Bethany was even in this situation.

Alexa had watched Bethany take heroin from when she was just seven years old. If she had been able to stop it back then, they might never have had to be torn apart. On the same day their mother died of a drug overdose Bethany had also overdosed. Bethany was in hospital for almost a month. When Bethany was released, she was technically free of heroin, but like the way she reached for a razor blade whenever life became too tough, Bethany reached for drugs to deaden her pain.

"I wish you could stay longer," said Bethany on Sunday night.

"I wish I could stay with you forever, Bethy, but I promise that I'll get us out of here," said Alexa firmly. "The Whites are pretty nice people and they said they'd help me get work in the summer holidays again – if they keep taking me back. Hopefully, by the time I finish school I'll have enough money that you can come and live with me. I know it's a long way off, but you just have to hang in there."

"I'm trying," said Bethany softly.

"I know, and I'm so proud of you," said Alexa, hugging Bethany tight. "You're amazing. I don't think I could fight this like you. I just know that I have to tell myself the same thing."

Bethany nodded in Alexa's neck and hugged her tighter. For the rest of the visit, they were nearly always in each other's arms. When Monday afternoon came around they held each other so tight that they had to be almost pried apart by Mrs Christie.

"Come now, Bethany, Alexa has to leave," said Mrs Christie, relief evident in her voice.

Neither let go as tears streamed down their faces. Alexa could feel her heart breaking and could not find the strength to release her grasp on Bethany. Eventually, Mrs Christie managed to separate them, literally pushing her arms between them and wedging them apart.

"I'll talk to you soon, okay. You take care, Bethy. I love you," said Alexa, stroking Bethany's face.

Forcing herself not to look into Bethany's eyes, Alexa walked away, tears falling uncontrollably down her face. Every step felt like walking through mud. Her legs were so heavy and the street so long. Her chest constricted with every breath, crushing her heart and squeezing her pain out her eyes.

"Lex!"

Alexa turned to see Bethany sprinting up the street. Bethany slammed into her, hugging her tight. The embrace was short, but fierce. With a shivering gasp, Bethany suddenly pushed away from her, turned and, without a word, ran into her house.

When the front door slammed closed, Alexa turned and ran towards the station, unable to stay so close to where Bethany was and not be with her.

***

Light was only just penetrating the curtains when Alexa woke the next morning to the sight of her foster sister's smiling face. She could not help but like Hayley who, at only a couple months off ten, with beautiful curly blonde hair and hazel eyes, thought the world of her.

"Why didn't you come and see us when you came home on Thursday?" asked Hayley, jumping on the bed next to her.

"I wasn't feeling too well and then you guys had to go and see your family and I went to see my sister," said Alexa, wrapping an arm around Hayley, to stop the bouncing as much as to greet her.

"Do you miss your sister?" asked Hayley curiously.

"More than anything in the world," Alexa replied truthfully, feeling her eyes sting.

"What about me? Do you miss me when you're at school?"

"I don't miss being jumped on in the morning," Alexa answered as she tickled Hayley, who giggled loudly. "But, yes, I miss you too."

It was true. Alexa enjoyed staying with the Whites. They were good, decent people and she had never felt more at home with a foster family, but it was Bethany who she truly wanted to be with.

"So I hear I'm taking care of you two for the rest of the week," said Alexa. It was the one condition Karl had laid down before she left to see Bethany. "What are we going to do?"

"I want to go to the movies, but Brett is being really grumpy. He doesn't want to do anything."

"Are your mum and dad still here?"

"Yep, it's only seven."

"Arrggh. You woke me up at seven! All right, I'll be down in a minute. And what's wrong with Brett?"

Hayley did not answer. She was already rushing excitedly down the stairs. Alexa followed at a much more subdued pace and managed to bid a tired farewell to Pam and Karl as they headed to work. It had not been her intention to come down late enough to avoid talking to them, but she was glad she had. The last thing she wanted to do was discuss her weekend with Bethany. Instead, she focused on finding out what had put Brett in such a bad mood.

"He got dumped," Hayley finally explained, as they walked through the shopping centre towards the cinemas. "That's why he didn't want to come today. I think she dumped him for his best friend or something and they're going to be here today."

Brett was walking several metres behind them. He had barely spoken to Alexa all day, which was quite unusual for him. Most holidays he asked all manner of questions of her, mostly intrigued about the trouble she had gotten herself into over the years. The worse it was, the more impressed he was.

Alexa slowed down so that Brett had no option but to fall into step next to her. He tried hard to ignore her so she decided to just ask straight out what the situation was.

"Did you get dumped, Brett?" Alexa asked as gently as possible.

Brett looked horrified by the question, before turning and glaring at Hayley. Hayley just stuck her tongue out at him.

"Can't you keep your mouth shut about anything?" Brett snarled, folding his arms and turning to walk the other direction.

"I'm sorry," said Alexa, chasing him down, but not letting the conversation drop. "She didn't really dump you for your best friend, did she?"

"For the most popular guy in the grade, actually," retorted Brett unhappily. "Can you understand now why I wanted to stay home? They're going to be here. I'm going to be a laughing stock."

"It won't be that bad," said Alexa, putting her arm around Brett's slouched shoulders as an irresponsible plan streaked through her mind. "I can help you save face if you're up for it."

"How?" asked Brett grumpily.

"I'll pretend to be your girlfriend," smiled Alexa mischievously.

"What?" Brett and Hayley said in unison.

"We're going to the movies whether you like it or not," Alexa explained with a casual shrug of her shoulders. "So you can either slouch in behind me and Hayley, or you can walk in with your head high, your hand in mine."

"It won't work," said Brett sceptically.

"Oh yeah it will."

Alexa took Brett's hand and walked towards the food court where they could have lunch before the movies. When Brett pointed out his ex-girlfriend amongst a group of teenagers, Alexa smiled and walked them to a table nearby.

"What are you doing?" hissed Brett, but Alexa only smiled.

It was stupid and juvenile, but this was a situation so far removed from the troubles of her real life that it felt happily surreal to pretend that she was just like every other girl her age; worrying about stupid things like being dumped.

Knowing that the other group would soon be looking their way, Alexa sent Hayley to buy their food and starting having fun with Brett. Alexa found it sweet how innocent Brett was and how awkward he looked when she ran her hands through his hair. However, egged on by the intrigued stares of his peers, it did not take long before Brett was acting all lovey-dovey back.

"You know dating your cousin's illegal," called a boy from the group.

"That's him. Karen's new boyfriend," muttered Brett, his shoulders hunching slightly.

Alexa smiled broadly. She ran her hand over Brett's cheek and brought his lips to hers. The kiss was not an awkward peck. Although Brett was clearly nervous, he knew how to kiss and make it look real – real enough to shock Hayley when she returned with a tray of food.

"It's okay," called Alexa, pulling away from Brett, though she kept her hand on his face. "He's not my cousin. He's my brother."

The howling response from the table next to them was too much for Alexa and she burst out laughing.

"You don't have another sister," replied one of the boys stupidly.

"I know," said Brett in a strong voice that surprised Alexa. He had seemed so timid up until that point. "She's my foster sister."

It was apparent that Brett had spoken to his schoolmates about her, and Alexa was surprised by the awed reaction that comment produced. No one ever reacted like that when they spoke about her.

"Oh yeah, Karrie, was it? I've been meaning to thank you, by the way," said Alexa, thinking they should milk this for all it was worth. Whatever Brett had said about her had not been mean and she appreciated that more than he would ever realise.

"My name's Karen," replied Brett's ex-girlfriend in a huff. "And why would you need to thank me? For letting you have my scraps?"

Alexa raised her eyebrows, wondering why Brett would care that he had been dumped by such an awful person. It made her more determined to do everything possible to allow Brett walk away from this as the hero. She did not care what she had to do to achieve it.

"Hardly," Alexa replied with a smug smile. "Brett mustn't have told you, but we usually hook up when I come home from boarding school. He told me he'd been trying to work out how to break up with you before I came home. Thanks to you, he didn't have to worry. Just had to act a bit sad for a few days to make sure your ego remained intact. He's a sweetie, huh?"

Karen was indignant, grabbing her stuff and storming off. Her boyfriend soon followed, but the other boys were slower to leave.

"Is it true you have a tattoo?" asked the stupid-sounding boy.

"Yeah," Alexa lied, smiling broadly, wondering what else Brett had said about her. "Brett's seen it, but it's not really on public display."

The boys all stared open mouthed for a few seconds before finally trudging off, constantly turning back around to take another look at them.

Alexa wrapped her arm around Brett's shoulders and hugged him, feeling his hands hold her tighter. Breaking away, she felt her cheeks blush at the fire that seemed to be burning in Brett's eyes.

"Let's eat, huh," said Alexa, distributing the food that still sat on Hayley's tray.

They ate quietly and, despite fearing what feelings she had stirred up in Brett, Alexa took his hand as they walked to the cinemas. He was a sweet boy and she knew there was a good chance his friends would still be around, waiting to catch them in their façade. Predictably, Karen and her group of boys followed them into the same movie, taking seats three rows behind them. Alexa disliked them immensely and was in the mood to have more fun. Whispering in Brett's ear to play along, she looked behind her to be sure Karen was watching before dropping her head against Brett's thigh.

Pinching his inner thigh, Brett pulled back and gasped dramatically. Alexa heard the frantic whispering and poked Brett again to make him shift in his seat. Hayley was looking on from the other side of Brett with a mixture of confusion and embarrassment. Alexa was sure Hayley understood that she was doing something vaguely sex-related, but was also sure that if Hayley really knew what she was pretending to do that she would have been screaming.

Catching on, Brett no longer needed Alexa's prodding. His hands stroked her hair gently as he agitatedly shifted his position as if trying hard to sit still. After a few minutes, Alexa sat up, smiling behind her. Brett reached his arm around her shoulders and pulled her gently into his chest before placing a very sweet kiss on the side of her head. Not even pretending this time, Alexa took Brett's other hand and held it in his lap, watching the rest of the movie from the comfort of his shoulder.

Chapter Eight

"BRETT," SAID ALEXA the next day when he returned from a walk with a bunch of garden-picked flowers for her. "You know nothing can happen between me and you, right?"

Brett shrugged his shoulders and walked off, leaving the flowers on the kitchen bench. Alexa went after him, closing his bedroom door behind her. Although Hayley had promised not to mention their antics at the movies to her parents, she could not really be trusted with a conversation like this one.

"I'm not really good enough for you, am I?" said Brett dejectedly. "I mean, I always knew that, but thought that one day you'd look at me as if I wasn't just a little kid."

"Brett, don't do this," replied Alexa, horrified by Brett's view on the situation. He was even more special than she realised. "You don't understand what kind of person I am. You are so great. You don't deserve someone like me. I'm not cool. I'm messed up. I like you – more than you know. I love that you even like me. That you tell people about me and not say mean things – that is almost the best thing anyone has ever done for me. You're my best foster brother ever. I want you to always be that – nothing more, because if it was ever anything more, I'd mess you up and you'd end up hating me."

"You were my first kiss, you know that?" said Brett with a soft smile. Alexa felt sad and delighted all at once. "I'm really your best foster brother?" Alexa nodded, her eyes stinging. "You're my best foster sister."

Alexa could not help it. She rushed forward and hugged Brett tight. He reciprocated the embrace, but thankfully kept it short and chuckled as he jokingly suggested that she was trying to give him the wrong idea.

***

Marcus looked at his watch again. Jackie was an hour late and her phone continued to divert to voicemail without ringing. He would have to face facts. He had been stood up. Pay back, he thought. Justified, he knew, but still, he would have preferred that

Jackie had not responded so pettily to his no-show the previous Thursday night. It seemed impossible that it had been just over a week since that horrible day.

Every day of the holidays had spent in fear of the phone. Marcus had been waiting for the call telling him that Alexa had been found dead somewhere, probably suicide. The call never came. It did not convince him of her welfare. It was just as likely that no one considered him anyone of note in Alexa's life to inform him of her death.

Putting his phone in his pocket, Marcus stood to leave. He wondered if Jackie was at home, waiting, or if she had gone out somewhere else to spite him. He was hungry, but did not want to eat alone. Looking around again, just in case Jackie was watching him to see how long he would wait for her, he finally decided to leave. Then he saw something that made his heart stuttered erratically, and forced his body to sprint down the street.

"Alexa," Marcus called, but she did not turn or even slow. "Alexa," he puffed, placing a gentle hand on her shoulder.

"Oh, hi, Sir," said Alexa pleasantly, looking up at him with surprised, soft eyes. It was not the reaction he had expected from her.

"What are you doing in the city?" asked Marcus as relief flooded his body. She was still alive.

"Oh, you know, finding a suitable bridge or building to jump off, that sort of thing," Alexa answered maliciously, all softness gone from her face, her eyes suddenly a cold steel blue.

The smile faded from Marcus's face and he felt tears build involuntarily in his eyes.

"That's not funny," he said, horrified by the way his voice broke.

"Yeah, well, it was nice running into you," said Alexa, turning her back and continuing down the street.

Marcus watched her walk off, his heart racing. He knew, after all she had said last week, that he should not go after her, but he also knew that he should never have let her go off alone just an hour after trying to take her own life.

"Alexa, wait," he said, catching up to her again. "It looks like I've been stood up and I'm starving. Have you had lunch?" Alexa shook her head, but did not look up. "Good. Are you hungry?"

Alexa still did not answer and when Marcus looked down he noticed how scared and uncomfortable she looked. A second later, all evidence of such emotions was gone, but his stomach tied in knots all the same. She still believed he would ask her for sex in return for his help. He had to change her perception of him, because he knew he had not done anything to give her that impression and whatever had happened to her was so much greater than anything he had suffered.

Determined that this time he would be able to help Alexa where he had previously failed, Marcus nodded for her to follow him. He guided her to a small café and sat them at a table near the window. Alexa took her seat in silence. He again noticed the discolouration on her cheekbone and felt another guilty knot tie in his stomach, knowing that he had done that to her.

"Order whatever you want," Marcus said, watching Alexa shift uncomfortably as she looked out the window. "I don't want to hurt you, Alexa. I know what you think I'm after from you and you're wrong," he continued, hoping that straight honesty was the best way to approach her. "I also realise nothing I say will convince you of that. So I'm just going to do my best to help you and, in time, I hope you'll realise that I don't want anything from you in return."

Alexa still did not answer.

"How've your holidays been? I have to say, I'm very glad to see you in one piece. I was worried you'd try and hurt yourself again."

"I went and saw my sister. We got to spend a few days together," replied Alexa, in a quiet and sad voice that made Marcus's heart ache. It was horrible that any child her age had already suffered so much.

"That's good to hear," Marcus nodded with supportive sincerity.

"So who stood you up?" asked Alexa.

Marcus knew it was a diversionary tactic, but also knew he owed Alexa a little bit of openness on his side. It was ridiculous to expect her to trust him in a situation like this without giving a bit of himself in return.

"My girlfriend," Marcus answered, trying not to sound too bitter. His relationship issues were not Alexa's problem.

"She can't be much of a girlfriend," said Alexa in a tone of casual criticism.

Marcus could not help but smile. Alexa could only say such a thing because she did not know Jackie. He may have been disappointed by Jackie's actions, but she was simply too perfect to blame for this situation. This one was all his fault.

"I actually think it's her revenge for Thursday night," said Marcus pointedly.

"Why? What happened Thursday night?" asked Alexa with dull curiosity. Marcus could only cock his head and raise his eyebrows, sure she must be joking. "Oh, that," she replied softly. "She was angry because you saved my life?"

"I didn't tell her about you," replied Marcus, shocking himself about the level of denial he was in about those events. "I told her I saw someone try to jump in front of a train, but that another man pulled them back in time. Once you left I found the nearest pub and drank until they kicked me out. Jackie and I were supposed to go out to dinner that night."

"Oh, right. It's good to know I have that effect on people, I guess," said Alexa tentatively, looking at the table now and refusing to meet his eyes. "Why didn't you tell her the truth? Why didn't you tell her about me?" she asked more forcefully.

That was a question Marcus had spent the whole week trying to answer and was not sure that he had yet come up with a suitable response. If anyone had ever given him this situation and asked him how he would have handled it, his answers would not have come anywhere close to resembling his actions. It disappointed him to know he was not the man he had imagined, and was much more flawed than he wanted to admit.

"I don't know exactly," Marcus confessed. "Your accusations cut pretty deep."

"Have you told the school?" Alexa asked with distrustful curiosity.

"No."

"Are you going to?"

"I am legally bound to do so," said Marcus, answering her questions as the better man.

"So why haven't you?" asked Alexa. It was almost an accusation.

Marcus hesitated. He was not sure he had a reasonable answer to that question either.

"I don't know," he replied, lying slightly as he formulated a new plan in his head. "I assume you'd prefer me to keep it to myself. If I don't tell the school – if I keep your suicide attempt secret – will you let me help you?"

Marcus watched Alexa's eyes grow slowly wider as he spoke before they flashed angrily.

"See, there's always an ultimatum. So much for trusting you," she spat, pushing away from the table.

"I didn't mean it like that. Shit!" said Marcus, realising how Alexa must have construed his comments. "I just want to help you."

"Well if you like ultimatums so much, then how about I give you one," said Alexa, her voice shaking. "If you tell the school about my suicide attempt, I'll tell them you made the whole thing up because I refused to sleep with you."

Alexa ran from the café and down the street, as Marcus sat frozen by fear. Part of him wanted to chase her down and force her to believe his good intentions, while the other part never wanted to lay eyes on her again. Knowing neither option was possible, he trudged home, terrified about what would happen when he returned to school.

Jackie was waiting for him when he arrived home, but Marcus was in no mood to see her. If she had just met him for lunch! Now he was really stuck. Alexa had stitched him into a corner. If he reported Alexa, as he should, she would accuse him of sexual harassment. If he did not report her – he could only imagine what would happen to her if she did not get the help she needed.

Marcus knew what he should have done. He should have fallen at Jackie's feet when she came to greet him, apologies written all over her face. He should have broken down and confessed everything. Instead, he packed his bag.

He was required at school the next day to register the returning students, but he had always intended to go in the morning. The tears that streamed down Jackie's face as he stormed around their apartment did not tear at his heart the way they usually did. All he could see was the horrible predicament he had put himself in, which he knew would somehow conspire to cost him the job – the career – that he loved.

Slamming his bag on to the bed, Marcus slumped to the floor of the small bedroom that adjoined his office. He was contrite now, but he knew his call home would not be enough to redeem him. Lying awake most of the night, staring at the ceiling, also did little to improve his mood. It made him about as grumpy and unapproachable as any of his students had ever seen him.

The result was that none of the returning boarders stayed in his office long after they had registered their arrival. Marcus was thankful. Never before had he disliked and distrusted his students the way he did now. He was terrified of what they were actually thinking about him, wondering if it was malicious and what they were planning. It was not fair. There was only one student he was truly fearful of, and every knock at the door made his stomach lurch, thinking that it would be her.

When it eventually was Alexa who walked through the door, Marcus felt his heart beat frantically and his stomach turn to lead. She was glaring at him. It was a warning and one he took very seriously. Alexa had nothing to lose by accusing him of sexual harassment. Redgrove might not like Alexa, but it would only take one person sympathetic to her situation to take her seriously and force him from his job.

"I'm just here to register my arrival," Alexa said coldly, pressing herself against Sam and away from him.

Marcus just nodded, his throat so tight that speech was impossible. Alexa turned to leave, but hesitated. Sam, who had come with her, acting as though he was her bodyguard, was standing his ground. With a nod from Sam, Alexa departed.

"You leave her alone," said Sam in a threatening voice, filling Marcus with dread. "She has enough to worry about without you hassling her."

"I'm worried about her, Mr Michaels. I want to help her," Marcus replied, stammering slightly. He wanted to know what Alexa had said to him. "Has Miss Samson spoken to you about her holidays?"

"She doesn't want to talk about them and, unlike you, I respect her wishes," spat Sam, throwing him a look of disgust. "I'm telling you now, don't mess with her. We've been real easy on you. We appreciate your support, but if you start harassing students you'll have us to deal with."

"I don't want to harass Miss Samson. I want to help her, but if she feels like I'm harassing her then, please, keep an eye out for her."

"Don't try and use me to spy on her. It won't work," Sam retorted, taking a step back as he shook his head. Marcus was beginning to think that he could say nothing right. "I owe you nothing. I'm warning you one last time. Lay off her."

***

Alexa sat at the far end of the library, in a corner where the shortened shelves did not reach all the way to the wall. It was in a rarely visited section of the library, so the structural anomaly remained unknown to most, but it was the one of the few places in the school where you could find solitude. However, Alexa was not alone for long. Sam sat down in the corner with her, leaning up against one of the shortened shelves.

Alexa and Sam understood each other in a way very few people did. Sam never pushed her into talking about anything and in the end she told him more about her and her life than anyone. They had known each other since year seven, when they had frequently met outside their year advisor's office after being thrown out of class, but it was not until year eight that they became really close.

Sam's parents were killed in a car accident halfway through the first term. Alexa knew what it was like to be alone and was one of the first to offer her condolences. The events and emotions that Sam experienced after losing his parents were very different to what Alexa had gone through after her mother died, but there were still many things that they suffered that none of their other friends came close to understanding, despite their best efforts to be sympathetic.

There had been a few tense weeks towards the end of that term where it was unclear if Sam and his younger sister, Melissa, would be able to remain at Redgrove. His parents' estate had been settled, but after paying off the debts from the farm, there was not enough left to continue paying their school fees. In a rare moment of humanity, Redgrove gave both of them full hardship scholarships. It was the only time Alexa could remember smiling and thanking Mrs Taylor.

By the end of year eight, Alexa and Sam were the glamour couple of the grade. They were each other's first love, and being with Sam was about the only thing that had made the months without any chance of seeing Bethany bearable. Sam was amazingly supportive of her situation and even welcomed Bethany warmly into his life and home when she and Bethany had run away from their foster homes to be together.

Their relationship lasted until year ten – until the dreaded night Ms Carter caught Alexa sneaking into Sam's room. That they had managed to remain friends through all that had happened since only made Alexa surer that Sam was one of the world's better people. She just wished that she could be the person he wanted her to be.

"Sam, tell me about your holidays. I don't want to be thinking right now," said Alexa, after almost fifteen minutes of silence, as she moved to sit in front of him. His arms instantly wrapped around her as she leaned against his warm chest.

"They weren't too bad," said Sam softly, pressing his cheek to hers. "Gran and Pop were happy to see us, as usual. They seem to be happier to see us every time we come back home."

"How's Mel?"

"Not so great. She was really upset these holidays. She wouldn't tell me why. She barely talks to anyone any more. Gran says she's just being a teenage girl, but I don't know. Something's wrong. I just wish I knew what it was."

"It can be tough here. We all wish we could go home at the end of the day, go out at night, go to the movies, all that kinda crap. At least we had some freedom during the holidays ..."

"Were they really that bad?" Sam asked when Alexa became suddenly quiet.

"Yes and no," Alexa shrugged. "I got to spend the first weekend with Bethy. She's been clean since I found her and I've wanted time with her more than anything in the world, but now it seems all it did was make the time away from her unbearable."

Alexa felt Sam's arms tighten around her as tears slipped from her cheeks on to his arms. She knew Sam understood and was glad that he did not ask any more questions. If he had asked her then what was really wrong, she may have answered and that was something she did not want to do.

The truth was that Alexa believed she could handle all her problems, including Ms Carter and Clinton, if she had Bethany by her side. Since they were first parted, Alexa had only ever felt half alive. Bethany must have felt the same, because it was only a few months after Alexa had first enrolled at Redgrove that Bethany began taking heroin again. Neither of them was fully functional when they were apart.

The trill of the bell signalling curfew filled Alexa with dread. She did not want to face Bianca. The agony of parting from Bethany had distracted her from the sadness of losing her baby in such a violent manner, but now she was back at school everything reminded her of it. Luckily, Bianca was in the bathroom when Alexa entered her room, and she feigned deep sleep when Bianca pulled back the curtains around her bed to talk to her.

Alexa knew Ezra and Bianca would be after her for information, but was not sure she was ready to explain what had transpired. The only way she knew to delay that inevitable conversation was to try and ignore them. At assembly, she sat with Sam and Chad and pretended to care about the crap Mrs Taylor spouted. It was harder to ignore Ezra and Bianca in class, but Alexa tried. It was odd acting interested in what the teachers were saying, and strange the way they noticed the change, calling on her to answer questions when they rarely had before.

Dashing from the classroom and hiding in the bathroom was the only tactic Alexa had to avoid them between classes. However, there was just no way she could keep that up forever.

"What's going on?" asked Bianca in a highly annoyed voice, finally catching up with Alexa when she got caught in the general rush from the classroom at lunch time.

"Nothing," Alexa answered as casually as possible, continuing to walk in the direction of the toilets.

"Then why've you been avoiding us? We have some really great news for you," said Ezra, trying to contain her grin.

"What?" asked Alexa scornfully. She did not want to be cheered up.

"First thing's first. What did you do with the lottery tickets?" asked Ezra, a hint of concern in her voice. "You didn't throw them out, did you?"

"I don't know, maybe. What's it matter anyway? We lost," muttered Alexa unhappily, not impressed by the direction of the conversation.

"No. We won," said Ezra quietly.

"No, we lost," said Alexa, not seeing the funny side of this joke. "I was there every time we checked the results. We didn't win anything."

"I know, but I forgot that I also entered the Easter Saturday draw. I saw that it was a big draw so I entered it as well. Just that after we lost those other draws and with everything going on with you, it kinda slipped my mind – until the draw," said Ezra with barely contained glee. "I would have called, but ..." she didn't have her number, added Alexa in her head.

Alexa had never given out the phone numbers of her foster families to anyone but Bethany. There just never seemed any point.

"Haven't you been watching the news?" asked Bianca, trying hard to disguise her incredulity. Alexa shook her head and wondered what world Bianca thought she inhabited. "It's everywhere. This massive win and nobody's claimed it."

"That guy in your dream was right," Ezra said in a kind voice. "Now you can take care of your sister and the baby."

Alexa could not speak. Her head was spinning. It was more than she could take in. The baby. Clinton's vicious assault ran through her body. It was all too late for the baby now. The memory of its painful death within her very own body made her want to vomit.

"You okay?" asked Ezra.

"Yeah, just can't believe it," muttered Alexa. "Better go find the tickets."

It took Alexa only a couple of minutes to reach her room. She had run to make sure no one came with her. Her mind was swirling and she needed the space to breath. Body shaking, she searched her room, trying to remember where she had stashed the tickets. It took her a minute of frantically tossing her belongings before she recalled where her hiding spot was.

There was a strange temptation to tear the tickets to shreds when she finally had them in her hand, but Alexa knew she would regret that moment of petulance later if this turned out to be real. However, right then, she was hoping it was all a sick joke.

"Should we go outside to check these?" asked Ezra, looking around the packed dining hall where Alexa had told them to wait.

They found a quiet place on the edge of the field. The day was cold and overcast so the grounds were empty. Ezra picked through the tickets until she found the entry for the Easter Saturday draw and then pulled a piece of paper out of her pocket with the winning numbers written on it.

"This could take a little while," said Ezra, looking at the rows of numbers. "Unless anyone remembers the numbers from Alexa's dream."

Bianca shook her head and they both looked at Alexa. Alexa did not reply. She sat unresponsive as irritation and guilt gnawed at her insides. This could not be happening.

"Eighteen, six, twenty-eight, forty-two, twenty-three," Alexa said after a long sigh.

Ezra looked up smiling.

"We have those numbers. The last one is four. So it must be the fourth game we entered," said Ezra, picking up the lottery tickets. "We won. Oh shit, we won. Do you realise how much money we won?" Ezra asked, her voice trembling. "Don't you understand? You don't have to worry any more. You have all the money in the world to take care of your baby. We just won twenty-five million dollars. There was only one winner. Us."

Chapter Nine

ALEXA FELT SICK. If she had just waited, if she had listened to Bianca, her baby would still be alive and she would be happy about the money. She leapt to her feet and stalked off. She wanted to escape, to run, to go anywhere, anywhere in the world, anywhere she wasn't. Self-loathing was consuming her and she wished there was some way of being someone else.

"Alexa, what's going on? Why aren't you happy? This is what you wanted," said Ezra, catching up to her.

"Yeah, what's wrong? Don't you understand? We're millionaires! Multimillionaires!" cried Bianca, twirling happily.

"That money can't help me. It can't get me out of here. It can't make me eighteen and old enough to claim it or take care of Bethy," Alexa snapped.

"But what about the baby?" asked Ezra softly.

"There is no baby. The baby's dead," Alexa replied harshly, storming away from them.

Bianca and Ezra did not try and stop her this time. They would be talking now, wondering how her situation had changed so dramatically. Alexa knew it was her fault. Of course they had been excited for her. They did not realise how badly she had ruined everything.

The back of the gym was as uninhabited as ever as Alexa sat down and pulled a razor blade out of her bag. She shoved the sleeve of her jumper up past her elbow and pushed the razor into her left forearm. Beads of blood formed along the cut as it circled her arm again and again. No tears fell as anger and self-hatred pulsed through her body. She felt her face warm and pangs of pain issue from her arm as the razor moved halfway down her forearm. Two inches from her wrist, the razor fell from her arm as all emotion left her body.

"You okay?" Ezra asked Alexa as they sat together in class the next day.

Alexa had not spoken to anyone yesterday and had barely slept, kept awake by her failing. She had hoped she would feel better today, knowing it was real, but that reality still only made her wish her suicide bid had been successful.

"Yeah, I'm fine," Alexa lied, without lifting her eyes, which were busy examining the different stains on the bench. The truth was simply not worth telling.

"What happened with the baby? How'd you lose it?"

"It doesn't really matter how. It's gone. I didn't need the money after all."

"Maybe it's for the best," said Ezra. Alexa liked that Ezra did not seem completely convinced by that idea. "You are only sixteen, after all. It's pretty young to be having a baby. Plus the money will still help you take care of Bethany. You wanted it for her too, didn't you?"

"Yeah, I know, but it'll be almost two years before we can get it. She may not last that long."

If Bethany felt anything close to how she did, Alexa feared she may not last a week. The money really meant nothing if they were both dead.

"We could claim it now," suggested Ezra, and Alexa was so grateful to her.

"Only if we have someone we trust," Alexa replied, shaking her head. "We're sixteen, with no legal right to that money and once it's claimed we can't force them to give it to us."

"We could sue them."

"No, we have to wait. I checked with my lawyer."

"Is that where you were last night? Bianca said you went missing," said Ezra.

Alexa nodded solemnly, but stayed silent. There was something in Ezra's voice that suggested there was more that Bianca had said.

"Maybe you should just tell Bethany about the money. It might help her stay clean."

"It's phantom money. Don't you understand? It doesn't exist except on paper. It won't protect her. She'll just be a heroin addict with a rich sister. You have no idea how different she is when she's using. She's not the same person. You'll never see two more different people in the one body."

"At least you know that when you get out of here you'll be able to help her. That has to help you make it through, doesn't it?" asked Ezra with genuine concern.

"It's phantom money to me too," replied Alexa, loving that Ezra was trying to understand, but hating that she couldn't. "I don't know how I'm going to survive this place. You just don't realise what a mess I'm in."

Alexa could see Ezra contemplating her response, wondering how much she should ask. It made Alexa wonder how much she would tell.

"There are plenty of places worse than here," said Ezra in a light voice after a long silence. "At least here you have a good chance of seeing someone set the chemistry lab on fire."

Alexa gave Ezra a weak smile. It was sweet that she was trying, but Alexa knew that she would never find the right words to say. The right words did not always exist. An uncomfortable silence fell between them as Alexa waited for Ezra ask the obvious questions, but they remained unasked. While she was glad Ezra did not probe, she wished she had someone to confide in. She wanted Bethany.

"So when did Bianca and Chris become an item?" asked Alexa, choosing diversion over wallowing. She had noticed them together at breakfast – and been thankful. It had kept Bianca away from her.

"During the holidays. They were some of the only year elevens that stayed at school. Apparently they hit it off pretty quickly," Ezra replied with a smirk.

"At least she'll have someone else to direct her attention to," Alexa sighed, trying hard not to sneer. "Who stopped her turning me in last night?"

"Martha. But that's not really fair. She's just worried about you. We both were. You can be a bit moody."

"She almost told a teacher I was missing last night. I would've been on detention for the rest of my life if they found out I snuck out again. I needed to make sure we could get the money – and I had to make sure the tickets were safe. You don't think I was just going to leave twenty-five million dollars sitting around for just anyone to find, did you?"

"Where did you put them?" asked Ezra, and Alexa was happy to hear that there was little distrust in her voice as she posed that question.

"With my lawyer – in a safe. Don't worry. It's all taken care of. Even if I die you and Bianca will still get your money."

"Planning on dying?" asked Ezra with raised eyebrows.

Alexa realised how foreign she must seem to Ezra at times. Their lives could not be more different.

"Not today, but it doesn't hurt to be prepared. Mainly I wanted to make sure Bethy would be taken care of."

Alexa was grateful when they were forced to set up their experiment. They had to concentrate, forcing the conversation away from the baby and the money. It was all just so surreal. Even her lawyer had been unable to believe it. Peter had tried to talk her in to letting him claim the money for her. He had even suggested she just take all of it and get her and Bethany far away from their present lives as possible.

The ferocity with which Peter protected her interests never stopped surprising Alexa. She was not even sure how she came to have a lawyer, particularly one who never charged her anything, but over the years she and Bethany had definitely needed him.

In the end, Alexa and Peter had settled on writing up a will. In the event of her death, Peter would be able to claim the money on her behalf with Bianca and Ezra on or after the date Ezra, the youngest of them, turned eighteen. Bethany would inherit Alexa's share. If she was underage, Peter agreed to be her guardian and would manage the money for Bethany.

Alexa tried to insist that Peter take a cut of the money, but he refused every time, asserting, with a wave around his office, that he was not in short supply of money.

It was strange the way Alexa had always trusted Peter. Perhaps it was because he had never wanted anything from her, and never shown much interest in her life. She was his client and he was just doing his job.

When the bell rang, Alexa's heart began to stammer. Ordinarily, she would make her way out of the school to meet Clinton, but she was not going anywhere he was. It was more frightening to walk to the dining hall for lunch than it ever had been sneaking out. Her heart beat so forcefully she was sure it would bruise. She could not help but be fearful that Clinton would arrive in the dining hall looking for her, but no one came.

Clinton did not appear at her room. Nor did Ms Carter. Breathing a shuddering sigh of relief, Alexa hoped that she had finally broken free. It was only one day, one week, but it was a step. Next week she could take another one, and if she kept taking those steps, week after week, it would not be long before Clinton and Ms Carter were so far away from her that she could pretend they did not exist.

The only problem seemed to be that whenever Alexa took a step away from one problem, she was bringing herself closer to some other dilemma. The source of her new troubles should not have been a surprise. Her problems with Bianca had always sat close by to her issues with Clinton.

Bianca had ignored Alexa at lunch, and then disappeared with Chris for the rest of the afternoon. At dinner, Bianca sat with Chris on the other side of the dining hall. It was not that Alexa missed Bianca's company. More that they had not really spoken since the discovery of their lottery win, and the longer it dragged on the bigger an issue it would become. It was more than Alexa wanted to deal with, so she decided to swallow her pride and make nice.

"New boyfriend, huh?" Alexa asked, sitting down on Bianca's bed when Bianca finally returned to their room just before curfew.

"You heard?" asked Bianca cautiously.

"Saw. It was kinda obvious when Chris put his arm around you at breakfast," said Alexa, forcing her voice to sound interested. There was a slight pause as she tried to think of what to say next. "Come on, you got yourself a boyfriend and you're a multimillionaire. You're well on the way to happiness, I'd say."

The smile could not be kept from Bianca's face then. Bianca's eyes glowed as she turned to face her.

"I just wish I could have it now, and then I wouldn't have to stay here," said Bianca with excited longing, all trace of her animosity gone.

"Makes little difference to me," shrugged Alexa. She had only wanted to stop this situation from ruining their friendship and could not really profess any great enthusiasm – about Bianca's relationship or the money. "I can't get custody of Bethy until I'm eighteen anyway. All the money in the world makes little difference to me now."

"But it's the silver lining, isn't it? You have to look at it that way," smiled Bianca, clearly trying to be encouraging and supportive. It was a nice gesture.

"Maybe, but you don't get to fly in the clouds until you die," replied Alexa, unable to see the situation through any lens but the reality of her life. "I just hope Bethy will still be alive for me to help and not floating around in my silver lining."

Alexa noticed the consternation on Bianca's face. She knew it was not the sentiment Bianca had been trying to convey, but she did not have the energy to try and explain further.

As she lay down in bed, Alexa was wracked with a precognitive ache that things were about to go very wrong. She had been so desperate to spend time with Bethany, but never realised how hard it would then be to be separated once more. She knew Bethany would be feeling the same way and that she would not cope if other things started to go awry. The only thing Alexa had to offer Bethany was the reassurance that she would be able to take care of her when she finished school, and so she got up and wrote the letter she swore she never would.

***

Despite the occasional quiet questioning of Bianca and Ezra, Alexa did not confide in anyone about the circumstances of her miscarriage, or tell anyone about her failed suicide bid. As she had heard nothing from the school or her social worker, it seemed as though Mr Knight had taken her threats seriously, and she hoped that would be the end of it. However, she found Mr Knight was keeping a very close eye on her.

During the first term Alexa had barely even noticed Mr Knight and wondered if she was just being paranoid now, but he seemed to be everywhere she turned. Each of his glances only earned him a hateful glare in return. It was less than she felt he deserved, but that was being handled separately.

Sam had noticed Mr Knight's constant watch of Alexa and promised her it would not go unpunished. It was the one thing the G7 would claim responsibility for. They were masters at wreaking havoc in the classes of teachers who had done them wrong. None of their behaviours were serious in themselves. It was more like waterboarding; slow, constant and torturous.

The worst part for the teacher was that once the G7 rallied against them, it was not long before others joined in, and not just within the grade, but across the whole school. The other students loved finding out another teacher was on the G7 hit list. They could do almost anything, knowing that with the right phrase they could get themselves out of everything. The teachers and Mrs Taylor never worried about discrediting such claims. They were happy to lay all the blame at the G7.

Rumours circulated that Mr Knight was different. He refused to let any of his students in other years blame their behaviour on the G7. There were minor revolts, which resulted in the G7 being hauled before Mrs Taylor and various punishments handed out, but for the most part the other grades pulled out of the dispute. That left things between the G7 and Mr Knight, and for the most part the G7 had the upper hand.

Mr Knight often appeared worn and fatigued. According to Lizzie, his classes were now strict and structured, but that only seemed to increase the opportunities to break the rules. When they had been more causal and relaxed, none of those behaviours had been punished. It was that fact that turned the other year eleven students against Mr Knight. In their eyes it was him who had changed, not them.

It was not within Alexa scope to feel sorry for Mr Knight for what he was suffering. As far as she was concerned, he had brought most of it upon himself. She also had more important things to worry about. Not only did she live with the constant fear of what Mr Knight could say and do, she spent every day concerned that she would run into Clinton. It was impossible not to catch glimpses of him around the school, but she worked hard at never getting close. Thankfully, she had Ezra and Bianca's support with that task.

On top of all that was the greatest burden of all. Bethany had not replied to Alexa's letter and it had now been over a month. Bethany had never been the greatest correspondent. Writing was not Bethany's greatest skill, but she had always made the effort to send something every few weeks. This silence was not like Bethany. It was not like the clean Bethany.

Alexa tried to reason the behaviour away. She tried to believe that things were going so well that Bethany had simply lost track of time. It was highly unlikely, but Alexa wanted to believe it was possible so forced herself not to panic – not yet.

However, it was not any of the things Alexa feared the most that shattered her fragile peace. It was Bianca. Despite all the warnings to be careful, Bianca did not listen and was caught sneaking out of the dormitories after curfew with Chris. Ms Carter was livid. Their whole room were called to Ms Carter's office, situated at the end of their floor. It was similar to the students' bedrooms, except that it had been split in two to create a separate office and bedroom. The five students stood in the centre of the office waiting for Ms Carter to turn from her desk and face them.

"I want to speak to Miss Ross alone first, and then I will talk to the rest of you," said Ms Carter, not turning to face them.

Alexa and the others stood outside. Martha and Natalie seemed very relaxed. They had been through this routine many times before as Alexa's roommate. Ms Carter loved trying to blame as many people as possible for an individual's behaviour. Lizzie was not used to getting in trouble and was a bit more anxious about the proceedings. Alexa could only wonder if Bianca's punishment would mirror what she had received for her similar indiscretion.

"How'd it go?" everyone asked at once, when Bianca finally emerged.

"I have to clean the dining hall after dinner every day for a week," groaned Bianca sourly.

Alexa felt a sudden stab of hatred towards Bianca before quickly quelling her anger. It was not Bianca's fault what she had suffered.

As predicted by Martha from her previous experiences, Ms Carter called them into her office to express her disappointment in them for not reporting Bianca's misbehaviour. It was short, to the point and on the whole much better than Alexa had expected.

"All right, back to bed then," said Ms Carter, releasing them. "Except Miss Samson, I need to talk to you about another matter."

Martha, Natalie and Lizzie exchanged curious looks as they left Ms Carter's room. Alexa's stomach churned. It seemed like the height of paranoia to assume this had all been about getting her alone, but she could not think of any reason why Ms Carter would need to speak to her.

"Well, well, well. Here we are, together again," said Ms Carter with a taunting smile. Alexa did not dare speak. "I'm disappointed to see that your bad habits are rubbing off on your friends."

"I can't control what Bianca does," Alexa cried before she could stop herself.

"Perhaps you'd better. It's your influence that has made Miss Ross behave in such a manner," snarled Ms Carter. Alexa found her breaths becoming more ragged. "Nowhere to run, is there? Where's your protection now?"

Ms Carter smiled and Alexa felt her stomach turn to lead.

"No, you can go to hell," said Alexa, running for the door, only to find it locked.

Alexa panicked as she fumbled with the handle. She was trapped. All of a sudden, a great force pulled her back by the hair. She did not remember Ms Carter being this strong. She tried to pull away, but couldn't. Her feet stumbled over each other as she was walked to the bedroom and thrown on to the bed. The air was cool on her skin as her shirt and jumper were yanked up over her head.

Struggling desperately, Alexa tried to wriggle out of Ms

Carter's grasp, but the weight on her arms and shoulders kept her pinned to the bed. Then she heard footsteps move across the room. Terror shot through Alexa. There was more someone else in the room.

"Do you want my help yet?" growled a menacing voice in Alexa's ear. Alexa felt her legs quivering as her head twisted from side to side in the blankets. It was not Ms Carter holding her down. "No? We'll see if we can change that."

A sharp pain ran down Alexa's back. It felt as though her back was about to burst open. Her mind was trying to process the pain of the strike when the cane came down again. The burning pain engulfed her as each new strike hit her back. She was not sure if Ms Carter was hitting her faster or harder. She could not even count how many times she was hit. All she felt was pain.

"You just say the word and I can make this stop," said Clinton softly in Alexa's ear. Alexa forced herself to remain silent. She could not stop the tears that were running down her cheeks, but she would not scream in pain and she would not beg for mercy. "Fine," Clinton barked, pulling her head up off the bed. "You might want this."

Clinton forced a piece of dowel between Alexa's teeth and pinned her back down on the bed. Alexa heard something shaking above her and automatically bit down hard on the dowel as pain seared through her body. Tears of agony streamed out of her eyes as her legs curled into her chest and her hands grasped the blankets in a desperate attempt to disperse the pain. The hold on her released and Alexa fell to the floor still writhing in pain.

Alexa did not know how long it was before she could face the torture of uncurling her body. Walking gingerly into the office, she could see Clinton and Ms Carter drinking coffee at Ms Carter's desk, a bottle of salt next to them. Alexa righted herself fully and crossed the room to the now unlocked door, never sparing them a second look.

"What happened?" asked Bianca in a concerned voice, when Alexa made her way slowly into her room. "Why have you been so long?"

Alexa did not answer or even turn. She walked straight to the bathroom and slammed the door.

***

The end of the week could not come fast enough for Alexa.

Though the wounds inflicted by Ms Carter's cane healed over relatively quickly, the bruising was much slower to subside. Her whole back was a swirl of red, purple, and yellow, but even as the bruises faded the pain remained. Moving was agonising, but sitting still was just as excruciating. Concentrating on anything beyond the pain was not something she was capable of, and she barely even tried to.

"Miss Samson, could you come here please," said Mrs Jackson halfway through maths. Alexa was not surprised. She had been shifting restlessly all class and her exercise book was completely empty. "Mr Knight wants to see you now."

Alexa sighed. She had been expecting this too. All week, Mr Knight's eyes had followed her pained body everywhere. She was just surprised he had waited this long to call her to his office. It made her sick to try and think of lies to cover the truth, so decided silence would have to be her tactic. She knocked and entered Mr Knight's office without waiting for a response, but stopped dead when she saw the two police officers.

"Sit down, Miss Samson," said Mr Knight in a concerned voice. "These officers want to talk to you."

Alexa hesitated. Perhaps Mr Knight had taken her blackmail threat more seriously than she thought. It made her wonder if she would stick to that story rather than tell the truth. It did not seem fair to take down an innocent teacher to protect a guilty one, but she was much more scared of Clinton than Mr Knight.

"I'm Constable Banks, and this is Constable Jacobs," said the friendlier-looking officer. "We need to talk to you about your sister."

"Bethy? Is she okay?" asked Alexa, her concerns about Mr Knight vanishing in an instant.

"We're not sure. She's been missing from her foster parents for just under a month now. They've had no contact with her. We want to know if you've heard from her," said Constable Jacobs, his voice lacking any real concern.

"No. I sent her a letter in week one but she never replied. I don't even know if she received it."

"We're pretty sure she did. Her foster parents say she disappeared a week after a letter from you arrived in the mail."

"In other words, they hid the letter and because it's gone missing they think she found it," spat Alexa, hating how far the Christies had gone over the years to keep her and Bethany apart. It made her wonder what else they had kept from Bethany.

"We just want to know what you wrote in the letter," said Constable Jacobs, ignoring Alexa's last comment.

"Nothing that would make her run away," Alexa asserted angrily. "Something must have happened."

"This is not exactly the first time she's gone missing."

"Yeah and I've always found her within days. How hard have you been looking for her? Why didn't you talk to me earlier?"

"We only just found out that Bethany is likely to have seen your letter. What did you write?" Constable Jacobs asked again.

"I'm her only family. You should have told me straight away!" Alexa cried, horrified that their kinship seemed to not mean anything to anyone. "And there was nothing in that letter that would make Bethany run away."

"Then you will have no problems telling us what was in it."

Alexa felt her throat constrict talking about the letter. It was one she knew she should never have written and that thought had plagued her since the day she wrote it. She had even tried to stop it being sent, but it had been too late. Now there was a chance it had done exactly what she had feared, even though she still could not think of anything within its contents that would make Bethany leave her home.

"I just told her that I had found a way of us being together when I left school and not to give up, okay," Alexa muttered, hating that she was even granting them an answer.

"How do you intend on looking after your sister?" asked Constable Banks.

"What does that matter? I didn't tell her," Alexa cried, terrified they would somehow find out about the money and steal it from her. "This is useless. You don't care. She's just another junkie to you. If you cared then you would've been here weeks ago. You would've been out on the streets looking for her, and if you were then you would've found her by now."

"Thank you for your cooperation. I assure you, we are doing our best to find your sister. We'll let you know if we find anything," said Constable Banks as he and Constable Jacobs left.

Alexa picked up her bag and turned for the door.

"I don't think you gave those officers much of a chance. They did come here to talk to you so they could find your sister," said Mr Knight.

"They're no more interested in my sister than you are," Alexa spat, turning on Mr Knight with vicious eyes. "She's just another junkie to them. They don't care if they find her or not. Argh, you heard me just say all this. What do you want?"

"A little less attitude might be nice. I want to make sure you are all right. You've seemed quite distressed this week," said Mr Knight firmly, appearing more angry than concerned.

"So?"

"I guess that means you're not going to tell me what's upsetting you."

"You're getting better at this, you know," replied Alexa acidly, exiting before Mr Knight could reply.

Alexa ran to her room and collapsed on her bed, her worst fears confirmed. Bethany was using again. If there was any other reason for her disappearance, Bethany would have contacted her by now. It left her with no option. If it was her fault that Bethany had run away, then it was her responsibility to find her. The police did not care. They had never cared and they had never once been the ones to bring Bethany home.

"Listen, I have to go out," Alexa said to Bianca as everyone was preparing to go to bed.

Bianca looked cautiously around the room, and Alexa realised that her other roommates were all listening in. It did not matter. It was probably better they knew her plans as well. She was only directing her request at Bianca because Bianca was the one most likely to dob.

"I will try to be back by Monday, so please, please try and cover for me until then. If I'm not back, then they'll find out soon enough. Please, just cover for me until Monday."

"Where are you going?" asked Bianca.

Alexa could see Bianca biting back a thousand other questions and warnings and was grateful for the effort. Martha shook her head disbelieving, as Natalie rolled her eyes and jumped into bed. Alexa smiled slightly. Martha and Natalie had always been good at providing question-free support.

"Bethy's missing. The police came to see me today, but they'll never find her. I have to try and get her back home," Alexa replied hurriedly, not liking that she was having to explain the situation.

"What if you can't find her?" asked Bianca, looking a little mortified by the answer.

"Then I'll keep looking until I do," Alexa snapped, before turning and hopping into bed.

Chapter Ten

ALEXA'S ALARM SOUNDED at three. She had not slept, but guessed Mr Knight would have been expecting her to leave straight away. She opened the window and manoeuvred her body out on to the window sill.

"Good luck," Alexa heard whispered from the darkness of her room. It sounded like Martha.

"Thanks," she whispered back before reaching out to the downpipe that ran down the wall half a metre from the window.

Alexa was glad that she was not afraid of heights. It was a long way to the ground from the fourth floor, and she was not sure anyone could survive the fall. It made her glad that she also was not afraid of dying. Part of her even welcomed the opportunity. Clinging to the downpipe, Alexa started the slow climb down. It took a while, but once she was on the ground, she started running across the grounds and out on to the street.

In the city by dawn, Alexa began her search by trekking to all the places she had found Bethany before, but with no luck. Many of the local drug users, and dealers, recognised her and helped as best they could. Some even openly wished their sister would come searching for them, but no one had seen Bethany recently.

The wind picked up as the sun set. It was going to be a cold night, but Alexa did not even consider going back to school. When the wind began swirling violently, she knew she would have to seek shelter and forget about finding Bethany for the moment. Wherever Bethany was, she would be bunkering down as well.

Alexa managed to stay dry, but struggled to find any sleep. Trying to stay indoors left her vulnerable to being moved along, and she knew she had to keep herself from being spotted by the authorities. She looked too young to be on the streets alone and she was not leaving them until she found Bethany. Unfortunately, Sunday was no more fruitful than Saturday had been. No matter where she walked or looked, no matter who she spoke to, she could not find Bethany anywhere.

Going to the bathrooms at the train station, Alexa washed her arms and face in the hand basin, ignoring the looks of strangers as she gulped down water from the tap. It would not keep her full for long, but it was better than a completely empty stomach. Moving to a cubicle, Alexa rested her head in her hands and felt her eyes slip closed.

Public toilets were not exactly the nicest place to sleep, but in a cubicle by the wall it possibly was one of the safest. While it was quiet, no one would be around long enough to know that she had been in there for an hour with her head resting against the wall.

The door slamming in the next cubicle woke Alexa with a start. Bags dropped on to the floor as the sound of a harried woman directing two small children echoed off the walls. Alexa was about to go back to sleep when she saw the open handbag near the gap under the dividing wall. It was horrible, but this woman had bags of possessions. Alexa had not eaten since dinner on Friday night. Seizing the opportunity, Alexa grabbed the exposed wallet and slipped quietly out of the bathrooms.

Jackpot! This woman had eighty dollars in cash on her. Pushing the cash into her pocket, Alexa walked straight to the supermarket. Grabbing a large baguette, she quickly paid for it and headed to the park. When she passed a post box, she dropped the wallet in, leaving everything but the cash. Credit cards, while useful, were too traceable. On the streets, cash was king, and Alexa now had a pocketful of it.

Alexa sat in the park and ate her baguette. It was the best tasting food she had ever had. The sun was out, and with no breeze it was quite warm. Sitting in the park like this, it was almost possible to convince herself that life had some beauty to it. There were other people snoozing in the sunlight – proper people, people in suits and fancy clothes – so Alexa decided it would not be too much of a risk to do the same.

"Oi! Hey, you," said a voice as something nudged Alexa's feet. "I think I saw your sister."

Alexa's eyes snapped opened as the words penetrated her brain. There was a young guy standing in front of her. Alexa had seen him around over the years and had spoken to him yesterday. When she did not move fast enough, he grabbed her hand and pulled her to her feet.

"Where is she?" asked Alexa, following the guy as he walked.

"Wrong park," he said. "Saw her at the Domain. Try there first. Then try the other parks. She likes them, your sister."

"Yeah, I know," answered Alexa. It was why she had been eating in Hyde Park – just in case.

"Don't give up on her," said the guy, stopping and pointing in the direction he had last seen Bethany.

"I won't," Alexa promised, reaching into her pocket and pulling out a twenty-dollar note. She shoved it into the guy's hand. "Take care," she said sincerely before dashing off.

It was strange the camaraderie that formed with other people on the streets. People Alexa had spoken to on Saturday now waved at her, calling her over to tell her of the rumours about where Bethany was. However, although there were now many sightings, they were all by others, not her.

Alexa glanced up at a clock as she passed a shop and tried to count the days. It had to be only Monday, even though it felt like a week since she had left school, perhaps because the bread roll in the park was the only time she had eaten. All her focus has been on finding Bethany and she was scared that the moment she turned her back, even just to eat, would be the time Bethany would pass her by.

The sightings became more recent and accurate as Monday progressed. Alexa knew she was getting close. She could feel Bethany in the air and let herself be dragged towards her, as though there was some internal magnetism between them. It was a useful connection they shared, but the first glimpse of Bethany late on Monday night was not as heartening as it should have been.

As soon as Alexa laid eyes on her, she knew Bethany had started using again. A wave of sadness washed over her as she watched her fourteen-year-old sister pack her needle and the rest of her kit away into a tattered plastic bag.

"Bethy," called Alexa, rushing over to her. Bethany looked up, but did not respond. "What are you doing, Bethy? What happened?"

"What do you want?" asked Bethany bitterly as Alexa tried to hug her.

"I want to get you home. I want to get you off these drugs," Alexa replied tenderly, stroking Bethany's face, trying to reach her sister buried deep within.

"No! I don't want to go back there," spat Bethany, throwing off Alexa's hand. "Leave me alone. Go back to your precious school. That's what you left me for."

"No, Bethy, no. I'm here, okay. I will take care of you, but you have to come with me. You have to get out of here."

"You're here now, but what about in a few days? You'll dump me at the Christies' then go back to school. You'd rather be there than with me."

"There's nowhere in this world I'd rather be than with you," cried Alexa, her heart tearing at the truth of that statement. "But where would we live? What would we eat? The Christies asked me to leave. I had no choice."

"Get away from me!" cried Bethany, pushing past her. "I'm not going back there. I want to stay here."

"You'll die here," Alexa said desperately. "Didn't you get my letter? I can take care of us – when I finish school – when I'm eighteen. You just have to hold out til then. Please."

"I am holding on. I'm doing the best I can, Lex," replied Bethany, her voice softer now.

Alexa knew she was getting through. Her beautiful sister was still under there, buried deep, but alive.

"What's going on here?" asked an angry voice

Alexa turned, expecting the police. It would not have been her preferred tactic to get Bethany home, but she was running out of options. It was not the police. It was the scruffy man who had been standing outside Bethany's school on the first day of the school year.

"Nothing that concerns you," snapped Alexa, turning back to Bethany.

"You're harassing my girlfriend. That is my concern," snarled the man, flinging Alexa around to face him.

"What? Shit, no. He's the reason you're here?" cried Alexa, grabbing Bethany's hand, refusing to be torn away from her like this.

"Leave Leo out of this," snapped Bethany, pulling out of Alexa's grasp and stepping in towards Leo.

"You bastard!" spat Alexa at Leo. She had never hated anyone the way she hated Leo in that moment. "You dragged her away from home for your own pleasure."

"Mutual pleasure," smiled Leo sickeningly, wrapping Bethany in his arms. "Now bugger off. I'm taking care of Bethany."

"Look at her goddamned arms. That is not taking care of her!"

"Just go back to school, Lex," said Bethany softly. "I don't want you here."

"No, Bethy, please don't do this. Don't trust him. I can help you. I won't go back to school. We can work things out together. Please," begged Alexa, stepping forward to try and grasp Bethany's hands again.

"Hey, you heard her," said Leo, pushing Alexa away as she tried to hug Bethany. "Get lost."

Alexa slapped Leo's hand away and saw his eyes flash dangerously. When Bethany again moved away from her and towards Leo, Alexa knew it was a lost cause. She reached into her pocket and pulled out what was left of the money she has stolen and thrust it into Bethany's hand.

"Buy food, buy clothes, buy whatever you need, just don't spend it on drugs, I'm begging you."

Bethany nodded, but Alexa knew she could not trust her. Now Bethany was back on drugs, there was no way Alexa could trust anything she said, but it might get her one meal before the rest went up her arm.

The walk back to school was the longest and loneliest Alexa had ever known. Tears trickled slowly down her face as her heart filled with grief and her stomach filled with guilt. She tried not to think about the next time she would see Bethany. Trying to pry her away from drugs and sex was pointless if there was nowhere to take her. Alexa knew she had no choice but to return to school and wait out her time. She was just not sure if Bethany could survive that long.

It was the early hours of Tuesday morning when Alexa finally snuck back into the school grounds. All she wanted to do was climb into her bed and sleep until the pain went away. As she approached the dormitories she noticed something across her window. Frustration and anger boiled over when she realised they had put bars across her window.

There was no way she could just walk into the building using any of the main entrances. They all were alarmed, but at that point Alexa was almost prepared to take the trouble she would be in just to sleep. Her body was aching with exhaustion, so much so she was sure she would fall asleep if she decided to simply curl up in the grass.

Looking up again at her barred window, it took Alexa's tired mind a while to realise that none of the other windows had bars on them. Climbing up the downpipe towards her room, Alexa stopped at the second floor and tapped on the window. A minute later a bleary-eyed boy opened the window and peered out.

"Let me in," Alexa whispered urgently, her body struggling to hold her weight.

Adrian moved aside and Alexa reached across and grabbed the window sill. Her body froze for a second, caught in an awkward position without the strength to alter it. Adrian looped his arm under one of hers, stabilising her position and allowing her to let go of the downpipe and climb in the window.

"Thanks," said Alexa, as she stepped into the room.

"No worries," replied Adrian, closing the window, yawning and hopping back in bed. "Sam's in the middle bed."

Alexa walked over to the third bed and sat on the edge. Sam woke and looked up at her with a tired smile on his face.

"Couldn't you get in your own window?" asked Sam, as Alexa stripped off her filthy clothes, leaving just her underwear. Alexa slipped under the covers and pressed in against his warm body. "They found out you were missing on Saturday. We tried to cover for you, but I think they expected you to disappear. Did you find her?"

"Yeah," replied Alexa sadly, Sam's arm wrapping around her. "She didn't want anything to do with me. I think she'd just scored. She has a boyfriend. He wouldn't let me talk to her. I don't know what to do. He must be at least twenty. She's not even fifteen."

"It'll be okay. I don't know how, but it'll work out," said Sam reassuringly, gently brushing the hair back off her face. "You're in a lot of trouble though. Mr Knight's furious. He hauled your whole room and the six of us into his office yesterday and demanded to know who knew about you leaving. No one said anything. I think Bianca wanted to, but Chris kept her quiet."

"She thinks she's helping me and I know she cares, but I just wish she'd learn to keep her damn mouth shut herself."

"She's quite pretty, though."

Alexa turned to see a sheepish smile spread across Sam's face.

"You like her? What is it with her? Everyone seems to like her," Alexa wondered. She had never found anything very attractive about Bianca.

"I know. Chad likes her too. If she's ever single, would you hate me for going out with her?" asked Sam, and Alexa was sure he was blushing as he spoke.

"No," she replied, hoping it was the truth. "It might be a bit strange, but I wouldn't hate you. I want you to be happy."

"Thanks," said Sam, kissing the back of her head. "We should get some sleep. I don't know how we are going to sneak you out of here."

Alexa needed no further encouragement and was asleep before her eyes were fully closed. When morning broke, Sam's roommates awoke to find her still asleep with Sam's arm wrapped around her. Chad dressed quietly as Adrian explained her appearance in the middle of the night.

"Sam, it's time to get up," said Chad, gently shaking Sam awake, waking Alexa as well. "Sleep well?" he asked, smiling down at them.

"I think I could sleep for another century," Alexa replied, stretching her arms, trying to convince her body that she could not do such a thing.

"How are we going to get her out of here?" asked Chad. "I took a bit of a stroll earlier and there're teachers everywhere."

"They start to leave after eight-thirty," said Sam, hopping out of bed. "We can wait til then. You want first shower?" he asked looking down at Alexa.

"Yeah, that'd be great," she murmured, but could not quite able to force her body to move.

"Oh yeah, I found Bianca and got you a uniform so you don't have to try and sneak into your room this morning," said Chad, handing Alexa a bag off his bed.

"Thanks guys. I'll make it up to you."

The shower was a long one, longer than intended. Alexa rested her head against the wall and closed her eyes. The next thing she knew Sam was shaking her and dragging her out of the shower.

"Geez, Alexa, can you not do that," said Sam, throwing a towel at her. "You're going to drown. Now quick get dressed while I shower."

Alexa was asleep on Sam's bed by the time he was out of the bathroom. His touch of her arm sent her scurrying across the bed away from him, but he paid no attention, sitting down on the bed and pulling her into his arms.

"I'll wake you when it's time for class," Sam whispered as he held her against his chest.

Alexa nodded, but was only semi-conscious. When Sam did try and wake her properly it was difficult and he had to practically carry her halfway across the school until she woke more fully.

"Ah, the traveller returns," said Mrs Jackson with a wry smile when Alexa entered her maths class thirty minutes late. "I assume you've been seen to by Mr Knight."

"Yes, Miss," said Alexa, taking her seat next to Ezra and Bianca.

"When did you get back?" asked Ezra quietly.

"Don't know, two maybe," Alexa answered, still feeling the lack of sleep in her body. It was hard not to just put her head down on the table and close her eyes.

"What'd Mr Knight say?" asked Bianca, who was looking a little pale.

"I haven't seen him," Alexa muttered, too tired to provide more details.

"But you just told Mrs Jackson –"

"I lied. I don't intend on seeing any teachers until I have to."

"He's really angry," said Ezra, giving Alexa a stern look.

"Yeah, I already heard that. Well, he noticed I left pretty quickly. We'll just have to see how long it takes him to notice I've returned."

It was a lot longer than anyone expected. By her last class of the day, Alexa was beginning to think that she may make it through the entire day without Mr Knight realising she had returned, but that would have been one miracle too far. She, Ezra, Lizzie and Natalie had set up their chemistry experiment for the day and were about to begin when there was a knock on the laboratory door. Lizzie nudged Alexa urgently. Alexa had not bothered to look up initially, but now saw Mr Knight standing at the door. He did not speak, only beckoned her with his finger.

Sighing heavily, Alexa picked up her bag and smiled at Ezra, walking through the room to the whistles and cheers of her classmates.

***

The office door slammed closed harder than Marcus intended, but Alexa did not flinch. She just sat diligently in the chair in front of his desk looking as defiant as ever.

"Have a nice trip?" asked Marcus, throwing himself heavily into his chair. Alexa had made him a laughing stock with her secret return to class and he was furious.

"I've had better," Alexa replied insolently.

"Do I really need to ask where you went? Or is it safe to assume you went looking for your sister?"

"Assume what you like," sighed Alexa, turning away from him.

"This is not a game," Marcus cried, Alexa's perpetually

unaffected demeanour only enraging him further. "The school is responsible for you. If anything had happened to you we would have been in a lot of trouble."

"Yeah, sweet, so it's all about saving your own skin. Well I don't really care how much trouble this school gets in."

"That much is evident," snapped Marcus, realising this one girl had the capacity to ruin his whole career and he hated her for it. He had really stopped feeling sorry for Alexa after this stunt. "Why you went looking for your sister when the police are searching for her is beyond me."

"Then you weren't listening very well last week, were you? She's been missing for over a month and they've found no trace of her, because she didn't walk into the police station and announce her presence. If they'd tried, they would have found her."

"So you found her, did you?" Marcus asked disbelievingly, his eyebrows raised.

"Of course I found her," spat Alexa contemptuously.

"Then where is she now?" Marcus retorted almost sarcastically.

"Where I found her." Alexa looked away from him as she answered. "Are we done yet?"

Marcus noticed Alexa's voice straining slightly, but it did not soften his resolve. He was sick of her sob stories. They were just covers to let her do whatever she pleased with little or no consequences.

"No," Marcus replied firmly. "Why just leave your sister when you went to all that trouble to find her?"

"Ever tried to reason with someone on heroin?"

Marcus caught his reply just in time. No, of course he had never tried to reason with a heroin addict.

"Fine," he said, changing the topic. Perhaps her life was complex enough to grant her some concessions. "Then how did you get back into the school?"

"Well, not through the window," Alexa replied, smiling hatefully at him. "Do you honestly think I can scale four storeys to climb in a window?"

"You're an amazingly talented girl. That much is evident," replied Marcus, straining to keep his frustration in check. "But the window is how you left the building so I can only assume you entered via a similar means."

"Says who?"

"The doors were alarmed and I know you didn't leave before

curfew."

"Whatever you say," said Alexa with a dismissive sigh.

"I want to know how you got in," Marcus asked with evident annoyance. It was infuriating the way Alexa could sit there so detached from the world.

"Why? Want to bar up a few more windows?" Alexa snarled.

"I think I've been more than tolerant with you this year. You have consistently walked out of our meetings without permission. You refuse to answer questions, you talk back and it is going to stop," replied Marcus, refusing to engage in her games.

"Feeling a little rejected, are we?" Alexa smiled.

Marcus was at boiling point. He stood up and walked across his office to try and contain his anger. He could feel Alexa's eyes watching him though she continued to stare at his empty chair. Feeling calmer, he leant against the front of his desk, positioning himself directly in front of Alexa.

"I am going to ask you how you got back into the school undetected and you are going to answer me," said Marcus in a tightly controlled voice.

"No," replied Alexa simply, looking him straight in the eyes as she did.

"We can stay here all day if you like."

"There's not a thing in the world that you can do to make me answer your questions. So why don't you just accept it and run along and find someone else to harass."

Marcus looked down at Alexa's taunting expression and felt the anger rising in him again. He stood up quickly, lifting his hand to brush the hair up off his face, but before he could he saw Alexa's eyes grow wide with terror. Her face turned away from him slightly, her eyes never leaving his raised hand. Marcus looked up at his hand and felt his heart sink.

"Alexa," said Marcus quietly, dropping his hand and crouching in front of her. "I wasn't going to – I would never hit you."

Marcus's anger evaporated in the face of Alexa's fear of him. As he watched her face, he noticed it quickly recompose and he wondered briefly if it had been an act, but although her face was calm, her legs were pulled into her chest and she was trying to shift her body away from him.

"Are you okay?" Marcus asked gently.

"I'm fine," said Alexa, hugging her knees tighter into her chest to move as far away from him as the chair allowed.

"All right, you can go back to class now. I will talk to you later," said Marcus, rising to his feet. He did not want to scare Alexa any more than he had.

Alexa stood, but turned back around at the door to face him.

"When are the bars coming off my window?" she asked forcefully.

"They aren't," Marcus replied flatly. He may have conceded one point, but would not concede them all. "I still think that's how you've been getting in and out of the school."

"This is bullshit. You can't bar up my window."

"If you didn't run away they would never've been put on," he replied simply.

"What would you've done?" asked Alexa, her voice almost desperate, as if begging for another solution. "Stand aside and let your sister die? She's going to overdose while I sit around in my caged cell."

"I understand how hard this is for you," said Marcus, as he moved across the room to Alexa and placed a comforting hand on her shoulder.

"You don't understand a thing, so get your goddamned hands off me," spat Alexa, pushing him away.

Marcus had not been expecting Alexa's aggressive reaction and stumbled backwards, tripping on his feet and hitting his head on the back of the chair she had just been sitting in. Landing hard on the floor, Marcus put his hand to his head and felt wet warmth seeping between his fingers and down his neck. He was about to stand when he felt his hair being parted and a wet cloth stroking his neck.

"I don't think it's a very big cut," Marcus heard Alexa say from behind.

Her voice was small and shaky, but somehow still controlled as she gently tended to him. It was such a contrast to the angry girl of seconds ago that it was hard to imagine she was the same person. Marcus reached back and wrapped his hand around Alexa's, gently pulling her in front of him. She was crouched and looked so timid and fragile, but that was not what disturbed him most. She did not even look like Alexa, but more like a shell she had retreated into. The change in her demeanour was not because she was ashamed of her actions, but because she was terrified of the consequences. Yet instead of running, she had helped him and put herself at the mercy of his response.

"I wasn't going to hurt you and I would never hit you. I just want to make sure that you know that," Marcus said softly.

Alexa would not meet his eyes and he could not be sure she believed him. He wanted to convince her, but knew it was dangerous to keep her with him in this state.

"I can take care of this. You go back to class."

This time Alexa did run.

Chapter Eleven

ALEXA DID NOT tell anyone what happened in Mr Knight's office – or explain how she had managed to get away with her three-day absence unpunished. It was impossible, and she did not expect to go unpunished. Every day she expected to be called into Mr Knight's or Mrs Taylor's office, but she never was. It did not put her at ease, but as they approached the last weeks of the term, she began to believe that the call might never come. Her spirits even rose slightly with the rest of the student population, with the prospect of escaping Redgrove for two whole weeks drawing nearer.

At the start of the second-last week of term Alexa received a letter from the Whites inviting her back for the holidays. She wanted to be happy, but had to settle for grateful. The Whites were a poor substitute for Bethany. She wished she did not feel that way. They had done more for her than any other foster family and they continued to ask her back each holidays despite the trouble she got herself into.

Bianca was again going to be left at school during the holidays, leaving her as one of the few glum boarders as the holidays approached. She became only more depressed when she found out that Chris would be going home for the holidays.

"This is great. I'll be here alone," Bianca moaned. "You don't even have a family and you have a place to go for the holidays," she added bitterly.

"I'm sure you won't be the only one here. I think Chad said he was staying behind," said Ezra, sparing Alexa from speaking the retort burning in her mouth.

"Yippee for me," replied Bianca sarcastically.

"Hey, Chad isn't that bad. Have you ever even spoken to him?" asked Alexa defensively, still reeling from Bianca's previous comment.

"I didn't mean it like that. I just wish I was getting out of here, that's all," added Bianca quickly.

Alexa knew how Bianca felt, but had little sympathy. To gain her own escape from Redgrove, she would have to see Mr Knight. She had not spoken to him since the day she split his head open and although he had not caused any trouble for her since, she was still nervous. Sam offered to go with her, but she declined, knowing this was one thing she should face up to on her own.

"Miss Samson, what can I do for you?" asked Mr Knight, when she entered his office.

Alexa had thought that Mr Knight would be angry the next time he spoke to her, but he appeared at ease with her arrival.

"I just need permission to go back to my foster parents' for the holidays, Sir," said Alexa timidly. She handed him the letter from the Whites and sat down in the chair in front of his desk. "I also wanted to apologise for what happened last time. I didn't mean for you to get hurt."

Alexa looked down when Mr Knight suddenly looked up at her.

"There's no need to apologise, Miss Samson," said Mr Knight in a gentle voice. "You were upset and I shouldn't have pushed you. I do realise that it can't be easy for you here." Alexa did not respond, though she felt his eyes looking intently at her. "It's good to see that your foster family is taking you back again. Are you looking forward to the holidays?"

"I guess."

"This is all fine. Here's your permission slip. I will see you when you return to school," said Mr Knight calmly, holding out his hand.

"That's all?" Alexa asked cautiously, taking the signed permission slip and letter.

"Was there anything else?" asked Mr Knight, and Alexa noticed he was smiling benignly.

"No, Sir. You just usually question me more than this."

"Perhaps I'm learning the lesson you and your friends have been trying to teach me," Mr Knight replied, still smiling.

Alexa did not understand, but would not pass up the opportunity to leave unquestioned. Thinking over just how generous Mr Knight had been to her – and the G7 – she decided to ask Chad and Sam to give him a break. If he betrayed their trust they could easily ramp things up again.

Returning to her dorm at the end of the day, Alexa was still relieved Mr Knight had not tried to probe her with questions the way he usually did, but it did not change her annoyance with him.

One glimpse of the bars on her window, and the reminder of her prison-like state, was almost enough to retract the concessions she had requested for him from the rest of the G7.

A large portion of Alexa's free time was now spent trying to find a way of dislodging the bars on her windows, but to no avail. Her roommates said nothing as she sat in the window frame hacking at the brickwork around the bars, but nothing she did had any real effect. She would need twenty years to get them off. The frustration over her failure continued to build to breaking point over the second-last week of term and she took it all out on her scarred upper arm.

Sitting, now calm, on the bathroom floor, Alexa let her blank mind wander, hoping a creative solution would soon come to mind. She found it staring at the bathroom closet. It was open and she noticed that the inside wall ended almost a metre from the outside wall. She knocked curiously on the internal wall of the cupboard and heard a hollow response. Encouraged, she pushed at the side panel with all her might but it would not move.

The closet had five large shelves, the highest only just within reach of her outstretched hand. The lowest shelf was hers, as she was the shortest of her roommates, so she pulled all of her belongings out of the way. With a clear area, Alexa kicked hard at the side of the closet and felt a softening in its resistance. Three kicks later the internal panel of the closet dislodged enough for her to peer behind it.

With her heart racing, Alexa pushed the side of the closet back far enough to fit her hand through the gap. Only emptiness met her probing hand as she felt around blindly. Pulling her hand back, she ran her hand along the wall that separated the closet from the bathroom, then pushed forward to meet the wall that was the outside of the room. She could not work out why there would be this large empty space, when they could have just made the cupboard larger. Then, as she pulled her hand back, it dropped below the level of the floor.

There was no floor.

Despite the hours spent in the bathroom, to the frustration of her roommates, Alexa was no closer to understanding the mystery of the empty space when she went to bed that night. The next morning at breakfast she snuck into the kitchen and stole a sharp knife off the counter. On her return, she spotted Chad and Sam.

"Sam," called Alexa, walking up behind him as he and Chad

hurried in for a late breakfast.

"Oh, hi, Alexa. We're running a bit late. Can we talk later?" asked Sam, piling toast into his hands.

"Can we walk and talk?" Alexa asked. Sam nodded with a slightly worried look on his face. "I found this hidden space last night and I want to find out what it is and if you guys have the same thing in your room."

"What hidden space?" asked Chad.

"It's in the bathroom, beside the closet, between the closet and the outside wall. There's a space – if you push the side of the closet off slightly – but there's no floor. I want to know if it goes all the way down to the ground floor."

"Planning another escape route, are we?" asked Sam, smiling slightly.

"I just want to know where this space goes. Will you help me?" asked Alexa with mild desperation.

"Yeah, we'll help you," answered Sam solemnly, before nodding to Chad and walking off.

Alexa did not miss the concerned looks they exchanged, and was glad they always just supported her and her crazy ideas.

Playful cries and bright light woke Alexa the next morning. The bedroom was empty. She had spent half the night before cutting a hole in the side of the closet large enough for her to squeeze through. There had been no sign of Chad or Sam all night and she planned to pester them after breakfast. She thought she would have less than half an hour's worth of work making the hole slightly larger.

An hour later and covered in dust, but having finally succeeded in creating a hole large enough to crawl through, Alexa jumped in the shower. Clean and refreshed, she hopped out only to realise that her towel was in the closet. Dripping water all over the bathroom floor as she knelt down to grab her towel, she almost slipped in fright when she saw a hand holding her towel up to her.

"I guess you're not decent then," called an amused voice from the somewhere behind the hole in her closet wall.

"Sam, is that you? You scared the hell out of me," said Alexa breathlessly, wrapping the towel around her wet body, including her red and torn arm.

"Sorry. Can I come in?"

"Yeah, come in."

The next minute a very blackened Sam crawled into Alexa's

closet and bathroom.

"Looks like we have ourselves a secret passageway," Sam said, smiling broadly. "It's pretty small so you can climb along both walls easily enough, but you get a little dirty."

"I can see that," Alexa replied in an amused voice. "So it goes right to the ground floor?"

"Yeah, though they still have the side of their closet attached. And you wouldn't want to fall. It's a fair way down."

"What's in there?" asked Alexa curiously.

"Pipes, there are just three pipes that run along the entire length up until your floor. I think they must be plumbing or something."

"How did you get out of your floor?"

"Same as you. We cut a hole in the side of the bottom shelf. It should be easy enough for you to get through," said Sam, and Alexa noted that he did not include himself in the need for the passage.

"Have you told anyone about it?"

"No, but I'm going to talk to Nick and Alan on Monday. I want to get some stuff to make steps."

"Who are you talking to, Alexa?" Bianca called from the other side of the bathroom door, causing both Alexa and Sam to jump in fright. They had not been making any attempt to keep their voices down.

"Nobody, I was just talking to myself," Alexa called back, pushing Sam back into the closet as they giggled childishly.

***

In that last week of term, Alexa felt as at ease as she believed possible. Despite the occasional muttered threat in the corridor, Clinton and Ms Carter had kept a low profile since their beating of her and her refusal to accept Clinton's 'assistance'. It made Alexa confident that they had finally realised that she would not play their games no matter how difficult they made her life. Beyond continually beating her, Alexa really could not think what more they could do to threaten her that did not risk exposing their actions.

On the freedom front, things were also going well. With the help of Nick and Alan, Sam made wooden steps in the secret passageway to allow them to move easily between their rooms. Alexa could now look at the bars on her window and smile. However, her newly-confident spirits were shaken on the last day of term when she was called into Mr Knight's office. There was only one thing she knew of that could get her into trouble, but could not work out how Mr Knight could have possibly discovered her secret.

Sitting in her usual seat, Alexa surveyed Mr Knight's young face. He did not appear angry – something he certainly would be if he had discovered her escape route. In fact, he looked nervous, even anxious. It made her apprehensive.

"I know you're probably wondering why I've asked to come here today," Mr Knight said gently, but Alexa did not respond. She did not want to give anything away. "I just wanted to check on you, to – to make sure that – are you feeling all right? I've noticed that you've appeared much happier this last week and I'm sure you're looking forward to the holidays." Alexa sighed in relief. "I'm still worried about you though."

"I'm fine. I don't need your worry," Alexa replied tonelessly.

"I do anyway. I still haven't forgotten how the last school holidays began and … I don't want to see anything like that ever again." Mr Knight's voice trailed off slightly and Alexa felt a spike of pity for him.

"I'm not going to kill myself," said Alexa in a soothing manner that greatly surprised her. She had never come into Mr Knight's office with the intention of offering him any sympathy.

Mr Knight nodded and allowed her to leave, which she did immediately. She did not want to feel sorry for him. She did not even want to think of him as a real person with real emotions. He was a teacher and she never wanted to get involved with a teacher in any way ever again.

What Alexa did want was to get well away from Redgrove for a while. As soon as the final bell rang, she rushed down to the dormitories, grabbed her bag and dashed frantically for the gates. She had only just opened the door to her foster parents' home when Hayley, who had turned ten a month earlier, greeted her with a crushing hug. Brett was nowhere to be seen. His newfound popularity since the Easter holidays meant that he was rarely home any more, much to his delight and his mother's anxiety. Despite this, Pam and Karl both smiled warmly as she sat down for dinner.

"How was school?" asked Karl.

"It was okay, I guess. Glad to be out for a while. Thanks for asking me back," said Alexa politely, though she did not quite raise her eyes enough to meet Karl's.

"We didn't have much choice. I don't think Hayley would have spoken to us again if we didn't ask you back," said Pam with a smile.

Hayley grinned broadly. Alexa tried to smile as a large knot twisted in her stomach. Though she could tell what Pam meant, she still wished there were some adults in the world who found her worthwhile.

"We had every intention of asking you back, Alexa. We're glad to take you in for the holidays," added Pam, as though reading her mind, but Alexa found it difficult to believe her.

"Do you have any plans for the holidays?" asked Karl in an overly casual manner.

Alexa just shook her head, realising the school must have informed them of her disappearance.

"Are you planning to go looking for your sister? We heard she was back on the streets," asked Pam, confirming Alexa's suspicions.

"I don't know," replied Alexa sadly, pushing her dinner across her plate. "I'm not sure there's any point. She doesn't want anything to do with me and she has a boyfriend now."

Alexa continued to stare at her plate. The thought of food made her want to vomit. Although she spent most of her time thinking about Bethany, she had tried not to think about the useless position she was in to help her. The Whites did not question her any more and as soon as dinner was over she escaped quickly to her room, not emerging again that night.

It was well past ten when Alexa woke the next morning. The house was quiet and so she showered and dressed before going downstairs to breakfast. There was a note on the kitchen table. They would be gone the entire day. Alexa ate slowly then walked aimlessly around the house. She found nothing to occupy herself with, so grabbed her bag and headed into the city, unsure of whether she was going looking for Bethany or not.

Alexa knew there would come a time when she could no longer run around after Bethany. A time when, like it or not, she would have to let Bethany make her own choices in life and pay the consequences. It was a thought that she had been mulling over a lot since their last encounter. There was just the question of how and when to make that decision. The problem was that she had spent her life protecting Bethany and did not know how to stop.

It seemed unconscionable to leave a fourteen-year-old to fend for themselves. Alexa was luckier than Bethany. Their mother had not started using drugs until after she was born. She had always wondered if it had been her birth that had driven her mother to drugs; her fault Bethany had been born addicted to heroin. Perhaps that would be taking too much responsibility for something she could never have controlled, but someone had to take responsibility for their lives and, in the absence of anyone else, Alexa knew it would have to be her.

As she strolled the city streets, Alexa knew it was not yet time to give up on Bethany, but nor was it the time to try and find her again either. There was just nowhere to take her and no way of looking after her. They would have to wait until she was eighteen and hope that their miracle windfall came through.

So the holidays passed without Alexa making any further attempts to find Bethany. Instead, she occupied her time by looking after Hayley while her foster parents were at work. It was not the holidays she desired, which made trying to be grateful more difficult than she wanted it to be. What the Whites gave her holidays after holidays was so much more than she deserved.

Pam and Karl were always kind. Brett was always welcoming. Hayley was just spectacular. Every day Hayley tried her best to keep Alexa cheerful and was, for the most part, quite successful, but despite her efforts Alexa could find no real happiness in her substitute family. She wanted it to be real, but it simply wasn't and it never would be. Just trying to be appreciative of their kindness often only made Alexa more angry and jealous of what she had never had. It made her thankful when it came time to pack her bags and head back to school.

Noise and clatter emanated from the dining hall as Alexa arrived at the start of lunch on Sunday. Bianca was already in the dining hall sitting next to Chad, with whom she appeared more than a bit friendly. Sam soon sat down beside them looking disheartened and only smiled weakly when Alexa joined them.

"Hi, Alexa. How were your holidays?" asked Bianca, much more upbeat than Alexa would have predicted before the holidays.

"Okay, I guess," replied Alexa cautiously, not really trusting Bianca's high spirits. "How about you? How'd you survive here by yourself?"

"She wasn't by herself," answered Chad with a smile, making Bianca blush.

Alexa was sure she did not want to know what was going on

between Chad and Bianca, and it was clear that Sam did not either.

"I have to go unpack," said Sam softly, pushing his plate away and walking off.

Alexa looked at her half-eaten lunch and then back at the departing Sam. Chad looked a little concerned by Sam's departure as well, but Bianca quickly diverted his attention back to her.

"I'd better go register. I'll see you guys later," said Alexa, jumping up from the table and walking quickly to catch up with Sam.

Sam was leaning against a window sill in the corridor leading down to the dormitories. His face looked determinedly blank, as though he was trying to deny whatever he was feeling.

"What's going on with those two?" asked Alexa as she leaned against the wall next to Sam and tilted her head back to the dining hall.

"They're going out now," Sam replied sadly.

Alexa had suspected that, but had hoped it was not true – for many people's sakes.

"What about Chris?" she asked, thinking about the intimate goodbye she had been forced to witness at the end of last term between Bianca and Chris.

"Like I give a shit about Chris," spat Sam, the blankness of his face cracking into anger

"Sam, I'm sorry. I know you liked her," Alexa said softly, realising he must have liked Bianca more than he had previously made out.

"Doesn't matter. Probably never had a chance anyway. Chad's the good looking one."

"Yeah, but you're the sweet one," said Alexa sincerely, taking Sam's hand and smiling.

"Doesn't get me very far though, does it? Wasn't enough for you either," replied Sam, throwing off her hand.

Alexa dropped her gaze and walked away. It not even close to the cruellest thing Sam could have said to her, and she was surprised he had not said worse before now.

"I'm sorry, that wasn't fair. I'm being an idiot," said Sam, catching up to her and grabbing her hand.

"It's okay. I'll talk to you later," replied Alexa softly, knowing full well that she had deserved that for all she had put Sam through. "I still have to go register. You want to come with me?"

"No, he's love sick as well."

"Who? Mr Knight?" Alexa asked enquiringly.

"Yeah. He proposed to his girlfriend in the holidays. Don't think we'll have to worry about him hassling us for a while," said Sam, before sulking off towards his room.

Chapter Twelve

MARCUS SMILED EASILY as he chatted to the students – female students – from his senior geography class. They had been asking him all about his engagement and he had given them some details. Though some, like Lizzie, looked at him with slightly gooey eyes, he knew that mostly they were interested in the romance, even if it belonged to someone else.

At least in this case, he had a romantic story to tell. He had arranged for his best mate Brandon to get Jackie out of the way for the day. He had then filled their apartment with candles and rose petals. When Jackie arrived home, Marcus had walked her blindfolded into the lounge room where he had spelt out the words 'marry me' in rose petals inside a candlelit love heart.

Though everyone, not just these young girls, gushed when he told the story, Marcus could still not help but feel like a fraud. It was not the way he had always imagined proposing. He had always wanted something simpler; in bed or while walking along the beach – no fanfare.

"Wow, I hope someone proposes to me like that," said one of the girls, but Marcus was not sure which. He had just noticed Alexa at his office door.

She looked awkward and was clearly confused by the easy smiling mood of the girls in front of her.

"Hi, Alexa. How were you holidays? Did you hear Mr Knight got engaged?" asked Lizzie excitedly.

"Yeah, I heard. Um, I just wanted to register my arrival," Alexa replied hesitantly.

Marcus could tell Alexa did not care to hear his story. It was clear she could not understand why anyone would want to hear his stories.

"That's all fine," he replied quietly.

Marcus watched Alexa leave and tried to rationalise his disappointment. He did not regret proposing to Jackie and when he looked at Alexa he did not have any interest in her that way. He could not understand why he then wished that it was her sitting in front of his desk talking happily to him and not the girls from his geography class.

There was no doubt that the events of the year had given Marcus a greater appreciation of the type of person Alexa must be. He could not truly fathom how complicated and difficult her life must be. Even her disappearance last term to search for her sister was something he looked on with something close to admiration – now that he had distanced himself from his anger over her defiance of him.

That was what he truly felt – admiration. He admired Alexa and wanted her to feel something less than disdain for him. However, admiration of a student was still dangerous and what he hoped for more than anything was that he would have as little to do with Alexa Samson as possible over the next year and a half.

***

As Alexa made her way through the dining hall for dinner, it was immediately clear that Sam was not the only person taking the news of Bianca's new relationship badly.

"So this is who you dumped me for?" spat Chris, standing over Bianca and Chad as they ate. "Do you just pick up a new boyfriend every holidays, then?"

Alexa sat down at the table and saw tears welling in Bianca's eyes. However, it was the look of shock on Bianca's face that surprised Alexa most, as though she had not been expecting Chris to be upset given how intimate they had been just a couple of weeks ago.

"I'm sorry, Chris. I didn't mean to hurt you," said Bianca meekly, but almost defiantly, not meeting Chris's eyes. "Things just happened. I didn't plan it."

"Yeah right. How long was it going on for? You acted all upset that I was going home for the holidays, but really you were glad cos you had Chad here waiting in the wings."

"Nothing happened with me and Chad until after I broke up with you," said Bianca, her voice shaking as tears began to fall down her cheeks, but Alexa was sure that they were tears of indignation rather than sadness or shame.

"Right, so you just can't go a couple of weeks without getting laid, then? Your boyfriend goes home for the holiday, so you just had to get it any way y–"

Chris did not get to finish his sentence. Chad practically leapfrogged Bianca to get to Chris and in a blink of an eye was on top of him, landing punch after punch. Chris quickly began his own assault. Seeing the confrontation, Alexa was surprised anyone could think that the G7 was a tight-knit group.

Alexa rushed around the table and tried to pull Chad off Chris, while Bianca sat in shock, tears streaming down her face. Sam stayed where he was until Alexa looked over at him with desperation. It took almost a minute to pull them apart, and Chad and Chris both sported cut lips and bruised faces when they sat back down at their respective tables.

Sam sat Chad down next to Bianca and made sure that he was okay before walking out of the dining hall in silence. Alexa made sure Bianca did not need her and ran out after Sam. When she caught up with him, she did not speak, but wrapped a consoling arm around his waist and led him to their quiet corner of the library. They sat down on the floor side by side and remained there in silence until curfew. Alexa knew it helped, because it had always helped her, and when they parted for bed Sam managed a genuine smile for her.

As the weeks rolled by, Bianca's betrayal remained the focal point of gossip amongst the year elevens and even though Bianca was her friend, Alexa was secretly relieved that everyone was gossiping about someone other than herself. It was selfish, but it was really the only positive she had to cling on to, so grabbed it with both hands.

The dynamics of their social group also changed with Chad and Bianca's relationship, but it was not all for the best. While it was nice to have Sam and Chad around more, Chad and Bianca were a very physical couple. It was nauseating and often put Sam in a terrible mood. It was nicer when Bianca went off with Chad and Sam, leaving Alexa alone with Ezra, but Alexa did feel sorry for Sam on those occasions.

Classes were also hectic. Unofficially, this was their last term of year eleven. They had to start their year twelve course in term four, which meant that their final exams were now just six weeks away. Alexa was grateful for the extra time she now had on Tuesday afternoons. She needed it. Her study habits to date had always been patchy at best and her frequent absences from school had left large gaps in her education.

Yet those hours on a Tuesday could not just be spent focused on her studies. There were too many memories of Tuesdays with

Clinton for Alexa to forget the threat he still posed. Though he had gone quiet last term, he was still around and just a glance from him was terrifying. Ms Carter's hateful glares did not help the situation, and as time went by Alexa could only be more concerned that something would happen that would once more leave her at their mercy.

On top of all of that were Alexa's constant concerns for Bethany. With Bethany living on the streets, Alexa could not even write her letters and stay in contact. There was no way for her to know if Bethany was safe or well. As the weeks passed by, her fears for Bethany's life not only consumed her days, but tortured her nights as well.

"We can take those bars off now," said Mr Knight smilingly, while Alexa stood at her window watching the colour fade from the sky.

"Why?" asked Alexa, astounded, as something far back in her mind twinging that this was not quite right.

"Because there're no more reasons for you to run away," replied Mr Knight happily.

"I don't understand. If you take the bars off, you know I'll go looking for Bethy," Alexa replied, staring at the bars once more, feeling their constraint.

"There's no need. Bethany's dead. You don't have to worry about her any more."

Mr Knight continued to look at her as though he was delivering good news, unaware of the way her heart was disintegrating.

"No, no you're lying," Alexa choked, as tears streamed down her face.

"She's gone. You can look after yourself now," said Mr Knight, as if he genuinely believed that was a good thing.

"No, no," Alexa cried, pushing past Mr Knight, running out through her bedroom door and straight out on to the city streets.

Alexa sprinted down the street, her body straining under the weight of her fear. It took many confused turns before she reached the place where she had last seen Bethany. Bethany was still there. Alexa felt as though her legs were filled with lead, with the last few metres seemingly impossible to traverse. Bethany was lying on the footpath, her body splayed out with a needle still in her arm.

"No, no please, Bethy, please wake up," cried Alexa, her heart feeling as though it might burst.

Alexa scooped up Bethany's lifeless body and cradled it softly, trying to will it back to life. Tears streamed down her face, bathing Bethany in her final shower.

Anguished sobbing woke Alexa from her sleep. It took her mind a while to realise that it was her body that was convulsing and that it was not just in her dreams that she had been crying. She looked desperately around the room, trying to reconcile reality with fantasy, but it was harder than it should have been.

This was not the first time that Alexa had dreamt of Bethany's death, but it was the first time since her dreams started coming true. If the dream about Ben and the marbles had been true then maybe this one was too. She could not take the risk. She could not stay and let Bethany die in the street.

Within seconds of making that decision, Alexa was out of bed and dressed. She threw the essentials into a bag, knowing she may never be coming back, and dashed into the bathroom. Climbing through the small hole in her bathroom closet, Alexa made sure she covered the hole again. Although she was not sure if she would ever be back, she did not want Sam or Chad being blamed or punished for her escape.

The steps that Sam had put in the passageway made travelling between the floors very easy. Alexa pushed aside the bags covering the hole on the second floor closet and climbed through, covering it again behind her. None of the boys woke as she climbed out their window, slipped down the drainpipe and hurried out of the school undetected.

By sunrise Alexa had reached the city. She rushed straight to the place where she had found Bethany last – where Bethany had just died in her dream – and there she was. Bethany was slouched on the footpath. There was no needle, but there were few signs of life either.

Alexa tried to keep her body moving forward, her heart pounding with fear. Whatever the reality was, she had to face it. Skidding to the ground next to Bethany, Alexa picked her up and held her tight, crying shamelessly.

"Get off me. What are you doing?" cried Bethany, suddenly thrashing her arms around.

Alexa choked on her sob as she sighed with relief, but she did not release Bethany. She couldn't. Bethany pushed out of her embrace enough to turn around. Alexa looked down at her, tears still slipping down her cheeks.

"What are you doing here?" asked Bethany, her voice

somewhere between petulance and glee.

"I had to see you. I had – I had a dream … you died. I had to make sure you were okay," replied Alexa, unable to hide her terror, and saw the faintest spark of a connection in Bethany's eyes before they glazed over again.

"And now you're going straight back to school – now that you know I'm not dead," spat Bethany, turning away.

"Not if you don't want me to," replied Alexa, stroking Bethany's once shiny brown hair. She knew now, more than ever, that she would have to live or die with Bethany on these streets. "You just say the word and I'll stay here with you."

Bethany laid her head back down into Alexa's lap. She was quiet for a while, then said in a firm voice, "Stay."

"Okay," nodded Alexa. "I'll stay."

Alexa took a deep shuddering breath as she processed that decision. This would be her new life. It was a choice she was making willingly, but it did not take away from their reality. They had no money and no home. She tried not to think about how they were going to survive, not just yet. Nothing was going to let her change her mind.

However, Alexa could not prevent her mind from trying to find some kind of solution that did not involve abandoning Bethany for her own comforts. She did not want to talk to her social worker, fearful that she would be forced back to school, but they needed somewhere to go. They needed money, but there was precious little work for sixteen-year-old street kids, especially ones that paid enough to keep her and Bethany fed and housed.

There was only one solution. Alexa had always known that, and perhaps that was what had stopped her from taking this step before. However, she was older now, old enough to know what she was doing, what she was deciding and what she was giving up with that choice.

"Listen, I have to go and try and get us some money," said Alexa when she had finally built up the courage to face her new future. "But I want to make sure that I'll be able to find you when I get back."

"Where are you going to get money from?" Bethany asked defiantly.

"I'll do what I have to do. It's not your concern, but no money I get is going to be spent on drugs," replied Alexa firmly. "I didn't agree to stay here to watch you die."

"How long will you be?"

"I'm not sure. Will you be here when I return?"

"I won't be far," replied Bethany. Alexa turned to leave. "Take care okay, Lex," Bethany called.

Alexa turned back and smiled, thankful that she could still reach Bethany, even full of heroin. It made what she was about to do almost bearable.

Trudging to another part of the city, Alexa was almost in denial over what she was about to do. It was surreal that it had come to this, but it was better than being separated from Bethany. With her heart beating hard in her throat, Alexa walked down a long street full of adult pleasures, trying to decide where to turn her future. A strip club caught her eye. There was no reason why it felt safer and more welcoming than any of the other places, but she would take any sign that her new life would not be as bad as she feared.

"I want to see the manager," Alexa said, as she walked up to the bar.

The barman looked her up and down a couple of times before directing her to a door at the back of the room. It led to a drab-looking hallway with several doors on either side. The last door on the left was ajar and Alexa headed towards it. Inside were two middle-aged men, one was sitting at a large desk while the other was standing in a corner talking in a low voice. Alexa took a deep breath, knocked and entered.

"What can I do for you?" asked the man seated behind the desk. His face was pleasant and not at all sinister as Alexa had expected. He had dark black hair, and stylish rectangular glasses framed his eyes.

"I need some work," replied Alexa nervously, knowing there would be no turning back after this.

"How old are you?"

"Eighteen," she lied.

"Do you have any identification?" asked the man, clearly sceptical.

"No."

"Sorry, I can't use you then," he replied dismissively, and turned away as though that ended the conversation.

"Okay, I'm only sixteen, but I need work," said Alexa, stepping forward. She did not know how to do this by herself.

"I can't put a minor out there," said the man firmly. "The police would have me shut down in a heartbeat."

"There must be other work ... private – not out there," said Alexa, not wanting to speak those other words aloud.

"What are you prepared to do?"

"Anything," she sighed, and it was true. For Bethany, she would do anything.

"You take drugs?"

"No, my sister does. I need to get her off the streets before she dies."

"So you want to put yourself on the streets instead?" Alexa did not answer, just stood defiantly. "Kid, I'm not going to do this. There must be other ways you can get the money."

"How? Last time I checked, McDonalds was still only paying seven dollars an hour."

The man searched Alexa's face intently before looking her up and down. She did not know what he was looking for. She had given him defiant and angry, but if he needed sweet and pleasing she would try.

"She certainly would be a drawcard with that baby face," he said in a low voice to the man in the corner. "Are you sure about this?" he asked, turning back to Alexa.

"Yes," Alexa replied softly, though she was anything but.

She wanted to run away screaming. She wanted to believe that this was all a mistake and somewhere out there were people who loved her and Bethany and wanted to give them a normal home and allow them to be average, boring children, but that was just a fantasy. This was her reality.

"When can you start?" asked the man.

"Right now," replied Alexa, stepping forward with shaking legs. She would not let this chance slip away.

"Right, well my name's Steve."

"Alexa."

Despite Steve's previous concern for her welfare, he still drove a hard bargain and Alexa only managed to secure a sixty percent cut of her earnings. She could not complain. Steve was offering protection and screening of her clients. She would work only in his club, the men would all use condoms and she could pull the plug if any of them refused to play by the rules. The money was also very good – even sixty percent of it.

"We'll give you a trial," said Steve. "Got someone tonight. Be a nice one to start with. So let's get you cleaned up."

Alexa nodded. She knew what she was agreeing to, but it still did not feel real. Steve showed her to the bathrooms where she could shower. There was an outfit waiting for her when finished. It did not make her feel sexy, but when she looked in the mirror she accepted that it accentuated all the right parts of her body.

Steve had food prepared for her. Alexa felt ridiculous sitting at a table eating when she was dressed in such revealing attire. When Steve looked at his watch, she knew it was time. Her heart started pounding painfully and her stomach swirled, making her wish she had not eaten. She was about to give herself to a man she had never met and it was the last thing she wanted to do. It was only the image of Bethany lying dead in the street that stopped her from fleeing.

They walked upstairs. It looked almost like a private residence, and Alexa could not be sure if this was a normal part of Steve's business or if she had presented him with an opportunity too good to resist.

"He's waiting for you," said Steve when they arrived at a closed door. Alexa nodded, but did not enter straight away. "Good luck. You'll be fine," he said as she placed her hand on the door handle.

Alexa nodded and breathed deeply before stepping into the room. It took her a moment to realise that her eyes were closed. Opening them slowly, she saw a man in his mid-forties with well-groomed brown hair, dressed in a black suit smiling at her.

"Hi," Alexa said softly. It sounded lame, but she really was not sure how else to start proceedings.

"Hello, I'm Martin."

"Alexa."

Alexa realised that she probably should have given him a fake name, but hardly saw the point. This name or another, it was still her body. And it was her body Martin was interested in. He seemed pleased by her youth as he moved in closer.

It's a job, just a job, repeated Alexa over and over in her head, trying to calm her pounding heart. She knew it was only sex, something she had had many times before, and tried to convince herself that this would be no different to those experiences. Martin's distinguished manner even reminded her a little of Clinton, something she found strangely comforting.

Leading Martin to the bed, Alexa undressed him gently, kissing his chest as her hands roamed lower. Martin moaned softly as her kisses moved below his waist. It was mechanical, and by focusing on Martin's pleasure, Alexa found she was able to make it very job-like in her head – until he touched her skin. That was when she remembered how little she wanted to be doing this.

"I'm ready," said Martin.

Alexa knew that meant she had to be as well, but it was difficult. Concentrating on relaxing her body to lessen the pain of the unwanted penetration, nothing she did could make the experience enjoyable. But she did not need to enjoy it. She just had to tolerate it.

When it was over, Martin dressed quickly and left the room without a backward glance. Alexa dressed slowly, her eyes completely dry despite feeling a piece of her soul break off and tumble into the abyss.

She was now a prostitute.

Chapter Thirteen

STEVE WAS SITTING behind his desk when Alexa came downstairs and sat in a chair opposite him. Alexa suddenly realised that her body was shaking uncontrollably.

"Here, drink this," said Steve, handing her a pale brown drink. She had not even noticed him leave his desk.

"Thanks," she said in a barely audible voice.

Alexa poured the drink down her throat, the taste causing her to shudder before she felt warmth spread through her stomach. She did not move. She did not know what she was supposed to do next.

"Here," Steve said, pushing money across his desk. "Like I explained before, this is a bit higher than the standard rate because you're young and girls your age are hard to find. I can get more from some of the more exotic clients, I guess you could call them, but you just let me know when you're ready. I won't give you any of them until you say so. Now, I think you should go home and come back tomorrow if you're still up for it."

Alexa did not answer, but nodded and took the money off the table. She did not want to come back tomorrow, but knew she would. With cash in her hand it was easier to believe the work was worth it. They were able to eat that night and the next day. It was not yet enough to house and clothe them, but that would come.

The next night Alexa saw four clients. The first two were of a similar vein to Martin; middle-aged, married men looking for pleasures their wives would not provide. The third client was a young, rich man, who could have not been much older than twenty. Alexa could not work out why he would pay for sex. He was not so ugly that no one would sleep with him and he obviously had enough money to make him attractive to any number of women. He was her worst client. He treated her with disdain, ordering her into different positions before resuming his violent thrusting. She hoped he would not return anytime soon.

By the end of that second night, Alexa felt as though her soul had completely died. She was instead filled with an emptiness she never knew existed, but if the price for Bethany's life was her soul, then she would sell it – destroy it – a thousand times over. However, Alexa knew there was more than just selling her soul involved in saving Bethany's life.

Straight after her shift, Alexa left work with one of the strippers from the club who lived in a boarding house three blocks away and had told her that there were rooms available. They were not spectacular. They were barely even basic, but they were affordable – just – and better than the streets. It was only Bethany who had to be convinced of that.

"I can't go yet. Leo isn't back," said Bethany, as Alexa tried to drag her back to their new home.

"This is not negotiable, Bethy. You know exactly what I'm doing for you. You wanted me to stay. You wanted me to help you and that's what I'm doing."

"I never told you to be a prostitute," retorted Bethany.

"How else did you think I was going to get us money? Besides, what I'm doing is not the point. The point is that I'm here to help you, like you asked me to, so now you have to accept a few of my conditions. I'm not going to do this to myself just to watch you die."

After again looking around for Leo, Bethany finally bowed her head and followed Alexa across town.

From the outside, the boarding house looked very old and run-down, which Bethany spitefully pointed out. The inside was little better and Bethany muttered as they made their way up the stairs and to the back of the house. However, when Alexa opened the door to their room Bethany's criticism stopped.

It was a very modest room, consisting of two single beds, a small wardrobe and two bedside tables. The floorboards were old and uneven and creaked with every step. Old and peeling wallpaper covered the walls, but there was a large window that lit the room and from a certain angle it gave the briefest glimpse of the harbour.

"This is ours?" asked Bethany, looking around. Alexa nodded. "And we're going to live here together? Both of us? Same room?" Alexa kept nodding. "Same bed?"

This time Alexa smiled. Her Bethany was coming back to her. They moved the beds so that they were right next to each other and positioned by the window. When they climbed in, they curled up in each other's arms on just one of the beds. It was the best sleep

Alexa had had in a very long time.

When they woke, the sun was starting to set and Bethany was beginning to shake. Alexa did not want to leave Bethany alone in this state, but it had taken nearly all the money she had earned to secure their room. Even so, working again could probably wait another day, except that it was Friday night. Steve promised her that Friday and Saturday nights would earn her more than the rest of the week combined.

"I have to work tonight, Bethy," said Alexa, making up her mind. This move was for the long term. If Bethany slipped up this weekend, she could take the whole week off if she needed to. "I really don't want you to leave, not until you're clean, so you have to promise you'll stay here and just fight it."

"I need it, Lex, I really do. I don't feel right without it," replied Bethany, her arms wrapped around her body.

It was a good sign. If Bethany did not want to withdraw, she would have been fighting her to get out of the room by now. Had they not been in the sanctuary of a room, with a bed and basic comforts, Alexa knew she would have had no hope of keeping Bethany clean. It did not make going to work any more enticing, but it did prove to her that she was doing the right thing.

"I know, but that will change," said Alexa, gently stroking Bethany's hair. "You have to remember what it's like without drugs. I'm here for you now. You're not alone. We can do this."

"You promise you won't leave?" asked Bethany, grasping Alexa's hand.

"I promise, Bethy. I won't leave you. I'm going to go and get you some food and water, okay. I'll be back soon."

It took Alexa almost an hour to get everything she needed to take care of Bethany. When she returned home Bethany was asleep, but still shaking as her body craved the heroin she was denying it. It was difficult to leave her like this. She never had before, but they had never been in this position before either. Knowing she had no choice, Alexa headed to work.

Steve was right. Friday and Saturday nights were busy. Alexa barely had time to think as she saw client after client, hour after hour. If she thought about anything, it was Bethany – her shaking body and the crawling hours that were slowly depleting it of heroin. She would not think beyond that. However, when Steve handed her an envelope full of money on Sunday morning, Alexa managed to crack a smile.

"You got a phone?" asked Steve. Alexa shook her head. "Then here, take this. I'll call you when I have work during the week. Just make sure you're around on the weekends."

Alexa took the little black box and examined it closely, completely confused. Steve laughed and explained that it was a beeper, not a phone, before showing her how to use it.

"So you don't think there will be much work during the week?" asked Alexa, looking back down at the envelope. There was more money in there than she had thought imaginable, but she could not be sure it was enough to take care of Bethany. "What if I need more work?"

"There will always be work. Half the guys you saw last night have asked about seeing you again. That's why I've given you that. Let's get you comfortable with some regulars first. It'll make it easier."

Alexa nodded, surprised by how kind and thoughtful Steve was. The concept of regular customers instead of constantly servicing new clients was appealing. It would make the whole process that much easier, and Alexa was thankful for even the smallest thing that would make her life more tolerable.

Running home, Alexa was glad to see that Bethany was still there. She was even glad Bethany was in a foul mood. It meant that the heroin was leaving her body. They were good signs, and Alexa kept reminding Bethany of that, even though all she got in return was a string of expletives.

They spent the whole day together, until Steve beeped. Martin wanted to see her again. Alexa considered saying no, but it was just an hour. Reassuring Bethany that she would not be long, she dashed back up to work, grateful that they were living close by.

It was better the second time. If Alexa thought too much about what she was doing, she could still find herself repulsed by her actions, but on a more global scale, it was actually not as bad as she imagined. Leaving with more money in her pocket, because all her clients had to pay in cash to avoid any record of her employment, she allowed herself to start thinking a little more long-term.

With prudent spending, Alexa knew she could easily earn enough to set her and Bethany up. Things would always be on the dodgy side while she remained underage and the work she was doing illegal, but she had met enough people who were prepared to ignore laws to reassure her that there would always be work. When she did turn eighteen, this world could be left behind her anyway. For the first time in a very long time, Alexa felt the uplifting effects of hope.

Bethany battled through her withdrawal despite Alexa's sporadic absences. Steve's requests for Alexa to work during the week were not as infrequent as she had imagined. She never turned him down. They needed the money. It was the only security they had, and Bethany seemed to understand that, never once complaining about her need to go to work, no matter what mood her withdrawal had put her in.

Alexa was heartened by Bethany's strength and will to beat her addiction. In the end, she knew she could not save them both by her will alone. Bethany had to want to get clean or it was all lost. Thankfully, it was something Bethany seemed to want. By Tuesday afternoon Bethany was out of bed, and by Thursday she feeling as good as she ever had.

"Thank you," said Bethany, dancing across the room and hugging Alexa.

Alexa could not believe just how different Bethany looked. Of course there was the showering, clean clothes and basic grooming that Bethany had been missing, but there was something more. It was really Bethany in front of her. The drugs and their physical occupation of Bethany's body were gone. Only Bethany remained.

"I would do anything for you," replied Alexa, stroking Bethany's hair that shone once more.

Pre-empting the beep that had already dragged her to work for two hours that morning, Alexa called Steve and told him she would not be in until Friday afternoon. She and Bethany were going to spend some long-awaited time together. It was the most fun they had had in a long time. They caught a ferry and ate food. They lounged in the park and walked along the foreshore. It really did not matter where they were or what they were doing. They were together.

If Alexa ever experienced a better twenty-four hours, she could not recall it. She was free, Bethany was clean and they had a place to live. It was more than enough of a reward for the work that was required to secure their new life and she knew it would not be forever. In a little over a year she would be eighteen, she would find Bianca and Ezra and they would claim their lottery win.

That miracle had never seemed so real as it did now, perhaps because Alexa no longer found herself reliant on it. It would simply cement the life she and Bethany would spend the next year building. Perhaps Bianca had been right about clouds having a silver lining after all.

When Friday afternoon rolled around, Alexa found herself more anxious about leaving Bethany than ever before. Bethany's more active state in many ways left her less immune to the temptation of drugs just outside the door. Bethany promised she would stay inside while she was at work. Alexa accepted this. There was no choice, but the weekend was much busier than Alexa anticipated.

There were breaks, but they were short and Alexa used them to get ready for the next client. After arriving at work at four on Friday afternoon, she did not leave again until ten the next morning. When she reached her own bed, she collapsed and fell instantly to sleep. The only consolation was waking up with Bethany's arms around her.

"What time is it?" asked Alexa sleepily.

"Three," answered Bethany, hugging her tighter.

"Urgh. Let's get up. I'm not going to miss more time with you sleeping. I can sleep when we're rich."

Bethany laughed and jumped out of bed. They grabbed some food from the supermarket and headed down to a park overlooking the harbour. They made huge, messy sandwiches, feasting until they both conceded defeat. Throwing it down with a bottle of juice, they could not help but laugh. They were living like kings.

Walking back up to their room, Bethany confessed her boredom. It was something Alexa had been thinking a lot about too. There was no way Bethany could go back to school. Not only did Bethany hate school, there was too big a risk that she would be discovered and their life together torn apart. Even Bethany getting a job posed similar risks, and Alexa was not prepared for Bethany to work in the same industry as her.

The only option left was to give Bethany money for her to do things and occupy her time, but that was almost as risky as all the other options combined.

"You have to learn to trust me eventually," said Bethany, as Alexa undressed on Sunday morning after another long night.

"I do trust you, but this isn't a matter of trust. I know how strong your cravings can be and one hit now would set you back so far."

"I don't want to take drugs. I just want to go shopping. I want to do something. It's so boring. You sleep all day. What am I supposed to do?"

"Okay, here take this," said Alexa, handing Bethany a hundred dollars. "Just know how much you will hurt me if you take drugs again. Like I said, I didn't come here to watch you die."

"I won't take any drugs, I promise."

Bethany kissed Alexa goodbye and rushed out of the room. If Alexa was not so exhausted, she would have expended more time being worried, but all she could do was speak a silent prayer before collapsing on the bed and falling straight to sleep.

The gentle rustling of plastic woke Alexa. The sun was setting, bathing the room in soft light. She rolled over to see Bethany trying on a new top.

"That looks nice," said Alexa smiling, her heart glowing. Things were finally starting to go their way.

"You can wear it too. I got stuff that would fit us both – and safety pins so you can pin the pants up," added Bethany with a smirk.

Alexa wrestled Bethany to the ground, play fighting as they rolled across the floor. They did not stop until Bethany's head clunked against the leg of the bed frame.

"You okay?" asked Alexa, though she was struggling not to laugh.

"Yeah, nothing in there anyway," chuckled Bethany in response, hugging Alexa tight. "Do you have to work tonight?"

"Later," grimaced Alexa. "But it's Sunday. Shouldn't be too hectic, and we have time now to get all dressed up and hit the town."

They smiled as they got ready. It was fun being together and having the means to do what they wanted, especially as what they wanted was never particularly extravagant. Every time they were out Alexa could not help but feel blessed. At times like these it really did not matter what her profession was. It was only when she was at work, with yet another man on top of her, trusting between her legs that she felt any kind of misgivings.

Bethany never asked Alexa much about her work, except for when she would be there. What she was doing was no secret, and she had even shown Bethany where she worked and given her Steve's phone number in case of an emergency. It was just something they knew was better left unspoken. Alexa could no more paint her job in a rosy light than she could tell the truth about how much she hated it at times for fear of the impact either would have on Bethany. It was a means to an end, nothing more.

That dichotomy of emotions towards her life was hard to reconcile, so as Alexa began the second week of her new life with Bethany, she stopped trying to. In many ways she stopped thinking all together. She rarely let herself think of the life she had left behind. The only person whose loss there was to mourn was Sam, but Alexa hoped that when she turned eighteen she might be able to see him again, and hoped that he would not be too disgusted in her.

The future was also generally off-limits for her thoughts, and many times Alexa did not want to think too much about the present either. So instead of thinking, she settled on simply living. It was a nice compromise, and allowed her to skip off from Bethany in the middle of the day with few qualms about where she was going. Her work was becoming more and more clinical and far less emotional by the day. It was unfortunate that it still had to be so incredibly physical, particularly with this client.

While Alexa had come to appreciate some of her regulars like Martin, who was gentle and kind, and so frequent she felt like she was starting to really get to know him, not all were as good as him. Phillip, the young, rich man she had serviced on her second night had also taken a liking to her, but he was so rough and vulgar that she had eventually found the courage to tell Steve that she did not want to see him again. Phillip responded by offering her more money, a lot more. In her present situation it was too much to resist.

Walking up the stairs, Alexa tried to clear her mind. Phillip had requested that she be dressed in a school uniform. The outfit made her ill. She reminded herself about how much this session would earn her, that it would end, and that afterwards she and Bethany would be free to do something really special together, all on him.

Phillip liked to have total control so Alexa waited for him to initiate the proceedings. He stood in front of her, looking down at her chest, before he ripped open her white shirt. He grabbed her breasts with his large hands, kneading them as though they were lumps of dough. Alexa complied when he pushed her towards the bed, lying down motionless as he tore the shirt from her body, yanked up her skirt and ripped off the underwear he had also insisted she wear.

Alexa always made sure that she was pre-lubricated after

learning the hard way how much a lack of arousal could hurt her. Situations like this were never going to turn her on and she did not want them to. Phillip spread her legs wide and thrust himself deep inside her. Alexa winced then drove all thoughts from her mind. In many ways, she found it easier to be with clients who liked to take control. That way she could just lay back and pretend it was not happening, rather than having to take an active role.

"Turn over. On your knees, bitch," Phillip snarled when he had had enough of the previous position.

Alexa hated the way Phillip talked while they had sex. He was actually much less vulgar before and after. He was like two different men and though Alexa did not like either of them, she could not help but empathise. This was not really her either.

***

The middle of the week quickly became Alexa's favourite time. It was quieter at work and she and Bethany got to spend plenty of time together, although they were also trying to slowly develop their own lives and routines. Alexa had started visiting the local pool, a pastime she had learned to enjoy from Hayley. Bethany had a strange fear of the water, so would rarely swim, though she always accompanied Alexa to the pool.

Bethany started drawing and painting. When they were out and about, Bethany always had a sketch pad and pencil with her. In their room, she had a corner dedicated to her paintings. They were abstract, and Alexa was sure would be considered nothing special from anyone else's point of view, but to her they were amazing. The emotion that Bethany was able to capture was breathtaking.

It made Alexa more comfortable leaving Bethany to go to work and giving her money to buy whatever it was she needed. Every day Bethany repaid her faith by being home when she expected, and always clean. There was simply nothing more she could ask for from Bethany.

For the first time, Alexa walked to work on Friday night not filled with disgust about what she was about to do. It did not matter any more. These men were funding her life – her wonderful life – with Bethany. It was almost laughable that they would walk away from her thinking they had the better end of the bargain.

Alexa practically skipped home on Saturday morning, but was caught short by Bethany's absence from their room. Bethany usually waited for her to come home before going out, but it was late and they were trialling not going everywhere together. Trying not to panic, Alexa climbed into bed and let herself sleep.

Bethany was still not home when Alexa woke. It was late. She had slept much longer than she usually did when Bethany was around. That realisation did not bring Alexa any comfort. It only took away from the time she had to look for Bethany before she went back to work. Determined to stay hopeful, Alexa checked all the places they had started frequenting since Bethany had been clean, but Bethany was nowhere to be seen.

A sick feeling settled in Alexa's stomach as she walked to work. It was the first time Bethany had not come home at all during the day and Alexa was sure it could mean only one thing. Throughout the night she tried to keep her hopes up and made excuse after excuse for Bethany's absence, but when Sunday morning came and there was still no sign of her, she knew there were no excuses.

Despite her exhaustion after another long night, Alexa forced herself across town and back to where Bethany had been living before. There were sightings. Bethany was definitely around, but Alexa did not find her before Steve beeped her back into work. She wanted to refuse, but the reality was that if Bethany was back on heroin, they would need all the money she could earn to tear her away from it.

That night was the hardest Alexa had faced since her very first. Selling her body had only ever been worthwhile if she could save Bethany's life. She was not sure she would be able to face even another hour if she did not believe that Bethany was still alive somewhere.

Trudging home in the early hours on Monday morning, Alexa tried to prepare herself for the emptiness that was occupying her room. It left her completely unprepared for the sight of Bethany and Leo in bed together.

Leo. She should have known. He must have found Bethany, because not once had Bethany mentioned trying to find him once she was clean.

"Get out," cried Alexa hysterically, pulling Leo out of the bed. She had never hated a person more in her life.

"Get your hands off him. What's wrong with you?" screamed Bethany, but it was not her, not really. This drug-affected girl was not the sister she loved.

"You promised me, Bethy, you promised," cried Alexa, as angry tears built in her eyes and desperation welled in her heart.

"You can't kick me out. This is Bethany's place as well and she invited me here," growled Leo.

"Don't you dare talk to me," Alexa spat hatefully at Leo. "You're the reason she's taking drugs again. She was clean! She was getting better. How dare you come here and tell me you have a right to be here. She's my sister, living with me and I will kick you out when you are putting her life in danger."

Alexa grabbed Leo by the arm and pulled him towards the door. If the only way to get rid of him was to physically throw him out of their lives then she would, but she was no real match for him.

"Get your goddamned hands off me," growled Leo, throwing her off him.

Leo shoved Alexa hard against the wardrobe before letting her fall to the floor. He stepped back as Bethany moved forward.

"Just stay out of my life, Lex. I can take care of myself," cried Bethany as she stood by Leo's side.

"You're a heroin addict. How are you going to take care of yourself? How are you going to keep a roof over your head or feed yourself?" asked Alexa, lifting herself off the floor.

"The same way you do," replied Bethany petulantly.

"No, Bethy, no. I won't have you doing that to yourself," cried Alexa, stepping forward, but Leo shifted his body between her and Bethany. "I'll look after you. I'll protect you, but you have to work at it as well. You have to want it too."

"You have to sleep. I'll get out of here."

"Bethy, no. Please don't go. Please don't go with him," Alexa pleaded, reaching out for Bethany's hand. Bethany did not take it.

"I can look after myself. You look after yourself," said Bethany flatly.

Bethany turned and led Leo out the door. The click of her departure was sickening. Alexa collapsed where she stood, tears of anger and fear spilling on to the floor. Everything had been going so well and now it had all fallen apart. It was never meant to have worked out like this.

Alexa did not stay curled up on the floor for long. If Bethany was on drugs, she had paid for them somehow. Terrified that Bethany had found her stash, she quickly checked her hiding spot. The money was still there. However, it was then that Alexa realised the rest of the room had been tossed. Bethany had been looking for the money. Alexa had to think quickly. There was always going to be the risk that Bethany would find the money, but if she split it up into smaller portions, she would not lose the lot in one raid.

Everything was going to have to be much more tactical from this point forward. Leo now knew where they lived, and there was no way they could outrun him. One weak moment from Bethany would always lead him back to them. It was probably better that they could not be taken by surprise, but the job of keeping Bethany clean was going to be so much harder with Leo around.

The beep of Steve's call was almost welcome as Alexa laid fitfully in bed, trying to string together a few hours of sleep. It would be nice to think about something other than Bethany and the horrible situation her relapse had put them in. Alexa even stayed after the client she was called in for left. There was rarely a shortage of men who would take the opportunity of sleeping with an underage girl when it was presented to them. It did not seem to matter to any of them that what they were doing was illegal.

Alexa had the feeling some of the men felt youthful having sex with her. Many often spoke of her as a conquest, despite the fact that they had won nothing and would not have stood a chance with her if they were not prepared to pay. They were simply taking what she had offered them. She only wished they had the ability to make her feel as good as she seemed to be able to make them feel. It would have been nice, for just one moment, to like her life.

"You work all night?" asked Bethany as soon as Alexa walked in the door late on Tuesday morning. Alexa could only nod.

Thankfully, Leo was not around, but it was obvious that Bethany had scored again. The sight broke Alexa's heart, but she loved Bethany so much that she could not stop herself from climbing on to the bed with her and wrapping her in her arms.

"I know you're just trying to help, but I love Leo. I can't be without him," said Bethany, hugging Alexa back.

"You love the drugs, not him," replied Alexa flatly. "You never spoke of him, thought of him, until he found you. He's the reason you're here. He's the reason I'm here. Please, this isn't the life I want, not for you and not for me. I'm only doing this to help you."

"Don't hate me, Lex. I'm doing the best I can," said Bethany in a small and desperate voice. It was the voice of her true sister crying out from the depths of her drug addiction, and Alexa held her tighter. "I'm not like you. I can't stop. I want to. I really do, but it's a part of me. I need it. I need it more than anything."

Alexa pulled Bethany down on to the bed, their limbs entwining with each other's, pulling them as close together as possible.

"I won't ever hate you, Bethy, never. I'm not going to leave you. I know this isn't easy. All I want from you is your best effort and I know that will be enough, because you've done it before. I can't get us out of here, not until I'm eighteen. I won't let them take you away from me, but it means you have to try too. You have to fight the temptation."

"I don't want to disappoint you, Lex."

"You won't. We'll make it through this. No matter how hard it gets, we're going to survive this. We'll have better lives than this, I promise."

"Okay," nodded Bethany.

Alexa knew Bethany trusted her, trusted her word. She just hoped she did not fail. It would all be for nothing if Bethany died, and the moment that happened, she would lose her one lingering connection to life. Nothing was going to tear them apart again. Not even death.

Walking to work, Alexa tried to rebuild her faith in the life she was establishing with Bethany. They had spent a nice afternoon together, but when Steve had called her in to work, Bethany immediately left. Alexa knew Bethany would score again before she next saw her.

It would not be ideal, but Alexa supposed that she could live the next year or so with Bethany as a heroin addict. If she gave her enough money to score, then there would be no reason for her to engage in any kind of behaviour that would risk her being arrested. There were still far too few options for them to get their life on track. These two weeks already felt like a lifetime. Alexa was not sure how old they would feel once they lived through another sixty of them.

Those musings took Alexa all the way to the door of her next client. She would work as long as Steve wanted her to tonight, but after that she was going to tell him she would not be back until Friday. She and Bethany needed time to really think about how they could set up their lives. Getting Bethany drug-free might have to wait for another time. Right now they would focus on keeping her alive, and keeping them together. That was all that mattered now.

146

The client had his back to the door and did not turn around when Alexa closed the door behind her. She did not care. She did not really look at them anyway. It was better she did not commit their faces to memory. The last thing she wanted was to recognise them outside of these four walls.

"Good evening, Sir. How are you tonight?" Alexa asked pleasantly.

"I'm fine. How are you doing?" replied a chillingly familiar voice.

Alexa looked up, her heart pounding painfully. Clinton just stood there, smiling menacingly.

Chapter Fourteen

"WELL, WELL, WELL, haven't you moved up in the world?" Clinton sneered, moving forward and brushing his hand lightly across Alexa's cheek.

"What are you doing here?" asked Alexa breathlessly.

"I've come looking for you. Mr Knight has all the teachers on the lookout for you. He is so very concerned."

"Then go back and tell him I'm fine and don't come and see me again," replied Alexa, stepping away.

"So this is what I was doing wrong all that time. You wanted to be paid for your services. I never even considered –"

"Go to hell!" spat Alexa. "I don't want anything from you, especially your money."

"Now, now," said Clinton in frighteningly calm reprimand. "I hope that's not the way they taught you to talk to your clients."

"Get out, before I kick you out," replied Alexa, pointing to the door. Her voice was holding strong and she was glad, because she did not want Clinton to know how truly terrified she was of him.

"Alexa," said Clinton in a silky voice. He was on top of her in seconds with his hand around her throat. "I think you're forgetting who you're talking to," he snarled menacingly.

Alexa tried to talk, but Clinton's grip was too strong. Instead, she kicked him hard in the shin. Clinton released her immediately, but before she could move he struck her across her face with the back of his hand. She was knocked to the ground. Scrambling to the bed, she fumbled desperately to reach the emergency button.

"Get up," growled Clinton, as he climbed on top of her and grabbed her by the collar.

"Get your hands off her," yelled Steve from the door, as two security guards pulled Clinton off Alexa and dragged him towards the door. "What the hell do you think you're doing?"

Steve moved between Alexa and Clinton and placed a hand on her shoulder. He squeezed it reassuringly as she tried to control the trembling of her body.

"Are you all right?" Steve asked her. She nodded, though it was a lie. "I don't ever want to see your face around here again," he barked at Clinton, who was wrestling with the security guards.

"You'd better let me go or I might just let the police know about your underage workers," said Clinton with a smug look.

Steve looked from Alexa to Clinton and signalled to the security guards to release him. Alexa's heart dropped.

"I am a teacher from Miss Samson's school and am here to escort her back. If you try and stop me I will call the police. Be thankful that I haven't called them already."

"Is this true?" asked Steve.

Steve's voice was not hard or unkind, but Alexa knew this was the end. She nodded slowly and heard him sigh heavily.

"Grab your stuff, kid, and go with your teacher."

Alexa walked towards the door, avoiding Clinton's gaze. She now realised that there were worse things in the world than selling her body. She would have had sex with a hundred strange men rather than go anywhere with Clinton.

As soon as they were out of the room, Clinton dragged Alexa down the stairs and around to a back alley where his car was parked, but Alexa had no intention of going with him. He may have just lost her that job, but she would find another. There was no way she was abandoning Bethany now.

"Get your hands off me," said Alexa, pushing Clinton off her as soon as they were on the street.

"Do you really think I am going to leave you here?" asked Clinton, his voice still silky.

"What does it matter to you? Go back and pretend you never saw me. I'm no concern of yours."

"I don't owe you any favours," growled Clinton in reply, making Alexa's heart thump erratically. "You're the one that owes me, or have you forgotten that?"

"Why are you doing this?" cried Alexa desperately, realising that this was not about her education.

Clinton smiled as he stepped closer. "Because no one dictates to me," he snarled. "No one ruins my plans, especially not you."

"What plans?" Alexa cried. "We never had any plans. I never ruined anything for you, so why are you going to ruin my chance to look after my sister? My life has nothing to do with you any more."

"You don't get to decide when I'm finished with you. I decide," snarled Clinton, his face just inches from hers. "And I'm not done with you yet."

Alexa knew Clinton was serious and that her only chance was to run. Pushing away from him, she sprinted down the street. Heavy footsteps closed in on her as her legs and lungs started to burn. The lights of the main road were visible when she felt pain surge through her head.

"Don't be so stupid," growled Clinton in her ear as he pulled her back by her hair.

"Get off me, get off," Alexa screamed, hoping to bring some assistance. She would even take police interference at this point.

"You are really going to need to learn to be more grateful," said Clinton calmly, the silkiness returning to his voice.

"I will never be grateful to you. Now get off me!"

Clinton dragged Alexa to his car, his weight too much for her to fight against, and the more she struggled the rougher he became. When he opened the front passenger door she pushed past him again, but did not get more than a foot away, pain tearing through her head as he once more pulled her back by the hair. She continued to struggle until the world began to spin and her legs gave way.

Alexa woke in Clinton's car. They were driving through deserted suburban streets. She touched the side of her head and felt a large, painful lump. All she could think about was Bethany, and how Bethany would believe that she had abandoned her. She wanted to get out and get back to Bethany, but her head ached so badly that she could not think clearly.

The towers of the school were soon visible in the distance and Alexa's heart rose slightly. She did not want to go back, but at least she knew she could escape from there. It did not matter how much trouble she was in – she would not be staying long enough to serve any punishment. Nothing was going to stop her from going back to Bethany.

Alexa was so busy formulating her escape that it took many vital minutes for her to notice that Clinton had driven straight past the school.

"Where the fuck are we going?" Alexa yelled, starting to panic. Clinton did not answer. She looked around and realised she knew exactly where they were. They were on their way to Clinton's apartment. "Shit. Let me out! Let me out, you bastard."

Alexa struggled with the door, but she could not open it. She took off her seatbelt and tried desperately to find a way out.

Clinton slowed down slightly, trying to pull her back into her seat, but she fought against him. The next moment she felt a blinding pain in her head and everything went black again.

***

"I see we're awake now," said Clinton in a gentle voice, entering his bedroom and turning on the light.

Alexa scurried to the top of the bed, curling her legs up in to her chest and covering her eyes with her arms to protect them from the blinding light. When she brought them back down Clinton was sitting next to her.

"So here you are once again. Good to be back, I presume?" Clinton asked with sick composure. Alexa did not answer, refusing to play his games. "I've missed having you here. I tried my best to get you back, but you kept resisting for reasons I will never understand."

"I don't want to be with you," said Alexa quietly, hoping that vocalising that fact would somehow make a difference.

"I don't think you ever really had that choice. I chose you. You should have loved me the way I wanted you to. You should've loved me so much you never wanted another man again. You should have felt privileged, but instead you threw everything back in my face."

"No, I did have a choice and I chose to end our relationship," Alexa said in a broken voice. "Don't you get it? I don't want to see you any more. I don't want anything more to do with you. I don't want anything from you, anything at all."

"I think it's you who doesn't get it. I will decide when our relationship is over, not you," said Clinton, his voice becoming more threatening. "I still expect more from you. I deserve more from you and I will get it, whether you want to give it to me or not."

Alexa did not like the sound of Clinton's threat. She wondered if anyone knew where she was. He could kill her and no one would ever know.

"I don't care what you think. You're getting nothing from me," breathed Alexa, jumping up off the bed and rushing for the door.

Clinton was on her in a flash. Her fingers tried to cling to the doorframe, as though if she could claw her way out of this room she could somehow make it to safety. Clinton was just too strong, and he dragged her back with ease.

"Don't you dare try and leave. One way or another, you will never want another man after me," Clinton growled his hand now firmly around her throat.

Alexa hoped it would be a quick and painless death, but if Clinton planned to kill her it was not the first thing he would do. He threw her back on the bed and climbed on top of her. She thrashed desperately to get him off her, but that only earned her another backhander across the face.

It took just three rips for Clinton to tear the clothes from her body. She fought hard against him at every step, but he was too strong and her head was too sore. With one of his hands pinning her arms above her head, there was just no way of fighting him off. Wrapping his other hand around her throat, Clinton plunged into her.

Despite everything Alexa had been through, every man she had been with, it had always been her choice. This violation was a thousand times worse than selling her body ever had been. Every violent thrust tore painfully not only at her body but at her will to live. She did not want to survive this experience.

When it was over, Alexa could do nothing more than curl up in a ball on the bed and pretend she was not alive. It worked until Clinton came back for more. This time he held her face down on the bed, preventing her struggles. It was not quick like the first time. He dragged it out, lording over her and cackling at her pain.

The third time, Alexa did not fight at all. Clinton was gentler then, praising her for finally coming to her senses. The way he stroked her skin, acting as though she could be somehow enjoying the experience, made her sick. It was almost worse than him hitting her.

"Let's get you cleaned up," said Clinton in a soft voice when he was finally finished with her.

Alexa did not have a chance to respond before he dragged her into the shower. He washed her roughly, removing the evidence of his crimes before forcing her to dress in the clothes from the brothel. She wondered if this was the point where he killed her.

Clinton seemed determined on dragging her torture out. He hauled her down to his car and pushed her in. She wished he would just pull out a gun and shoot her in the head. She did not want a painful, violent death. All she wanted was for it to be over, but when Clinton spoke she realised he never intended on letting her off that easily.

"You will meet me next Tuesday and every Tuesday after that or next time it will be a thousand times worse," he growled.

Alexa knew Clinton was not joking and hoped that something would save her – or better yet kill her – between now and next Tuesday.

***

Marcus stood behind Mrs Taylor as Clinton Marsh brought Alexa into the office. She looked terrible, but from Clinton's description of where he had found her and of her activities in the city, he guessed he could not expect any better.

"I found her early this morning in the city. It appears that she's been supporting herself by rather unsavoury means," said Clinton callously, before retelling the story he had told them by phone early that morning.

Alexa sat quietly. Her head was hung and her hands were in her lap. Marcus could not fathom what she was thinking. That she had willingly and knowingly sold herself into prostitution was still beyond his comprehension. There was just no reasonable explanation for such behaviour when she had so many other options at her disposal.

A professional whore, he scoffed. Perhaps it had been too much seeing the wealth of her schoolmates and she had needed to compete. Maybe she found some pleasure in being used by multiple men. Whatever her reasons or excuses, he could not think of her as a decent person any more.

"You seem to believe that this school is your own personal hotel, where you can come and go as you please," said Mrs Taylor sternly. "This school has been more than lenient towards you because of your situation, but that is going to change. If you leave these school grounds again without permission, you will be expelled. Is that understood?"

Alexa did not look up or respond. Something inside told Marcus that things were not quite right, but he was too angry and disappointed in Alexa to care. Whatever it was, he was sure it was nothing he could or would help her with. He had given up on helping her this time.

"I asked if you understood, Miss Samson," said Mrs Taylor angrily.

"Yes, ma'am," Alexa responded tonelessly, never looking up.

"Fine, get out of my sight."

Alexa stood up and walked towards the door.

"Miss Samson, I want you to head to my office," said Marcus in a harsher voice than he had ever used on a student.

Alexa did not show any signs of recognition as she left the room.

"I hope you are finally on my side when it comes to these students," said Mrs Taylor in superior tone.

"If Miss Samson puts a toe out of lie, I will not hesitate. I will expel her myself," replied Marcus, looking straight at Mrs Taylor. "But don't expect me to involve any of the others. We still disagree there."

Marcus left before he got himself into another argument with Mrs Taylor. This grade was doing very little for his prospects of promotion within the school. He guessed the only reason Mrs Taylor had not yet sacked him was because he was still the only teacher willing to be the year advisor to Alexa's grade.

Alexa was sitting on the floor outside his office when he arrived. He stepped over her as he entered his office and waited for her to join him. Alexa's disappearance and subsequent discovery in a brothel had affected him in a way he never expected. Her disappearance had come out of the blue and he had believed Sam and Bianca when they told him they were just as surprised as he was by her sudden departure.

Marcus's best guess was that Alexa had gone to find her sister. In the evenings and on the weekends, he had spent much of his spare time searching for her. He was sure there had to be a better solution to their situation than constantly running away, even if it did not involve her returning to Redgrove. However, he never found any trace of Alexa.

He had not checked the area that she was found in. Such thoughts had never crossed his mind. Despite all his confusion over the way he felt for Alexa, he had never thought of her sexually. Now when he looked at her, he could not stop himself from thinking about the things she had done and it made him sick. It made him wonder how he could have possibly thought that she was somebody outside of the ordinary.

"You can head back to your room after this meeting," Marcus said in a calm, but stern voice when Alexa finally sat down in her usual seat. "You don't need to go to class until tomorrow. I will have your teachers compile the work you have missed. Come back in the morning to pick it up."

Alexa still did not raise her head.

"I don't suppose there's much point in expecting an explanation from you," he continued, but Alexa remained unmoved. "I didn't think so. You may as well leave then. Nothing anyone has done for you seems to make a difference. You seem hell bent on throwing your life away, but make no mistake, if you put another foot out of line you will be thrown out of the school. No one has had as many chances as you, Miss Samson."

Alexa left without a word. Marcus had never seen her so silent. It crossed his mind that perhaps she did not want to be back at school and he half expected to hear that she had disappeared again the next morning. However, she was there outside his office at the appointed time and in her school uniform.

The sight of Alexa, hunched and reclusive made Marcus's heart ache in a strange way. Something was very wrong, but he was determined not to care. He had been sucked in once before and he refused to let his life and career be torn apart by one girl who continually rejected the help she so desperately needed.

"I have the work you missed while you were away," said Marcus, placing a large folder of papers on his desk in front of Alexa. She did not look up, her head was hung and her hands sat in her lap. "If you fail these final exams the school will have no choice but to cancel your scholarship. So I suggest you start spending every spare second catching up."

Alexa shook her head as she finally looked up to meet his face, though she did not meet his eyes. The sight shocked Marcus slightly. She looked half-dead – not physically – just only half-alive somehow.

"If you're so desperate to expel me, then why don't you just do it? Why set me up to fail?" Alexa asked, her voice desperate. It was the most emotion Marcus had ever heard from her.

"You are the person who has consistently thrown away the chances that you've been given," Marcus pointed out.

"You make it sound like I have a world of wonderful choices in front of me. I don't get a choice. I never asked to come back here. I was brought back against my will and now you set me up just so you can expel me. Why the fuck did you even bring me back?"

"You had better mind your language –"

"Why? Because you'll expel me?" asked Alexa spitefully. "Well fuck this, fuck this shit and fuck you."

Alexa grabbed the folder and stormed out of the room,

slamming the door behind her. Marcus was fuming, but there was a part of him that was rational enough to realise that Alexa had never had an outburst like that before. As angry as she had been in the past, she had never sworn and she had never lost control of her emotions so forcefully.

Then Marcus considered more carefully what Alexa had said. Brought back against her will. He had considered the idea that she would try to run away again, but had not really entertained any thoughts that she had not come back willingly. He just assumed that, if Alexa left, it was because she would rather leave than face any punishment.

What did she mean? Had she really wanted to stay on the streets? Had Clinton physically dragged her back? Alexa was sixteen. They had no rights to force her anywhere. Marcus had always just assumed that she would want to return – have a roof over her head and food on her plate rather than live on the streets.

Marching after her, Marcus was disappointed he had given Alexa so much of a head start. He headed towards her room, but halfway there he saw her from a window, disappearing behind the gym.

He walked purposefully, breathing deeply and calming his mind. He had to give Alexa a chance to explain her situation. If she did not want to remain at Redgrove, he would organise … something. He could hardly think what. However, all his plans for Alexa's future were driven forcefully from his mind when he turned the corner around the back of the gym. Alexa was over ten metres away, but he could clearly see the cuts ringing her arm and the blood seeping from them.

Alexa's startled eyes suddenly met his. She quickly began packing up her belongings and pulling on her jumper. Marcus grabbed her before she could stand and saw a razor fall to the ground. He pulled the jumper off her arm and felt his heart stick in his throat. Alexa's arm was completely covered in blood and cuts.

Alexa tried once more to collect her things.

"No, you sit down," said Marcus breathlessly, pulling Alexa back down to the ground by her bloodied wrist. "You are going to explain this right now."

"Let me go," said Alexa, trying to pull her wrist out of his grasp. "Let me go!" She took a swipe at his face with her free fist, but he grabbed it easily. "Let me go!"

"No – not until you tell me what the hell this is all about."

"Stop pretending you care," Alexa cried, trying to free her legs from under her body. "Expel me and be done with it. Now let me go!"

Alexa continued to struggle against him, but Marcus easily held her against the gym wall.

"Please, let me go," begged Alexa meekly.

Tears began to fall down her cheeks. Marcus looked into her eyes for the first time since she had returned to school and what he saw broke his heart. All the anger he felt disappeared in an instant. His grip on her wrists loosened, but he continued to restrain her.

"What happened?" he asked, his voice gentle and caring. Alexa just shook her head. "If you don't tell me what happened I can't help you."

"You can't help me," Alexa cried.

"I can," Marcus replied earnestly. "You have to trust me. If you don't tell me, I have to take you to Mrs Taylor." He did not care if he had to use blackmail. He would find out what was wrong with Alexa this time. "Tell me what happened."

"He – I don't – I can't do it – I don't want to do it any more," Alexa sobbed, as her chest heaved.

"Do what, Alexa?" Marcus asked breathlessly. She did not reply and he became alarmed. Something truly terrible must have happened for Alexa to openly weep in front of him. "Come on, Alexa. What don't you want to do any more?"

Alexa looked up at the sky. She was trying to ignore him, he thought. Then she spoke.

"He raped me … because I didn't want to see him any more. If I don't see him again he said it would be worse next time."

Alexa's voice was soft, but steady. Marcus could hardly breathe. It had to be a lie. She had to be trying to find a way out of trouble. Yet it seemed so extreme to claim such a thing. Then he thought about her blackmail attempt. Perhaps she would go that far.

"Who? Who are you talking about, Alexa?" asked Marcus cautiously.

"Clinton," she breathed.

"Clinton? Clinton Marsh, the history teacher?" Marcus asked, still not sure if he should believe her. Alexa nodded, still avoiding his eyes. "When?" he choked, feeling ill.

Marcus may not have been sure if Alexa's claim was true, but that was only one part of his brain. The rest had no doubts about her truthfulness, and it hated him for it.

"Tuesday night," answered Alexa softly, her voice steadying just slightly.

"But he didn't find you until Wednesday morning – yesterday morning," replied Marcus, desperate to find a hole in her story – desperate for it not to be true. Alexa just shrugged her shoulders. "He told us he found you on Wednesday morning. Why didn't you say something in Mrs Taylor's office or to me afterwards?"

"Would you have believed me?" Alexa asked scathingly.

Marcus wanted to say yes, but he remembered how angry he had been and wondered if he really would have believed her. He looked at the tear-stained and bloodied Alexa and wished that he had been more open and available. There had to have been some way that he could have prevented this.

Looking down and realising that he still had hold of Alexa's wrists, Marcus quickly released her. He did not want to be restraining her if she had already suffered so much. Alexa pulled her hands to her face and her knees into her chest. She looked so fragile. He wanted to hold her and comfort her, but he knew that would be wrong in so many ways.

Taking a step back, Marcus tried to rationalise what was happening. Alexa had just accused another teacher of raping her. He weighed this claim up against the threats she had made against him. He did not want to be party to destroying an innocent man because of one child's vendetta. Yet Alexa had never lorded her threats over him. She had thrown them at him in the hope that he would be so distracted by them that she could escape. This was completely different.

Alexa's whole body was shaking. Her head was tucked into her knees and her arms were curled over her head, shielding her from the world. A troubled and troublesome student, there was every reason to disbelieve her. Then Marcus thought of Clinton Marsh. Smooth and powerful, he was practically untouchable in the school. That made a girl like Alexa the perfect victim.

"All right, put your jumper on," said Marcus gently, finally making up his mind.

"What are you going to do with me?" asked Alexa.

Marcus could hear the fear in her voice. When she looked up at him her eyes were full of terror.

"I'm going to get you cleaned up and then I'm taking you to the police station," Marcus replied firmly, hoping Alexa believed him.

He did not want to have to force her to go with him.

"No, I don't want to go to the police," Alexa replied, curling her body back into a ball.

"What? Why? Alexa, you have to tell the police. You can't let this happen," Marcus urged desperately, as he knelt down in front of her.

"There's nothing they can do. What proof do I have?" murmured Alexa into her knees. "He'll kill me if he finds out. Please. I just want things to be over between us. That's all."

"Alexa, this man took advantage of you. He raped you. You can't let him get away with this. You're going to tell the police. I will be there. Nothing will happen to you, I promise," swore Marcus sincerely, determined that nothing would allow him to break this promise.

Chapter Fifteen

THE CORRIDORS WERE empty as Alexa followed Mr Knight through the school. She hesitated at his car, hoping she was not being a fool to trust him. What if he just wanted his bit of her? She was not sure she could handle much more, but felt she had no choice. There was nowhere else for her to go. Nowhere else she could run.

Alexa was almost surprised when they did pull up outside the police station. They walked in silence and Mr Knight sat her down on some seats and went up to the reception. A few minutes later he returned with a female officer.

"Come through, Alexa," the officer said in a pleasant voice. They walked through the station to a small room with a table, several chairs and a large tape recorder. "Now how old are you, Alexa?"

"Sixteen," she replied softly, not looking up.

"We really need to have a parent or guardian present when we question you."

"I want my lawyer," answered Alexa quickly. She did not know how much trouble she was in, but knew it was enough to call for Peter. "I don't have any parents, I'm a ward of the state and I don't want you to tell my foster parents. I just want my lawyer."

"You don't need a lawyer, Alexa," the officer said.

"I want my lawyer."

"Listen, I'm her year advisor. While she's at boarding school I'm the closest thing to a guardian she has. Can't I sit in?" asked Mr Knight.

The officer looked at Alexa for an answer. She did not want Mr Knight to stay and hear the details, but would concede to get what she wanted.

"But I still want my lawyer," Alexa said firmly

The police gave in when she responded to every other question with stubborn silence, ignoring them as completely as they were ignoring her request.

It took Peter only thirty minutes to arrive. Alexa knew he must have cancelled meetings to come so quickly and thought she would have to remember to thank him. She had known him for as long as she could remember and he had always helped her when she needed him. She tried to make sure she rarely needed him. She owed him too much already.

Peter Lam walked in with a calm, detached look on his face. He was a tall and lean man in his late thirties with dark black hair and was dressed in an expensive suit. When Peter sat himself down next to Alexa, the female officer introduced herself as Senior Constable Lewis and she was joined by Constable Banks. Alexa recognised Constable Banks from his visit to the school to ask her about Bethany's disappearance. Mr Knight stood silently in a corner.

"Okay, Alexa, now what is it that you have to tell us. Your teacher here claims that another teacher raped you. Is that true?" Senior Constable Lewis asked.

Alexa did not answer. She did not want to recount the story again. It had been hard enough telling Mr Knight and she had left out all the details, so simply nodded.

"We need you to answer, Alexa," urged Constable Banks gently.

"Yes," Alexa murmured, not looking up from the table.

"When did this happen?" asked Senior Constable Lewis.

"Tuesday night … in his apartment," Alexa sighed, knowing there was no escaping this now. She closed her eyes, laid her head on her arms, and pretended that the room was empty.

Alexa recounted in detail how Clinton had found her in the city, though she decided to omit any reference to her work place. Steve had given her work when she had needed it and although he had made her go with Clinton, it was not his fault she was raped. She then recounted the horrifying details of the rapes. It took a long time as she paused frequently, trying hard not to let her emotions spill over. She was trying to disconnect the emotion from the memory.

The constables asked Alexa questions about her relationship with Clinton and she spoke truthfully about everything, except Ms Carter. Alexa wanted to tell them about Ms Carter, but thought that it would all sound too farfetched, too unbelievable. If they believed her about Clinton then that would be enough.

"Wait here, Alexa," said Peter, putting a comforting hand on her shoulder when the interview had finished. "I'm just going to talk to the officers for a minute."

"You did very well, Alexa. You should be proud of yourself," said Mr Knight when they were alone.

Alexa remained silent, looking away from Mr Knight. Divulging the details of the rape was like being stripped naked and she did not like it. She wanted desperately to try and erase every memory of the last few days from her mind forever and wanted to believe that Mr Knight would do the same.

"I need to talk with Alexa alone," said Peter solemnly, as he re-entered the room.

Alexa saw Mr Knight's hesitation so nodded her ascent. She really did not need Mr Knight getting all protective over her now.

"So what now?" Alexa asked when Mr Knight had left.

"That's up to you," replied Peter, taking his seat next to her and watching her carefully.

"What do you mean?"

"It's your word against his. Essentially, there's no proof that he raped you," explained Peter softly, making Alexa's heart sink. "There's no proof that the two of you even had a relationship. I assume he never wrote you any love letters?" Alexa shook her head despairingly. "I didn't think so."

"So all this was for nothing? I didn't want to even come here. He made me come, saying that I had to, that I couldn't let Clinton get away with this, but he will anyway. Why did I even come here?" Alexa cried softly, pulling her arms around her chest and curling her body into a ball on the chair.

"Your teacher was right. You did the right thing," replied Peter in a determined voice. "They will investigate your claims. Believe me, the police have no intention of letting this matter rest."

"Investigate? How the hell are they going to investigate? Do they think they can just ask him and he will admit to it? Don't you understand? He will kill me when he finds out."

"Alexa, your first memory of your childhood, how old were you?" asked Peter suddenly, practically cutting her off.

"I don't know," answered Alexa, thrown by the question. "Seven. Maybe eight."

Peter nodded thoughtfully.

"Any chance you will take me up on that offer to get you that money and get you the hell out of here?" Peter asked, a slight pleading in his voice.

"What's the use? I have nowhere to go," said Alexa in a

defeated voice, curling her body into a tighter ball.

"You're sixteen. We can set you up in your own place."

"Will they give me Bethany?" Peter shook his head. "That money is only a third mine. I can't take it all. It wouldn't be fair."

"What has happened to you isn't fair," retorted Peter forcefully.

"And you expect me to do that to other people? I won't do it. None of it matters if they won't give me Bethy."

Alexa buried her head in her knees to hide her tears. Peter's hand rubbed her back gently. He rested it there until she composed herself.

"There is another way we can get Clinton, but it won't be easy, especially for you." Peter paused, but Alexa did not speak. "Would Clinton admit to you that your relationship existed?"

"Yes, of course he would," Alexa murmured.

"Would you be prepared to see him again to get the evidence you need? Could you talk to him on the phone? Or write to him? Email?"

"We've never spoken on the phone or written to each other."

"Would you agree to see him again in person to get the evidence?"

"What – wait until he rapes me again?" asked Alexa spitefully. She really meant nothing to anybody.

"No, you would wear a wire and we would record your conversation," replied Peter reassuringly. "We will never let him hurt you like that again. I promise."

Alexa thought for a long time. If Clinton found the wire he would kill her for sure, but if she did not do it she would have no proof that she was telling the truth. Yet if she went back to school with nothing but her unsubstantiated accusation, she was in just as much danger. Clinton had left her in a no-win situation.

"What if he finds it?" asked Alexa, reasoning that if there was a chance to get rid of Clinton completely she may as well take it. It was over anyway.

"We won't be far away."

Alexa shuffled the pens left on the table from hand to hand. She really did not know how to make this decision. All she wanted was to close her eyes and be back with Bethany. She would even live with Leo if she had to. Anything was better than this horrid reality.

"Alexa, I know you don't want to do this and I can fully appreciate why, but I want to see this bastard rot in gaol for what he did to you," said Peter in a voice that barely masked his anger.

"This is the only way we have to get the evidence we need. You don't have to go through with it and I would understand if you can't, but he deserves to be in gaol."

"You believe me?" asked Alexa, burying her head once more in her knees.

Peter's hands were suddenly locked on either side of her face, turning it forcefully to face his. Alexa kept her eyes bowed, but Peter just pulled her head up further and lowered his gaze until their eyes met.

"Every. Single. Word," said Peter, not breaking his gaze.

"Okay," replied Alexa after lengthy consideration. Peter sighed heavily and released her face, his hand moving on to her back and rubbing it gently. "But I won't go back to his apartment. I won't ever go back there."

"That's okay. You won't have to. We'll work something out."

Alexa nodded, then looked back up at Peter. He looked anxious, almost like he was arguing with himself about something.

"I want something else – if I do this – from you," Alexa said determinedly.

"Anything," replied Peter, squeezing her shoulder solemnly.

Alexa told Peter where her secret stashes of money were in the boarding house and its address. She had been gone long enough that she knew Bethany would have raided the place and probably found some of the cash. Worried about Bethany's relapse, she had even left smaller amounts of money more accessible. It was better than losing it all, because she knew no one was going to let her just go back to her illegal street life now.

"Find it, before she does," Alexa commanded. "Pay the rent with it for as long as it lasts. Just find it before she shoots it up her arm."

"I'll take care of it. I promise," said Peter, nodding assuredly. "As soon as I leave here, I will sort it out. I'll take care of it until you can."

***

The next morning, Alexa showered and dressed before her roommates had even woken. Breakfast was quiet. No one spoke to her as she sat slowly turning her toast to crumbs. She did not look at any of her friends or roommates to explain why she did not move when they did. She was to wait in the dining hall until Mr Knight called her to his office so that was what she did.

Senior Constable Lewis was waiting in Mr Knight's office with two other male officers Alexa had never seen before. The four of them moved into Mr Knight's bedroom to attach the wire to her chest, while Mr Knight waited in his office. He had been very kind since her confession, but Alexa still struggled to trust his motives. Surely he was only biding his time until Clinton was out of the way before he could have his slice.

Alexa felt her body shake as she was forced to strip off her shirt, leaving her standing in front of strangers in just her bra. All the officers looked curiously at the cuts that wrapped around her left arm, but said nothing as they taped the wire to her chest and fastened the battery pack to the inside of her skirt. Senior Constable Lewis stayed close and held her hand as the men worked, but did not seem to realise that Alexa hated her presence as much as the other officers.

"Okay, now remember that everything you say today is going to be recorded. Do you know when you plan to see him?" one of the male officers asked as they re-entered Mr Knight's office.

"I have sixth period free," Alexa replied, pulling her cardigan tighter over her chest to try and dissipate the exposed feeling. "He has it off too. Otherwise, I'll see him after school. He'll need to go back to his office before he leaves."

Ten minutes later, Alexa was allowed to leave. Peter arrived just as she reached the door and gave her an encouraging smile and pat on the back.

"Did you do it?" Alexa asked forcefully.

"Yes. I took care of it," replied Peter.

Alexa could see the curious looks of the officers on the other side of the room and wished she could have some time alone with Peter, but realised it was probably not a good idea. If she started thinking about Bethany now she might be tempted to just run back to the city, grab Bethany and keep running.

With her first period free, Alexa went straight back to her room. She did not want to be running into anyone today. The minutes dragged by painfully. She could not concentrate her mind on anything but what was going to happen that afternoon. A sense of dread was filling her body. It was not going to work out. Things with Clinton never did. She had been so sure that she would be able to blackmail him into supporting their child, but it only resulted in the death of their unborn baby.

When Alexa did go to class, she did not speak to anyone. The teachers left her alone completely and she wondered if Mr Knight had tipped them off. Her classmates seemed to know her well enough to not even try and approach her. She had not spoken to any of her friends since her return. Not even Sam. There just did not seem to be anything to say any more. This world was so divorced from her life that she was not sure she would ever be able to relate to any of her friends again.

The day dragged by so slowly that Alexa was surprised when there was suddenly only five minutes until the end of maths – five minutes until she had to face Clinton again. The bell rang and Alexa packed her bag at the normal rate, her heart now pounding heavily in her chest.

She wanted to speak to Bianca and Ezra, thank them for their friendship, but no words came out. She walked out in silence and down the corridor, everything moving at light speed. Having dawdled for most of the day, time was somehow flying now and she was outside Clinton's office in what seemed like a second. She took several deep breaths and knocked.

"Enter," said Clinton blandly from behind the door.

Alexa walked in and closed the door behind her. Clinton glared at her before looking back down at the papers on his desk.

"I don't recall organising to meet you today," he said dismissively, not looking at her.

"I know," Alexa answered, her voice barely above a whisper. "I thought I should tell you in person that I'm not going to be there to meet you this Tuesday … or any other Tuesday."

Anger flashed across Clinton's eyes briefly as he looked up at her before he smiled menacingly.

"We're not going to go through all this again, are we?" asked Clinton, his voice silky and threatening. "I explained to you the other night how bad the consequences would be if you decided to continue defying me. Now you don't want to go through that again, do you?"

"It would be no different if I came voluntarily," Alexa cried. "You don't care about me. You just care about the sex you can get from me."

"Now, now, now, that's not very fair. I rescued you from that brothel you were calling home. You're ungrateful. That has been your problem from the start."

"Ungrateful? You fucking raped me, you bastard. What part of that was I supposed to be grateful for?" cried Alexa, her body shaking.

"That's some nasty language you've picked up while you were away. You never were one for swearing, but I have noticed a significant increase these last few days," said Clinton in a frustratingly condescending tone. "I don't think there's anything more to discuss. I will see you on Tuesday afternoon or I will organise to find you alone."

"You lay a hand on me and I will report you," replied Alexa threateningly.

Clinton laughed merrily, never taking his eyes off her.

"Really? To who?" he smiled, throwing his arms out and looking around the room. "Who is going to believe you? You, who a few days ago was selling their body on the streets? Who will ever believe you over me?"

"You have no idea the trouble I could cause you. If Sam ever knew –"

"Ah, yes, the infamous G7. What a joke. You think that you and your pathetic band of friends could ever touch me?"

"We've gotten rid of every year advisor we've ever had. Do you think you would survive?"

"Oh, please. Don't make me laugh," retorted Clinton seriously. "No group of students could ever have me thrown out of here. What proof do you have? Prove that we ever had a relationship. Prove that I ever laid a hand on you. Prove that I ever had sex with you."

Alexa was stung. The anxiety of being in Clinton's presence and fear of what he would do to her had made her completely forget about the wire taped to her chest. Being in the same room as him had erased her mind of everything but trying to stop him ever touching her again.

"I have all the proof I could ever need," Alexa retorted. "Our baby."

Terror flashed across Clinton's face and Alexa smiled triumphantly.

***

In the unused drama room across the school, questioning looks flew across the room. Alexa had never mentioned a child at any point in the interviews. Marcus felt ill. Listening to Alexa's conversation with Clinton was much harder than he had ever expected. He had assumed it would be a mere formality after listening to her recount of events, but Clinton's threatening nature added a whole other dimension to the situation.

Marcus wanted to kill Clinton. He wanted to destroy him for what he had done to Alexa, because there was no doubt in his mind that Alexa was the one telling the truth. Looking across the room, he realised that Mrs Taylor did not feel the same way. She was sitting there in reluctant silence after her attempts to have Alexa's accusations dismissed out of hand failed. He knew that nothing Mrs Taylor heard today – excepting a straight out confession, and perhaps not even that – would convince her that Alexa was not lying.

Peter was in the corner. Marcus watched him. Peter, along with the three officers who had prepared Alexa had been in the room all day, listening intently to Alexa's silence. Marcus had just joined them. They were all confident that what they had heard would be enough to convict Clinton, but it was the news of a baby that had the room abuzz.

"What baby?" asked Senior Constable Lewis.

"Did she ever mention a baby to you?" asked Detective Jallon, one of the male officers.

"No. This is the first I have heard of it," replied Marcus, while Peter looked out the window.

***

"You don't honestly believe that after you caused the miscarriage of our baby that I would simply flush it out to sea, do you?" asked Alexa in an angry sneer.

Clinton looked terrified, but anger soon replaced his terror as he slammed his fist down on his desk.

"I told you that that child was never mine," he snarled. "You're a slut. That child could've been anyone's."

"And like I said, a simple DNA test will prove me right."

Clinton was standing now.

"Don't you dare try and threaten me," he growled, pointing his finger threateningly at Alexa. "You remember what happened last time you tried that, you came off second best."

"How can I forget? That was the day you killed our child."

"Listen to me, you ungrateful little slut. I have done more for you than anyone around here and I have not yet been fully repaid. You will give me what you owe me and nothing less."

***

Marcus listened in horror. He now understood why Alexa had said the things she had on the day of her suicide attempt. If he had only known then. If only he had been able to persuade her to tell him what was wrong, then perhaps none of the last three weeks would have happened.

***

"No, I will never give you anything again. I will report you if you lay a single finger on me," said Alexa defiantly.

"With what proof?" Clinton asked menacingly, as he stood less than a foot from her.

"I told you, our child –"

Alexa did not get to finish her sentence as Clinton grabbed her by the throat and pulled her face within inches of his.

"There is no child. You're bluffing. If you had the proof you wouldn't be here."

Alexa was terrified, Clinton had called her bluff and she had nothing else. She had still not remembered that the entire conversation was being listened to. She was too scared of what was about to happen.

"But seeing as though you are here, you may as well work off a bit more of your debt."

***

Everyone's ears pricked up. They could not believe that Clinton would possibly try to rape Alexa within school grounds.

"Do something! Didn't you hear him? You have to – we have to go. We have to stop him," said Marcus frantically.

He had promised Alexa that nothing would happen to her. They were on the other side of the school.

"No, we should wait. If we can catch him in the act –" Senior Constable Lewis started.

"And what about the goddamned wire? If he sees that –"

"You can't let this happen," said Peter, pushing himself out of the corner. "Call it off," he demanded.

"We won't let it get that far," Detective Jallon said. "We'll be in that room in a flash."

***

Clinton released his grip on Alexa's throat and dragged her by the upper arm to the adjacent bedroom.

"No," cried Alexa, struggling against him, but he clasped his hand over her mouth to silence her.

Alexa bit down on Clinton's finger as hard as she could, and he released her instantly. He looked at the bite mark, then struck her across the face with the back of his hand.

***

"This is ridiculous. We have to go now," cried Marcus in response to the noises they were hearing.

Peter was already at the door.

"No, not yet," replied Senior Constable Lewis.

***

Clinton dragged the stunned Alexa across the bedroom and threw her down on the bed. She tried to push him away as he climbed on top of her, but her head was ringing and he was just too strong. He pushed her skirt up and tore at her underwear. His belt was soon undone and he ripped open the fly of his pants.

"No, please, don't," cried Alexa. "Please don't."

Clinton moved his hand across her chest and ripped open her shirt. A look of anger and terror tore across his face.

"What the hell is this?" Clinton roared.

Alexa looked down and saw the black wire across her chest. She knew she was vindicated. She knew she was dead.

Chapter Sixteen

THE DOOR TO Clinton's office was not locked and Constable Desani and Detective Jallon burst through the door in front of Marcus and Peter. Clinton was standing just inside the bedroom, to the right of the office, his hands wrapped around Alexa's throat.

"Let her go," yelled Constable Desani, storming into the room.

Clinton turned to find himself confronted by Constable Desani and Detective Jallon wielding a baton and capsicum spray. His hands released Alexa immediately and she fell without resistance to the floor. Constable Desani rushed forward and handcuffed Clinton. Marcus pushed past everyone to Alexa. The way her body had collapsed was sickening and he prayed that she was not dead.

Marcus placed his ear over Alexa's mouth, but felt no breath. He frantically tried to recall how to perform CPR. It was not coming back to him clearly and he hoped the paramedics arrived soon. He did not want Alexa to die because of his incompetence.

"She has a pulse," said Marcus, breathing a brief sigh of relief as his fingers rested on her neck.

Marcus checked Alexa's breath again, hoping that he had been mistaken, but she was definitely not breathing. Peter, Constable Desani and Detective Jallon watched on nervously as he performed mouth to mouth until he felt a faint breath across his ear and saw Alexa's chest rise slightly by itself. He rolled her into the recovery position and kept a light hand on her ribs so he could feel the rise and fall of her chest. She had still not recovered consciousness, but she was alive.

"Ambulance is on its way," Detective Jallon said quietly.

"Just a few more minutes," hissed Marcus in a low voice. "A few more minutes and she would've been dead."

"We had no idea he would react so violently," said Detective Jallon, and Marcus thought he sounded a little defensive.

"Why not?" cried Marcus. Everyone else had thought it disturbingly obvious what was about to happen. "He raped her and she came here because we said that we'd protect her. You had all the proof you needed and you let it go on and on. For what?"

Marcus was angry and he wanted to stay that way. It covered the fear that was pulsing through his stomach – and the guilt. At so many points during the year, he could have done something differently and prevented Alexa from ending up here. Piecing it all together in his head over the last twenty-four hours, he realised how truly vulnerable Alexa was and how Clinton must have groomed her, leaving her with nowhere to turn. Redgrove had a lot to answer for in this case and Marcus hated that he had played a part in Alexa's suffering.

Ambulance officers arrived within minutes. They worked to stabilise Alexa before she was placed on the stretcher and wheeled out of Clinton's office still unconscious. Marcus followed. He did not look at Clinton, who was sitting handcuffed at his desk, watched over by Constable Desani. Marcus knew he would not be able to control himself if he looked at Clinton now.

A crowd of students had gathered outside Clinton's office, attracted by the ambulance officers and the numerous police officers crowding the steps. Towards the back of the crowd Bianca, Chad and Sam were trying to make their way through the throng of students to the dormitories. Marcus caught Sam's eye and his gut turned to ice. Sam looked over at the stretcher and his face fell. Bianca was suddenly engulfed in tears as Sam shook her roughly.

A look of realisation fell upon Sam and Chad, and they pushed their way towards Marcus, looking mutinous. Marcus was sure Sam was about to hit him when Constable Desani and Detective Jallon led Clinton out of his office. The two boys immediately turned their attention to Clinton. They landed several punches before anyone could react. Marcus did not move. They were doing what he wanted to do.

It took six officers to pull Chad and Sam off Clinton as Constable Desani and Detective Jallon rushed Clinton back into his office. Marcus knew he should have directed Chad and Sam to his office to discipline them for their actions, but he did not want to face their questions – or his guilt. All he could muster was a half-hearted reprimand, before he demanded all the students go home or return to their dormitories immediately. Once they had complied, Marcus headed straight to the hospital.

The wait to see Alexa was going to be a long one, but Marcus did not leave. Alexa had been taken to the intensive care unit after her heart twice stopped beating – once in the ambulance and again on arrival. It made Marcus sick to think that she may actually die because of Clinton's assault.

Back at the school, Alexa's foster parents and social worker were meeting with Mrs Taylor to decide her future, but Marcus did not know of or care for their plans. There would be no need for plans if Alexa did not survive this, and it seemed ridiculous that they would now all convene and act as though they had all previously cared about Alexa's welfare. Marcus choked on a guilty sob as he recalled all his previous anger and frustrations with Alexa. It all seemed so petty now compared to what she had endured.

Shortly before midnight, Marcus was eventually allowed in to see Alexa. She was still unconscious, but she was alive and they expected her to pull through. A monitor by her bedside beeped with every beat of her heart, while an oxygen mask helped her breathe. Her face was so pale and with her eyes closed she looked so fragile and so very young.

The sight made Marcus want to vomit. As he sat by Alexa's bedside, he tried to decipher just how he felt. Guilt was the most prominent emotion, but beyond that were emotions he feared were too deep. He wanted to protect Alexa, hold her and shield her from the world. He wanted to convince himself that there was nothing physical or sexual about his feelings for her, but when he looked at her all he could think about was Clinton's hands on her body, Clinton on top of her, Clinton inside her.

Whatever it was that Marcus felt for Alexa, he knew it was more than a teacher should feel for any student, but he was also partly responsible for her being in this hospital bed. So although he knew he should leave, he just moved to a chair in the corner of the room and fell asleep to the beeps of Alexa's heart.

The nurses did not try to wake Marcus and he slept through the night, his body and mind completely exhausted. He woke stiff and sore, stretching out of his contorted position before moving over to Alexa's bedside.

Alexa remained as pale and fragile as the night before. The monitor continued to register every heartbeat, noting its irregular rhythm along with the occasional flutter. Marcus wanted to hold Alexa's hand so badly that he did not dare touch her. He was determined not to do anything which could be misconstrued. He was nothing like Clinton Marsh, he told himself.

There was a steady stream of police to check on Alexa's condition throughout the day. Peter came briefly to see how she was doing, but appeared too agitated to stay. Only Marcus remained by her side the entire time. He could not leave. Jackie called several times and offered to come by to comfort him, but he declined. He did not want to test the nature of his feelings for Alexa by having them in the same room together.

There were no other visitors for Alexa. Her foster parents did not come to see her and Marcus doubted that her sister would even know that she was in hospital. He looked at his watch. It was almost seven. Marcus knew he would have to go home eventually, but was reluctant to leave. Alexa's heart was now beating regularly and her breathing was less laboured. They were all good signs, so good the doctors were preparing to transfer her to a normal ward, but still he was worried.

Marcus walked over to the bed and sat down next to Alexa. She seemed less pale, but no less fragile or young, so very young. He sat there for almost ten minutes before he decided that he had to leave. He would be back tomorrow.

As he stood to leave, he took one last look down at Alexa's face and noticed her eyelids twitching slightly. He sat back down immediately and took her hand.

"Alexa? Alexa, can you hear me?" Marcus asked softly, his heart pounding.

Alexa's eyes began to blink open and her fingers wiggled slightly in Marcus's hand. The touch of Alexa's hand on his made Marcus's heart swell so much he thought it would burst, so he gently placed her hand back down on the bed. It took almost five minutes for Alexa to wake fully.

"I will go and get the nurse," said Marcus softly when Alexa's eyes met his.

Alexa looked much more alert when he returned with the nurse, who gave her a quick once over.

"How are you feeling?" asked the nurse kindly. Alexa tried to reply but could only grasp her throat. "I'll get you some ice," the nurse said, seeing Alexa trying to talk.

"Where am I?" asked Alexa a few minutes later, still sucking on a cube of ice. The nurse had left, leaving her and Marcus alone.

"You're in the hospital," replied Marcus.

"What happened?" Alexa asked, clearly confused.

"What's the last thing you remember?" asked Marcus. He did not want to have to explain how they had failed her – how they had heard Clinton's threats, heard her pleas, heard his assault and let it happen.

"I don't know," Alexa replied, shaking her head. "I don't know. I don't know what is what. Just tell me what happened."

"Perhaps we should leave it for a while. Your memory will come back in time."

"I want to know why I'm here," she cried, her voice failing her on the last words.

"Do you remember coming back to school?" asked Marcus, realising Alexa did have the right to that kind of information. Alexa nodded her head slowly. "Do you remember telling me about Mr Marsh and what he did to you?"

"You took me to the police," said Alexa softly, though her words felt strangely like an accusation.

"That's right. Do you remember what happened after I asked you to come to my office on Friday morning?"

Alexa stopped nodding. She simply laid there, her eyes glazed. It felt like hours before she spoke.

"I told you he would kill me," she said in a soft, stony voice.

Marcus did not know how to reply, but was saved the trouble of doing so. Alexa turned her head away from him and closed her eyes.

Walking slowly back to his car, Marcus stopped halfway and vomited in somebody's front lawn. It was close to midnight. The sky was moonless and dark. He felt sick and lost. He did not expect that Alexa would have forgotten what had happened to her. Thinking back, he did not understand why. Perhaps it was because he could not forget, because he could not stop seeing her lying unconscious on the floor of Clinton Marsh's bedroom.

He had remained by Alexa's side despite her continued silence. When a bed became available in a regular ward, he was told he would have to leave.

Jackie was fast asleep when Marcus arrived home. He undressed in the dark and hopped into bed beside her. She did not wake. He looked up at the ceiling exhausted, but unable to sleep. Alexa floated across his view again and again. Though he tried to divert his mind, when Marcus rolled over and wrapped his arm around Jackie, it was Alexa he was thinking of as he held Jackie tighter.

Marcus woke alone. Light blazed through the open curtains and for a blissful moment he had no recollection of the last few days. The reprieve was not long-lasting. Within fifteen minutes he was showered, dressed and preparing to make his way back to the hospital.

Jackie was in the kitchen cleaning up after her breakfast. She looked so beautiful. Marcus had fallen in love with her at first sight and now, five years later, he was preparing to marry her, but that morning he barely even looked at her.

"Hey, baby," said Jackie, as Marcus walked into the kitchen. She walked over and slipped her arms around his waist and planted a loving kiss on his cheek. "Did you sleep okay? What time did you get in? I didn't even wake up."

"A bit after midnight, I guess," Marcus replied in a distracted voice. "Have you seen my keys?"

"They're next to the TV. Why?"

"I have to go back to the hospital."

"Why? Has something else happened?" asked Jackie in a concerned voice.

"No. I just need to be there."

"You've barely been anywhere else. I don't think you should go just yet. It's not even nine," said Jackie, restraining him just slightly with her arms around his waist. "Why don't we do something this morning and you can go in this afternoon?"

"No, I have to be there. I have to check on her," Marcus replied insistently, frustrated by any delay in returning to Alexa's side.

"And you will. This afternoon."

"Why are you trying to stop me?" cried Marcus, stepping away from Jackie's embrace.

"Because I don't think it's healthy," replied Jackie forcefully. "This grade and especially this girl have become an obsession for you. You need to relax, step back a bit and get some perspective."

"I have perspective," replied Marcus, trying to keep his voice from filling with the swirl of emotions inside of him. "That girl is in hospital because I finally convinced her to trust me and it almost got her killed."

Jackie did not respond. Marcus had not yet told her everything that had transpired. He had barely had five minutes alone with Jackie since Alexa's return.

"Go to the hospital then, if it'll make you happy," sighed Jackie, waving her hand in defeat as she turned away from him.

Marcus found his keys, wallet and mobile and prepared to leave.

"I'll probably stay at school most of this week. There's going to be a lot to deal with. I'll call you when I get the chance," he said distractedly, as he kissed Jackie on the cheek and then headed to the front door.

"I love you," Jackie called after him.

"I love you too, baby," Marcus replied, turning and smiling.

It was the first time he had really looked at Jackie all morning and he felt a jab in his heart at the disappointment on her face. He knew he was being unfair to her, but he needed to go to the hospital. He needed to be with Alexa.

As Marcus walked up the stairs towards Alexa's ward, every step caused his heart to pound harder in his chest. He was a mixture of anticipation and fear, terrified about how he would feel when he saw Alexa again. The images inside his head were always the same – him holding Alexa, protecting her and caring for her. He tried to comfort himself with the knowledge that there was nothing more physical in those images, because what he felt was bad enough.

Alexa was in her bed looking out the window. Marcus stood at the door watching her and was glad that most of the anticipation fell from his body on seeing her. She was awake and looking defiant now, a sight that was much less enticing than her unconscious or in pain.

"Good morning, Miss Samson. How are you feeling? Did you get a good night sleep?" asked Marcus, his voice thankfully calm.

"I'm okay. Why are you here?" Alexa asked pointedly. It reminded Marcus of her asking what his price would be for his help.

"I wanted to make sure you were all right. You gave us all a pretty big scare," he replied, trying to smile reassuringly.

"Have I been expelled?"

"Expelled? Why would you've been expelled?" he asked, thrown by the question.

Marcus remembered now why he had always found Alexa so difficult to deal with. She saw situations through completely irrational eyes. There was absolutely no way they could expel her now, no matter how much Mrs Taylor wished she could.

"Because of the trouble I caused and you said if I didn't pass the exams I'd be expelled. I didn't think I had much chance of passing before, but I don't think I have any chance of passing now."

Marcus's heart sank. He had completely forgotten about that

conversation and how angry he had been. It made him sick to think that that was what Alexa remembered of their conversations leading up to this.

"No, you've not been expelled, nor will you be, irrespective of your exam results," Marcus said firmly. He had no authority to make such a promise, but he would do anything he had to, to ensure it was true. "Saying that, I will also do all I can to make sure you pass."

"I don't need your help. I can do the exams myself," said Alexa defensively, shifting her body away from him.

"I didn't mean anything by that, Alexa."

It was a reckless thing to say and Marcus was cursing himself for it. Looking in Alexa's eyes, he was sure he had wounded her. The bruising on her neck should have been all the reminder he needed not to offer her help.

"I spoke to the doctor on the way in," Marcus said brightly, changing the topic. "They're planning to release you tomorrow, pending some tests and a psychiatric evaluation."

"So that's how you plan on stopping me from returning to the school?" asked Alexa scathingly, shaking her head slowly.

"Alexa, I explained earlier that you're not in trouble. You're not being expelled. No one wants to stop you from coming back to school."

"Really? So Mrs Taylor's going to be waiting at the gates with open arms?" she retorted.

"No, I doubt it," Marcus replied cautiously. It would do him no good to let the students know how much he disliked and disagreed with Mrs Taylor. "But there're no grounds to keep you from returning to school."

"Then why the test?" Alexa spat accusingly.

"You've been through a very traumatic experience. The doctors want to make sure you're all right and that you're not a danger to anyone, particularly yourself."

Marcus looked at the healing cuts on Alexa's arm as her head fell back on the pillow. There had been no hiding them in the hospital and Alexa's mental state was immediately called into question, with concerns she would attempt further self-harm if she survived.

"Are you going to tell them about before ... at the train station?" asked Alexa in a detached voice, not looking at him.

"I have considered it," Marcus answered truthfully. It had been on the tip of his tongue the whole time he had been at the hospital. "If anything happened because I didn't –"

"I'm not going to kill myself. You don't have to tell them anything."

Marcus knew that this was not a request. It was a command, but how serious it was he could not tell, because Alexa would still not meet his eyes.

"How do I know that?" he asked.

"Because I am still here," replied Alexa firmly, finally looking at him.

Marcus knew what he should do, but he was finding it harder to garner the strength to go against what Alexa wanted from him. Part of him wanted to just give her everything.

***

All the medical checks came back clear the next day and lunchtime saw the arrival of the psychiatrist for Alexa's evaluation. Alexa had been awake all night working on a way of proving herself sane and safe. She had never been very good at lying to people she cared about, but in situations like this her proficiency for making people believe what she wanted them too was much greater. She had no intention of being kept in hospital any longer than she had to be, and so told the doctors exactly what she knew they wanted to hear. This was a process she had been through too many times in her youth to not know how to play the system.

Mr Knight arrived at the hospital just after five-thirty. Alexa was ready to go as soon as he entered the room. However, something about his face made her immediately realise that the doctors had relayed what she had said about him. He did not look smug or victorious or anything Alexa could even really describe, but she knew she wanted to get away from him.

They did not speak as they walked back to the car and Alexa kept her eyes to the ground. She was not sure what to feel. The idea of going back to school – that life she had once lived – seemed like such a foreign concept. There was no doubt that everyone would already know about her and Clinton, and she wondered what else they knew.

"What do you want for dinner? I thought we might grab something to eat on the way back to school," said Mr Knight, breaking the long silence. Alexa looked at him sceptically. "It was just a thought. I'm sure you would prefer to eat dinner in the dining hall."

"Fine, whatever," replied Alexa, feeling instantly ill. "I don't care, but I'm starving so just find something quick, okay."

Mr Knight did not respond and Alexa turned away from him, not caring where they were going and trying to ignore the fear that was building as she contemplated what was coming next.

Alexa did not know the place they stopped at and followed Mr Knight grudgingly into the tightly-packed Chinese restaurant.

"Order anything you like," said Mr Knight.

Alexa continued to stare at the menu, but took none of it in. She did not want to owe Mr Knight any more than she already did – not even a meal.

They were silent for a few more minutes, before Mr Knight finally guessed that she was not hungry. He took her menu and ordered directly from the restaurant manager. Alexa watched Mr Knight's every move, trying to work out when the attack would come.

"I think we need to have a little chat," Mr Knight said, resuming his seat and pouring them both some tea. "I'm gathering that everything you told the doctors about being able to trust me was a lie to make sure you were released, because you won't even look at me let alone let me buy you dinner. I do understand why you don't feel like you can trust anybody and why you don't want to trust me, but you can."

Alexa looked up and glared right through Mr Knight. She wanted what he was saying to be true, more than she could explain, but she could not take that risk.

"Does everyone know about Clinton and me?" she asked tentatively, before looking back down at the table.

"Yes, I'm afraid so," replied Mr Knight gently. "There was not much chance of keeping that under wraps."

"Do they all blame me?"

"Blame you? Alexa, no one blames you for what happened," replied Mr Knight as though that were really true. "Mr Marsh took advantage of you. You didn't do anything wrong."

Alexa bowed her head further, resisting the temptation to cover her ears. There was no point in believing his carefully structured lies.

"What about the other stuff? When I was away. Does everyone know about that?" Alexa asked timidly. She was not sure she wanted to know the answer to this question, but at least she could prepare herself.

"No. Mrs Taylor and I, along with Mr Marsh, are the only ones who know about … know where you were found. I have done all I can to keep that secret and will continue to do so, all right?" asked Mr Knight, bowing his head to meet her eyes.

Alexa nodded, but refused to meet his eyes. She knew that it was all probably just a ploy to sucker her in. She could feel Mr Knight watching her and she kept her eyes averted until the food came. So much food came. Mr Knight began eating immediately, and with absolutely no reference to her, filling his bowl and shovelling ravenously.

"Sorry, did you want some?" Mr Knight asked after ten minutes. "I was starving, but I think my eyes were bigger than my stomach. You should try these – pork buns. Very nice. You ever had them?"

Alexa shook her head and Mr Knight pushed the plate towards her, then carried on eating. It was rude, but so peculiarly normal that she was comforted by his behaviour. Picking at the food, she found it tastier than she expected and ate more than she intended. When she saw Mr Knight's smile as they got back in the car, she felt ill again.

It was dark when they pulled up in the school car park. Alexa jumped quickly out of the car, rushing towards the dormitories before the car had even come to a complete stop.

"Stop," yelled Mr Knight, jumping out after her. "I will walk you back to your room."

"I don't need an escort," Alexa spat angrily to cover her vulnerability.

"No, but I want to make sure you don't make any unnecessary detours," replied Mr Knight calmly.

"Fine, then fucking hurry up."

Mr Knight did not hurry and Alexa stormed off.

"That language is going to stop," said Mr Knight, catching up to her before she had gone ten metres. "I am your teacher and you will speak to me with respect. Is that understood?"

Alexa did not answer. She owed Mr Knight more than she had ever owed Clinton. Mr Knight seemed kinder than Clinton ever had, but it did not matter. He would want the same thing in the end and would take it by force if she chose not to give it to him – just as Clinton had.

Chapter Seventeen

THE NEXT MORNING arrived quicker than Alexa liked. Her roommates were only just waking when she swung her bag over her shoulder. It was too early for breakfast and too early for her meeting with Mrs Taylor, but she could not lie in bed and pretend it was not all coming. She sat in the slowly filling dining hall barely touching her food. She sat alone. No one joined her.

At five-to-eight Alexa picked up her bag and headed out of the now full dining hall. She was almost at the door when she was swung around and embraced tightly.

"You should've told me. I would've been able to stop him. I wouldn't have let him do this to you."

Alexa recognised the voice immediately, dropped her bag and reciprocated Sam's embrace.

"I didn't want you to do anything that would get you kicked out. I couldn't handle this place without you," Alexa replied, trying not to cry.

Sam stroked the back of her head as they continued to hug in the middle of the dining hall. Alexa eventually pulled away from him, but he would not let go completely and held tight on to her hand as he led her back to his table where Chad was finishing his breakfast. Chad hugged her and kissed her gently on the cheek.

"Good to have you back," said Chad sincerely. "Sam and me got a few good punches in for you as they brought Mr Marsh out. They had to take him back into his office and he needed an escort of fifteen cops to get him out of the school."

Chad smiled victoriously at Alexa and took another bite of his toast. Sam sat behind her with his arms around her waist. It made her wonder if she would be allowed to leave his side that day. She wasn't.

Sam escorted Alexa to Mrs Taylor's office and waited outside during the hour-long meeting – just to give her a hug at the end of it. Bianca and Ezra tried to cheer her up and convince her that everything was going to work out. Alexa did not believe them, but was thankful for their support.

They all wanted her to promise that she would stop running away now that Clinton was gone, but it was a promise she could not keep. Bethany was, and always would be, her first priority and she did not want to have to choose between her friends and her sister. As soon as she could face her life back in the city, that was where she would be.

"Hey, Alexa, you have a letter," said Natalie as Alexa walked into the bedroom at the end of the very long day.

Alexa recognised the handwriting immediately and rushed to her bed, pulling the curtains around her.

My dear Lex,

I know what happened and why you left. I spoke to Steve and the news of Clinton was everywhere. I hope you're okay. I found your money and used it to get me a smaller room here.

Please don't come back. Not til you're eighteen and can get me out of here. I can wait. I can hang on til then. Don't write. Don't visit. It's too hard. You won't leave if you came back. You deserve more than this. If you want to help me then stay at school. I hated knowing what you were doing for me.

Love you always Lex.

Bethy

The night air was cool and Alexa pulled her jacket around her to keep the wind out. The tears that fell from her eyes dried almost instantly in the wind, but new ones continued to fall over the old. It was a beautiful night. The sky was cloudless and the last rays of light were colouring the far horizon. Alexa looked up at the night sky, saw a lone bright star above and prayed.

"Please, please, please keep Bethy safe. I know I can help her. Just keep her safe til then," she gasped.

"What you doing out here on a cold and lonely night?"

Alexa turned around to see Sam standing in front of her. He looked sad, but his smile was genuine.

"I'm surprised Mr Knight didn't have a teacher tail you to make sure you didn't run off again," joked Sam, though it was a legitimate point.

"I'm not going anywhere – not any more," Alexa replied, her voice shaking as she tried to convince herself for the hundredth time that that was the right decision. She was still not convinced, but the thought of another man touching her was still far too terrifying to contemplate. Until she could handle such intimate contact, she knew she had no choice but to stay at school.

"Because Bethany asked you not to?" asked Sam cautiously.

"Yeah. It was killing both of us, but a big part of me wishes I could face it all again. Why do you look so down?" Alexa asked, quickly changing the subject.

She did not want to talk about that other life with Sam. He was the only one she had shown Bethany's letter to. She and Bethany had run away to his grandparents' farm enough times for him to understand their situation. Sharing that letter had resulted in Sam asking many questions, but she had never confirmed any of his suspicions about how she had supported herself and Bethany. He may have forgiven her for her affair with Clinton, but did not think even his kind heart could forgive the choices she had made in the city.

"I'm worried about Mel," said Sam, answering her attention-deflecting question. "She's been funny ever since this thing with Mr Marsh. I know he was her year advisor and I guess it came as a bit of a shock, especially because she knows you through me. He was pretty nice and supportive after our parents died. I think she feels really let down. I get the feeling she may have admired him a bit."

"She wouldn't have been the first person to make that mistake," Alexa shrugged, though she was not sure she had ever admired Clinton. Thankfully, everyone had accepted the theory that Clinton had groomed her into their relationship on his own and she had never had to explain to anyone what Ms Carter had done to her. "At least Mel just thought he was a nice teacher. I was the dumb git that dated him."

"He's gone now," said Sam tenderly. Alexa looked away, scared that Sam would want what she was no longer capable of giving him. "C'mon, I have my soccer ball and a bit of one on one action will do you good," he smiled, pulling at her hand.

Alexa dribbled the ball up the field towards Sam and the goal posts. Ten metres out from goal he ran out to challenge her, stealing the ball easily. She ran after him and pushed him out of the way, stealing the ball back to the sound of his loud and profane protests.

"Cheater. I can play like that as well as well, you know," Sam puffed as he grabbed Alexa around the waist, arms and all, and swung her away from the ball.

Alexa stumbled to the ground. Sam offered an apologetic hand to help her, but she only smiled as she flicked her leg behind his knees, sending him crashing to the ground next to her. She shuffled quickly into his arms and laid her head on his chest.

Sam's arms immediately wrapped themselves around her body. It was so nice to be held without the fear of anything more happening. If there was one person in the world Alexa trusted not to harm her, it was Sam. She just wished the reverse was true, but she knew how much she had hurt Sam with everything she had done and could barely believe that he was so kind-hearted as to continue to be her friend.

"Oi! What are you two doing out here this late?"

Alexa and Sam sat up, startled, to see Mr Knight striding towards them.

"I would've thought you two would be spending your time a bit more constructively than this," snapped Mr Knight in an angry tone.

"Don't you have a fiancée to be getting home to?" asked Sam contemptuously, clearly agitated by the interruption. "We have a right to be out here. There's over an hour to curfew."

"That may be all right for you, Mr Michaels, but Miss Samson has over three weeks of work to be catching up on."

"We're just hanging out," sighed Alexa. She was not worried by Mr Knight while Sam was with her.

"And if you knew anything, you'd know that Alexa's been up since six this morning catching up on her work. She's been working all week to catch on the three weeks of work she missed," added Sam derisively. "So why don't you run along home and let me take care of her."

Sam laid back down and pulled Alexa down with him, wrapping his arms around her chest and turning her head away from Mr Knight. She closed her eyes and reciprocated Sam's embrace as they both completely ignored Mr Knight's continued presence.

"Miss Samson, my office, now," said Mr Knight firmly, turning and walking away.

"What?" cried Alexa and Sam together.

"Now!"

***

Alexa did not hurry. Marcus sat at his desk waiting, trying to justify the jealousy that was pulsing through his body. He did need to speak to Alexa, but it could have waited. It made no sense for him to be so angry, so desirous to rip Alexa out of Sam's comforting arms. He should not be wishing that it was his arms that were comforting her. She was sixteen! And he did not even want her. He wanted Jackie. He knew that as surely as he knew the sun would rise again in the morning, so could not explain the effect Alexa's appearance had on his body.

"Close the door. I need to talk to you about the upcoming holidays," said Marcus as Alexa lingered at the office door, glaring at him. He would ignore everything – every feeling – and concentrate on the reason he would have had to call her into his office anyway.

"I assume that means the Whites don't want me back," replied Alexa quietly as she took her seat, and Marcus could not help but be touched by her resignation. It did nothing for his determination not to care too much for her.

"They were upset about what happened to you," he acknowledged.

"Yes, but that wouldn't have stopped them from asking me back. You told them where Clinton found me, didn't you."

"I didn't, but they do know," Marcus clarified. He had promised Alexa he would not disclose that information to anyone and he had kept that promise. Even Jackie did not know that part. "While you were in hospital there was a meeting between your foster parents, your social worker and Mrs Taylor to determine your future."

"Determine my future?" cried Alexa. "What the hell do you mean determine my future? How are any of them qualified to determine my future?"

"There were some concerns about your return to school and whether you'd be better served being placed permanently in a foster home and attend a day school instead of a boarding school."

"Right, I get it. The Whites didn't want me and it was determined that after my activities in the city that I couldn't be trusted anywhere where I couldn't be caged in."

"I don't think it was like that," said Marcus reassuringly, but supposed that was probably a lie. He had avoided knowing too much about those conversations, because on this point he was much more on Alexa's side.

"I don't really care what it was like," Alexa said angrily, walking towards the door. "You can tell the department I'll stay at school for the holidays. They can find me another foster family for the Christmas holidays."

"Sit down," called Marcus, standing, ready to block Alexa's exit if he had to. "You can stay here if you like, but your foster parents have agreed to take you back – with some conditions."

Alexa sat back down. She crossed her arms and glared at him. Marcus could really not blame Alexa for her attitude in this case. She had been through hell the last few weeks, and now her life was being dictated to her without the slightest attempt at consultation with her. When he had mentioned that Alexa should be involved in some of those discussions and decisions, Mrs Taylor had disagreed in the strongest way. It was just not worth his job to argue.

"What conditions?" spat Alexa.

"You're not to go to the city at any stage during your stay," Marcus replied, deciding to ignore Alexa's contempt. He would just tell it as it was. "You're also to be escorted to and from their house. If you travel to their house or back to school unaccompanied they won't have you back."

"This is bullshit. So who's accompanying me? The cops?"

"No. I've agreed to take you to your foster parents' house on the last day of term and they'll bring you back for the start of next term."

"This is crap. I'm being treated like a child," cried Alexa.

"You are only sixteen," replied Marcus, just managing to stop himself from pointing out that she was still a child. "I don't think there's anything very unreasonable about your foster parents' conditions."

"I'm seventeen and I don't need to be escorted anywhere. I can take care of myself."

Marcus looked down at Alexa's file. Today was her birthday. He looked up at her, but her angry stare into the distance made it clear she was not looking for his best wishes.

"Well, are you staying here? Or going to stay with your foster parents?" Marcus asked simply, refusing to engage with Alexa's sullen distrust.

"I'll go," replied Alexa, her voice cold and distant. "Gets me away from here."

Marcus was not surprised when Alexa stood and stormed from the room. He did not try and stop her. There was no point. He just looked back down at her file and felt a small glow in his heart and a slight easing of his conscience. Seventeen was so much better than sixteen.

***

Alexa sat on her bed wondering if she was really looking forward tomorrow. They had finished their exams that morning and tomorrow was the last day of term. It would be a chance to get away from Redgrove for two weeks, but her life on the outside was a bigger shambles than her school life. She was not sure if she knew how to exist outside of school without Bethany. She was not even sure she knew how to exist at all.

The only reason Alexa could give to how she had survived her return to school was that she did not have to truly engage with her life here. Everything was decided for her. She did not have to think for herself. All she had to do was move along in the direction she was pointed. Perhaps going back to the Whites, with all their new rules, would be the same; an automated conveyor belt she just had to sit on.

"Oh hey, Alexa, guess what," said Bianca, bounding excitedly over to her bed. "I forgot to tell you. I'm getting out of here these holidays. My parents are going to be in the country and they arranged it all last week. I'm so happy."

As if to prove the point, Bianca twirled a couple of times before sitting smilingly on the edge of Alexa's bed.

"That's great. Have you told Chad?" asked Alexa in a concerned voice.

"No. Why should I?" retorted Bianca in an annoyed tone.

"Because he told his parents that he was going to stay at school to keep you company."

It was hard for Alexa to keep her voice from being a sarcastic sneer, though she knew Chad had wanted his staying for the holidays to be a surprise. However, if Bianca had known last week, Alexa could not comprehend how that had not come up in conversation with Chad. Chad had been talking excitedly just that morning about what he had planned for him and Bianca in the holidays.

"Oh, I didn't know," said Bianca softly, biting her lip.

"And his parents went on holidays so he can't go home either," Alexa added so Bianca understood just how much she had stuffed Chad up.

"Shit! Why didn't he tell me?" asked Bianca, looking around the room. "Well it's hardly my fault if he doesn't tell me. Who's going to choose to stay at school? I sure wouldn't."

"I guess he wanted to surprise you," replied Alexa, biting down on everything else she wanted to say.

"Urgh, I'll just go down and tell him now," sighed Bianca unhappily, pushing off the bed and striding towards the door.

"You can't. It's almost curfew," said Alexa, feeling her heart stammer erratically. She did not need another meeting with Ms Carter now.

"What's the big deal? It's only a few minutes. Besides, I'm the one who'll get in trouble, not you."

"Yeah, right," said Martha, moving towards the bedroom door with Natalie. "I don't know what kind of school you used to go to, but here we all pay for your sins. If you didn't notice last time, the rest of us were all hauled in front of Ms Carter because of you."

Alexa was grateful for Martha's interference. Martha and Bianca had never really gotten along and it was nice that when Bianca stomped back to her bed it was not just her she was annoyed at.

"Yeah, well when Chad gets the shits at me tomorrow, I'll let him know that it was you guys who stopped me from telling him tonight," huffed Bianca, pulling the curtains around her bed closed. "Never seem to have an issue when it's us getting in trouble for Alexa though," she muttered from behind the curtains. "Don't see anyone standing up to stop her from sneaking out."

"Yeah, well, when you're an orphan who's just trying to look after your little sister, then we'll step aside," said Natalie, returning to her bed.

Martha muttered her own response that Alexa did not quite hear, but was happy to think that it had been more supportive of her than Bianca. However, their support did not do much to change Chad's situation, so when Lizzie emerged from the bathroom, Alexa rushed in and locked the door. To avoid suspicion, she turned on the water in the shower before uncovering the hole in the side of the closet. Within minutes she was pushing open the hole in Sam's closet, hoping to find the bathroom empty.

"Hey, who's there?" a voice called from the bathroom.

"It's just me, you idiot," Alexa replied, as Sam helped her out of the closet.

"What are you doing here?" asked Sam with a sweet smile.

"I need to talk to Chad."

"And here I was thinking you wanted to see me. Hey, I've been meaning to ask you, is this how you got out that night you ran away?"

"Yeah, you guys sure are heavy sleepers. I was pretty upset that night I don't think I remembered to be very quiet, but no one heard me leave."

"What made you go?"

"Later, I need to talk to Chad."

"All right, I'll make sure everyone is dressed." Sam opened the bathroom door and stuck his head out. "Lady coming through, guys."

"Hey, Alexa, what brings you down here?" smiled Chad.

"You, actually," Alexa grimaced. She hated being the bearer of bad news. "Bianca's going home for the holidays. I only just found out. She didn't know that you'd arranged to stay at school with her."

"Oh," said Chad, sitting down on his bed and ruffling his hair. "Looks like I'm gunna have two very quiet weeks then."

"There's no way you can meet up with your family?" asked Alexa, sitting down next to him.

"Nah, they've already gone. They were going to wait for me in case I changed my mind, but I told them to go."

"I'd offer you a place with me, but I'm not sure that foster care is all that appealing," said Alexa remorsefully.

"Come with me, come to my grandparents', they'd be stoked to see you," said Sam excitedly.

"I'll never get permission. Tomorrow's the last day of term and Mr Knight will never approve," said Chad unhappily, because he seemed very happy about Sam's offer.

"I know who could get him to approve it," said Sam with a broad smile, looking directly at Alexa. She glared back at him with a warning look. "Come on, Alexa, you know Mr Knight likes you. He's intent on solving your problems and fixing your life. You're like a project to him. If you ask him to do this, you know he will."

"I don't know if Sam's right, but will you try? Please. I don't want to be stuck here alone," pleaded Chad, falling to his knees in front of her and holding his hands in prayer.

Alexa felt sick. It seemed ridiculous to owe one person so much and go back and ask for more, but for Sam and Chad she would do almost anything.

"Fine, I'll try," Alexa sighed reluctantly. "I don't think it'll make much difference, but I'll do what I can."

190

"Thank you, thank you, thank you," said Chad, kissing her hand.

Alexa sighed again, trying not to think about what she was getting herself into. This was really not making the prospect of waking tomorrow any more enticing. Walking back to the bathroom, she was trying to resist the urge to back out of her promise when Sam grabbed her hand and pulled her back towards him.

"Stay, stay with me tonight," he urged, stroking her face.

"Okay," replied Alexa softly, though she knew she should say no. "I'll come back. I have the shower running."

Alexa would have snuck straight back down, but the bathroom was in constant use after her return, and it was too risky to try anything before the lights went out. Waiting as her roommates, one by one, succumb to their tiredness was difficult when she was so tired herself, but after an hour of waiting Alexa thought it was safe to creep into her bathroom and out of Sam's.

"I didn't think you'd come," mumbled Sam, shuffling over to make room for her to slide in next to him. His arms wrapped immediately around her body and held her tight. Alexa felt his lips press against the top of her head and she snuggled in closer.

"I shouldn't be here," she said, hating that it was true.

"Why not?" asked Sam in sleepy sincerity.

"You deserve to like someone better than me. You should hate me."

"I love you, Alexa. I could never hate you."

"Don't, don't love me. Please don't," Alexa cried softly, tears burning the sides of her eyes.

"Shh. I know we're just friends. I love you more than that, in more ways than that," said Sam tenderly, holding her tighter. "We're best friends and I'm going to take care of you – just like you took care of me when I needed you. Me and you, we're forever – through everything – boyfriends, girlfriends, school, afterlife. I don't care where we are, we're always going to be friends and I am always going to love you."

Alexa did not reply. She just pulled in closer and let Sam's chest soak up her unworthy tears.

Chapter Eighteen

CHAD, SAM AND Alexa all woke early the next morning. Alexa scurried back up to her room and dressed undetected. She was nervous as she met Chad and Sam outside Mr Knight's office. If she was going to help Chad, she knew she had to do it properly. Taking a deep breath, she tried to focus her mind on making sure she smiled at Mr Knight when she saw him instead of scowling the way she usually did.

Chad knocked tentatively on the office, but there was no answer. Knocking harder, he tried again, but the result was the same. Sam stepped forward and banged heavily on the door.

"Maybe he went home last night," said Sam, but just as he finished his sentence, a bleary-eyed Mr Knight opened his office door.

Alexa was glad Mr Knight looked at Sam and Chad first. It gave her time to rearrange her features and had managed an awkward smile by the time he looked at her.

"What's wrong? What time is it?" asked Mr Knight, shaking his head slightly.

"Ah, it's a bit before seven," said Chad, looking down at his watch.

"Okay," said Mr Knight, dropping his head. "Is it urgent?"

"No, not really, we can come back. It's okay," said Alexa in a pleasant voice, pulling Sam and Chad backwards. "We shouldn't have woken you."

"Look, just give me five minutes to get dressed," replied Mr Knight with a sigh.

"Thanks, Sir," said Alexa, smiling again. Perhaps she could convince him after all, she thought happily, but then her eyes caught Mr Knight's. Her heart stopped and her stomach rolled over as something warm tingled through her veins. "Let's go," she said anxiously, pulling Sam and Chad even harder.

***

Marcus waited curiously at his desk for Alexa, Chad and Sam to return. He had been looking forward to this day for weeks –

looking forward to the hour he would spend alone with Alexa driving her home. His disgust in himself over this was no small thing. He was no longer sleeping well, often felt nauseated and was vomiting on a regular basis.

All Marcus could do was remind himself that he was not interested in Alexa sexually. He was concerned about her welfare and wanted to help her – nothing more.

"So what is it that you three need at such an early hour?" he asked, as Chad, Sam and Alexa walked into his office at a quarter-past-seven.

"It's about the holidays. I don't want to stay at school any more," said Chad as he sat down in the chair in front of the desk. Sam sat down in a spare chair next to him, while Alexa stood in a corner of the room behind them.

"I'm sorry, you really should've organised that last week at the latest. It's the last day of term," said Marcus, feeling let down. Tedious administration, that was what they wanted from him. "How am I supposed to approve anything today? Do you have a letter from your parents?"

"No, but things have changed and Sam said I can go home with him. My parents are overseas and I don't want to stay at school alone."

"Ah, so I'm guessing this change of heart would have something to do with Miss Ross's parents asking for her to be allowed to leave these holidays."

Chad did not answer.

"But her parents didn't write, did they? They called and arranged it all over the phone," said Alexa from the corner.

"Yes, but I don't see what that has –"

"Why can't we organise this over the phone?" challenged Alexa. "We can call Sam's grandparents, they'll tell you that Chad is allowed to stay and then we can call Chad's parents and they'll say that Chad can go to Sam's place for the holidays."

"That's not really the way it's done," said Marcus, keeping to the official line. This was not what he wanted to deal with on the last day of term.

"You can leave any time you want. We're stuck here," retorted Alexa with more passion than Marcus had ever heard from her. "Now Chad has a chance to get out and you'd prefer him to be stuck here alone because it's a little inconvenient for you to organise permission."

"I never said that," replied Marcus pointedly, trying to mark his authority on this issue.

"You didn't have to. I'm not the only student in this grade that needs help."

Marcus looked at Alexa, waiting for more, but she stayed silent.

"This is not to become a common occurrence. This is a one-off. I hope you understand that," conceded Marcus after a lengthy pause. He was terrified that Alexa somehow knew how he felt about her. If she did, he knew she was not above using that information to her advantage. She had already shown her propensity for blackmail.

"Yes, Sir. Thank you so much," said Chad, grinning broadly.

"I suppose we should clear this with your grandparents first," said Marcus, pushing his phone towards Sam.

It took less than three rings for Sam's grandmother to answer the phone.

"Hi, Gran," said Sam pleasantly. "Um, Chad has nowhere to go these holidays and I was hoping he could stay with us."

"Just Chad? What about Alexa?" asked Gran, her voice loud enough for everyone to hear. "Does she have anywhere to go? You make sure she comes out here with you if she doesn't have somewhere nice to go."

"No, no, it's just Chad," smiled Sam, looking over his shoulder at Alexa.

"You sure? Is she there with you? Put her on."

"Alexa, Gran wants to say hi," said Sam, grinning knowingly as he held out the receiver to Alexa.

Alexa waved her hand. Sam dropped his outstretched arm and just waited. Alexa stared at Sam for a moment before sighing heavily and stepping forward. Sam grabbed her hand and sat her on his lap before handing her the receiver.

"Hi, Gran," said Alexa pleasantly, pushing her body closer to Sam's as his arms snaked around her waist.

"How are you, dear?" Marcus heard Gran ask. "I hope you're recovering well."

"Yeah, I'm okay."

"Do you remember much of what happened? He didn't leave any permanent marks on you, did he? Are you sure you're doing all right?"

"No, I don't remember much. There were no scars and I'm okay, I promise. Sam and Chad have been good. Sam's always there for me."

Watching Alexa speak to Sam's grandmother astounded Marcus. He had never seen this side of her before and he was amazed and impressed. Alexa always spoke to him with a hint of sarcasm in her voice and was always on guard, but now she spoke so comfortably and freely. There was no hesitation in her answering and Marcus wished she would speak to him like that – normally, just normally.

"Okay, I will talk to you again soon," said Alexa, standing up from Sam's lap, her eyes a little sadder than when she had walked in. "I'm glad you're both well. Bye."

Alexa handed the phone over to Marcus. He smiled at her, but she just glared at him and returned to her corner. It was a far cry from the smile she had given him when he had first opened the door. It made Marcus think that there was a very different side to Alexa, one more beautiful and enticing than the girl he knew, and it made him desperate to get to know that other girl.

Horrified by how desperately his heart was yearning for the opportunity to truly know and love Alexa, Marcus quickly turned his mind back to the task at hand. He wanted to ensure that Sam's grandmother was truly happy to have Chad for the whole holidays. Gran was a pleasant woman and Marcus could see why Alexa would feel so comfortable talking to her.

"So I can go with Sam?" asked Chad eagerly as soon as Marcus hung up the phone.

"As I just told Mr Michaels' grandmother, we will still need permission from your parents before I can allow you to go," said Marcus firmly, still not prepared to concede everything to these students. "So we had better call them next."

Chad looked miserably down at his mobile. He dialled their number slowly on Marcus's phone and put the receiver to his ear. The ringing continued and the phone remained unanswered before the line finally went dead.

"I know you don't want to hear this, Mr Olsen, but I can't allow you to go with Mr Michaels without your parents' permission," said Marcus, lacking any real concern. Chad crossed his arms and stared angrily back at him. "I'm sorry."

"Sure you are," spat Chad.

Chad rose from his chair and headed towards the door. Sam followed. Alexa met them at the door then sat down in the chair Chad had just vacated.

"So that's all you're going to do?" asked Alexa, folding her arms and sinking lower into the chair.

"What else do you think I can do?" Marcus asked incredulously. He thought he had been incredibly generous already.

Alexa smiled and slid Chad's mobile across his desk.

"You can keep trying and you can stop when you've finally spoken to his parents," replied Alexa simply.

"You want me to spend my whole day trying to get in contact with Mr Olsen's parents?" asked Marcus, confused by Alexa's determination "Why does this even matter to you? He's not staying with you."

"It may be a strange concept to you, but I care because he's my friend," replied Alexa, sneering slightly. "Plus, I know what it's like to be stuck somewhere you don't want to be."

"All right, I'll keep trying," sighed Marcus, realising that if it had been Alexa not Chad begging to be allowed to get out of Redgrove for the holidays he would have done whatever he could. However, he still did not want to lock himself into anything. "But just realise that I'm not promising anything," he added sternly.

Marcus wished he could promise Alexa the world, but this situation felt dangerous. Alexa smiled smugly and her eyes flicked back to Chad's mobile as she stood and left. She did not say anything before slamming the door closed behind her. The whole situation made Marcus feel manipulated and once again suspect that Alexa knew how he felt about her. However, thinking back on all his interactions with Alexa, he chose to hope that she was just trying to use the inherent fairness when dealing with his student that he prided himself on to her advantage; something he could not blame her for. Either way, he would have to step very carefully in the future if his feelings for Alexa, whatever they were, were to remain undiscovered.

***

Alexa opened the curtains to allow the sun to shine on her while she lay on her bed. Stripy shadows fell across the bed, but she took no notice of the bars on her windows. They made little difference now. She was not going to run away again and even if she had to, she had another exit.

The warmth of the sun on her skin was soothing, but it did nothing to relax her jittery mind. Alexa could not understand why her had body reacted so warmly to Mr Knight's glance. Was it because she had smiled at him? Let down her guard and tried to be nice? She could not have feelings for Mr Knight – Marcus, she sighed involuntarily, and felt her stomach twist warmly.

This was a disaster. It was as though she had she not learnt anything from her affair with Clinton, but she was both relieved and terrified when she made the comparison between the two teachers. Mr Knight had never really tried to be manipulative or controlling like Clinton. All Alexa could accuse Mr Knight of was trying too hard to help. And he did help her. Despite her threats and allegations, Mr Knight had never stopped trying to help her. He had even protected her in her nightmares – months earlier, when she had seen him as nothing more than an annoyance – he had protected her and Bethany from the menacing shadow of her nightmares. He had died for them – and she had cried for him.

Alexa did not understand what this all meant, but she knew it was trouble. She was determined that she could not like Mr Knight and, even if she did, she was going to bury those feelings so deep even she would not know they existed. She would not touch him and he would never lay a hand on her. Of that, she was absolutely certain.

"Alexa, Alexa!" cried Chad, rushing into the room with Sam right behind him.

"What?" she asked, sitting up and looking between their bewildered faces.

"I don't know what you said, but I'm indebted to you forever," said Chad, smiling broadly.

"Why, what happened? Can you go to Sam's for the holidays?"

"Yeah, he can come, but that's not the amazing part," said Sam, sitting down on the end of her bed. Chad looked too excited to sit.

"What's the amazing part?" asked Alexa, a little annoyed that they would not just tell her.

"What Mr Knight did to track down Chad's parents," answered Sam, though it explained very little.

"Well?" Alexa asked, frustrated by the silence. "Am I ever going to get the whole story or do I have to ask you questions every time you stop talking?"

"Okay, okay," said Chad, finally sitting on the end of her bed next to Sam. "I was sure that I'd have to stay at school because I hadn't been able to contact my parents and their mobile was the only number I had for them. But Mr Knight called my house and luckily the housekeeper was there. She was supposed to be on holidays, too, you see. That's why I never bothered calling home."

"You have a housekeeper? I never knew that," said Alexa in an awed voice.

"Anyway," continued Chad, waving off her comment, making her wonder just how different she really was to all her schoolmates. "So it turns out my dumb parents left their mobile at home. Mr Knight asked Janie, our housekeeper, if she knew where Mum and Dad were. She gave him the number for their hotel in New Zealand and then he rang them there and got their permission for me to stay with Sam for the holidays."

"And how is it that I have anything to do with this?" asked Alexa, somewhat impressed by what Mr Knight had done, but not really believing it had anything to do with her – hoping it had nothing to do with her.

"You don't honestly think Mr Knight did all this for me, do you?" laughed Chad with merry scepticism. "He wasn't even going to try and call my parents when Sam and me left his office."

"Look, I'm glad that you get to go with Sam, but you're really giving me too much credit," said Alexa, wanting it desperately to be the truth.

"I don't care what you think. Mr Knight put in that extra effort because of you," said Chad dismissively. "Just remember to say thanks. This could be a real source of gold."

"And how do you want me to thank him?" Alexa asked, suddenly furious. "The same way Clinton expected me to thank him?"

"No! I never meant it like that. I meant to say thank you, that's all," cried Chad, rising from the bed horror-struck.

"As long as you get what you need, right? It's a good thing that Clinton was never your teacher. Imagine the things I could have done to get you some extra marks. But hey, now I have Mr Knight on side you guys are sure to be top of geography, right?"

"That's not what he meant and you know it," said Sam angrily.

"I don't really care, okay, just go and have a good holiday together," Alexa snapped defensively, waving her hand as she rushed into the bathroom.

When she eventually emerged, her red and torn arm hidden under her jumper, Sam and Chad had gone. It left her in a very disagreeable mood as she carried her bags towards Mr Knight's office. She was upset at what Chad had said to her and
198

disappointed that the last words she said to Chad and Sam were angry. She was just so scared that what they said was true, and now she had to spend an hour alone with Mr Knight.

"Are you ready to go?" asked Mr Knight as she entered his office.

"Yes, Sir," Alexa murmured quietly, not raising her eyes to meet his.

"Good. I'll just pack up. I had to drop Mr Michaels, Mr Olsen and Miss Michaels into the city so they would make their train."

"Why'd you do it?" Alexa asked immediately, her fears overcoming her determination not to talk to him.

"Do what?" asked Mr Knight, looking up with a confused expression on his face.

"Why'd you make such an effort to get Chad permission to leave for the holidays when you didn't even want to see us this morning?"

"I thought about some of the things you said and considered things from Mr Olsen's point of view."

Alexa waited for further explanation, a qualification, but Mr Knight's answer sounded completely reasonable that she had no choice than to accept it. She could not exactly accuse him of wanting to sleep with her again.

"Well, thanks, it was a nice thing to do," she said, hoping that would appease Chad.

"It was my pleasure. It's not often I get to please three of the toughest students in the grade at once," replied Mr Knight with a slight smile. "Okay, let's get out of here."

The lights blurred in Alexa's eyes as they drove. People on the streets walked along, oblivious to the pain inside her. They walked free while she felt more trapped than ever. She wanted a choice, any choice, but a real choice. She wanted some way to feel in control of her life. Her hand slipped into the pocket and her fingers ran along the edge of a razor.

It was a bad sign that she felt the need to use it again so soon after her cutting that afternoon. A session such as that usually provided protection for at least a day from her emotions.

"How you going over there?" asked Mr Knight, after almost twenty minutes of silence. Alexa did not answer or show any signs that she had even heard him. "I really don't think you have to be so worried. Your foster parents don't resent you coming to stay. They're just worried about you. They don't want to see you back in the predicament you got yourself into in the city."

"I never thought of it as a predicament. It was a choice and I made it. Just because other people don't agree doesn't make it wrong," snapped Alexa, hating the way everyone viewed her life.

"So you would honestly prefer being back in the city selling yourself than going to your foster parents' place for the holidays?" asked Mr Knight incredulously.

"It wasn't about me and what I preferred. It was about what was right."

"How could that've ever been right? Where do you think prostitution was going to get you? You would've ended up dead in a gutter next to your sister," retorted Mr Knight, annoying Alexa with his condescension as much as his concern.

"I would have ended up in a nice home with my sister and I would've been able to get her clean."

"That is a fantasy. You're seventeen, you were sixteen, and the choice you made was going to get you nowhere but dead."

The lights ahead were red. Mr Knight stopped at the last moment and Alexa took her chance. She jumped out of the car, walking between the other stopped vehicles and on to the footpath. She did not know where she was or where she was going and she did not care.

"Alexa, stop!" called Mr Knight from behind her, but she did not turn and headed towards the park in front of her.

She went straight towards the play equipment, grabbed the monkey bars and swung her legs above her head. She wrapped her knees around one of the bars and pulled herself up.

"I'm not a child, you know," Alexa called down to Mr Knight who was now standing below her, his worried face looking up at her, making her stomach twist in spite of itself. "My decisions are my decisions and I don't regret them just because you don't agree."

"You have seen more and been through more than most people your age, but you are still only seventeen and that is so very young," replied Mr Knight, and Alexa thought he sounded almost pleading.

"I can take care of myself."

"I know you can and I think that if you were the only person you thought about, you would do very well."

"That's not an option I have."

"I think it's an option you've just never considered," replied Mr Knight seriously.

Alexa did not answer. She did not want to talk about this with him. She did not want to hate him because he could not understand. But more than that, she did not want to risk him understanding and risk her liking him more than she already did.

In response to her unmoved silence, Mr Knight walked to the end of the monkey bars. He lifted himself up on the bar at the end and slowly pulled himself along the top until he was sitting next to her, facing the opposite direction.

"I just want life to be simple and not so complicated," Alexa sighed, feeling compelled to speak even though – or maybe because – Mr Knight said nothing.

"I wish I could tell you that life gets less complicated, but it only gets worse. I guess, as you get older, you have had more experience and learn how to deal with the complications a bit better. I wish my life was less complex too."

"What's so complex about your life?" asked Alexa scathingly, though she knew she should not judge. Anything could be going on in his life and she could just be making it worse.

"Ah, well …" replied Mr Knight before hesitating for many moments. "Well, you know that I got engaged earlier this year?" he continued, though his voice wavered slightly. Alexa nodded, her gut turning to stone even as she told herself how stupid she was. "We've been going out for a long time and Jackie's really great, but I've been … distracted lately."

"Distracted? Like you're engaged, but you want to screw around as well?" asked Alexa, wanting to find out now that he was a bastard who could not be trusted.

"No, not screw around," replied Mr Knight, shaking his head and smiling, before his face became serious again. "I haven't been looking elsewhere in general, but elsewhere in particular."

"Then why not break it off with your fiancée and go with the girl you like?" Alexa asked tentatively, her body tensing, ready to run.

"Because I can't have the girl I like."

"Why not?" she asked breathlessly. Her heart was beating double-time, but she knew she was being an idiot. Mr Knight spoke as if he liked this other woman – really liked – and that could not be her. He would never like her, not like that. If he wanted her at all it was only to make use of her body.

"She's just not available. She's seeing someone else – a mate," explained Mr Knight hesitantly. Alexa's stomach loosened at these words. He was not talking about her. "And that's not the complicated part. I don't even know how much I want her, but I want to be with her – in her company – and I want to talk to her and get to know her. I can't do that without being suspicious, but how will I ever know how I truly feel if I never get to really know her?"

"Does the other girl know how you feel about her?" asked Alexa timidly.

"No," answered Mr Knight firmly, shaking his head. "And I'm not going to tell her. It wouldn't be fair."

"I still think my life beats yours hands down," replied Alexa a little scathingly. She was glad Mr Knight had no interest in her, but could not understand how he thought his situation was anywhere near as complex as hers.

"I don't know many people with lives as tough as yours, but you're also a lot stronger than most people I know, so I know you'll make it through all right," said Mr Knight sincerely. It made Alexa's heart involuntarily soften for him. No one ever really complimented her. "Come on, we'd better go. You need to get to your foster parents' place and I have to see my fiancée."

Alexa slipped nimbly between the bars, then waited for Mr Knight to climb awkwardly down. She felt a little more at ease now, knowing he did not care about her and that she could think of him nicely without any danger of him knowing, or wanting more. However, the rest of the trip was still spent in silence until directions were required.

"It's down that street," said Alexa quietly, as Mr Knight drove slowly along the poorly lit road. "This house here."

They stopped in front of the Whites' house. It was a homely two-storey house with a blue picket fence and a light lit up the front porch. Alexa jumped out of the car and grabbed her bags from the back seat.

"You don't have to come with me," she said, seeing Mr Knight out of the car.

"Actually, I do," Mr Knight answered determinedly. "It was part of the agreement."

"Fuck the agreement."

Alexa walked quickly to the door and knocked impatiently. Pam opened the door with a smile that quickly faded when she received Alexa's harsh glare. Alexa stalked into the house and waited a few metres inside the door.

"Marcus Knight," said Mr Knight, holding out his hand.

"Pam White," replied Pam, shaking his hand. "Would you like to come in?"

"No, thank you. I'd better get going," said Mr Knight, making Alexa wonder if he would have said yes if she had been nicer to him. It made her determined not to be nice to him again. "I just thought I'd introduce myself. I hope we aren't too late. I got a little caught up at school."

"No, it's fine."

"Here," said Mr Knight, pulling a card out from his pocket. "I'll give you my contact details in case you need to talk to me for any reason."

"Thank you," said Pam, looking down at the numbers.

Alexa stood behind Pam, scowling intently at Mr Knight. She was ready to explode. She did not want Mr Knight to be in any way a part of her life outside of school.

"Alexa!" yelled Hayley, who rushed over to her unaware of the hateful expression on her face.

Alexa dropped her bags and turned and hugged Hayley warmly.

"How you doin', Hayley?" asked Alexa, stroking Hayley's face tenderly.

"I'm good. Aren't you glad it's the holidays?" replied Hayley happily, intent on ignoring the growing tension in the room.

"I'm glad to see you," Alexa answered sincerely, then realising that Mr Knight was still at the door with an astonished look on his face, she spoke harshly once more. "I thought you were leaving."

"I am," Mr Knight muttered, quickly backing away. "I'll see you back at school. Nice to meet you all."

"Alexa, come up to my room," said Hayley excitedly as soon as the door closed. Apparently Hayley thought Mr Knight was intruding as well.

"No, we need to have a chat with Alexa before dinner," said Pam in a slightly strained voice. "Why don't you get cleaned up and we'll call you and Brett down when it's ready."

Alexa rolled her eyes and walked towards the lounge room as Hayley trudged angrily upstairs.

"I assume your teacher explained our conditions for your return to this house, but I would like to reiterate them so there's no mistaking our position," said Pam in a serious and stern voice

Alexa rarely heard from her, as Pam walked into the room right behind her with Karl by her side.

"Is this really necessary?" asked Alexa contemptuously.

"Yes, it is," replied Karl firmly.

"We don't want you leaving this house unaccompanied. So if you're going anywhere you're to be with one of us or Brett and Hayley," said Pam.

"What!" cried Alexa. That had not been on the original list of rules.

"Second, you will not discuss any of the activities you engaged in while you were away with either Brett or Hayley. They also don't know anything about the situation with you and your history teacher and we would like it kept that way," said Pam firmly.

"Do you honestly think I just go around talking about that shit? Fuck!" Alexa snapped, furious that they thought they could order her around like she was one of their real children.

"There'll be none of that language either," said Karl harshly.

"And if you break these rules, we will not ask you back again no matter how much Hayley pleads," said Pam.

"You didn't want me back this time. Why the hell do you set all these rules when you don't want me here in the first place?" Alexa muttered, folding her arms angrily. "Just send me back like everyone else does."

"If we didn't want you here, believe me, you wouldn't be here," said Karl in a stern voice. "This is not about punishing you. It is about protecting you."

"You don't care about protecting me. You want to protect Brett and Hayley from me," Alexa sneered. "The only reason you keep asking me back is because Hayley asks you to and it kills you that she likes me."

"We keep asking you back in the hope that you will eventually accept more than Hayley into your heart," snapped Karl.

"What do you care if you're in my heart or not? I'm not part of this family. I'm simply a guest four times a year. You don't want me to be a part of this family."

"That is what you say to make yourself feel better. The truth is you won't allow yourself to be a part of this family," said Karl angrily. "We have invited you to every family event and have never excluded you. You won't let yourself be a part of this family because you think that will mean you've abandoned your sister. Your sister is the reason you identify with Hayley. Hayley is the next best thing. You feel like the sister you want to be when you are around her. The rest of us are just surplus."

Alexa slumped down on the lounge. She had no answer to that. Karl had rarely involved himself when it came to her, but he clearly understood her and how she reacted to things.

"We did want you to come back here," said Pam, sitting down on the lounge next to Alexa. "We even considered having you stay here permanently after you ended up in hospital, but given all the turmoil, we thought it was best that you stayed with your friends."

"We've been harsh on you because we want what's best for you. You're not a bad person, Alexa," said Karl gently, taking a seat next to Pam.

"Even after everything I've done?" asked Alexa, not daring to look up.

"You're not in an easy situation and we don't envy your position," said Pam sincerely, tucking Alexa's hair behind her ear. "I wish there was a simple solution for you and that you could have the family you crave, but in the meantime I hope you'll make an effort with the family that's on offer."

Alexa did not speak. She felt empty. Everything Pam and Karl had said was right. She could not allow herself to be part of the family, because Bethany was not with her and it felt too wrong. The problem was, it still felt wrong.

Chapter Nineteen

THAT NIGHT MARKED a turning point for Alexa and the Whites. Although the Whites did not relax their new rules and Alexa still did not consider herself part of the family, she involved herself more with the family and tagged along to family outings, much to Hayley's delight. Brett also enjoyed her company, but he was now fifteen and was trying to spend as little time with the family as possible. He even jokingly thanked Alexa for taking the pressure off him and allowing him to escape more often. Alexa was glad she could help, but would have been happier if she could have escaped too.

While Pam and Karl had to work through the holidays, and with Brett out and about, Alexa spent most days with Hayley, taking her out shopping or to the movies. At night, Alexa worked on her assignments. They were a good excuse to avoid too much time with the whole family. It was still just far too awkward.

The days rolled quietly by until there was just under a week left before the end of the school holidays. Alexa finished her assignments, but made the mistake of telling Hayley. After that Hayley accepted no excuse for Alexa not to hang out with the family. However, Alexa still felt uncomfortable and out of place with the Whites, making dinner on Tuesday night a quiet affair. Only Hayley was prepared to brave the tension and talk, detailing her day at the pool with Alexa.

"And I beat Alexa in a race," said Hayley proudly.

Alexa wished she could have believed she had let Hayley win, but although she could keep herself afloat and stroke with basic competence, Hayley was a much better swimmer than her.

"Wow, well down," said Pam, smiling at her beaming daughter. "Oh, we wanted to talk to everyone about the rest of the holidays," she added quickly, as if finally finding the best time for this conversation. It made Alexa's heart stammer and she kept her head down as Pam continued. "Aunt Shirley's invited us up to her place for the rest of the week and I said we would go. So we'll drive up tomorrow night after work. Alexa, are you going to come?"

"Is this the same aunt that disapproved greatly of my presence before last Christmas?" Alexa asked.

It had been the meeting that had pretty much put an end to Alexa doing anything family-like with the Whites. Pam and Karl's families had been very sceptical of the types of children they would be given as foster parents and Alexa's arrival seemed to have confirmed all their fears.

"Yes," replied Pam hesitantly, her eyes flicking to Karl.

"And I'm guessing she still doesn't approve of my presence?" asked Alexa pointedly.

Neither Pam nor Karl answered, but their look was enough. Alexa supposed she should have been thankful that they had continued to ask her back despite their families' disapproval, but it was difficult to be that grateful when she was being asked to be subjected to their displeasure again.

"What happens if I don't go?" Alexa asked tentatively.

"There are a few options," said Pam quickly, as though they had been expecting this question. "We can drop you off at school tomorrow night on the way or your year advisor, Mr Knight, is returning to school on Friday and will pick you up on his way."

Neither option was particularly appealing, but Alexa supposed she had to return to school eventually.

"So you'll let me stay here for a day by myself?" she asked sceptically.

"Yes, we think you can be trusted for a day," answered Karl with a nod.

"Do I have to stay inside the house?" Alexa asked, wondering just how much they trusted her.

"No, but that does not mean you're allowed to go wandering around the city either. If you do leave it's only to go somewhere local," answered Karl. It was more leeway than Alexa had expected.

"I'll go back to school on Friday with Mr Knight," Alexa nodded, wanting to test the true depth of their trust in her before she agreed to possibly coming back for the long summer holidays.

Pam and Karl immediately nodded their consent to her choice. It was a concession she would never have expected to be granted at the start of the holidays, and wondered if they were trying to prove that they did have some faith in her. It was nice, but Alexa thought it was probably misplaced. Whether she meant to or not, she would disappoint them.

The only person not happy with her decision was Hayley, who spent all of Wednesday trying to convince her to change her mind, but it was to no avail. Alexa was not going to subject herself to anyone's disapproval if she did not have to, but felt bad telling Hayley that she did not like her extended family.

"Are you coming back for the summer holidays then?" asked Hayley sulkily, finally conceding defeat on Aunt Shirley.

"I think so," replied Alexa tentatively. It did no one any good to be too confident about these things. "Your mum and dad have said that it'll be okay and they have work lined up for me as well, like they did last summer."

"Are you going to be here for Christmas as well or are you going to leave like last year?" asked Hayley in a huff.

"Will it make you happy if I stick around on Christmas Day?" asked Alexa hesitantly. Hayley nodded her head. "Okay, for you, I'll be here for Christmas."

"Promise?"

"I promise."

Hayley lifted her head to reveal a broad smile. Alexa was glad she could make Hayley happy so easily. It was even nice to find that there were others who were almost as pleased by her decision.

"I'm glad to hear you've decided to be here for Christmas," said Karl, as Alexa helped him pack the car on Wednesday afternoon.

"Hayley was really upset about me not going up with you so I had to make it up to her somehow," replied Alexa with a dismissive shrug of her shoulders.

"Hayley's the only reason?"

"Yeah," Alexa answered softly, nodding her head. "I know what you said was right, about why I'm not part of this family, but I can't change the way I feel. I'm lucky, and I know it, to have been placed with you and Pam, but it doesn't change the fact that I would do anything to be with Bethy."

"As long as you know that we're always here for you if you need us," said Karl sincerely, holding Alexa's gaze and nodding as if to emphasise the point.

"Thanks," Alexa replied in a small voice, feeling like the Whites had just given her the first Christmas present she had ever received.

***

Marcus pulled up nervously in front of the Whites' house. He looked at the clock – twenty to ten. He was early. That would not make him popular, but he had not been able to sit in his apartment any longer – waiting.

With a deep breath, Marcus knocked on the front door and waited. No one came. His heart started beating harder as he wondered if he had gotten his wires crossed. He knocked again, starting to panic, then he heard movement. Five seconds later Alexa appeared at the door, but the sight shocked him. Alexa was dressed in her pyjamas, with her haired pulled hastily back in a messy bun.

"Hi, sorry. I guess I'm a bit early," said Marcus awkwardly.

"Well, I never thought between ten and eleven included half past nine," muttered Alexa darkly.

"Sorry," Marcus replied automatically, though he noticed his watch now read quarter to ten. "Did I wake you?"

"Yes," answered Alexa, walking back into the house, allowing him to follow. She strode into the kitchen and pulled out the kettle and toaster.

"How were your holidays?" asked Marcus politely, realising Alexa was not happy about his arrival.

"Shorter than I expected," quipped Alexa, piling food on to the counter. "Tea, white with two sugars, toast not too dark and not too much butter."

"Sorry?"

"When you hear the shower stop you can put the toast and the kettle on. Help yourself if you're hungry. If you put one foot on those stairs I will call the police."

Marcus stood stunned for a moment. Alexa's calm, cold and thoroughly untrusting manner intrigued him. He boiled the kettle and made himself a coffee, trying not to analyse too much. He could hear the shower running and tried even harder not to think about Alexa naked underneath it. When the shower stopped he was glad to have something else to think about as he set about making Alexa's breakfast. Alexa arrived in the kitchen just as he finished putting the vegemite on her toast.

Alexa nodded her thanks and ate in silence. Fifteen minutes later they were walking out the door. Marcus was surprised. It was only just after ten. He had never known any woman to be ready so quickly. He heard Alexa sigh as she slumped further into the passenger seat of the car. He wanted to sigh too, but he guessed for very different reasons and he cursed himself for it.

"Can't we ..." Alexa said softly, her voice almost inaudible as she spoke to her feet. "Couldn't we just go somewhere ... until lunch time or something?" Marcus felt his heart beat double-time. "I just don't want to go back to school yet. People should be at the beach on days like today, not at school, especially when it's really still school holidays."

"You know I shouldn't. I'm not really allowed to take you places when it's not school-related," Marcus answered, thankful the correct response came out of his mouth.

"You've taken me to *dinner*," replied Alexa, though Marcus was glad there was nothing malicious or accusing in her tone.

"I know," he nodded, but he knew he was not supposed to have done that either.

Mrs Taylor had given him specific instructions that Alexa was to be brought back to school for dinner from the hospital after Clinton's attack, but he knew that was just Mrs Taylor's spite and he would not concede to that. This was completely different. He had no way to justify taking Alexa out now, but he wanted to – so much.

"You're going to have to promise not to tell anybody," said Marcus, before internally cursing himself for allowing such words to be spoken. He was really much better off with Alexa thinking of him as a heartless bastard. "I could end up in a lot of trouble."

"I promise. I won't tell a soul," replied Alexa solemnly.

Marcus had the strange feeling he could trust Alexa's word on that. Now all he had to do was not give her any reasons to distrust his word.

"Where do you want to go?" he asked, hoping he could comply.

"The beach? I haven't been since – since before my mum died, I guess," answered Alexa softly, her eyes downcast.

Alexa's answer was strangely heartbreaking. It was such a simple request, and one Marcus could easily fulfil.

"The beach it is then," he smiled. Alexa did not smile back.

Alexa remained quiet as they drove, but Marcus did not mind. It was not the angry silence he was used to and he was glad he could do something to make her happy, but was worried about being seen with her. He was on a very slippery slope right now and even occasionally acknowledged that had it not been for Alexa's affair with Clinton, he may have considered tempting fate and testing the depth of his feelings for her. He liked Alexa, he could no longer deny that, but he wanted nothing else – except to keep her safe until she left Redgrove and walked away from him forever.

***

Alexa looked out the open car window, feeling the hot breeze whip against her face. It was nice knowing that she was not going back to school right away and was grateful to Mr Knight for taking her out. However, that feeling did not last long after he suddenly pulled into the car park of a small apartment complex.

"Hey, what are we doing?" Alexa asked anxiously.

"It's okay. This is my place," replied Mr Knight. Alexa shifted uncomfortably in her seat. "I just want to pick up a couple of things, but I'm in someone else's spot so can you wait here in case they come back?"

Mr Knight jumped out of the car, leaving Alexa alone. Alexa wondered what to do. Mr Knight had not asked her to come in, but she could not understand why he had brought her to his place. Looking around frantically, Alexa tried to work out where Mr Knight had gone and which directions he could approach from. There were no geographical landmarks that could tell her where she was. All she was left with was fear.

Knowing it was far too dangerous to stay, Alexa jumped out of the car and grabbed her bags. She would run first and work out where she was going later.

"Going somewhere?"

Alexa turned quickly to see Mr Knight standing behind her. He had a bag on his shoulder and two towels in his hand.

"I just – I was ..."

"I know what you were doing and why. Hop back in the car," said Mr Knight gently. "I didn't mean to scare you. I just needed to pick up a few things."

Alexa hesitated. She was still sure it was safer to run, but Mr Knight was blocking her exit. He did not reach out for her or try and force her into the car.

"I'm sorry, please," said Mr Knight sincerely. "It's okay. You can trust me. I won't hurt you. Just hop back in the car."

Alexa still did not move. Her body was shaking. Mr Knight looked contrite, but she could not trust him.

"Okay," he murmured, ruffling his hair as he thought intently. "We can catch the train back to school. I will see be able to supervise your travel, but we will be in public and you won't have to sit with me."

Mr Knight nodded, as though convinced by his own plan. Alexa watched him as he muttered, moving around the car, grabbing his personal belongings from the car and dumping the other bag and towels in the boot. It took Alexa a moment to realise that he had left her exit unguarded as he did this. She tensed to run, but caught his eye as he turned to her, ready to walk to the train station.

It was the height of reckless idiocy, but Alexa found her body turning back to the car and sliding into the passenger seat. She kept her body pressed against the door and away from the driver's seat, but that would really not spare her when Mr Knight eventually turned. She was risking her life every time she was alone with him anyway. It seemed ridiculous not to get something she wanted out of the transaction before the inevitable ending.

"I am very sorry, Alexa," said Mr Knight sincerely when he slipped back into the car. "I should've warned you, but I was afraid you mightn't believe it was innocent."

"Were you really in someone else's car space?" Alexa asked, trying to control her shaking voice.

"No, I had to tell you something. I really had no intention of … of anything. I would never hurt you, Alexa."

Alexa nodded and pulled her knees into her chest. They drove for another twenty-five minutes, but every minute felt like as lifetime as she wondered what was coming next.

"All right, we're here," said Mr Knight somewhat hesitantly.

Alexa did not move to begin with. There was no beach in sight. She wondered why Mr Knight made it so difficult to trust his word. When he explained that they had to walk a little bit, Alexa decided to grab her bags and follow him. Out of the car, she could run if she needed to.

They walked through a small park and came to a cliff top. Below was a small bay with no sand, but there was a large rock ledge. It was beautiful. There were only a three people in the water; a small number given the heat.

"This is the place," said Mr Knight. She thought he looked a little bashful and wondered why. "Or there's a proper beach a few minutes away."

"Why'd you bring me here?" Alexa asked distrustfully, needing to know Mr Knight's motives.

"First, so that we were less likely to be seen and, second, because this is where I come when I'm by myself. It's much more relaxing than the beach, less people, more space."

Reasonable. Both were perfectly reasonable answers, thought Alexa. Though the first answer could have double meaning, she liked the second answer a lot.

"Okay, we can go here," she nodded.

It took them a few minutes to walk down to the rock ledge. Mr Knight laid out the towels in the shade and unpacked his bag. Alexa watched, slightly amazed, as he pulled out an array of food from his bag. Then she looked around the beach.

"No bathrooms?"

"No, I … sorry, I forgot," said Mr Knight, blushing as he began to repack his bag. "I usually just change under a towel. Come on, we'll go back to the main beach. I'm sorry. I completely forgot."

Scrutinising his face, Alexa eventually decided to believe Mr Knight had genuinely forgotten. That or he was a very good actor. She should have distrusted him, but she really did like it here and did not want to be around a lot of people right now. If the worst came, she would push Mr Knight into the water and run for her life.

"No, it's okay," said Alexa, grabbing the larger towel and pulling her swimmers from her bag.

She walked a few metres away with her back to Mr Knight. There really was nowhere private to go. Wrapping the towel around her waist, she pulled her swimmers up under the towel. When she looked up she saw Mr Knight looking away, making her stomach swirl. Rearranging the towel so she could pull the swimmers over the top half of her body, Alexa pulled off the rest of the clothes and walked back over to the picnic Mr Knight had set up on the remaining towel.

"Are you hungry?" asked Mr Knight, looking strangely unsure of himself as she examined the food.

"Yeah, but I'm going to swim first."

Alexa dropped her stuff at her feet before walking over to the rock ledge, diving straight in. She loved the rush of cold water over her body. This was perhaps one of the finer moments of her life, but could not decide if she was grateful or resentful that she had Mr Knight to thank for that. It would be better if she hated him, but she did not want to think that everyone was horrible. It would be nicer to believe that there were some pockets of kindness in the world.

It seemed strange to Alexa that she could accept Steve as being a good man for the kindness that he had shown her, yet she was also fully aware that Steve was knowingly and illegally exploiting her for monetary gain. From the start, Steve was someone she should not have been able to trust, but he had been good to her, better than he needed to be. Mr Knight was someone who had only ever done the best by her, but he was someone society said she should trust. They were the people Alexa had always distrusted the most.

Jumping out of the water, Alexa was determined that no matter how nice Mr Knight was, no matter what he did, she would not like him. She would not put her faith him and she would not trust him. He would be the nothing he had been up until the start of this year.

"I'm starving," said Alexa, grabbing her towel and standing over the food, dripping water all over it.

Alexa grabbed a paper plate and piled it with food before sitting down in a small patch of shade away from Mr Knight. She sat and ate for almost half an hour before laying her towel out on the rocks to sun herself.

"You should put some sunscreen on. Your face is already a little red," said Mr Knight, throwing her a bottle of sunscreen. Alexa covered her face, arms and legs then threw the bottle back towards him. "Do you want me to put some on your back?"

Alexa told herself not to be suspicious. It was an innocent question, but she did not want Mr Knight's hands anywhere near her so declined the offer.

"Here," said Mr Knight, and he threw her his shirt. "Use that to cover your back."

Alexa smiled, threw the shirt over her shoulders and rolled on to her stomach. Mr Knight had not been angry at her refusal and she felt her stomach twist warmly about his compromise. Turning her head so that she could assess Mr Knight more closely, Alexa realised that he was much better looking than she had ever noticed before and started to appreciate Lizzie's crush. This was really not the best way to turn her heart against Mr Knight, and without her noticing, Alexa found her mind thinking kindly of him again. It was frustrating, but it took more energy than she wanted to expend trying to be angry and distrustful of Mr Knight while he was being so good to her. She would worry about ignoring his existence when she got back to school.

After about fifteen minutes, Alexa rolled over on to her back and laid Mr Knight's shirt over her face to keep the sun out of her eyes. This was just too perfect, lying here and enjoying the moment, but it was not long before she was hot again.

"You coming for a swim?" Alexa asked, walking over to where Mr Knight was sitting, staring out to sea.

"What?" he replied, shaking his head slightly.

"I just asked if you were coming for a swim," Alexa said again. Mr Knight looked up at her, his hand shielding his eyes from the sun. "Come on, you can't come to the beach and not swim."

Alexa took Mr Knight's hand from above his eyes and pulled him to his feet, tingles travelling from his hand up through her arm and into her stomach. Their eyes met briefly and Alexa felt the most intense surge of warmth her body had ever known.

"I have to get changed first," said Mr Knight, releasing her hand casually.

Alexa's stomach turned to lead. Mr Knight must have noticed her growing infatuation and was trying to dismiss her gently. As much as that thought hurt, Alexa was glad. She liked him all the more for it.

***

Marcus watched Alexa dive into the water before changing. She was swimming near the mouth of the bay. Daring, he thought, but he was not concerned. He was not sure that he had ever met a stronger woman than Alexa. Woman, he scoffed. Alexa was just a girl, little more than a child. But somewhere along the line things had changed and his view of Alexa had gone from that of an intriguing schoolgirl to a strong, beautiful woman. Just being close to her, while she was being so nice to him, made his heart ache in a way he had convinced himself it never would for her.

Swimming around the bay, Marcus kept well clear of Alexa, but always had an eye on her. Watching Alexa, he could not help but think of the life they would never have after she left school. He could think about it, he justified, because it would never happen and even if by some miracle it did, it was okay because he would no longer be her teacher.

They would meet unexpectedly. Alexa would ask him if he wanted coffee and they would talk for hours. Then she would invite him back to her place. She would make more coffee and they would sit on the lounge talking and laughing. He would put his cup down on the coffee table and move in closer …

Marcus forced himself to open his eyes. He could not think about that. The eighteen-year-old Alexa of his fantasies looked exactly the way she did now. The slippery slope had suddenly been greased with extra oil. Sighing, Marcus looked around the bay, but realised Alexa was no longer in the water. Scanning the rock ledge, he noticed that her bags were gone from their picnic area. Swimming quickly to the edge, he jumped out of the water and on to the rocks. He ran, searching for her, cursing his stupidity.

After throwing everything into his bag, Marcus rushed towards the steps leading up to the car, constantly looking around for Alexa. There was little chance he would catch up to her. She could have gone in any number of directions, and Marcus was not even convinced that she would be heading back to school. This day had suddenly turned into a disaster. Scanning the bay again, he rushed up the stairs.

Alexa was gone.

Marcus was at the top of the stairs when he looked back down and scanned the bay again, his mind struck by the horrific thought that Alexa had not run away, but had drowned – silently slipping under while he indulged in immoral fantasies. Torn between the possibilities, Marcus was almost at the point of despair when he saw something white wedged between the rock ledge and the cliff above, just a few metres from where they had been sitting.

Running down the stairs two at a time, Marcus stumbled and grabbed the railing just in time to stop himself tumbling headfirst down the stairs. A minute later he was back on the rock ledge trying to find where he had seen the white between the rocks. He threw his bag down and dropped to his knees to look along the bottom of the cliff and there, just three metres away, was Alexa, asleep in a small gap at the bottom of the cliff. One of her bags was under her head the other was hugged into her chest. She was still wearing his shirt.

Marcus shuffled along until he was in front of where Alexa was laying and rested his head against the cliff face. Relief washed over his body as he sat and watched her sleep.

"Do we have to go?" asked Alexa sleepily.

"You're awake," Marcus sighed. Alexa was still lying down in the small gap, too small for her to sit up in. "You scared me half to death. I thought you'd run off."

"I thought you saw me," replied Alexa in a small voice. "You were looking this way when I came under here. I just didn't want to lie in the sun. It was too hot."

"It's okay. I should've been paying more attention, but we do have to go. It's almost two."

***

The drive back to the school took almost an hour. Alexa rested her head against the window and watched Mr Knight's hand as he changed gears. He had nice, strong, tanned hands. Her eyes wandered up his equally tanned arms and on to his still bare chest. She watched his chest rise and fall with each breath, her stomach swirling with tension and arousal. His hair stuck out at funny angles, tussled by the salty water, but his face remained as smooth as ever.

Alexa looked up at Mr Knight's eyes. She did not want to be caught looking at him, but she needed to look into his eyes, to try and determine the nature of her feelings for him. He turned and looked at her, but she chickened out and quickly flicked her eyes down to the floor.

It was now two-thirty and Mr Knight's open window allowed the cool change to flow through into the car. Alexa turned and took a jumper out of her bag.

"Are you cold? Do you want me to wind the window up?" asked Mr Knight with concern.

"No, the fresh air is nice," Alexa replied, not looking up at him or smiling at how courteous he was being. She just laid her head back against her window and watched him from the corner of her eyes.

When the tall towers of the school came into sight Alexa's heart dropped. She did not want to go back to her prison cell. Ten minutes later they pulled into the school car park. Alexa did not look over at Mr Knight. It felt strange being with him like this at school.

"Um, thanks for today. It was a really nice thing to do. I really liked it," said Alexa nervously, not game enough to meet Mr Knight's eyes as she grabbed her bags.

"I'm glad you had a good time," replied Mr Knight, nodding slightly.

Nothing else. No conditions. No demands. It made Alexa nervous.

"Is it okay if I just go straight to my room?" she asked, waiting for the inevitable ultimatum.

"That's fine," answered Mr Knight.

Alexa took her chance. She grabbed her bags and rushed to her room, her heart thrumming erratically. Dropping her bags on the floor, she collapsed on to her bed and cursed herself. No matter how hard she tried, she could not hate Mr Knight. Every thought of him was a tender one, and caused her stomach to squirm warmly.

It was a disaster. Alexa could not comprehend how she had let this happen. Perhaps it was just because she had spent so much time with Mr Knight – with Marcus, she sighed, thinking of him as a person and not just a teacher – but that was something she could change. If she stayed out of trouble, she would have no reason to see Mr Knight. Her feelings would pass. Mr Knight would return to being nothing. There was no choice. She could not face the consequences of dating a teacher again.

It was a fear that kept Alexa in her room most of the weekend. She did not want to see Mr Knight at all, and kept her head down whenever he was near. If time was going to help her feelings subside, then she needed it to pass much quicker than it was, because without classes to focus her mind on all she thought about was him – how kind he was to her; how supportive and understanding he continued to be; how he saw her as nothing more than a student; but mostly about how nice it was for a decent guy to think of her as an okay kind of person.

Sam and Chad returned to school just before lunch on Sunday. Alexa saw them from the common room window as they walked towards the dormitories. She was not sure what to say to them given the way they left things at the end of term, and the way her feelings for Mr Knight had developed since then. It made her avoid them for as long as possible, but they were not prepared to ignore her and quickly tracked her down after lunch to sort things out.

"I'm sorry about the things I said. I really didn't mean anything by it," said Chad, squeezing Alexa's hand.

"It's okay. I shouldn't have snapped," Alexa replied as her heart fluttered frantically. "I'm just glad that you didn't stay mad."

"We could never stay mad at you," said Sam, pulling her into a hug. "How were your holidays? Did you survive the foster family? How'd things go with Mr Knight?"

"Holidays were okay, considering the two assignments I had to do. The foster family was fine. We had a bit of a discussion on the

Friday night, but everything's fine. They're having me back for the summer holidays at least."

"And Mr Knight, did he hassle you at all?" asked Chad.

"No, there were no problems," Alexa answered, though she did not look at Sam as she spoke.

"You sure?" asked Sam, forcing her to face him.

"Sam, he didn't do or say anything inappropriate, I promise," stated Alexa, looking him directly in the eyes.

It was true. Mr Knight had been entirely appropriate. It was her who had the inappropriate feelings for him.

Chapter Twenty

AT THE GRADE meeting on the first day of term four, Mr Knight reminded them all of the importance of the next year and that he was always there if they needed to talk. Alexa paid no attention to him, preferring instead to doodle on scraps of paper. She would speak as few words to Mr Knight in her remaining year as she could get away with.

"Well that's about all. I think you can all head to recess," said Mr Knight, wrapping up the meeting.

"Don't you want to see any of us individually?" asked Sam as the grade began to disperse, six other students waiting for Mr Knight's answer.

"No, I don't think there's any need for that. I don't think there's anyone in this grade who'll cause me trouble this term. Did you want to see me about something, Mr Michaels?"

"No, it's just that we usually have extra meetings after grade meetings," answered Sam, pointing out their reality.

"I realise that. It's what I was advised to do when I took the job, but I don't think there's any need," said Mr Knight, before looking like he might have said too much. "Unless of course you are planning to cause trouble for me this term, then we should go and have a chat," he added with a quick smile.

The G7 students all shook their heads and made their way quickly to the door. They knew to take their chances when they came. It was likely to be a short reprieve, but it was a reprieve all the same, and Alexa headed to class more than a little relieved that she did not have to spend any extra time with Mr Knight.

"I can't believe this is our last year – that there's only a year to go," said Bianca as they walked out of the meeting.

"A year plus our final exams, I think you'll find," said Ezra.

"Yeah, see it's the exam part that worries me, not the year," said Alexa.

A day, a month, a year. Without Bethany, it all felt the same. Until she turned eighteen, time meant nothing. It may as well not be passing at all. It never brought anything good with it.

"But this also means that it's only a little over a year until we get our money," said Bianca giddily. "Multimillionaires in just over a year!"

"I think the first thing I'll buy is an apartment. Something by the sea would be nice," said Alexa wistfully. She did not want that to be her last carefree swim in the ocean.

"I don't know what I'd buy first, but a car would be good, I guess, maybe take a holiday," said Ezra.

"I'm going to go into the city and go on a massive shopping spree with my Mum," said Bianca excitedly. "After that I'm going to hire a boat and fill it with food and drinks and spend the night cruising the harbour with all my friends.

"In the morning, I'll have a long relaxing, massage before going shopping again and then going and booking a first-class trip around the world. But," Bianca quickly added. "Before I go, I'm going to throw the biggest party and invite everyone I know."

"We certainly have everything planned, don't we," smiled Alexa.

"Haven't you been thinking about what you'll do?" asked Bianca incredulously.

"I think about it, but it's just so much money I don't know where to start," smiled Ezra. "I want a giant Lindt Easter egg."

"I've barely thought about it at all," said Alexa solemnly, her smile from Ezra's comment fading. "It's always felt so far away and useless."

"Far away, maybe, but useless, never. We really need to discuss this more often if you two are struggling so badly to find ways to spend this money," said Bianca.

"I'm sure once we have it we'll find a million things to spend it on," said Ezra as the bell rang for class. "I still think the hard part is where to start."

"I don't think that's the hard part.," said Alexa softly, almost to herself. "Once I finish school I'm homeless. I really will be looking for an apartment."

The discussions about what to do with their fortunes continued well into the first week of term, though it really only made Alexa notice just how different she was to Ezra and Bianca. Her reality was such a stark contrast to theirs and though they seemed to try, they could not understand why she did not want to make grand plans. They were sure that money was all it would take to solve her problems.

Money would certainly give Alexa some stability and a degree of certainty about her basic needs, which had always been such insecure resources in the past. However, the thought of Bethany still addicted to heroin and with an endless supply of cash terrified Alexa, and in many ways she thought they may actually be better off without it. It left her as fearful of her future as she was of her present.

However, Alexa found herself able to stick to her one plan for the present. She was keeping such a low profile that her teachers sometimes did not even notice that she was in the class, but the approach did help her stay out of trouble. It meant she only caught the briefest glimpses of Mr Knight, but every time she did see him her stomach leapt up into her chest. In spite of this, school life had never been so relaxed and carefree.

With Clinton gone, Ms Carter had slunk off in to the distance. Alexa did worry that it meant Ms Carter had just found herself another victim within the scholarship population, but she did not think it possible that Ms Carter could hate any student more than her and did not want her mind to linger on the bad when things were finally going well.

Chad and Bianca were as passionate as ever after their holidays apart, so Alexa often found herself alone with Ezra. Alexa had forgotten how tranquil it was with just Ezra. They occasionally talked about the money. Ezra's plans were nowhere near as grand as Bianca's, but it was still a long way from her world and Ezra quickly realised that she was not interested in those conversations. That future was so distant and unreachable.

The more immediate future was now Alexa's biggest concern as teacher after teacher started returning their exam results. Alexa sat nervously in each class, worried about what mark was going to be placed before her and if Mr Knight had really been telling her the truth when he had said her scholarship would not be revoked no matter how poorly she did. To her relief, and utmost surprise, she had managed to scrape a pass in every subject. She was tempted to go up to Mr Knight's office and throw her exam results back in his face, but she did not want him to be happy with her efforts any more than she wanted him to be angry with her petulance.

Ezra did consistently well, as usual, while Bianca's marks were a bit more hit and miss, practically topping one exam while barely passing another. Sam, Chad, Lizzie, Nick and Alan all blitzed the exams, with Nick and Alan beating out the other three to top the grade.

"You should've heard Mr Knight talking today," said Sam as they all ate lunch. "He was so happy that three of his geography students were near the top of the grade."

"But I think he was happier that it was some of the G7," said Lizzie. "I heard him say that he felt vindicated for taking the grade that no one wanted and especially for constantly defending the G7."

"He's only defended us once," said Alexa, feeling the need to minimise Mr Knight's deeds.

"No. Apparently, some of the staff have been really angry about you guys and the things they think you get away with, especially you," said Lizzie, looking at Alexa. "Apparently, he had to fight really hard to keep you in the school and loads of the staff think you should've been expelled by now."

"We knew he had a soft spot for Alexa ages ago. That's why we used her to get me out of school for the holidays," laughed Chad.

"It's not just Alexa he's been defending though. Mrs Taylor wanted to cancel Sam's scholarship for constantly withholding information about Alexa, where she is and how she keeps getting out of school."

"How do you know all this?" asked Bianca.

"I don't know," shrugged Lizzie, though she was smiling proudly. "Mr Knight chats a lot. He gets really stressed and just spits it all out. He says he really likes our year."

"He may like us, but I'm not sure that he'll be back next year," said Sam.

"Why not?" asked Ezra. "He's made it this far."

"Lizzie's right," said Sam. "You haven't seen how stressed he's been. He was really shaken up after Mr Marsh tried to kill Alexa. I think he'll go away for summer and decide our grade's not worth the hassle. I just wonder who else'll be willing to take us."

"But no one's planning to try and make him quit are they?" asked Lizzie, concern clouding her voice.

"You shouldn't believe even half of what Mrs Taylor says we've done," said Alexa, trying hard not to roll her eyes. Lizzie's crush was really kind of cute.

"And we only ever really turned on teachers if they went along with Mrs Taylor in blaming us for everything," said Sam.

"So as long as we can keep Alexa out of trouble, we should be able to keep Mr Knight," said Lizzie in an upbeat voice.

"I am keeping out of trouble," sulked Alexa.

It was true. Four weeks had passed and she had kept her word. There had never been a time she had gone so long without getting into some sort of trouble. No one could say anything while she stayed so quiet in class, though some of her teachers had started to threaten her with disciplinary action if she did not start participating more. It was an empty threat. They all preferred her silent.

Over those weeks, Alexa had still only caught rare glimpses of Mr Knight, but the reaction of her stomach was always the same. It was terrifying. She had never been so scared of her own mind before and was horrified when Lizzie noticed the way she looked at Mr Knight.

"Finally noticed, then?" smirked Lizzie.

"What?" said Alexa frantically.

"That Mr Knight's hot," Lizzie grinned. Alexa stammered a denial, but Lizzie only shrugged. "I sometimes wish I got in as much trouble as you. It'd be nice to have an excuse to be near him so often."

"What?" replied Alexa again, this time truly bewildered. "Trust me, it's not really that great."

Lizzie sighed and Alexa laughed, loving the way Lizzie was able to normalise her feelings for Mr Knight. It was a relief and she enjoyed the conversations she and Lizzie shared about Mr Knight. It made her feel almost normal.

"You've just got to wonder what he's like under those clothes though, don't you?" said Lizzie wistfully.

"No, I don't like to think of him that way," replied Alexa truthfully, but then remembered her day at the beach. "He does have a pretty good chest, actually."

"What? How do you know that?" cried Lizzie, sounding horrified that she had not previously shared that information with her.

"I, um, I –" Shit, thought Alexa frantically. "Oh, it was when he was taking his jumper off. His shirt went with it. I only got a glance."

Lizzie sighed dramatically and over the next few days made Alexa describe the sight in intimate detail. Alexa's descriptions were vague, but not because she could not give more detail. She could give too much detail. It scared her and what she wanted to be able to do more than anything was tell Lizzie that her feelings for Mr Knight felt like more than a crush and that she wished they would go away. It was an impossible revelation, so that truth stayed her secret as she was forced to engage in more trivial conversations with her friends.

"I can't believe it's going to be Christmas soon," said Sam as they all ate their lunches in the warm sunshine.

"I hate Christmas," replied Alexa instantly, hoping that profession would change the topic quickly. She hated the thought of another Christmas without Bethany.

"We don't celebrate it," added Ezra in an unconcerned voice.

"Well, I'm still looking forward to Christmas," said Sam tersely, before continuing in a more upbeat voice. "You can come to my place for Christmas, if you like. My grandparents would be stoked and you could help me cheer up Mel."

"I can't. I promised Hayley I'd be there for Christmas," replied Alexa glumly. Christmas sucked no matter what happy family she spent it with, but thought it might have been more relaxing at Sam's than at the Whites'. "What's wrong with Mel?" she asked quickly, thankful for the chance to change the topic of conversation.

"I don't know. She's been really up and down this year. Super happy, then really reclusive," answered Sam with genuine concern. "I thought she started to cheer up during term three, but became really down after that thing with Mr Marsh."

"What about now?" asked Alexa.

"Now, she barely talks to me. Her friends say she's perking up, but I can't see it. I just don't understand and she won't talk to me," said Sam, his voice tainted with anguished frustration. He and Mel had always been really close. "It reminds me of what you were like last year – you'd get down and distant and push me away, but then for no reason you would start to thaw and get back to yourself and be my friend again."

Sam's last comment felt like a slap in the face. Alexa's mind swirled and she hoped she was wrong, but she remembered Sam telling her that Mel had admired Clinton. Alexa had never thought Clinton had seen their relationship as long-term, just one that he wanted completely on his terms. If he had lured her into the relationship through Ms Carter, there was no reason to believe that he would not have tried it with another student – another scholarship student, alone, parentless.

Perhaps Mel was the reason Ms Carter was no longer giving her any trouble. Alexa did not know how the dynamics of Ms Carter's assaults would be altered by Clinton's absence, but Ms Carter had never needed reasons to torture scholarship students. She had needed restraining and the only person who had been capable of that was now gone.

The consequences of this situation for Mel were unclear, but Alexa knew she could not sit back and do nothing. It had been her decision not to implicate Ms Carter in Clinton's behaviour towards her, and it would be her fault if Sam's sister suffered now. The only problem was that Alexa was not sure that she had any chance of stopping Ms Carter, but for Sam she would try.

Alexa waited until ten minutes before curfew to leave her room and head down to Ms Carter's office. If Mel was not Sam's sister, she knew she would not be making this trip.

"Come in," called Ms Carter gruffly in response to Alexa's knock. Alexa took a deep breath and tried to calm her pounding heart as she entered. "Miss Samson, to what do I owe the displeasure."

"I know that you and Clinton teamed up on me to get me to go out with him and I know you were trying to do it to another student," said Alexa, trying to sound confident. "Clinton's gone now and you'll be too if you continue."

"What a brilliant imagination you have," said Ms Carter, smiling and rising from her desk. "I think you should be careful about the accusations you make. You may have gotten rid of Clinton, but your name's still mud in this school."

Ms Carter walked towards Alexa. Alexa stood her ground, but did not know what else to say or do. Pain suddenly speared down the left side of her back, bringing her to her knees. Ms Carter's hands groped her back and stomach. Alexa could not work out what was going on, but then suddenly realised that Ms Carter must be looking for a wire.

"Would you like to indulge me with whom this other student might be?" asked Ms Carter smugly, seemingly satisfied they were not being recorded.

"You know I'm talking about Melissa Michaels," spat Alexa. Ms Carter may not be afraid of her, but just in case, she was going to make it clear that Mel was off-limits.

"Miss Michaels, like you, is a student in need of discipline," replied Ms Carter with a sinister smile.

"You were setting her up for that bastard, just like you did me!"

"Now, now, let's not have that sort of language. I've never heard any other student refer to Clinton Marsh as a bastard. It seems that you brought out the worst in him, like you do in everyone you meet," sneered Ms Carter viciously.

Alexa was livid. She wanted to inflict so much pain on Ms Carter and it was taking all her energy and resolve to restrain herself.

"If you think that Miss Michaels is being hard done by, you are free to take her punishment yourself," said Ms Carter with a slight smile, as though she would enjoy such a thing.

"If you lay a hand on Mel, or me, or any other student, I'll have you thrown out of this school just like Clinton," spat Alexa, hoping that was true.

"With what proof? Like I said, your name is mud in this school. You can never touch me. I will be here when you name is a mere shadow of a memory."

Alexa did not answer, taking her chance to leave before the conversation became too hostile. It did no good to provoke Ms Carter. Alexa did not believe she had scared her, but hoped she had put her on guard. It was the best she could do. It was all she really wanted to do. If she never stepped foot into Ms Carter's room again it would be too soon.

However, there was one more person Alexa had to talk to. She needed to let Mel know that she was not alone, and now had some small measure of protection from Ms Carter. In a selfish way, Alexa was glad she was not the only one to suffer this way.

"Hey, Mel, can we talk a minute?" called Alexa as Mel walked towards the dining hall for breakfast the next morning.

"What?" replied Mel in a surly voice.

"Look, I know about Ms Carter and Mr Marsh," said Alexa quietly, pulling them to a quiet corner of the corridor.

"Know what about them?" asked Mel agitatedly, taking a step back. Her reaction was confirmation enough for Alexa.

"I know that Ms Carter assaulted you and that Clinton was there for you when you thought all was lost," Alexa said sympathetically. "Clinton's gone, but I spoke to Ms Carter last night and I don't think she'd be game enough to do anything now. I just need you to promise me that if she touches you that you come and see me straight away. Mr Knight will believe you – and me."

"I don't need your help. I have all the help I need," spat Mel, taking another step back.

"I know what you're going through. I know what you would've ended up going through," cried Alexa, grabbing Mel's hand to try and make her see reason.

"You have no idea what I'm going through. You ruined everything!" replied Mel, pulling her hand back.

"What are you talking about?"

"You! I told him he could never trust you – that you and Sam would never stop loving each other."

"What?" gasped Alexa, not quite believing her ears. "You were feeding his paranoia? Do you even realise what he did to me because of that?"

"Nothing more than you deserved," snarled Mel. "You never deserved Clinton. You never loved him. You could never've been as good to him as I would've."

"What are you talking about?" Alexa asked, confused by the turn in the conversation. "He raped me and tried to kill me. Don't you understand? He would have done the same to you."

"No! You're a liar. You're nothing – and that's how he treated you. He would've never hurt me, because I loved him. I never would've betrayed him."

Alexa was gutted. She wanted to scream at Mel that she was wrong, but such a big part of her could not help but believe what Mel was saying.

"Don't you understand? It was all a set up. Clinton, Ms Carter, it was all designed to get you into bed," Alexa cried, desperate for Mel to understand.

"No. Ms Carter's a bitch and everyone knows it. She hates us because we're scholarship students and we hate her, but Clinton's different. Clinton would never've hurt me. You were just – I was the one for him. I could've been happy if it wasn't for you. We could've been happy. He should've left you in the brothel. It's where you belong."

The world was falling out from under Alexa's feet. She could not believe what she was hearing. She picked up her bag and stormed back into her now empty bedroom. She wanted to scream. Mel's words stung her so badly. She tried to convince herself they were not true, but it was difficult. They fit every worthless image she had of herself.

In the distance, the bell for class rang. Alexa cursed loudly as she picked up her bag and slammed the door behind her. The anger and pain was almost blinding. She did not notice anyone as she walked towards her class and was halfway to chemistry before she realised that she had her first period free.

"Fuck!" Alexa yelled, scaring a few eighth-graders walking nearby.

"Miss Samson." Alexa's stomach churned uncomfortably. She did not want to see him now. "My office, thank you."

Alexa turned and followed Mr Knight into his office, dropping unhappily into her usual chair.

"Would you like to explain that display of profanity?" asked Mr Knight sternly.

"I just got my timetable mixed up," Alexa replied angrily.

"All that for a timetable mix up? What's wrong?" Mr Knight asked in a kind, compassionate voice.

It did not escape Alexa's notice that Mr Knight was asking what was wrong first before telling her off or accusing her of wrongdoing, but she did not want him to be nice to her. She needed to hate him the way she once had.

"Nothing. Can I go now?" Alexa muttered angrily.

"I thought we had gotten somewhere on the whole trust issue."

"Well you thought wrong," she replied contemptuously, grabbing her bag and walking to the door.

"I did not say that you could go," said Mr Knight, blocking the doorway before she could leave.

"Get the fuck out of my way."

"You will not speak to me like that. Now sit down," he said firmly, pointing back at her chair.

"No! Get out of my way," Alexa yelled, pulling hard on the door handle. Mr Knight pushed the door closed again and pulled her hand off the door. "Get your goddamned hands off me." Alexa pulled her arm out of his grip, slamming it hard into the door. "Fuck!"

"Are you all right?" Mr Knight asked kindly, only terrifying Alexa more.

"Stay the fuck away from me and keep you fucking hands off me, got it?" she spat, before grabbing the door handle with her other hand and rushing out the door, slamming it behind her.

Alexa expected Mr Knight to come out after her, but he must have gone to class. She ran back to her room, locked the bathroom door and grabbed her razor.

Alexa spent the day in an angry silence. She did not want to talk to anyone, especially Sam. She could never tell him what Mel had said. It would break his heart. She was also scared that if Sam knew all Mel did he would think as poorly of her as Mel did.

"I'm going to get a drink. Want to come?" Ezra asked Alexa quietly as they sat in the quadrangle at lunchtime.

Alexa shrugged and picked up her bag. They were about to walk off when they heard a large explosion that shook the ground beneath them. They were exchanging confused looks when Chad, Sam and Bianca came running into the quad.

"What was that?" asked Chad.

"I don't know, but whatever it is we're going to cop the blame, so we'd better find out," replied Alexa gruffly.

"Don't move!" called a voice from the second floor. The group looked up to see Mr Knight pointing down at them. "Stay where you are."

"What happened?" asked Sam.

"I don't know yet, but I don't want you three anywhere near it. Where are the others?"

"How are we supposed to know?" spat Alexa angrily.

"I think Nick and Al are in chemistry with Mr San," said Sam. "I don't know about Chris and Stacey. I think they usually eat near the oval."

"All right, stay there until I come back," said Mr Knight before rushing off.

Alexa threw her bag down and sat beside it, her mood not improved by this latest drama. Chad, Sam, Bianca and Ezra sat next to her, discussing what the explosion could have been. They watched as groups of students began to pour into quad with distressed looks on their faces.

"Hey, what happened," Sam asked a group of anxiously chattering students.

"A bomb or something went off in the middle of this group of year nines, I think."

"Were they hurt?" asked Bianca.

"I think so. A whole lot of students went over to help, but they had to clear everyone away cos there were more bombs or something. It's crazy."

Sam and Chad exchanged worried looks before looking over at Alexa who nodded slowly. They picked up their bags and began to walk towards the chemistry rooms.

"I thought I told you three to stay put." Mr Knight was walking towards them from the oval looking very pale. "You have to go to the Principal's office now. I will meet you all there in a minute. The others are already on their way."

"We didn't have anything to do with the bomb," snarled Alexa.

"How do you know it was a bomb? Doesn't matter. Just go to Mrs Taylor's office," ordered Mr Knight.

Nick and Alan were already sitting in Mrs Taylor's office, looking confused, when they arrived. Mr Knight arrived a few minutes later with Stacey and Chris in tow. Both were covered in blood and looked dazed.

"I want to get these two to the hospital as soon as possible," said Mr Knight firmly, as he guided the pair to empty seats.

"They will go when we find out why this seven thought bombs would be a fun thing to bring to school," said Mrs Taylor angrily.

"I don't think you can blame my students," cried Mr Knight. "Mr Olsen, Mr Michaels and Miss Samson were all in the quadrangle seconds after it happened. Mr Poulos and Mr Chan were having extra lessons from Mr San and were with him when the bomb went off, and Mr Appen and Miss Verloc were having lunch on the oval and went to help the injured students straight away."

"Just because they didn't set them off does not mean they didn't have a hand in making and distributing the bombs," said Mrs Taylor.

"You've got to be joking," yelled Alexa. Her temper had been at boiling point all day and this had pushed her too far. "Why the hell would we make bombs? Don't you get it? We haven't been responsible for half the things that've happened at this school, but you're too stupid to realise it. We don't make and distribute bombs."

"You can sit down, Miss. I have little interest in what you have to say," snarled Mrs Taylor.

"We have little fucking interest in what you have to say, but we have to sit and listen to your bullshit," Alexa retaliated hatefully.

"Miss Samson, sit down," warned Mr Knight.

"No! I want to know what evidence she has of our involvement," Alexa cried, throwing out her arm.

"The victims, for starters," said Mrs Taylor firmly. "One of them was Con Poulos."

"What?" exclaimed Mr Knight and Nick in unison.

"Is he okay?" asked Nick, his voice breaking.

"Not the victim you intended, hmm?" asked Mrs Taylor in a

sickly sweet voice.

"There were no intended victims. We didn't have anything to do with this. At what point are you going to get it through your thick head that we don't go around trying to cause trouble," continued Alexa, her anger ever rising.

"You can deny it all you like, but I know that you lot are responsible. It is hardly beyond Mr Poulos's and Mr Chan's capability to make bombs, given their prowess in chemistry," said Mrs Taylor with slightly flustered authority.

"It is hardly beyond my capacity to strangle you with my own bare hands, but it doesn't mean that I will," snapped Alexa.

"Miss Samson, sit down now!" yelled Mr Knight, but Alexa was not listening.

"You have two students that need medical attention and another whose brother's in hospital and yet you have us all in here, blaming us for something we didn't do," Alexa continued, sick of being blamed for things they had nothing to do with while their own suffering was ignored.

"You had better watch yourself, young Miss, if you want to keep your place in this school," warned Mrs Taylor.

"I don't give a fuck about staying in this school," Alexa cried angrily. "Throw us all out, that's what you've always wanted and then you can find out how wrong you are about us, how wrong you always were. You care more about the teachers and the school's goddamned reputation than you do about your students. If you knew anything about what happened in this school you wouldn't see us as the enemy."

"I know exactly what goes in this school," said Mrs Taylor sternly. "You just like putting the blame on everyone else for the trouble you get yourself in. It doesn't wash with me. I know exactly what kind of person you are."

"And I know exactly what kind of person you are, you –"

Chapter Twenty-One

"GET OUT!" CRIED Mr Knight, pulling Alexa by the arm and forcing her out of Mrs Taylor's office. "You wait for me outside my office. Now!"

The look on Mr Knight's face told Alexa not to challenge him. She turned and stormed towards his office, kicking everything she came across. When she reached the lounge outside his office, she collapsed on it and pressed her face into the cushion, almost hoping to suffocate and end the misery of her life.

"They called the police," said Chad, as he approached Mr Knight's office ten minutes later, the rest of the G7 close behind. "Mr Knight agreed and everything."

"I don't care about the police. I just want to see Con. Did you guys see him? Was he okay?" asked Nick anxiously, turning to Chris and Stacey.

"It was kinda hard to tell who was who," said Chris slowly.

Stacey burst into tears and Chris wrapped his arms around her to comfort her, a single tear falling from his eye.

"You're in a lot of trouble," Sam said quietly to Alexa.

"I don't care," Alexa replied flatly. "I don't want to stay in this shithole any more anyway."

"What happened today? What made you so angry?" asked Sam urgently.

Alexa could not answer and was spared more questions by Mr Knight's arrival. Mr Knight ushered them all into his office. Chris and Stacey sat in the two chairs while Nick paced anxiously. Alexa slumped down the wall and on to the floor. Sam and Alan sat on either side of her, Chad just in front. They felt like bodyguards, and she wondered who they thought they were protecting.

"I've organised for Mr San to take the three of you to the hospital," said Mr Knight, looking at Stacey, Chris and Nick. "He should be here any minute. Your parents are being contacted and except Chris's, will probably meet you at the hospital. You're bound to be released before your parents can make it, but I'm sure they'll visit you here."

"Are you coming to the hospital?" asked Stacey softly.

"I'm planning to. I hope to be able to bring Chris back to school tonight, depending on his parents' wishes. However, I have quite a job here to do. Mrs Taylor is still convinced the seven of you are involved. Hopefully, the police investigation will prove her wrong and she will accept it. Keeping Miss Samson in school may be a more difficult task."

"Don't bother," muttered Alexa, meeting Mr Knight's eyes. All traces of her crush were gone, hate and anger filling her instead.

A knock at the door signalled Mr San's arrival, at which point Stacey, Chris and Nick left without a word. Another knock at the door announced the arrival of the police. Alexa recognised the officers immediately and they recognised her.

"The Principal said the suspects were in here," said Constable Banks as he entered the room.

"They're over there," said Mr Knight, pointing to the four of them on the floor. "But Mrs Taylor is the only person who suspects them. None of them were near the scene. The only two that were, were some of the first to offer assistance."

"We still have to investigate all possible suspects. Some of the victims are in a very bad way. We might start with Alexa. The rest can wait outside," said Constable Banks.

Mr Knight looked uncomfortable with the plan, but nodded and instructed Chad, Sam and Alan to wait outside.

Alexa refused to move out of the corner to answer Constable Banks' questions and he seemed content to let her stay there. The questioning was short and to the point. Alexa really could not give them any information other than what had been given to her by others.

"So why does Mrs Taylor suspect your involvement?" asked Constable Banks.

"Because she's a paranoid bitch," replied Alexa harshly, looking up into Constable Banks' eyes to see his surprise. "Go ask her, then. Go and talk to her and see how much sense you get from her. Sometimes it's easier to create a lie than face the truth."

Constable Banks looked over at Mr Knight, but it was clear Mr Knight was not going to give his opinion in front of students. With a shake of the head and a sigh, Constable Banks walked over to the door and called the others in. He asked them all the same questions he had asked her, but their responses were much more bitter and sarcastic than hers had been.

234

"Cut the attitude," snapped Constable Banks. "And stop wasting my time. I just need to know what you know."

"We don't know anything," answered Alan passionately. "We can't tell you anything. We weren't there. We weren't involved. Ask as many questions as you like. The answers will still be the same."

Constable Banks dismissed the four of them with an agitated wave of his hand. Alexa stormed straight out and marched towards her room. Sam called after her, but she ignored him. She did not want to be near people today. What she wanted was to close her eyes and for the whole world besides her and Bethany to simply disappear.

***

"Alexa, wake up," said Bianca, shaking Alexa awake. Alexa flinched, her arm flinging up defensively as she scurried away from Bianca.

"What?" mumbled Alexa, realising what was happening and trying to turn away to go back to sleep. She did not even know what time it was or what day and she did not care to.

"You have to get up. Mr Knight wants to see you."

"Tell him I'm asleep," Alexa muttered.

"No, I think you need to go. It's about yesterday. You have to see Mrs Taylor as well," said Bianca anxiously.

Alexa rolled on to her back and looked up at the ceiling. Yesterday, for those few brief moments she had forgotten that day ever existed.

When Alexa arrived at Mr Knight's office all the boarding members of the G7 were already there. She sat down on the ground away from everyone. Mr Knight was seated at his desk, while the three boys, Chad, Sam and Chris, were sitting in chairs in front of his desk.

"You'll be happy to know that the police have all but cleared five of you of involvement in yesterday's incident," said Mr Knight with a heavy sigh, his face worn and anxious.

"What do you mean five of us?" asked Sam.

"They're still talking to Nick and Alan. It looks like Nick's brother, Con, made the pipe bombs himself and brought them into school. They had six with them yesterday. It's not clear what they were planning to do with them, but one went off while they were inspecting them."

"What does that have to do with Nick and Alan?" asked Chad.

"The bombs were all made, it seems, from material from Nick and Con's home. We all know that Nick and Alan are the ones capable of making bombs. The police just want to make sure they weren't involved."

"If Nick and Alan had made those bombs, none of them would've exploded accidentally," said Alexa from the floor.

"That may be true, but we have five kids in hospital. Three of them, including Con, are in very serious conditions," replied Mr Knight in a tightly controlled voice. "All possibilities have to be explored."

"So what happens now?" asked Chris.

"For you boys, nothing," answered Mr Knight with a grim smile. "I thought you'd want to know as soon as possible, so you didn't have these accusations hanging over you."

"What about Alexa?" asked Sam in a concerned voice.

"What about me?" Alexa snapped.

"Your outburst yesterday was completely unacceptable," said Mr Knight.

"So were the fucking accusations," Alexa replied in a low voice.

"I don't really care what you're accused of. You're going to have to learn to hold your tongue," replied Mr Knight firmly. "If you honestly think that swearing at Mrs Taylor and I is the best way to stay in school, you're severely mistaken."

"Well how about I save you the trouble of expelling me," Alexa snapped and stalked out of the office. It was not what she had wanted to do, but she did not want to be expelled. At least this way it was on her terms.

"What's going on?" asked Bianca, as Alexa stormed into their room and started gathered her belongings.

"I'm done."

"What? What do you mean? Did they expel you?"

"I'm not giving them the chance," Alexa replied, angrily throwing more belongings into her bag.

"You don't have to go. You don't know that they'll expel you," Bianca tried to reason, but Alexa did not care. "Where are you going to go?"

"I don't care. Anywhere's better than here," Alexa answered, as she zipped up her bags and threw them over her shoulder.

The click of the door behind her made Alexa's heart sink. When she looked up along the corridor she saw Mr Knight striding angrily towards her. She bowed her head and tried to walk straight past him.

"You had better be walking towards my office," said Mr Knight sternly.

"Why? So you can expel me? No thanks," Alexa replied angrily.

"You, come with me now."

"No, you cannot threaten me and you cannot touch me," Alexa responded, turning and glaring angrily at Mr Knight.

"Fine, you want to throw your future away. I have all the forms in my office. Let's go," snapped Mr Knight. "In fifteen minutes you can be walking out those gates."

Clouds of anger and confusion carried Alexa back to Mr Knight's office. Mr Knight waded through sheets of paper in his desk before tossing the appropriate forms at her and slamming himself into his chair.

"You are really something, you know that?" said Mr Knight, but Alexa did not look up from the forms she was angrily completing. "I spent two hours this morning arguing with Mrs Taylor to keep you in this school and it's not the first time I've had to do it. Do you want people to feel sorry for you, because I really don't any more. I've seen you work your way out of everything. Somehow, every time you're facing serious punishment, you manage to bring out a major tragedy so we can all feel sorry for you again."

"You'll soon be the year advisor Mrs Taylor wanted you to be. After me, Nick and Alan, there'll only be four left. Do you think you could take them all out in the year you have left?" Alexa snapped at Mr Knight.

"I just told you that I fought for two hours to keep you in school and I will do the same for Mr Poulos and Mr Chan," cried Mr Knight. "You want to be angry at the whole world. I have only ever tried to help you."

"I never asked for your help and I don't owe you anything," replied Alexa, her voice and body shaking.

"No, you don't owe me anything," said Mr Knight with calm sincerity. "But you do owe a lot to yourself. Let me help you with that."

"I don't want your help and I can do just fine without it."

"Without it you wouldn't be anywhere but in a coffin, and that's just where you'll end up when you walk out of here," snapped Mr Knight, slamming his hand on his desk. "Where do you think living and working on the streets in going to get you?"

"It will get me away from here!" Alexa cried fiercely, looking up at Mr Knight, her eyes stinging with angry tears. She quickly looked back down and signed the forms.

"I want five minutes of honesty from you," Mr Knight said seriously. Alexa looked up, but did not respond. "Straight answers, no sarcasm, no crap, just the truth. Do you really want to leave school?" Alexa looked past him and out the window. "I just want some honest answers, Miss Samson, then you're free to go. Do you really want to leave school?"

"Yes and no," she said after another long pause as she sat still looking out the window. "Would you want to stay if you were me?"

"Will you stay here at school?" asked Mr Knight in a softer voice.

"No, I think it's best I go," Alexa answered truthfully.

"Would you've said that if all this happened last week and not yesterday? What happened yesterday to make you so upset?"

Alexa could no longer keep the emotion from her face as it filled with anger and her heart pierced with sadness.

"What happened, Alexa? Let me help you," pleaded Mr Knight.

"You can't help me," she cried softly. "There's nothing to be done. I just want to go."

Alexa grabbed her bags off the floor and headed for the door.

"Stay, face the punishment. It won't be as bad as you imagine. Don't throw away your future because of one bad day," said Mr Knight, rising from his desk and approaching Alexa, though he did not touch her or block her exit. "I'll always be here. You have a whole lot of friends who care about you. Don't just walk away from it all."

"Why stay? Everyone thinks the same way about me, the same way Mrs Taylor does, and the way you do. I deserve everything that's happened to me," Alexa snapped, hunching her shoulders.

"You have made choices, some of them were not the best choices, and you have paid dearly," replied Mr Knight after a moment's hesitation. "But you do not deserve the treatment that you and the rest of the G7 receive from Mrs Taylor and other staff. You also didn't deserve any of the things Mr Marsh did to you."

"That's not true. If I was a better person, then none of these things would've happened."

"Well you are about to make another bad decision," said Mr

Knight determinedly. "Don't walk out that door. Stay. Come with me, apologise to Mrs Taylor and accept the punishment, then get on with your life. You only have a year left, don't throw it all away."

Alexa stood rooted to the spot. She did not know how to make this decision and in the end Mr Knight made it for her, taking her bags off her shoulder and guiding her towards Mrs Taylor's office.

"Come in," called Mrs Taylor. Mr Knight guided Alexa in the door. "Ah, Miss Samson. Come to apologise, I assume."

"Yes ma'am," said Alexa quietly, not looking at Mrs Taylor, who was smiling victoriously.

"Well, I am waiting."

"I just wanted to apologise for speaking to you so rudely yesterday," said Alexa flatly. "It was unacceptable and I'm sorry."

"That was better than I nothing, I suppose," said Mrs Taylor in an unimpressed voice. "Your behaviour is so often unacceptable and I suggest it stops this instant. I have already lost one very good teacher because of you, but Mr Knight argued very hard in support of you and your place in this school. I would like nothing more than to see you gone.

"However, since I have no proof of your involvement in yesterday's horrible incident, your scholarship remains. You will, however, serve afternoon detention every afternoon for the rest of the year – in Mr Knight's office."

Alexa noticed Mr Knight's surprise at her punishment and realised this was about penalising him as much as her. The stony look on his face as they returned to his office so she could collect her bags assured Alexa that she did not have to worry about him ever wanting to help her again. If he did not already hate her very existence, she was sure he would now, but she also knew that he could not be dreading this punishment more than she was.

The anxiety of being trapped in such close vicinity to Mr Knight made Alexa vomit several times over the weekend. Only her razor could calm her down enough to stop her from fleeing in fear of her punishment. Dread filled Alexa's body as the minutes ticked by and brought Monday afternoon ever closer.

Through every class on Monday, Alexa feared the sound of the next bell. When the final bell for the day rang, her heart pounded frantically. She was tempted to run from the school and never look back, but she somehow forced her feet towards Mr Knight's office. She entered without knocking and refused to look at Mr Knight.

"Close the door behind you," said Mr Knight firmly. "I borrowed a fold up desk so you can do your homework. No point wasting your time here."

Alexa looked over and saw a desk folded up against the wall. She set the desk up and pulled out her maths textbook.

"Can I get some water?" she asked after fifteen minutes.

Mr Knight brought her a cup of water from the adjoining room. She accepted it and did not speak again until detention was over.

Closing her bedroom door behind her, Alexa sighed heavily. She had survived. She wanted to keep hating Mr Knight, but while he did not pressure her in any way, her anger could only last so long. Hating him was so draining when liking him came much more easily. However, Alexa was determined to squash all kind feelings she had for Mr Knight. She would feel nothing – neither hate nor like. Despite her desire to watch him and talk to him, she would resist. She would ignore him.

Alexa was determined that if could ignore Mr Knight for one afternoon, she could ignore him for another twenty-four. It would have been easier to believe such a feat was possible if her stomach did not squiggle with the very thought of seeing him again tomorrow.

"Well, well, well. Haven't we found a nice new way to be with another teacher? Detention every afternoon."

Alexa turned as she headed for dinner to see Mel leaving her bedroom. There was no one else around and Alexa wondered why Mel was not up in the dining hall already.

"So is Mr Knight paying you like your other clients, or do you give it away for free to all teachers?" asked Mel spitefully. Alexa turned back around and headed back towards her room. "How much sympathy do you think you would've gotten if everyone knew what I knew?" hissed Mel, flinging Alexa around to face her. "You set Clinton up just to keep your filthy secret. You can trust me. It won't be a secret much longer."

Alexa pulled free and dashed into her room, slamming the door behind her. She marched towards the bathroom and locked the door. Sitting on the cold tiled floor, she pulled out her razor and slashed violently at her arm. They were not the precise cuts that she usually made. She hacked at her flesh time and time again to try and disperse the fear and anger that was building inside her.

Alexa hated Clinton for what he had done to her – and to Mel. She desperately wanted to hate Mel for the things she had said, but mainly she hated herself for the truths that lay in what Mel said.

"Miss Samson, are you in there," called Mr Knight.

Alexa looked down at her bloody arm. She quickly threw her razor blade back into the cupboard and wiped her arm of blood. There was nothing in the bathroom to cover her arm, so she splashed water on the cuts, but they continued to bleed.

"I'm just in the bathroom," Alexa called, hoping to stall for more time and keep Mr Knight from entering her bedroom.

"Open the door please, Miss Samson," called Mr Knight firmly.

"Yep, one minute," replied Alexa, trying to sound calm and unflustered. She rushed to her bed and found a jumper, pulling it over her head despite the warm weather. "What's up?" she asked casually when she opened the door.

"Why aren't you at dinner?" asked Mr Knight sternly.

"Oh, I'm not really hungry," Alexa replied dismissively, trying to close the door again, but Mr Knight held his hand against the door to stop her.

"Cold?" asked Mr Knight, looking down at the jumper. Alexa glanced down at her arms and shrugged defiantly. "Is there anything you want to talk about?" he asked more kindly.

"I'm fine," Alexa replied through clenched teeth.

"You don't look fine," continued Mr Knight in a concerned voice, refusing to let this situation go like other teachers would have. "You look like you've been crying."

"I'm fine," Alexa repeated more forcefully.

"All right, then head up to dinner before you miss it," said Mr Knight, pushing her bedroom door fully open and gesturing for her to leave.

"I said I'm not hungry."

She crossed her arms and stood her ground on the bedroom-side of the doorway. It no longer felt so impossible to hate Mr Knight.

"I know what you said, but I don't believe you, so head up to dinner."

Mr Knight looked unprepared to back down. He continued to hold the bedroom door open with one arm as the other directed her to the dining hall. Alexa glared as she stalked deliberately past him, never turning to see if he was behind her. If he spoke too kindly to her any longer she was afraid she would be tempted to accept his comfort.

In an unwanted development, Tuesday's detention started

straight after lunch and continued through until six-thirty when dinner was served. Five hours. Five hours that Alexa had to force herself silently through. It was made easier by the mostly-silent state she spent the rest of her time. However, there was one person who would not accept her silence on the issue of her detention. Lizzie wanted details, and was mortified by how little Alexa had taken advantage of the time she had been spending with their mutual crush.

"You don't talk?" asked Lizzie incredulously. "You've been going to detention for over a week with a teacher you like and you haven't spoken to him?"

"I don't know, I haven't really thought of him that way lately," murmured Alexa. "I've generally been too pissed off to care. I think my crush is over."

It was mostly true. Alexa was terrified that if she tried to be nice, that Mr Knight would reciprocate and her feelings would return. It was safer to stay angry and avoid any chances for Mr Knight to be nice to her.

"I still think you could try saying hi," said Lizzie, looking like she was holding back more detailed instructions about what Alexa should do. "It couldn't hurt. I mean, I'd be saying more than hi if I was you."

"No you wouldn't," replied Alexa seriously. "People are probably already thinking that Mr Knight and me are on together. Still, it's better than some of the other rumours people could be spreading."

Alexa had been worried all week that Mel would spread the news of her prostitution in the city. Thankfully, it seemed to have been a baseless threat. Rumours spread fast at Redgrove and Alexa was sure that if Mel had said anything she would have heard it by now.

Despite her talk with Lizzie, Alexa was still not looking forward to her detention. Mr Knight was sitting behind his desk marking papers when she entered his office. She set up her desk in silence, her plans to try speaking – even just to say hello – withering in her throat.

"I want you to take your jacket off," said Mr Knight suddenly, forcing Alexa's eyes up from her books, her heart racing.

"Excuse me?" she stammered.

"Take your jacket off, Miss Samson," repeated Mr Knight firmly. "It's almost thirty degrees. There's no need for you to be wearing a jacket."

"What I wear is none of your business."

"Right now it is. Take your jacket off."

"No," Alexa said stubbornly, not prepared to concede defeat on this.

Alexa knew Mr Knight would not understand what she did or why. He would want to fix her, deluded by the belief that he could make her life bearable. No matter what he said, Alexa was determined not to comply. He would have to rip her jacket off her himself and she hoped that was one line he was not prepared to cross.

"You take it off now or we go to Mrs Taylor's office," threatened Mr Knight.

"You can't do this. What I wear is my choice."

"You do have a choice. You can deal with this with me or we go to Mrs Taylor's office and we deal with it there. Or we can go back to the hospital and deal with it there."

"That's blackmail," Alexa gasped.

"You would know," replied Mr Knight pointedly. "And I don't really care what it is. There is a situation here that needs to be dealt with. How it's dealt with is completely up to you. It's your choice. Me. Mrs Taylor. Hospital."

Alexa's heart pounded. Mr Knight did not look like he was bluffing, and Alexa hated that he was turning it back on her. She detested every one of his options. She did not want to go back to the hospital, nor did she want to see Mrs Taylor, so reluctantly pulled her cardigan off. Her right arm was soft and pale, but Mr Knight's eyes were on her other arm. Slowly, Alexa pulled the cardigan off completely to reveal a red arm with the barest patches of white. Fresh, deliberate cuts were mixed with the older, frenzied slashing of the previous Monday night.

"Happy?" she asked, picking up her pen and looking back down at her homework.

"No, Alexa, the sight of your arm torn up does not make me happy," replied Mr Knight, his voice trembling slightly. "Why would you do this to yourself? This is no way of coping."

"You're right. I should just make my way down to the nearest bar and drink til the barman refuses me service," Alexa retorted maliciously.

"That's not fair," murmured Mr Knight as though she had truly wounded him, but right then she did not care if she did or not. She just wanted to be left alone and not be continually tortured by society's double-standards.

"How?" Alexa asked seriously. "Why's it okay for you to get blind drunk, but not for me to cope my own way. Mine is far less destructive."

"Less destructive? Your arm is covered in cuts."

"These cuts will heal and they'll heal more completely than your liver."

"What you're doing is self-mutilation," cried Mr Knight. "You're not in control of yourself."

"I have total control. This is ultimate control."

"Control? How is that control? Something goes wrong and you slash your arms to ribbons. That is not control."

"It's no worse than getting drunk or taking drugs and it's my life," Alexa said firmly, looking back down at her book, hoping the conversation was now over.

"I don't think drinking or taking drugs are good coping methods either," said Mr Knight in a softer voice, as though conceding one point. "But slashing your arm is no means of control."

"Really, have you tried?" Alexa retorted. Mr Knight shook his head in horror. "Then how can you say it's not controlled?"

"Explain it then."

"Because physical pain means nothing to me," Alexa said, hoping there was a slim chance Mr Knight would accept her reasoning. "It's a simple transfer of pain. If I can't handle the emotional pain I convert it to physical pain. The more it hurts the more I have to cut."

"There are ways of dealing with pain that mean you would never have to cut yourself," replied Mr Knight after being momentarily stunned into silence.

"Like what?" Alexa asked sceptically.

"Talking."

"I don't need to talk. I don't care what you think. This is my life, my body. These cuts will heal. There is no problem."

It was a statement Alexa hoped Mr Knight would heed. She did not need more trouble than she was already in. She did not want to talk about her life to people who had no interest in finding solutions that actually addressed her situation.

Mr Knight seemed determined to pay no attention to her wishes. In stony defiance of her demands, he walked around his desk and crouched in front of her, pulling her red arm straight.

"This is a problem," said Mr Knight feelingly, his voice shaking slightly. "You're just inches away from your wrist. What happens when you have a really bad day? Will you just slide that razor down a little and slice across your wrist?"

"And what does that matter to you?" Alexa questioned coolly. "What do you care if I live or die?"

"Of course it matters to me," cried Mr Knight. "You mean everything to me."

Chapter Twenty-Two

ALEXA LOOKED UP at Mr Knight's startled face. He released her arm and walked straight out of the office. She buried her head in her hands, her whole body shaking as she waited for Mr Knight to barge back in and demand she give him what he desired. She sat and waited, glued by fear to her seat, but Mr Knight did not return.

When the clock hit six-fifteen, Alexa decided she could leave without anyone questioning why she was not in detention. She was too distracted to notice the looks her roommates were giving her as she walked into her room and dashed to her bed, pulling the curtains around it. Her whole body shook as she rocked back and forth, waiting for the moment Mr Knight would come to claim her.

At six-thirty they all walked to the dining hall. Alexa did not care to eat, but was too scared to remain alone in her room. It was not unusual for her to remain in stubborn silence, so no one questioned her mood as she walked behind Lizzie and Bianca, oblivious to the pointing and talking that was going on around her. Sam and Chad arrived a few minutes later looking as worried as Lizzie and Bianca.

"How was detention?" asked Sam.

"What? Oh, fine," Alexa replied in a distracted voice, putting her head back down. She did not want to talk about Mr Knight, but it seemed everyone else did.

"How are things with Mr Knight?" asked Chad more pointedly.

"What do you mean?" asked Alexa, looking up to see Sam, Chad, Bianca and Lizzie all staring at her with worried faces. "What's wrong?"

"There isn't anything going on between you two is there?" asked Sam cautiously.

Alexa wondered how they could have found out about Mr Knight's confession. She had not told anyone and doubted he would have.

"No, of course not," she said defensively.

"I guess that means you haven't heard what all the students are saying, then?" said Bianca softly.

Alexa's heart sank. Mel must have told people about her prostitution as she had threatened to.

"What are they saying?" Alexa asked quietly.

"That you and Mr Knight are on together. That you offer yourself to any teacher willing to pay," said Sam as gently as possible.

Alexa dropped her head on the table as Bianca put her arm around her shoulders. Sam moved to sit in front of Alexa and held her hands gently. Alexa could not take it. It was horrible knowing that Sam was only still her friend because he did not know the truth about her. She rushed towards the door, not willing to be there when he did find out. Halfway there she looked up slightly to see Mel smiling hideously in front of her.

"I told you that you'd pay for the things you've done," said Mel viciously.

Alexa could not speak. She hated that Mel was Sam's sister. All she could do was stand there and wait for Mel to stand aside. Physically forcing Mel out of her way would not help her situation.

"You okay?" asked Sam, taking Alexa by the hand.

"She's fine. She's just getting her just desserts," said Mel.

"What are you talking about? Alexa doesn't deserve this," said Sam, stunned by Mel's taunts. "She's done nothing wrong."

"When are you going to stop sticking by her? Look at the way she uses you. She uses everybody and twists everything to get what she wants," argued Mel passionately.

Sam stared at Mel in disbelief, as Alexa just stood there, pale and shaking. She could not bring herself to defend herself to Sam against Mel.

"Come on, let's go," said Sam, pulling Alexa by the hand. "I'll talk to you later," he hissed at Mel.

They walked out on to the oval. It was a mild night, but Alexa still shivered in Sam's arms as he held her close, tears slipping continuously down her cheeks. Sam wanted to stay with her and comfort her, but she felt so unworthy of his kindness.

Rushing back to her dormitory, Alexa pulled the curtains around her bed and ignored everyone who came to check on her. She was thankful when the lights finally went out, but sleep would not find her. All she could do was lay there, listening as Mel's hateful words and the sniggers of students filled her ears in the blackened silence. When the taunting darkness suddenly reached out and grabbed her, and it took all her restraint not to scream.

"Shhh," whispered someone next to her, restraining her gently as she tried to scurry away. "It's okay. It's just me."

"Sam, what as you doing?" Alexa asked in a whisper as her heart settled back into its normal rhythm.

"I just want to be with you," replied Sam, as he slipped between the sheets and snuggled in next to her. "Let me stay."

Alexa managed to smile just slightly. Sam knew very well that she would never kick him out of her bed. She needed to be with him too. Shuffling over so Sam could lie comfortably in the bed, Alexa snuggled back into him and buried her head in the crook of his neck. Sam's arms wrapped around her body as he kissed her on the forehead and stroked her hair gently until she finally fell asleep.

***

Marcus sat at his desk waiting for Alexa to arrive. His hands kept fidgeting as his heart pounded and his stomach churned. He did not understand how he had let this happen. He had always promised himself that, no matter what, he would never allow Alexa to find out that he had feelings for her. Now she knew and rumours were rife among the students and staff that she had been making moves on him. Worse still, they were insinuating that Alexa was prostituting herself for him. It made him feel sicker than he already did.

Throughout the day Marcus had been defending Alexa – and himself – against the rumours. They were just as discrediting to him, but he did not feel like he deserved defending, not after what he said to Alexa yesterday. That was completely unforgiveable, and part of him no longer cared if she turned him in. It was what he deserved at this point.

A knock on the door broke his thoughts and Alexa entered his office without waiting for his response. She closed the door behind her but did not move further in to the room, keeping a firm grasp on the door handle. Marcus looked up at her, feeling more wretched than he ever had before.

"Alexa, I just want to apologise –"

"I want to ask you something and I want you to answer honestly," Alexa said, cutting him off. Marcus was not sure what she would ask, but knew that with everything she was going through the truth was the least he could give her. "That night – in the park on the way to my foster parents' – you said that there was someone else that you wanted, but couldn't have. Were you talking about me?"

"Yes," Marcus replied softly, nodding.

Alexa gripped the door handle harder as he slowly raised his head to look into her frightened eyes.

"What are you going to do with me?" Alexa asked, her voice shaking.

"Nothing," replied Marcus breathlessly. "Alexa, I will never, ever lay a hand on you. I don't want that. What I said was wrong. I do care about you – very much – but I don't want a relationship with you."

Alexa relaxed her grip on the door handle, but did not move.

"Promise?"

"Alexa, I swear. I will never act inappropriately towards you," Marcus said with the firmest sincerity. "The last thing in the world I want to do is hurt you. Nothing will ever happen between us – ever, I swear. I don't want that. I don't *want* to be with you. Please believe me."

Alexa nodded her head once and sat in the chair in front of his desk.

"I am so sorry, Alexa," said Marcus, desperate for her to understand how horrible he felt about this situation. Part of him wanted to try and explain how he felt, how much he liked her, just not in that way, but knew better than to go down that path. The truth was that he had no idea how to describe his feelings for her. "This never should have happened."

"It doesn't matter. The rumours would still be there, even if you didn't say anything," replied Alexa in a sad, defeated voice.

"You heard them too?" sighed Marcus heavily.

"Who hasn't?"

"They'll pass in time. People will find other things to talk about, especially with Nick and Alan returning to school," he said, hoping it was true.

"Are they in trouble?" asked Alexa, looking up briefly, before quickly averting her gaze.

"No, the police have cleared them of all involvement," Marcus answered flatly. Alexa and the G7 had not deserved that situation either. He could still not understand why he had had to fight so hard for all their places in the school when there had never been any evidence of their involvement. "It became clear fairly quickly that Con was responsible for making the bombs."

"I don't think their return will stop the rumours," sighed Alexa, returning Marcus's thoughts to the real problem. Him.

"I wish there was something I could do to help you," he choked, just managing to hold back the guilty sob in his chest.

Alexa smiled weakly up at him. It was a very generous gesture, but not one that he could reciprocate. He had never felt like smiling less than he did right now.

"Do you have something to drink?" asked Alexa softly, again surprising him.

Alexa normally responded to him with sarcasm or silence. Yet today, after he had betrayed her trust in the worst possible way, she was being responsive in a kind and gentle manner. It only made him more in awe of her.

"How about hot chocolate?"

Alexa nodded slightly and Marcus quickly made her the drink. It was not much, but he felt better doing something nice for her.

"You did believe me when I said that I wouldn't do anything to you, didn't you?" he asked, sitting back down at his desk.

Marcus knew he had no right to request such reassurance from Alexa, but the words had forced themselves out like so many others that should have stayed forever silent.

"I want to," replied Alexa weakly. Marcus dropped his head, but when he tried to speak she cut him off. "I don't distrust you. It's just that I don't trust most people. I'm just scared – after Clinton and all."

Marcus nodded. Of course she compared him to Clinton Marsh.

"Can I ask you something?" Marcus queried tentatively. Alexa shrugged her shoulders, suddenly looking fearful. "It was kind of forgotten in all the drama of what happened, but I wanted to know. When you went to see Clinton Marsh that afternoon, you talked about a baby. And, well, is it true? Was there a baby?" Alexa did not answer, but nodded slowly, her eyes on her hot chocolate. "What happened?"

"I tried to blackmail him," replied Alexa, her voice barely above a whisper. "I wanted money to look after the baby in return for keeping the paternity a secret. Clinton didn't take it too well and so he punched me, then kicked me to be sure."

"When?" asked Marcus. He was almost certain he already knew the answer, but he wanted to hear it from Alexa. He wanted to torture himself with the full extent of his depressing failures.

"The last day of term one."

"The day you tried to kill yourself," he gasped, his hand over his mouth as if to stop the words escaping. "Why didn't you tell me?"

"I didn't know you. I'd already gotten myself in enough trouble. I couldn't risk you being like him," replied Alexa softly.

Marcus did not reply. He felt ill. Alexa finished her drink then set up her desk and pulled out her maths books. Marcus could only look down at his desk and stare blankly at the assignments before him.

"I don't think you're like Clinton," said Alexa suddenly, looking up from her books.

Marcus met her eyes. She was smiling lightly. There was a tiny glint in her eye he had never seen before. He felt his heart warm instantly at Alexa's words and her smile. Alexa smiled again before returning to her work. Marcus watched her surreptitiously for a few minutes, but she did not look back up at him.

Alexa stayed as silent as she usually was in his company, yet it was somehow different. It was not hostile. It was so pleasant that it even started to ease his swirling guilt and allow him to concentrate on his work. They worked in silence until six-thirty when Alexa packed up her books and headed to the door.

"You still promise, right?" Alexa asked, a hint of fear creeping back into her eyes.

"On my life," Marcus nodded sincerely.

Alexa smiled just slightly and left. It did not matter that he had had to reassure her. The important thing was that for a short time she had believed him – trusted him. He would reassure her as many times as he had to, while ensuring he never came close to breaking his promise, until she could believe forever that nothing would ever happen between them.

***

As Mr Knight had predicted, Nick and Alan's return to school replaced Alexa as the main talking point among the students, but they brought with them uncomfortable news. Con was permanently blinded. As much as the G7 members despised being blamed for the bombs, they thought Con's punishment more than severe.

However, Alexa knew this news would not steal her limelight for long. Despite that, she found herself almost looking forward to the end of each day and to her detentions with Mr Knight. It was a change Lizzie was particularly happy with. It made Lizzie feel vindicated in her original advice to talk to Mr Knight, but that was something Alexa still had not yet really done.

"Good afternoon, Miss Samson," said Mr Knight warmly, once she had finished unpacking her schoolbooks and sat down at her fold-up desk.

"Hi, Sir," Alexa replied with a sweet and genuine smile. Then she put her head down and stayed silent.

After Mr Knight's promise that he would never touch her, Alexa found her heart inadvertently opening to him. That one promise allowed her to feel safe in her affections for him, because she knew nothing would ever happen between them. She could love Mr Knight as much as she wanted and it would hurt nobody. She could love him forever if she wanted and it would never be taken away from her, because they would never be together.

However, that would only be true while she remained silent. If she spoke to Mr Knight, she risked him finding out something that would take away his inexplicable attraction to her. It would also risk her finding out something bad about him.

Loving Mr Knight and allowing herself to believe that there was true kindness and goodness in the world was all Alexa really wanted. She did not want to be with Mr Knight either. The thought of his hands on her made her insides quiver, but she did like that he was capable of liking her.

So for three hours they worked in silence. At the end of it, Mr Knight wished her a good night, offering her a tender smile with it. Alexa reciprocated, walking from detention in another world. The walls no longer felt so dark and encasing, they held a warmth in them. They held Mr Knight – Marcus – within them.

Sitting down in the dining hall, Alexa did not notice the bemused looks of Bianca or Chad or the brooding mood Sam was in as she played absently with her food. She was nowhere but with Marcus, and it was a nice place to be.

"Come for a walk with me?" asked Sam, as they finished their dinners.

"Nah, I'm okay. I might just head to bed get an early night," Alexa replied. She wanted time alone with her feelings.

"Please. I need to talk," urged Sam.

"Okay," smiled Alexa, looping her arm into Sam's as he led her out of the dining hall. She would do anything for Sam if he needed her to.

They strolled in silence, but Alexa did not care. Perhaps Sam just wanted some company, and she could understand that. It was nice just being with him.

"What's going on with you and Mr Knight?" asked Sam suddenly when they reached the empty oval. There was anger and deep resentment in his voice, pulling Alexa quickly out of her fantasy world.

"Nothing … I …"

"There are all these rumours and we all take your side, back you up and then it turns out they're true. So don't lie to me any more," snapped Sam. "What's going on with Mr Knight?"

"The rumours are true, is that what you think?" asked Alexa, cut deeply. Her heightened emotions from earlier in the night made the crash down that much harder. "So you think I'm prostituting myself out to all the teachers? What? You think Mr Knight was the highest bidder?"

Alexa turned and walked away, a large lump obstructing her throat. Her lungs started to push against her ribcage, but she resisted to the urge to sob. She would block this pain, ignore it, shut it down and never feel again.

"Alexa, no," cried Sam, running and pulling her back by the hand. "I'm not talking about that. I was talking about the rumour that you and Mr Knight were on together. God, Alexa, when did this happen."

"Never. Nothing's happened. We're not on together," Alexa gasped, shaking her head. She could defend herself against that allegation.

"Don't lie. I know you and I know something's going on," continued Sam, his grip on her hand more restraining than comforting.

"It's not what you think. Nothing's happening. I just … I …"

"You what?"

"I … I think I love him."

Alexa stopped dead. She could not believe what she had just said, but she could not take it back either. Sam stood in shock, clearly hoping that she would laugh and say that it was all a joke, but she did not move.

"No, Alexa, no," said Sam, placing a gentle hand on her face and forcing her eyes to meet his. "Please, Alexa, don't do this."

"I'm not doing anything," she said, her voice shaking. "I don't want to feel this way. I don't want this."

"Make it stop, then," pleaded Sam desperately.

"I can't."

"You did with me."

"No, I didn't. I could never stop loving you. I love you as much today as I did when we were going out, just not in the same way."

"Then do the same thing again with him," cried Sam, throwing his arm out towards Mr Knight's office. "Please don't do this, Alexa, please. I can't watch you go through that again."

"I'm not going to do anything. I could never do that again," Alexa replied earnestly, still shaking her head. "I don't want to be with Mr Knight, I don't, but I can't help how I feel."

"What about him? What does he want? Does he love you too?" asked Sam in a harsh, sceptical voice.

"I don't know," Alexa lied. "He cares, we know that and probably more than he should, but he has a job, a fiancée. He's not going to throw it all away for me. Nothing will happen, I promise. I won't make that mistake again."

"I just don't want you hurt. I don't want to lose you," said Sam, pulling her into a crushing embrace.

Alexa wrapped her arms around Sam and cried softly into his neck, while fearful tears fell slowly down his face as he stroked her long soft hair.

"Please, Alexa, I'm begging. Make this stop," said Sam, his voice shaking as he hugged her tighter.

"I can't," she replied truthfully. "I need to – I just want to feel – it's not real, but I need to pretend it could be. Please, Sam, don't take this from me."

Sam sighed heavily, heaving slightly as his embrace loosened and his hands began to stroke her arms and hair. When he finally released her, he quickly wiped the tears from his face and they slumped down together on the oval.

Alexa was glad that Sam knew. She was glad that she would not have to hide from him and glad that he cared so much.

"I don't care how much you like him, if he ever touches you, I will kill him," said Sam in a determined growl. "I'm not going to let anyone hurt you."

"I will never stop loving you, you know that? No matter what happens in this world, I will never stop loving you. You'll always be my first love. I wish I could've given you what you deserved," Alexa said sadly.

"We were kids, we're not much older now, but we couldn't

expect it to last forever. It would have been nice though, but ..."

"I know."

And she did. Barely a day passed that Alexa did not wish that she could recall the feelings she once had for Sam. He was her soul mate and she had destroyed their love. Now she was hurting him more with every choice she made.

Alexa wished with all her heart that she could make her feelings for Mr Knight go away, but every afternoon her heart stammered in anticipation of seeing him again. The prospect of spending those hours of blessed silence in his company was just too great to resist. It gave her one tiny thing to look forward to in her days full of bleakness.

However, as much as Alexa wished it could, the silence was not able to last forever. As the end of the term approached, there was simply not enough work to fill all the hours. She tried to pretend that she was doing work, but she could not help but sneak looks at Mr Knight. Whenever he saw her watching him, he stopped working and gazed up at her. Sometimes he would talk. Other times he would just smile.

Alexa hated it when Mr Knight asked her questions. She hated that there was a part of her that wanted to answer him, because she knew there were so many parts of her life that she did not want him to see – that he would not want to see.

"How is your first term of year twelve work going?" asked Mr Knight, starting their conversation innocently enough on Monday afternoon of the last week of the school year.

"Okay," Alexa replied, trying to decide how much to say. "I still feel lost from all the work I missed. I hate feeling lost."

"How often do you feel lost?"

"All the time when I'm here," she shrugged.

"What about when you run away?" Mr Knight asked curiously.

"No, I feel found then," Alexa replied, trying not to smile. Mr Knight would never understand how little she belonged to this world, or how much more comfortable she felt on the streets than most of the students felt at Redgrove. "I don't run away without a reason. So when I'm gone there's always a purpose," she said, trying to explain in a way he might understand.

"What about last time, when you ..." said Mr Knight, though he could not bring himself to actually ask the question.

Alexa looked up and examined Mr Knight's face. She had to see the look on it when he spoke about her time as a prostitute. There was no disgust or revulsion, just deep sadness, which intrigued her. That time in the city was when she had felt like she needed his pity least.

"You see me differently because of what I did, don't you?" she asked, though she was not sure why. This was the reason she did not want to talk to Mr Knight. It did neither of them any good to expose truths that were better left unsaid.

"I think it would be a lie to say no," answered Mr Knight slowly.

Alexa was surprised by his honesty. She had expected him to make up some pathetic lie to try and spare her feelings.

"Does it make you sick?" asked Alexa, her curiosity piqued by his honesty.

"It makes me sad. I couldn't imagine – I think you're too young to have ever seen or experienced such things and I'm so sorry that you felt you had to," answered Mr Knight solemnly.

"It wouldn't have been forever and if it'd gotten Bethy off drugs I wouldn't have regretted it for a second," Alexa replied straightforwardly. It was nice that he was not revolted by her, but doubted he understood just how empowered that job – and the money it supplied – had made her.

"Is there anything you wouldn't do for your sister?" asked Mr Knight seriously.

"Yes," Alexa answered honestly. "But not much."

***

Marcus could not help but wonder what the few things were that Alexa would not do for her sister, because he had the feeling she would even die for her. It was a level of devotion he could only admire, despite knowing the actions it inspired were often misguided at best. However, the more Marcus had tried to see things from Alexa's point of view over the last few months, the better he could comprehend the siege mentality she continually locked herself into.

Over the next few days Marcus tried constantly to understand Alexa more completely. He asked her about her family and her past. He wanted to understand what she had been through. Reading her file was one thing, but hearing it from her, even just bits of information, gave much greater insight into her life.

Marcus wanted to understand how Alexa had not just survived an upbringing like hers, but also pushed through to become such an amazing person. Despite her anger and attitude, he was realising that underneath that was a beautiful and tender heart. The way she gave herself to those she loved was truly incredible

Alexa refused to respond to any of his questions. Whenever he shifted the conversation away from the mundane, she shut it down immediately. If he pushed too hard, she clammed up completely and refused to speak again. She was stubborn enough that even returning to normal conversation could not coax her out of her silence. It was an impressive level of obstinacy that Marcus knew he would never be able to match.

Marcus knew he should have been satisfied chatting to Alexa about routine, irrelevant matters. Up until this point she had barely even spoken civilly to him, and it was clear that she did not want to talk about those things. However, the one concession Alexa granted him when his questions crossed the line was a mischievous smile that made his stomach twist upon itself. It made him occasionally ponder if it was her smile that kept him talking when she wanted him to be silent, because he knew he would ask a thousand unwanted questions just to see that smile again.

Chapter Twenty-Three

ALEXA WOKE ON Friday morning with a strange sense of release. She had made it. One more day and the school year was over. She had survived – just. It seemed such a long time ago that she had left the Christies' and wandered nonchalantly into the dining hall. So much had happened this year, yet somehow everything was the same. Bethany was back on the streets and she was involved with a teacher.

Thinking back, Alexa tried to remember what deluded state of hope she had managed to get herself into on this day last year. But she had not been hopeful last year. She had been barely clinging on, scared that she would not be able to spend enough time with Bethany to keep her hopes up, worried about returning to the Whites', yet wondrous that they had even invited her back and had organised work for her during the holidays.

It seemed strange that she could even be hopeful now given all that had happened since then, but she was. If she could survive a year like this one, then perhaps she would be able survive the coming one. She did not even have to make it a whole year. Eleven months. Eleven months and she would have finished her exams, turned eighteen and collected their lottery win. She would be an adult and the law would finally be on her side.

The dining hall sounded like the student population had doubled overnight as everyone chatted animatedly about their holiday plans. There was not a tired set of eyes in sight. In under eight hours they would all be free.

The destinations of Redgrove's students were far flung and very few of the students saw each other outside of school; the boarding students all saw enough of each other in school. Even Chad, Ezra and Alexa, who all lived in the city, never caught up during the holidays. Their lives outside of Redgrove were all very separate. Sam and Lizzie were returning to their country homes, and Bianca was joining her parents in Europe where her father worked as a pilot, so Alexa did not expect to see any of them until school returned.

It made Alexa a little reminiscent for the holidays where she and Bethany had run away to Sam's place and hidden out with him for as long as they could. His grandparents had always welcomed them, no matter what time they had arrived or in what state. When Alexa had arrived alone, her state was almost always guaranteed to be worse than if she had Bethany in tow. Shaking her head, Alexa pushed those thoughts away. It did no good to dwell on bad memories.

"Hey, Alexa, Gran and Pop asked if you wanted to come out for some of the holidays," said Sam loudly across the table as soon as she sat down with her toast.

"Really?" asked Alexa, thinking Sam had to be psychic. "Ah, crap, I don't know if I can. Pam and Karl have organised some work for me. I'm not sure if I can ask for time off."

"I'm going," smiled Chad. "Last week of the holidays. Bianca's going to try and come as well."

Bianca rolled her eyes and nodded. Alexa was grateful Chad did not see it, but she noticed Sam stiffen slightly.

"Please," begged Sam.

"I don't know," Alexa replied with a slight smile, realising Sam was really not keen on spending a week with just Chad and Bianca.

"I don't know why you're even working," said Bianca. "Why would you want to spend your only weeks of freedom working? What do they make you do?"

"Karl's friend owns an company. They do a lot of business over Christmas and January. I pack lots of boxes for not a hell of a lot of money, but it adds up in the end."

"Jeez, why bother. Sounds like crap," replied Bianca dismissively. "No way I'd let my parents make me do shit like that."

"Not everyone's lucky like us," said Chad in a quiet voice as Alexa bit down on her retorts.

It was a strange response, given that Alexa knew Chad's parents made him work for them during the holidays when he was home. However, it had the effect of shutting Bianca up, for which Alexa was eternally grateful.

"Please, Alexa. Gran and Pop really want to see you again," said Sam, taking her hands to turn her eyes back to him and away from Bianca.

Alexa tried not to grimace. It was not just the work that was making her hesitant. Although things had settled down over the last couple of weeks, she knew Mel had not yet forgiven her for the events surrounding Clinton and she did not want things to become confrontational. She did not want Gran, Pop or Sam to find out about the flame Mel held for Clinton.

"What about Mel?" Alexa asked tentatively, hoping Sam would understand. "She seems to have a pretty big problem with me at the moment."

"Forget Mel," he replied immediately, and Alexa knew he was not just being dismissive. "Anyway, I think she's planning to stay at one her friends back here for the last couple of weeks."

"Okay," smiled Alexa, thinking of all the good times they had had together out on his farm. "I'll see if I can get the time off and see if Pam and Karl will let me go. Mr Knight still has to drive me to and from school. They still don't trust me."

"They'll let you, don't worry," smiled Sam happily. "If not, I'll put Gran on to them and that'll sort them out."

Alexa smiled and squeezed Sam's hands. She really would like to see Gran and Pop again. Every time she left them she feared it would be the last time she ever saw them.

The prospect of spending a week at Sam's farm helped to propel Alexa through the last day. She was disappointed that her teachers did not yet seem to be in holiday mode and were determined to work them right up to the last bell. Their insistence that this was not the end of their year, but the middle of it did not please any of the students – nor did the three assignments they were given for completion by the end of the holidays.

When the bell rang at the end of the day, Alexa raced down to her room to collect her bags hoping this Friday would be shorter than the previous four. Bursting into Mr Knight's office with a hopeful look on her face, she was horrified to see him behind his desk with a stack of papers in front of him.

"I'd make yourself comfortable if I was you," said Mr Knight, glancing up at her, before looking back down at his work.

"But I thought we might be able to leave early today," Alexa replied in a quietly pleading voice she hoped might convince him to change his mind about her detention.

"I thought that too, but Mrs Taylor had other ideas," Mr Knight replied slowly. "She spoke to me this morning and said that under no circumstances was your detention to be cancelled."

"But can't we just go?" Alexa asked with a sly smile. "She'll never know."

"Actually, I will," snarled Mrs Taylor from behind, making Alexa flinch and step further into Mr Knight's office to get away from her. "If you want to break the rules then you will face the consequences, and if Mr Knight insists that you be kept on at this school then he will not mind enforcing that punishment."

"Neither of us has a problem with that," said Mr Knight diplomatically. "Miss Samson was just putting her bags down."

Alexa grudgingly put her bags down on the ground and stormed over to the chair. Mrs Taylor smiled as she left.

"She is such a –"

"Let's not get into what Mrs Taylor is or isn't," said Mr Knight quickly, cutting Alexa off. "The fact is you have detention today, whether we like it or not. So why not make yourself comfortable, because we have three whole hours to waste."

Alexa folded her arms angrily as she scowled, making Mr Knight smirk as he continued to mark his papers.

"Year eight," he said pointing at the papers. "They're terrible."

"Shouldn't they be done by now? Year's over."

"Second chance papers. I have until Monday to complete them – and I'm not really allowed to fail any of them. It's harder than it seems at times."

"Is that why I passed my exams?" asked Alexa, feeling sick.

"No," replied Mr Knight solemnly. "It's sink or swim in year eleven and twelve – which is setting many of these kids up to fail – and there's no preferential treatment for scholarship students ever."

Alexa decided not to question the system more. She already knew it was unfair.

"Hot chocolate?" offered Mr Knight, as though it was some kind of consolation.

Alexa drank in silence, trying to draw out every sip. It was not until she noticed Mr Knight looking at her with an exasperated smile that she realised she was slurping loudly.

"Sorry. Bored."

"You looking forward to the holidays?" asked Mr Knight, talking as he marked. She liked that he was not staring at her as he spoke. "It's good you're able to go back to the same foster family."

"They're good people," nodded Alexa.

That really understated the situation. Pam's letter to invite her back had been nothing but kindness and had included a letter from Hayley, who was brimming with anticipation of her homecoming.

It made her return that much easier, because it was still not where she really wanted to be, and she could not afford to get close to the Whites. She knew how these things always ended.

What Alexa was looking forward to was the fact that the Whites would have no choice but to let her travel alone to and from work and give her back some of the freedom everyone had been slowly stripping her of this year. It would be nice to feel vaguely independent again.

Looking up at the clock, Alexa was horrified by how little time had passed. Determined not to do any school work on the last day of the year – and after the school day had officially ended – she looked around trying to find something to occupy her mind, but Mr Knight's office proved to be incredibly boring. It seemed devoid of any form of entertainment.

Walking around the room, Alexa let her fingers trace imaginary lines in the wall. When she reached the sideboard behind Mr Knight's desk, she started looking more closely at the few photos he had sitting in wooden frames. It was strange to think of him as a person who had a life outside of school. It made her wonder if she would like the man the rest of the world knew.

"Is this your family?" Alexa asked, holding a photo of him with an older man and woman and a young lady.

"That's me with my mum and dad and little sister, Rhianna," Mr Knight nodded, not appearing completely comfortable with her question.

"Nice. Is that your fiancée?" queried Alexa, pointing to a picture of a woman on his desk. Alexa thought she looked very pretty.

Mr Knight nodded silently and Alexa could see his discomfort so walked back around to her chair. He was not paying attention to his work any more. He had picked up the photo of his fiancée, tracing her face with his finger.

"It's our six-year anniversary next week and then Christmas the week after," said Mr Knight in a distant voice. "I always used to look forward to this time of year."

"I've always dreaded this time of year," Alexa replied simply, hoping Mr Knight would not think to change the topic of conversation to Christmas.

"So I am this year," he replied with a grim smile. "It's been a tough year and we're not coping too well. Sometimes I wonder if it's worth it, wonder if we should just stop trying."

Alexa shifted uncomfortably in her chair. It was one thing for her to like Mr Knight and even for him to like her, but to listen to their feelings destroying his relationship was more than she wanted.

"I'm sorry, Alexa. I shouldn't be saying these kinds of things in front of you. They're my problems, not yours," said Mr Knight firmly, nodding as he put down the photo. Alexa remained silent. She was starting to feel like a home wrecker. "Do you have plans for the holidays yet?"

"No, not really, but Hayley has plenty," Alexa replied, thankful for the change in topic. "She wants to go shopping and swimming and probably wants to see some more silly children's movies."

"You like Hayley. I was surprised by that. I thought you would've shied away from another little sister," said Mr Knight, showing much more insight than Alexa would have expected from him.

"There's nothing to dislike about Hayley. I did try at first, but she won me over pretty easily. I like the fact that she'll never be like me. Why did you take us on?" asked Alexa quickly, changing the subject before Mr Knight could ask her more questions.

"I didn't think it was as hard as everyone made it out to be," Mr Knight laughed. "I taught you and nearly every other member of the G7 in the junior years. None of you seemed too tough. I thought it was all just hype."

"And now?" Alexa asked curiously.

"It wasn't what I expected. It was more work than I expected. I see dozens of students every day and I ended up staying here much more than I ever expected. And that's just the normal work. Add on to that the trouble with you running away and Nick's brother. It's been a tough year."

"So tough you won't do it again?"

"Ah, yes, the infamous battle," smiled Mr Knight, before pausing for a moment. "I really don't know. There are some very good reasons for me not to."

Alexa knew he meant her and it did not make her feel good. All in all, he had been a good year advisor and the rest of the grade loved him. If he did not return next year it would be all her fault.

"But there are also many reasons why I should come back," Mr Knight added suddenly, before falling silent again.

"So what are you going to do?" asked Alexa, wanting the heads up for next year.

"I don't know yet."

Mr Knight looked down at his desk, his eyes resting on the photo of his fiancée. Alexa felt supremely uncomfortable once again. She stood up and examined the contents of the bookshelf at the back of the room.

"There has to be something to do in this room," she said, frustrated as she looked at the clock. There was still over an hour of detention left.

"I have a few games on my computer, if that will help," offered Mr Knight. Alexa shrugged. She had never played any computer games before. "Bring your chair around here and I'll set it up for you."

Alexa lifted the chair over the desk to Mr Knight and he moved his chair further down. She quickly bored with the computer games. There were none that she knew how to play and those that were easy enough to understand were not particularly engrossing when matched with her complete lack of skills. It made her wonder how people could play them for hours on end. It took her less than fifteen minutes to be thoroughly over them, but she did not leave her seat. It was too nice being so close to Marcus, she thought sweetly, before catching herself. Mr Knight, she told herself. He always had to be Mr Knight.

The clock clicked over to six twenty-two and Alexa could wait no more. She turned her chair to face Mr Knight and laced her fingers together as if in prayer.

"Yeah, screw it. Let's get out of here," replied Mr Knight, looking over at the clock, making Alexa smile broadly.

When they reached Mr Knight's car, Alexa threw her bags on to the back seat, while he piled his belongings into the boot. Minutes later they were on the road and the school was quickly out of sight. Alexa turned and faced the road ahead, breathing a heavy sigh of relief. Now it really was over.

They drove in silence, but for once, Alexa wanted to know what Mr Knight was thinking. She knew she had less than an hour to make things right between them.

"Can I talk to you honestly about something?" Alexa asked, her heart pounding.

"Sure," replied Mr Knight with a nod, though she noticed him pale slightly as he waited for her to continue.

"You should make the effort with your fiancée," she said decidedly. "You don't want to throw away everything because of someone you can't have, especially someone like me."

"Alexa, please don't put yourself down like that. I –"

"I'm not," Alexa said quickly, cutting Mr Knight off before he said something too nice. "But I'm your student and a messed up one at that. Neither of us really wants to feel this way about each other – and nothing can happen anyway. We promised nothing would ever happen."

Mr Knight turned to her with wide and surprised eyes. It took Alexa a second to work out why. This was the first time she had confessed the mutuality of their feelings. It was strange. She had felt horrifically transparent over the last few weeks.

"I just think we're both better off trying to forget how we feel," continued Alexa, deciding against backtracking and trying to deny the truth. "We need to go back to our lives and you need to realise that you have everything you could ever want."

"I wish it were that simple, Alexa, I just –"

"I never said it was simple, but it's the right thing to do," Alexa continued firmly. She could not understand why Mr Knight was making this so hard. It was nonsensical that he would really like her that much. "You know you won't do anything about how you feel and I … I can't go through anything like that again."

"You're right," replied Mr Knight firmly after a moment of silence. "We're just indulging in an infatuation. The break will give us the perspective we need."

They both fell into a contemplative silence. Alexa wanted to know if Mr Knight would really stop liking her, if he ever truly did care for her to begin with, because she was not sure how to stop loving him. She just needed him to believe she had. She wanted to know that he would go on to live a happy life without her, even though her heart ached slightly at a vision of her future without him in it.

When they turned off the main road, Alexa began directing Mr Knight through the suburban streets. The sound of his voice accepting her directions warmed her more than she believed possible, and it made her consider another future. If she could convince Mr Knight that she felt nothing for him, then perhaps he would never see her as a threat. Perhaps they could be friends and she could hear his voice whenever she needed. There were no laws against friendships. She could have Mr Knight – Marcus – in her life without destroying his. The perfect compromise.

The car stopped and Alexa jumped out. She opened the back

door and grabbed her bags. Mr Knight was staring straight ahead. She wondered if she should just leave, but if they were friends, she could never be so rude.

"Um … thanks for the lift," Alexa said softly. Mr Knight turned to face her on hearing her voice. "Have a good Christmas," she added, smiling warmly.

"You too, Miss Samson," Mr Knight replied sombrely, his smile more of a grimace. "I'll see you next year."

Alexa waved and closed the door. Mr Knight's car immediately sped off. She watched him drive away, but felt something slam into her before he was even out of sight.

"Alexa!" cried Hayley, hugging her warmly. "It's so great you're home. Dinner's ready. We're all really glad you're home."

"Thanks, Hales," replied Alexa, returning Hayley's hug as her heart warmed unintentionally.

Perhaps there really was reason to hope.

Sitting on her bed later that night, wrapped in Mr Knight's shirt from their day at the beach, Alexa looked up at the moon, hoping Mr Knight was looking up at it right then too. She wondered if he would be married the next time she saw him and how much it would hurt if he was.

It would be possible to stop loving Mr Knight if she had to. She had learned well enough that you could stop loving anyone if you tried hard enough. The problem was that she wanted to love Mr Knight. She did not need him to love her back. It was better for everyone if he didn't. However, that Mr Knight could like her in spite of knowing her and the things she had done meant that he deserved to be loved in return, and she was determined to do so until she found someone she could love more.

With her love for Mr Knight, the Whites' genuine smiles at her return and Bethany's continued existence, Alexa found herself almost glad she had survived this year and those moments of near-death. Perhaps now, with something to hold on to, she could hope that there would still be others in the world who would love her despite all she had done and feared she still may do.

Smiling up at the moon, feeling its light shine down on her, Alexa dared to hope that in her future she may yet know true happiness.

www.ingramcontent.com/pod-product-compliance
Lightning Source LLC
Chambersburg PA
CBHW021002120726
47905CB00009B/2807